Good Morning, Dr. Brantwood

Taryn Peters

Courthouse Publications
Alberta, Canada

ISBN: 978-0-9917726-0-5

Copyrights

To Rowena.

And to all who, like Abraham,
have the courage to remain true to their faith,
even when it means placing their own hearts on the altar.

Preface

The 1960s were wonderful, if stormy and tempestuous years. The baby boomers were teenagers. Change was in the air. In no place was the unrest that permeated the atmosphere—the desire for reform—felt more than in our universities. On these campuses there was a literal revolution of ideas, which challenged and changed the way men and women looked at themselves and at their world.

In 1964, student demonstrators at Berkeley University in California led the idea revolution. With the introduction of the Free Speech movement, the world spotlight was focused on the need for universities (and society in general) to reassess their position on political activism and become involved in such issues as civil liberties and the war in Vietnam. Hippies on and off campuses advocated personal freedom to follow their own path to peace by resisting 'outside' restraints and authority. Women's Lib was gaining momentum. Martin Luther King paid the ultimate price for his key role in furthering civil rights.

Much good was accomplished by this great ideological ferment—this change in thinking. But with the good came increased skepticism. God was dead. Humanity was in charge. Progress was orchestrated by mortal not divine means. Secular humanism, the reliance on human reason to define moral and ethical conduct, gained supremacy. Rationalism reigned the undisputed queen of modern thought from shore to shore.

The result? Traditional values bit the dust in unprecedented numbers. Faith in God was sorely tested, and casualties from loss of belief mounted. Those who did maintain their faith did so at the peril of appearing intellectually stagnant.

Such was the tumultuous decade in which this story is set. Such is the decision we all still must make. Is there or is there not a power beyond the world of man? Is there a God?

Acknowledgements

I wish to acknowledge the Supreme Creator: He who made the world, the sun and the stars: He who bestowed life upon his children, thus enabling them to know love and to value liberty.

Special appreciation to Carmen, Adlai, Anna, Lesley, and especially my son Aaron, for their encouraging support, as well as much thanks for the invaluable assistance of Chris, Mara, Debbie, & Rob O'Byrne at JETLAUNCH.net; my husband Lowell, Jim Kotyk, and Bernie Koltun. In addition, I would like to thank my faithful pooch, Hedgy, for keeping my feet warm on long, cold winter nights.

"Now we have received, not the spirit of the world,
But the spirit which is of God, that we might know
the things that are freely given to us of God.
Which things also we speak,
not to the words which man's wisdom teacheth.
But which the Holy Ghost teacheth
—1 Corinthians 2: 12-13

Good Morning, Dr. Brantwood

Whate'er the theme, the maiden sang
As if her song could have no ending;

—William Wordsworth: *The Solitary Reaper*[1]

It was autumn—a carillon of wind and spirit, strength and compassion: the perfect time.

Walking across the grounds of Western University to register for my final year in Honors English, I was glad. It was impossible to be anything else. The robust vitality of the fall season literally sang into my senses, the beauty of the campus cascading around me in harmonious chords of vibrant, living color.

Enchanted, I looked at the row of aging maples hedging the Medical building. In their solemn vigilance, the maples looked like ancient sages chanting in ascetic unison of the glory and goodness of life.

Oblivious to the wisdom of the stately tree choir, a group of medical students, neatly dressed in white, was walking across the center green. Although just past seven o'clock, it was no surprise to see them. Early morning was their time to be out, but not for long. After furtive flights outdoors, most disappeared back into their quiet study ponds with the speed of flying fish.

The thought made me smile. While not a medical student myself, I was aware we shared similar characteristics. Academically reclusive, I was content to study and let the world take its course for good or ill. A sudden doubt pricked my conscience. Perhaps my self-imposed isolation was, as Adrianne claimed, a disguised but virulent form of social leprosy. I discarded the thought. If I was a social leper, today was not the time to worry about it.

Today was the time to meet my favorite analyst and closest friend, The Miss Adrianne Eaton. I was especially looking forward to seeing Adrianne this term, as she and her twin brother, Warren, had been away all summer working in B.C. for Parks and Recreation; during which endeavor, I hadn't the slightest doubt, Adrianne would have completely restructured, redesigned, and reinvented the whole operation.

Miss Eaton was not a young woman to let well enough alone. The wise adage, "If it's not broken don't fix it," would never have occurred to Adrianne. First and foremost, she was a reformer. If anything looked even remotely mossy around the edges, or smacked—however faintly—of status quo, Adrianne would fly into action. To Adrianne, a modern activist and true child of the liberated 1960s, status quo was always smug. Adrianne had no time for smugness, for self-satisfied complacency. What the world needed, according to Adrianne, was change—and plenty of it.

I smiled again. How different we were—polar opposites, really. I hadn't spent my summer attempting to change the world. I'd remained quietly at home assisting Father, a history professor, with his research paper, "Ethnic Groups in North America." Adrianne had eloquently given me her opinion on that score.

In contemplative moments, I wondered why Adrianne kept up our friendship. That she deserved full credit for our continued association was no secret. She simply refused to go away and give up on me. Her confident prediction made in second year still tantalized my mind.

"Someday, someway, Diana Lynn Esther Collingsgate, you're going to emerge from your isolated academic cocoon. When you do, I want to be there—to see if you've turned into a butterfly or a pterodactyl."

In spite of Adrianne's contagious enthusiasm, I rather doubted such a transforming metamorphosis would ever happen. Even so, I kept my doubts to myself, not wishing to put a damper on my friend's optimistic hopes for my social rehabilitation.

So musing, I walked up the broad cement steps of Admin and entered the dimly lit lobby. Not seeing Adrianne, I proceeded to the lone east window that afforded a clear view of students approaching across the green. It appeared the early arrivals were mostly first-year inductees, not a few of whom wore expressions reminiscent of lost children walking on acorns in their bare feet. Others projected a cultivated boredom, amusingly presented as the *coup de maitre* of sophistication.

I didn't mind waiting for my friends; it gave me a moment to reflect quietly in the autumn loveliness. The beauty of the campus grounds always lifted my spirits—especially the location. The founder of the university, Palmer Rolfson, was thought to be eccentric in demanding the site be located on the lonely crest of the foothills twenty miles downriver from the city. All the same, the passage of time proved his wisdom, the intervening distance being since reduced to half by city expansion. While this argued the inevitable absorption of the campus into the suburban sprawl, it would be distressing to see that day. Nestled on the gently molded toes of the mountains, the university was a distinct and separate community. It was a real, not an artificial, oasis.

At barely ten minutes to eight, Adrianne and Warren swung into sight. As usual, Adrianne was leading the way. Wondering what earth-shaking reforms Adrianne would embark upon this year, I went to meet my friends.

"Dia Mia," Adrianne greeted, shaking a small finger while stepping briskly forward to give me an energetic hug. "Punctual as usual. I see that crazy clock you call your mind is still ticking." Smiling disarmingly, she added, "So what've you been doing all summer?"

It was indeed Adrianne. I nodded a helpless but fond hello. "Do you think I should go out and come in again, Warren?" I asked, offering Adrianne's smiling brother my hand.

Warren's big hand closed comfortably around mine. "If Addy wasn't keyed up over something, it wouldn't be Sis," he laughed. "She likes to keep the furnace stoked."

Holding the door open in the easy, gallant manner of a more dignified age, Warren left us to ourselves and to our greetings. Every year I waited for Adrianne in Admin, and every year Adrianne chaffed because I arrived first. It was a yearly ritual neither of us would have felt complete without. Passing through the foyer of the main office, Adrianne pointed to the cork bulletin board.

"That one's for you, Diana Duckling. Just what you need to cap your education. But first you'll have to scrap that brown missionary sackcloth you're wearing for penance."

I looked from Adrianne, dressed in a stylishly modern blue shell blouse and swinging Colquhoun tartan skirt high above the knee, to the bulletin board. On the far right corner of the board, on red construction paper, was printed: Wanted: Male or Female to room with three others of the same. All Facilities Shared. Phone 492-0678. No references required.

As the bulletin boards on campus often sported such ads, I wasn't shocked as Adrianne hoped. Neither would I have commented, had she not been tapping her red, leather-clad toe. When Adrianne tapped her toe, it was my cue to respond immediately, or before.

"If I answer that ad I could change my sackcloth easily enough, but not my fame," I said truthfully. "Best to tag around with you until I learn to dress smarter."

"Don't bluff me, Dio. You know your outfit is lovely as usual, especially the yellow scarf. You always did know how to dress—even if you don't know where your skirts should end and your legs should begin. Come, let's begin the hassling. I hope this year isn't typical and we can register without bloodshed. C comes before E."

With cheerful efficiency, Adrianne directed me to the correct line in front of the Arts Faculty wicket.

My own registration cards were delivered promptly. All were in order. I moved to the glassed portion of the counter and waited for Adrianne to receive her cards. The clerk, a thin, middle-aged woman with yellow, over-permed hair, took Adrianne's name and disappeared into the file room. A moment later, she returned.

Handing Adrianne's ID back to her, she said, "I'm sorry, Miss Eaton. We have no record of your registration. If you wish to take the matter up further, please consult the Dean of your faculty. Next please."

If the student facing the wicket had been anyone but Adrianne, the innocently officious clerk might have been left to finish the day in peace. However, as the irate young woman facing the wicket was Adrianne, the clerk was predestined for a battle. Adrianne had had dealings with the registration department before. She had never lost. Neither did she harbor any sympathy for what she termed the "blatant bigotry of classless incompetence." Nor did she now hesitate in conveying to the surprised filer the explicit reasons why her cards should be immediately located.

Adrianne was not above pulling strings, and she had connections. Mr. Howard Eaton, Adrianne's father, was on the WU Board of Directors. Knowing this, I felt a pang of sympathy for the newly initiated file clerk, who went scurrying back into the file room, this time in a sincere attempt to locate the missing registration. Half a dozen phone calls later, she reappeared.

"Your cards, Miss Eaton," the subdued lady explained politely, "were misplaced with the foreign students' registration on the second floor. One of the secretaries is bringing them down."

Her suspicion of mismanagement confirmed, Adrianne didn't budge an inch from in front of the wicket. "I'll wait right here thank you," she said firmly.

Marveling at Addy's indomitable spirit. I found a seat out of the way and prepared to wait as well. Only five-foot one, Adrianne was not tall. Paradoxically, her passionate personality aroused the impression of a much taller person. Adding to this illusion was her striking copper hair, which she, unlike the famed Anne of Green Gables, didn't mind in the least. Adrianne was realistic enough to know the vivid color matched her ardent nature too well to pretend otherwise. "My hair is red, and so is my spirit," she admitted frankly, "so why complain?"

I looked with renewed admiration at my remarkable friend. Today she seemed transformed by an inner light, her intelligence sparkling in her lovely green eyes. In spite of her small stature, she did indeed make a large impression on the mind.

Warren, although Addy's twin, was the extreme opposite of Adrianne in nature and appearance, except that he too retained the bright copper hair. In contrast to his sister, Warren was tall and muscular, his build typical of all football players. Interestingly, from a distance of more than a few feet, Warren's deep brown eyes were barely distinguishable from the mass of freckles that covered his face and extended down his arms to the backs of his hands. As surely as Warren's complexion contrasted with Adrianne's, so his temperament was much less volatile, igniting long after his sister's fury was a fiery spark of righteous indignation on the pages of history.

Warren, who had won a sport scholarship to the university, was a credit to his faculty where he was training to be a physical education instructor. Well suited to his career choice, Warren had the type of enviable disposition that could elicit excellence from others without creating undue tension. Easygoing, Warren was nonetheless capable of intensity when the need arose.

I sometimes envied the Eaton twins, who were as close as only twins can be close. One might say they were a team. More correctly, Warren was the team and Adrianne was the captain. While Warren towered more than a foot above his petite sister, she considered him her responsibility. Presuming to look after his welfare, she fancied herself his protector—a very indignant one if he so much as chose a date without her approval. Amenable to his sister's directing influence, Warren sometimes stood in as a partner for Adrianne. That he was her escort even rarely, was due to Adrianne temporarily having no interest in the selection offered, rather than any lack of available candidates.

A clipped comment from Adrianne to the clerk brought me back from my reveries. "Be sure these are filed under E in the Arts Faculty. Disorganization costs the tax payers money."

A rueful smile crossed my mind. The last thing Adrianne should be concerned over was money. That she was sincerely concerned on behalf of society, made me feel more than a little guilty. Unlike Adrianne, I wasn't an outspoken advocate for social justice.

Silently, we left Admin together and headed northwest across the center lawn toward the Arts building on the riverside of Edward's library. Out in the crisp autumn air, Adrianne's displeasure vanished like the morning mist.

She laughed. "Do you remember third year registration, Di?"

I raised a tentative eyebrow.

"Oh, you know," she urged. "You must remember the creative cutie who was convinced I was a first year Ag student. Can you imagine me an Ag student?"

I could, but didn't argue. I could imagine Adrianne as anything she chose to be.

Adrianne swung her purse over her shoulder with dramatic constraint. "All this frustration every year just to register," she sighed. "Every year we dutifully fracture our nervous systems—and for what? So we can be packed away into the proper slots. Just so many simpering sardines in cans."

Pausing, Adrianne slanted her almond eyes at me and deigned me a histrionic grimace. "Students are the original 'Lost Ten Tribes.' It's a miracle anyone has the effrontery to live in this mental muddle . . . this bramble briar of tangled intentions." Adrianne looked defiantly at a passing group of happy students.

"What time do you have English 550, Adrianne?" I asked.

"Nine, by the ding dong—of all the hideous hours. When does the disaster strike you?"

"Same time."

"What? You're taking 550 from Steele Man, too? Not 'The' Dr. Steele? Whatever possessed you? Haven't you heard? His class is completely unethical. You won't get any soul food there." Adrianne eyed me suspiciously. "You're joking, right?"

"No. I heard a new professor is teaching the class—so I signed up. It—"

"It will be dull. Same as every other course in this inept, bureaucratic, grind-your-brains mill. Anyway, I don't believe you. Where'd you hear that? This come from your crafty father? If I'd known Steele Man wasn't teaching, I'd have taken the class later in the term. Or better still, not at all." Adrianne threw her arms upward to heaven, supplicating what divine intervention I couldn't ascertain, as she didn't believe overly in God.

"Great," she protested. "I'll bet the new prof is a 101-year-old impeccably boring oddball with 101 impeccably boring ideas for impeccably boring students to death. Wicked Dr. Steele, how could you desert us?" Adrianne looked at me distrustfully. "Why did he desert us, Di? Your tricky dad tell you that?"

I swallowed, hesitating. Diplomacy wasn't foreign to me. It was just that with Adrianne, you had to be at least a ten-star ambassador to hold your ground.

"I believe . . . Dr. Steele felt a change of universities would—"

"No way! Don't pad. He got kicked out. Didn't he! Once every mildewed millennium we get a prof who's really where it's at, an intellect for our time. And what does this stuffed-turkey administration of ours do? Send him to the opposition." Adrianne flung herself grandly down on a bench. I was concerned to get to class on time but didn't want to leave Adrianne in her self-generated dither.

"He—" I began lamely.

"He led a student riot. So? Everyone knows he was in favor of strong student government. He felt campus life would be improved if students had more power. He was before his time. The rights of minorities before the wrongs of majorities. Simple humanitarian logic."

I knew better than to take the bait but asked anyway. "What did he offer to improve minority rights, Adrianne?"

"Himself, Di, himself. The inner man stripped of pomp and ceremony, unbound by ritual, unfettered by tradition. The individualist not yet molded to the decayed ruin of rigid institutionalism. His own free spirit."

While I couldn't disagree with Dr. Steele's being a free spirit, Adrianne was still exasperated.

"Look. Just because he spent the night with the Beta Sigma Phi sorority girls, singing mildly unpatriotic songs over the loudspeaker, he should be dismissed? Why should freedom of association be confined to the daytime?"

My personal opinion was that Dr. Steele was not as interested in freedom as he was in license, but I kept my peace. He had intended the display to emphasize his contempt for university stratification. Professors and students belonged to different hierarchies. They didn't, as a rule, socialize—at least not extravagantly. I doubted very much that Adrianne was herself deceived. Having a minister's penchant for championing the underdog, Adrianne put her head and heart behind her causes, but she also liked opportunities to rail at the university. Privately, I suspected she was more delighted to have new ammunition for her cause against the establishment, than she was downhearted at Dr. Steele's dismissal.

Adrianne paused on the wide steps of the Arts building and gazed in the direction we had come across campus. There was an exiled and lonely look on her face. Feeling the poignancy of her expression, I followed her gaze, but the truth that separated our perspectives was reserved for her sight alone, for I couldn't see what she saw.

Her mood changing with characteristic abruptness, Adrianne swung up the steps with a determination that allowed little room for even a reflective grievance and asked cheerfully, "All your classes in Arts, Di?"

"No," I answered, marveling at her resilient nature. "Psych in Ed, and two classes in St. Mark's."

"St. Mark's? You planning on joining the Grey Nuns?"

"No," I said, laughing. "That's where Philosophy is held. How about you?"

"Three in Arts, one in Math Physics, and two in Ag. Got to pick up Bugs and Bot this year. Been putting them off. Formaldehyde makes me almost as sick as some profs I know. Can you imagine me with a group of first year idealists?"

Again, I could, but said nothing, knowing it would be much harder for the freshmen to imagine Adrianne. Passing through the outer lobby of the Arts building, I noticed that the large gray metal clock was, as it had always been, a good half-hour slow. As though aware of the discrepancy, the round bland face smiled fastidiously. Adrianne granted me a wink at the clock's meticulous falseness.

"We're early, Di. Class won't begin for thirty-five minutes. Let's see if the chocolate milk in The Pit has curdled along with everything else here."

Not waiting for consent, Adrianne was halfway to the Arts lounge when I caught up with her. The lounge, nicknamed *The Pit* for obvious reasons, served as a student-gathering place. Located in the basement of the Arts building, The Pit was too small to accommodate the droves of students and teachers that tried to force their way in to get a cup of coffee or chocolate during the breaks between classes. Those in the coffee line-up, which often extended out the lounge door and down the hall like the rolling body of a Chinese dragon, frequently discovered, to their disappointment, that the coffee ran out before their turn came.

Adrianne didn't particularly like chocolate milk, but she preferred anything to waiting a whole break in the never-ending line in front of the coffee machine. This morning there was no line-up—only a few students milling about the machine. Maneuvering adroitly past the straggling students, Adrianne put her dime in the coffee slot.

"No use getting spoiled," she reflected, eyeing the cold, muddy water that came through the service spout. "It's worse than last year. Must be the leftover embalming fluid from the lab."

Seeing Adrianne's plight, a grinning attendant took a carton of unopened chocolate milk from his crate. "We're cleaning the machine," he said. "Would you prefer this?" Adrianne accepted the carton with tactful self-possession.

We found a table, but Adrianne didn't take a chair. "Di. Isn't that Nelson Cruthers? You remember. The student who did yoga in Soc. 340. He'd make a great prof, eh? Let's say hi."

"You say hi, Adrianne," I declined. "I never really knew him."

"You should have," she returned tartly. "He sat two chairs down from you."

I shook my head. "I'll go up to class. It's past time."

"Okay, my lovely armadillo. I'll go alone, as usual." Adrianne smiled goodbye, and I left my adventurous friend to her inscrutable machinations.

The lounge always seemed empty and cold without Adrianne. Today I noticed, as if with new eyes, the severity of the surroundings. The recently completed Arts building had all the trimming university funds would allow, but it was undeniably sparse in design and decoration. The box-like classrooms were designed for serviceability, not aesthetic appreciation—adequate, but not beautiful.

I thought wistfully of the vibrant, colorful autumn day outside. All the rooms in Arts were painted a bland cream-beige, which Adrianne referred to, not unfairly, as "melted ice cream" décor. The Pit was the exception. However, the deep green walls and black leather furniture did little to relieve the pervading gloom felt there. It was true that neither the classrooms nor the lounge were attractive, but this wasn't important. What was important was that there was a place for classes to be held. The door to the wonder of learning led through the mind, not the building.

Room 39, where English 550 was to be held, was on the second floor. This was good because it allowed access by the stairs when the elevator was crowded. Another advantage was that the windows of Room 39 faced west, affording an excellent view of both the river valley and the mountains beyond.

The door to Room 39 was open when I arrived. Instead of the usual one-armed desks, a long table occupied the center of the room. Somewhat surprised, I stepped inside and surveyed the interior. Even more surprisingly, around the table were comfortable chairs placed an agreeable distance apart. It was obvious someone had carefully directed the arrangement of the classroom. I wondered who and why.

There were other changes as well. On the side of the table nearest the board there was the standard plywood platform for holding the professor's notes, but there was also a teacher's desk by the window. This was most unusual. Most classrooms didn't have desks for the professors, who were as itinerant as the students.

Taking a chair where I could see out the window, I dropped my purse to the floor and placed clipboard, pencil, and admission card on the table. There were only three other students in the room, but this was to be expected, as it was still a few minutes to nine o'clock. Depending on the professor, formal lectures didn't usually begin until the second day.

At nine fifteen, five more students arrived. A few minutes later the door opened to admit Adrianne. She jerked an elbow amiably at me, dumped loose-leaf, purse, and a half-eaten package of red licorice on the table, then looked briskly around the room.

"Think I'm going to like this prof after all," she effused. "He's so delightfully considerate! Here it's twenty after the bell, and he still hasn't depressed us with his presence. My profound congratulations to him/her/whoever."

Having shared her take on the situation, Adrianne turned her attention to the other students in the room. As in all groups, there were those who didn't need to be named to be noticed. They stood out against their fellows like lone fence posts on the prairie. Two such students, a man and a woman, were conversing at the far end of the table. Though they were talking to one another, their voices were clearly audible to the other students in the room, who had no difficulty in catching their names.

The woman was Janice Suffolk, the man Harris Saunders. Tanned a deep golden-brown from the summer sun, Janice was sitting cross-legged in a half-lounging position. Dressed in a mini-skirt, Miss Suffolk's manner was one of practiced sophistication, emphasized as she crossed and uncrossed her legs with the preciseness of a priestess performing a religious rite. Passersby, if they could have seen up to the third floor, would no doubt have the impression she was a store window mannequin advertising nylons for a summer garden party.

With her long blond hair catching the sunlight filtering through the window, Janice held the attention of many of the students in the room. Yet at least one observer was not admiring the black lace under the tiny, yellow mini-skirt. Adrianne was a modern woman, but she fervently despised what she termed "vulgar display." Wrinkling up her nose, she studied Janice, a dangerous glint in her eye.

"She must think this is some bleak coast out of "*Ulysses*" for sirens to wail upon. And would you look at that mountain goat next to her. He looks like he's going to molt!"

"Adrianne. Mountain men don't molt."

"They do if they haven't the sense to stay out of the fire."

"Mr. Saunders looks capable of defending himself," I said honestly.

"If that's what's on his mind," Adrianne returned grinning, "but only if he stays behind that beard and cigarette."

Thankfully, a slender East Indian lady gracefully eased the tension with an introduction. "I am Kumari Nagarsenkar," she said, smiling as she extended a slim brown hand first to Adrianne and then to me.

"Kumari. What a lovely name. I'm Adrianne Eaton, and this bashful debutante is Diana Collingsgate. Haven't seen you around campus. This your first year here?"

"My husband and I are attending your fine university this term," Kumari replied graciously. "We're impressed with both the campus and Canadians." Kumari's manner was refined, her pronunciation too genteel for her to be native born.

"Kumari," Adrianne enthused, "that's the most beautiful sari I've ever seen. Is it from India?"

Kumari nodded. "Yes. It's Indian silk. I had it made before I left."

"Do you always wear a sari?" Adrienne pursued.

"Yes. As you wear skirts and blouses."

Adrianne looked down the table at Janice and rolled her eyes.

"Not any more than necessary, obviously." Kumari smiled, wisely ignoring Adrianne's reference to Janice's skimpy attire.

I looked at Kumari. She was lovely. More than ordinarily attractive, Mrs. Nagarsenkar's face reflected a quiet self-respect. One could guess she was well educated, even without seeing the mark of her caste, a red ruby, in the center of her forehead.

Adrianne, her pert eyebrows arched, looked intently at the ruby. I had seen that look before and was immediately uneasy. It was my turn to intervene. Turning to the student on my left, a pale girl in a pastel suit, I introduced myself. Before I had time to introduce Kumari and Adrianne, the girl began a nervous concert of questions.

"My name's Neila Connaught. Do you think the prof will come soon? I'm so worried. The texts I ordered haven't arrived, so I couldn't do the pre-session studying. Do you think the first exam will have much bearing on the final mark?" Neila's questions came in short, little bursts of energy, like the excited puffs from a child's toy steam engine. She was in a state of high tension and greatly needed calming.

"No," I said honestly, hoping the small, inadequate word would provide the calming needed. Neila's face darkened.

"Of course," I added, "it depends on the professor, but usually the first exam is only lightly weighted. Are you from out of town?"

"Yes," she said, "that's why I'm so worried. I don't know the system. Have you done all the reading?"

To say that I had would have disturbed Neila even more. Stumped at what to respond to ease Miss Connaught's distress, I was grateful when Mr. Stewart, a middle-aged man I'd seen a few times in Edwards Library, interposed. Taking an unlit pipe out of his mouth, he said confidently, "A bright young woman like you shouldn't worry. I haven't been able to acquire the texts myself. The professor will understand the tie-up is at the bookstores." Mr. Stewart gave Neila a patriarchal smile of approval and replaced his cold pipe.

"But I've been to all three bookstores in the city and *none* of them have the texts," she said, her tone reflecting the plaintive, wistful quality of a lost kitten. It was clear her concern was not to be dislodged by logic alone. Not wishing to add to Neila's burdens, I left her in the care of Mr. Stewart.

Oblivious to my presence, Adrianne and Kumari were engaged in an enthusiastic discussion about caste. I felt an unspoken reprimand to my cautiousness on the subject in Adrianne's lively questions and Kumari's straightforward responses. Thankfully, neither appeared offended by the topic.

I looked around the room, noting that there were other students who preferred to sit quietly by themselves. With these independent souls, I felt an unseen bond uniting us in silent community. An attractive black lady, with exquisite, finely sculptured features, sat unobtrusively by herself near the door, next to a Japanese gentleman. Both students were engaged in checking their registration cards, with clearly no desire to converse.

Two more students entered at quarter to ten. One of them I knew. She was Daphne Englesby, called "Jingle Bells" by Adrianne in fond exaggeration of Daphne's irreverent approach to life. Stylishly nonchalant, if Daphne said what she thought, she managed to avoid giving offense, perhaps in part because of an attitude as mottled as floral print.

The student accompanying Daphne, I'd seen on campus the year before, but had never met. She had an air of competence, everything about her shouting efficiency. Impressed, the thought occurred to me, that even in a more congruent age than ours, this woman could have worn shoes that didn't match and would still appear masterfully confident. Intrigued, I watched her stride with calm assurance to a vacant chair. She was forty-five minutes late, but her manner made it clear there were exonerating circumstances. Slightly in awe of such visible self-possession, I wondered if she ever felt unequal to any task.

By now, a few of the students were beginning to speculate on what was detaining the professor, as class was scheduled to last ninety minutes, and the time was more than half spent. Possibly, it was nothing to get excited about—only the maiden confusion over scheduling that occurred regularly every year, so most of the students didn't show undue concern. Neila Connaught was the only student who appeared overly anxious. Looking uneasily from her watch to the clock on the wall, then back to her watch with each sound in the hall, she fretted the minutes away.

Adrianne, for different reasons, was also growing steadily more interested in the tardy professor. In his seeming contempt for routine, he was in grave danger of becoming a symbol of emancipated intellect to Adrianne.

Offering me a piece of twisted licorice, she remarked, "Di Doll, do you know, for the first time in my life, I think I'm really in love. But how could anyone keep from loving such a temperate person as our absent mentor?" Satisfied with her own assessment, she bit off a piece of licorice with deft finality, observing the remaining portion in her hand with alert, undeceived eyes. "Think I should tell him of my passion as soon as he arrives, or let him guess?"

"What if he doesn't show?" I suggested.

"Then my heart will be lost forever to a man I've never met."

I shook my head helplessly at Adrianne's incorrigible spirit.

At ten to ten, Adrianne was forced to abandon her hope of *avant-garde* leadership. The door opened to admit a young, but respectable-looking professor. Adrianne eyed the new instructor's conservative green tie and outmoded white shirt with suspicion. In her questioning eyes was a look dangerously similar to the one she gave me when she was attempting to visually exorcize my soul of the "fetters of tradition."

"He's young as Steele Man and much prettier," she approved. "But he looks like a prof. Wouldn't you know it? Just like a prof!" Adrianne crumpled the empty licorice wrapper and jammed it unceremoniously into her purse.

The traditionally, almost staidly, dressed instructor walked purposefully to the blackboard. He did appear competent. At least in this, Adrianne was not mistaken. Picking up a piece of chalk, he wrote the name Dr. G. L. Brantwood on the board in large, clearly legible letters. Looking at the graceful writing, I had the strange sensation the letters had been created, not written. It was hard to pin point, but there was something about this professor that reminded me of a motto I had learned as a child: "Don't just be counted. Be counted for something."

Dr. Brantwood's hands caught my attention. Myself a musician, I'd often observed others' hands. Had even, while in high school, made a private study of hand types to see if they revealed anything about character. At the time, I concluded they did not. Still, Dr. Brantwood did have beautiful hands. The thought made me strangely uncomfortable.

"It seems I was issued a private cell," Dr. Brantwood said calmly, turning to face the class. "It is progressive of Admin to assign students to one room and professor to another. Hopefully the practice will take; it's a commendable idea."

"Hear, hear!" Harris Saunders applauded, slapping the table.

If Dr. Brantwood intended his remarks to be amusing, he wasn't smiling. There was clearly commitment in his eyes. Intrigued, I noticed he had a focused objectivity, similar to the peculiar facility of a minister whose attention seems to be riveted on you alone, when in reality he is observing the whole congregation. It is a look that carries neither praise nor blame. Perhaps, because such a look offers no judgment, you are persuaded to judge yourself. It was an attractive quality, but this further discovery made me even more uneasy. I blanched; such bold thoughts were decidedly uncharacteristic.

Mercifully, Adrianne distracted me from further speculation with a poke in the ribs, observing, "So, Dio. Looks like we've caught a live one. Perhaps there *is* life after Steele Man. What's your take?"

"The new professor does appear to be breathing," I conceded warily, hoping Adrianne hadn't sensed the unintended admiration of my thoughts. She gave me a quizzical look, the way she always did when she knew I was avoiding her interrogations.

"Hmm," was all she said.

Dr. Brantwood finished alphabetically arranging the admission cards on his desk. Reading aloud the surnames, he paused briefly after each to locate the respective student. "Anderson, Buckles, Collingsgate, Connaught, Englesby, Eaton, Nagarsenkar, Saunders, Stewart, Suffolk—"

"Jan, please," interrupted a languid voice from across the room.

Dr. Brantwood glanced briefly from the card to Janice, and then continued without comment. "Hito and Weiss," he finished.

"Mrs. Weiss," corrected the self-composed student at the end of the table opposite Janice.

"Surely you don't expect me to remember which students are married and which are not?" Dr. Brantwood replied. "One student looks like another to me."

That the professor meant the mild rebuff seriously was difficult to say. Most of the class accepted the comment on face value and laughed appreciatively. The notable exceptions were Janice and Mrs. Weiss, both of whom looked rather put off. Janice was exceptionally beautiful, and Mrs. Weiss had unmistakably strong features.

Ignoring their unspoken objections, Dr. Brantwood continued amiably. "There are thirteen students and twelve cards. I don't object to someone auditing the course. You're welcome. However, you will be expected to complete the same assignments—without the same credit—as registered students. Your marks will not affect your GPA, but you will have to write the exams. Still game?"

A youth, who had entered late, verified the missing card. "Yeah, man! I've got the pass, you've got the class," he drawled, strutting up with his permission slip. "Name's Bob Davis."

Dr. Brantwood nodded, his expression neutral. For the moment, all eyes were focused on Bob. A thoroughly modern young man, Bob wore his hair hippie style, hanging in lost wisps about his shoulders. I suspected he would have had a beard, had he been able to grow one.

"Yes, Miss Connaught?" Dr. Brantwood said, recognizing Neila who was urgently waving her arm.

"When is the exam?" Neila asked. "None of the bookstores have the books. Will we be penalized?"

"There will be no exam," Dr. Brantwood replied. An audible sigh of relief spread through the class, but the easing of tension didn't reach Neila.

"Yes, but what about the books?" she asked tightly. "Won't we have to know what's in them?"

"It's not my concern whether you read all the listed texts or do not," Dr. Brantwood rejoined. "The anthology provided is a guide. The reference texts will be your choice."

Harris Saunders gave a snicker. He, at least, liked the idea of *carte blanche* on study materials. It was, however, too much for Neila. Sinking into a small nervous huddle, she wrote down every pellet of instruction. Wrapped securely in self-inflicted stress, she looked again like a lost little kitten. My heart went out to her, but there was little I could do.

"How will you know we haven't already studied the texts?" Mrs. Weiss asked. Integrity appeared to be her concern.

"All the better," Dr. Brantwood said, with a half smile. "The material studied in this course is the responsibility of the student. If you didn't learn it the first time, here's your chance to redeem yourself." He didn't wait for the amused titters to die down.

"As you know, this course is an overview of English literature from the fifteenth century to the present. So choose a work from that time frame and have at. First presentations in two week's time."

Seeing Neila's dismay, Dr. Brantwood added, "You may select any type of work you wish: bawdy, saintly, rowdy, conformist. You may even write your own, if you have the compunction and fortitude." There was a brief chuckle of delight from the class.

"But what if we choose the same book as someone else?" Neila asked.

"In which case, Miss Connaught," Dr. Brantwood replied patiently, "you need only concern yourself that you don't say the same things."

"How will you know the paper is ours?" Harris interjected.

"The last time I received a paper not written by the student, I gave myself an A for writing it," Dr. Brantwood said tersely. "The student was expelled."

The class laughed. Even Neila had to appreciate the humor in someone being naive enough to hand a professor his own paper.

"It wasn't that I didn't appreciate the compliment," Dr. Brantwood mused. "It was that the student hadn't done his research. He should have known whose paper he had pillaged. If I'm going to be publicly vandalized, I require the notoriety of having my name published."

"Are you stipulating no quotations?" Harris asked skeptically.

"Certainly not. Quote away. But be honest. You want to give me a playback of my opinions—or anyone else's—go ahead. Just don't present another's work as your own. Give credit to the source of your ideas. That's standard procedure in all classes, be they English, American, or Civilized." Dr. Brantwood paused, then added, "If you must parrot my ideas, would you please improve on them. Seems hardly worth my time to read what I already know."

Raising his hand to stem the tide of Neila's rising concerns, Dr. Brantwood continued, "Term work will follow a rotating plan: lectures alternating with presentations by class members." Realizing this information hadn't dislodged Neila's anxieties, he added pleasantly, "If this isn't clear, please see me after class."

Organization of the term work completed, students left for their next classes. Janice and Harris strolled up to the professor and offered to treat him to coffee.

"If you want to do me a favor," Dr. Brantwood said, "throw me the dime and let me gulp my coffee in peace." Harris nodded without offense and left the professor to Miss Connaught. Janice shrugged and strolled into the hall after Harris.

I admired them both for losing like sports. Unless the professor was unduly vain, 'prof pandering' was a risky endeavor, even for a student as attractive as Janice.

Once out in the hallway, the students disbanded quickly. Adrianne, Kumari, and I walked together as far as the main entrance.

"What do you think of that blue-eyed shark offering to take the prof to coffee first thing?" Adrianne said. "I'll have to teach her about prof polishing. You'd think she'd have the tact to——"

"Ask the rest of the class along?" Kumari interposed, smiling.

"At the very least," Adrianne returned, laughing. "This prof has possibilities, but I am disappointed. Anyone who wears a plain narrow tie in the heyday of the psychedelic bib is strictly past tense."

We parted at the door. Kumari went to see about housing accommodations, and Adrianne whisked off to attend the Student Union meeting. She'd discovered in her chat with Nelson Cruthers that he was running for president, and had spontaneously promised to help with his campaign. Adrianne, who was never one to leave a quiet crustacean to his own watery resources, but must always dive in and badger the poor maladjusted recluse into taking a greater interest in the community at large, would be an efficient and enthusiastic campaigner. Even Adrianne's detractors, if she had any, would have to admit she held an impressively honest, if somewhat intense, interest in community affairs.

Chapter Two

This is my Father's world, and to my listening ears
All nature sings, and round me rings the music of the spheres.

—Maltbie D. Babcock: *This is My Father's World* [2]

Classes finished by noon, I decided to walk home along the river. My home was shared with Father, my sister Ginny, and Aunt Amy. These humans were presided over by Aunt Amy's cat, Mephistopheles, and Ginny's loquacious canary, Carlyle. Collingsgate itself was two miles south of the university by the road, or three miles by the river route, that curved in a lazy S.

The walk home was always invigorating, but today it held a new vitality that was spiritually renewing. The leaves of the birch trees, clumped together in strands along the river's edge, were just beginning to change color; yellow-green leaves cavorting cheerfully on the back of the breeze, like myriads of tiny cowboys riding miniature flying horses. The small cowboys waving and tossing so lightly in the wind seemed to be laughing at the crows, that fretted and cawed even on this lovely afternoon. The more the crows complained, the more the leaf cowboys laughed.

I smiled. It would have taken more than a few discontented crows to disrupt the serenity of such a day. Refreshed by the walk, I passed the last bend in the river before my home and paused to rest beside a slender birch. A piece of lined, white bark fell off at my feet. It looked strangely out of place among the leaves. Picking it up, I felt the smooth surface lines between the raised welts with my fingers. For some reason, the picture of Dr. Brantwood writing on the board came to mind.

I could well imagine Adrianne's comment. "You've got a problem here, Didillo? Better watch that garrison you call your heart, or you may find it breached." Shaking off that nonsense, I continued walking. It would be pleasant to stay longer in the autumn wonder, but I knew Ginny and Aunt Amy would be waiting supper.

My sister Ginny and I were as different in appearance and disposition as the sun is from the moon. Observing this, Father called us *Sunlight* and *Moonlight*. I had to agree we suited his description. In height, coloration and personality we were notably different. To someone who still retained the imagination of childhood, Ginny might be thought to be a forest sprite; but in reality, at eighteen years of age, Ginny, whose full name was Virginia Elizabeth Ellen, was a swiftly blooming young woman.

Personally, I regretted to see how quickly the years were leaving Ginny's girlhood behind. Becoming increasingly the subject of admiring glances, it was to her credit that was she was not vain. Feeling her nose made her plain, she had at age nine confided that if she could just have a proper nose, she would be satisfied with her other deficiencies—deficiencies which neither Father, nor Mother, nor I, could ascertain. Father, in particular, was perplexed that Virginia Elizabeth Ellen ever gave her pretty little nose a moment's thought.

"Sunlight," he said, "what has the size of your nose got to do with the size of your soul?" If something didn't make sense to Father, he didn't waste energy on it. Not that he was unkind. However foolish Ginny's woes, we all—including Father—did our best not to scourge the wound. Rather we loved her more for her silliness, for hers was a warm and friendly nature which attracted the friendship of old and young.

When Ginny was fifteen, a small boy followed her adoringly all the way home from school. Little Fred arrived at the back door just a few steps behind Virginia. His courageous devotion won the brave fellow, who was all of six years old, a cookie and glass of milk, before Father drove him home. Ginny wanted to keep 'Fearless Fred' for supper, but Father firmly refused her request.

"No, Virginia," he directed, "Stray puppies we can keep, but not others' wayward children. Lost little boys must be returned at once."

Perhaps Ginny's most ardent admirer was Father, who cultivated her company as carefully as if she were one of the prize roses in his garden. Father's passion, if he had one, was roses.

Home from his day of teaching history at the university, Father had arrived ahead of me and was tending his roses in the front yard. As usual, he was wearing his old brown corduroy jacket. Ginny and Aunt Amy had both threatened many times to burn the relic of a coat, but it had somehow survived destruction and was still Father's favorite garden attire. He leaned on his spade as I came down the walk.

Not bothering to say hello, he asked, "Crossing R. chinensis with gallicas and centifolias produced what?"

"Hybrid chinas, forerunner of hybrid perpetuals," I answered correctly. The slanting rays of the sun tinged the gray-blue of Father's eyes with silver.

"And what was the advantage of that?" he humphed, disgruntled he hadn't caught me unaware.

"A stronger, longer-lasting bloom," I answered, pleased I'd won that round.

"Hmm. I see you still have something useful in your head," he said. "I was fearin' you'd become too sophisticated for practical things."

Screening the hummingbird quickness of his mind, Father's eyes were twinkling, as they always did when he indulged in talk that was half play, half serious. We stood a person apart, admiring the rose garden together in silence. Noticing the sun was about to disappear behind the mountains, Father picked up his spade and went back to work.

Our home, which had been called *Collingsgate* since it was built, had survived many generations of active Collingsgate children and was still sturdy. Finished in grey stone slab, laboriously hauled from the mountains before the turn of the century, the old house was the only home Ginny and I had ever known. Father himself was born on a cot in the kitchen during a winter blizzard. The thing I liked about Collingsgate was that it was spacious enough to allow all family members their privacy.

When Father married Elizabeth Kathleen and brought her home to Collingsgate, she convinced him to remodel the main floor. Previously, Grandfather Richard had modernized the home, adding electricity and plumbing conveniences; but kept the old wall lamps in case the new lights, which he never quite trusted, should fail. Father would have taken the lamps down, but Mother prevented him, saying they gave the home character.

The one-time attic, which had long ago been converted into a study for Father, was the most interesting part of the house, at least to me. Father had built windows into the ceiling to form a skylight that gave an impressive view of the stars and constellations on a clear night. Through the window on the west wall, Father could see the mountains. It was his practice to leave his study to remind us that the sun was setting with particular splendor over the jagged peaks; or to inform us that there were clouds forming on the mountain tops, indicating snow or rain; or to simply alert us that the mountains were more brilliantly visible than they had been in recent days.

From the west window of my room, located on the second floor under Father's study, I could also see the mountains. "Sentinels of Solitude," Father called them. They did appear that. To the north I could also see the lights of the university; which, patently ignoring the mountains' isolating reserve, shone faithfully every night.

While Father had his room and study and we girls had our rooms, Ginny controlled the remaining space in the house. Even when Aunt Amy was present, Ginny was the true mistress of Collingsgate. From the kitchen, Ginny could direct the household and enjoy the company of Carlyle, whose cage hung in the window by the potted geraniums.

Ginny's favorite spot in the kitchen was an old rocking chair, in which she liked to recline after supper and play her guitar. Both Father and Aunt Amy encouraged this pastime, but it was Ginny's canary, Carlyle, and Aunt Amy's cat, Mephistopheles, who formed her most faithfully attentive audience. Carlyle would listen with her head to one side, as if Ginny's playing was for her benefit alone. Mephistopheles, a silky black Persian named after the devil in Christopher Marlowe's *Dr. Faustus*, would wind around Ginny's legs and purr.

Greeting me at the kitchen door, Ginny called, "Hurry up, Diddi, or supper will be all 'hot cockalorum,' which does mean burnt to a cinder!"

Wishing to oblige, I hurried in to wash. Father joined us at the table.

"So how was your first day back?" Father asked, smiling. "Did you navigate the shoals of registration without shipwreck this year?" Father knew something of registration day difficulties, himself being a permanent fixture at the university.

"Yes," I replied, "fortunately I had Adrianne along to keep score and tally the results."

"So what was the score and who won?" Aunt Amy asked cheerfully, with cultivated innocence.

"The students outmaneuvered the system one more time. We're all registered, I'm happy to say."

"That means the score should be about even," Aunt Amy said, smiling.

"Could be," I admitted. "But Dad, did you know there's a new English professor on campus?" I felt silly for asking, but also a desire to know what Father might readily supply.

"Yes," Dad said, "I understand someone from Ryerson University in Toronto has been bribed to take Dr. Steele's place. The board must have done some fancy talking to convince him to leave RU and come here. Wonder what bait they used? Whale hooks, no doubt."

"Perhaps he just wanted to see the West," Ginny suggested.

"Which he could no doubt do and get paid, rather than throwing his fortunes to the wind in this duck pond," Father said. "Must be a terribly unfrugal man."

Father liked to make out that Western University was the backwash of civilization. In reality, Professor Collingsgate was happy at his work and quite content to spend his life "muddling along in the mental muskeg," as he described life on campus.

"You know you love the Duck Pond, Poppa," Ginny sassed. "Wherever are they going to get someone to take your place when you retire?"

"I had hopes that one of my insufferable children might be tempted to do something with her mind," Dad said. He spoke to Ginny, but he looked at me.

"The acorn never falls far from the oak," Aunt Amy reminded us, giving Ginny a supportive pat on her hand. If Ginny had plans for a professorship, she didn't comment.

Supper over, Ginny ordered us out of the kitchen. From an early age, Ginny had personally taken responsibility for supervising all household activities. She even managed Aunt Amy who had a mind of her own, but who had taken to Ginny so strongly that there was little, if any, disagreement between them. Aunt Amy had come to Collingsgate shortly after Mother's death. Although outspoken, she was warm-hearted, and her presence at Collingsgate had been a blessing.

Directly after cleanup, Ginny took her usual place in the rocker, but for some reason she didn't sing. I watched her fondly as she rested in the large old chair, playing on the guitar with artless skill, her fingers pressing the strings with sober detachment. In her thoughtful mood, Ginny seemed a little sad, like the young ladies in Reynold's *The Age of Innocence*, a print of which hung over the mantelpiece in the front room. Ginny was not often downcast. Inheriting Mother's cheerful nature, she didn't indulge in moodiness or worry over things needlessly. Tonight, however, she was noticeably pensive.

"Anything wrong, Ginny?" I asked.

"Not really," she replied dreamily. "Do you know a law student at university named Neal Allen?"

"No . . . Perhaps . . . That is, I think there was a Neal in one of my classes. Do you?"

"Yes. He came to Hazelmere High last week. Gave a guest lecture for career day. Funny guy."

Knowing Ginny, 'funny guy' could mean just about anything. I decided not to pursue the topic. There were books to review before tomorrow's classes.

Seated at the desk in my room, my mind wandered from my studies. An incident from childhood emerged from the past, dominating my reveries. It was Father's habit to wake before sunrise and go for a stroll along the river. Frequently, when Ginny and I were younger and Mother was alive, we would all accompany Dad on his sojourns to greet the day. In my mind's eye, I could see Father leading the way; his Elizabeth Kathleen tucked on his right arm; Ginny on his left, her chubby fingers curled securely around the index finger of Father's brown hand.

Walking by the river in the early morning stillness that couldn't be shattered by even the piercing racket of the birds, I discovered hidden treasures: flowers, trees, birds, animals, and my first breathtaking glimpse of a mind that sincerely reverenced the wonders of nature. It was a mind that knew the common and Latin names of every tree, shrub, flower, and weed along the way.

On those walks, Father often commented on the fragility of life. His appreciation for life's transience made both nature and those he loved very dear to him. His favorite exhortation if anyone quarreled was always, "Why waste a good friendship? Quarrel after you're dead—if you must." I smiled at the recollection.

Valuing life made Father observant. His keen eyes would often detect some natural wonder we others missed. Sighting a lone flower half-hidden from view, he would point it out, raising his eyebrows in bemused concern that we'd failed to spot the notable specimen ourselves. Many lovely things would have escaped notice, but for Father's practiced eye.

Over the years, thanks to his tutoring, growing things became more than simple vegetation. Of endless variety and intricacy of design, the world of nature emerged symbolic of the depth and magnitude of the original creative mind—the mind of God. With Father's guiding interest as an active catalyst, the marvel of life upon Earth began to proclaim the wonder of the infinite, as every new flower, its loveliness articulated in awe, expanded the dimensions of my universe.

Encouraged and challenged by my own growing interest in the natural world, I spent many happy hours learning all I could. Eventually, I mastered the difficult Latin names and could classify most wild plants native to our vicinity with some degree of accuracy. I carted home flowers and weeds alike to compare with the charts in Father's study. Learning was gentle; the hours never grew tedious. The path to understanding is not difficult or wearisome when it is lined with bluebells, wild honeysuckle, and love.

The one difficulty that plagued my young life was that I couldn't always get to the plants when they were freshly picked. The reason for this delay was that I had to wait until the study—Father's special domain—was available. I didn't mention my projects to Father, but listened quietly, my own interest camouflaged by Mother's and Ginny's more raucous appreciation of Father's botanical discourses. In those first years of awakening, I felt an ironbound solemnity in Father's presence, no matter how engrossing the discussion or how captivated my attention. Over time, when I came to know of Father's ingenious subtlety, his ploys to further our acumen, I felt less reticent around him.

My discovery of this hither-to-hidden facet of Father's personality occurred one morning as we were walking by the river shortly after sunrise. Ginny, catching sight of a long-stemmed flower growing on the bank, pointed it out to father with pride. Father smiled his approval, then after studying the flower intently for a few seconds, pronounced with usurped authority, as devoid of guilt as the fresh spring day, the most diabolical lie ever concocted upon the banks of the entire river. Father termed a common Monkshood, *Dionaea muscipula.*

Not aware of the deception, Ginny bubbled her appreciation. Stunned, I knew from a book I'd been reading that Venus Fly Trap was incapable of surviving the winters in our area, growing in its native state only on the coasts of the Carolinas. I couldn't move from the spot, my gaze riveted in silence to the now sickly looking, purplish flower. Father had deceived them; he'd deceived his own wife and daughter.

With the knowledge of the deception tearing at my mind, the walk became increasingly unbearable. Crossing a small hillside stream, I noticed Father bend to point out something growing at the stream's edge. Motioning to me, he called me over. The half-inch bloom of the bluish-white flower, shaped in a monk's cowl, was horrid to my sight.

Deeply insulted, I said tersely, "The correct name is *Aconitum napellus.*"

Father returned my reproachful gaze quietly, his eyes thought-fully scanning my face. Straightening his back, he sportively winked his eye at me. "That's correct," he commented calmly. "Monkshood really shouldn't be growing here, either. Its natural habitat is the eastern coast. Do you think you can remember that, Moonlight?"

In that instant my heart exalted above the dungeon into which it had sunk, as into my mind flashed an understanding as radiant as the early morning sunlight. So that's what Dad meant when he told us to "verify for victory." He was admonishing us to do our own research: to never depend on others, however emulated, to define the truth for us.

It is possible a strict devotee of facts only, with no generosity of nature, would deem Father, in his single-minded devotion to inspire others to do their own digging, either illiterate or a liar. Neither was true. He just wanted us to corroborate the truth of things for our-selves. If a little hornswoggling helped us learn to think independently, then hornswoggling there would be. If his methods at times resembled intellectual larceny, Dad never did anything without good reason. He was not one to be concerned with the criticisms of those whose "glaciated analysis" stemmed from "perpetually frozen minds." If anything, he was less exact in the classroom than at home.

Not surprisingly, it was around the dinner table at Collings-gate that we got to know Father best. Immediately after grace was finished, he would dredge up the most clearly implausible histori-cal apparitions that ever strolled across a dining room table. But through his designed artistry, history came alive; and for myself, the peerless specters of the past became more than welcome guests—they became friends who allowed me to feel more a part of the family. When these charming ghosts of Father's fertile imagination were present, it was as though there was an unseen bond between us.

In later years, when I discovered Father also puzzling students and colleagues alike with his wily woolgathering, my appreciation of this exclusive commodity of his character grew even more. It was not unjust. Those who trustingly believed his creative philandering were not injured, as they had no real desire to know truth. Those who did seek truth accepted his methods for what they were intended to be—a mentally stimulating game of cat and mouse.

Chapter Three

Pictures are intended to be looked at, not smelled.

—Rembrandt, *Harmenszoon van Rijn*[3]

Monday was another glorious autumn day. The fresh fall wind gusted against my face as I walked across the campus. In the Arts building I met Adrianne on her way to the lounge for breakfast. She was wearing a sari exactly like the blue silk she had admired on Kumari Friday, and looked so greatly changed in the Sari, that even with her copper hair, I almost failed to recognize her.

Seeing my dismay, she beamed happily. "You'll never guess?" she teased, twirling in front of me. "Kumari gave me her sari to keep. It seems the enchanting custom of her homeland is for the *complimentee* to give the *complimenter* the *complimented*."

I shook my head mystified at the hopelessly Adriannized grammar.

"Oh, you get it Diogenes," Adrianne urged. "I said I liked Kumari's sari. So she wrapped it up for me. Which reminds me, don't ever let me compliment Suffolk on her mind."

"Nor mine either," I assured her. "I need all my synapses this year. It's a heavy term."

"Your mind is perfectly capable of doing a little extra sculling, Di. Brains. But you can keep it. It looks good on you."

I couldn't help laughing. Adrianne was such an entertaining, if outrageous, mixture of wine and vinegar. I watched her strut off down the hall in her sari. As unpredictable as the ice on the Bow River in the winter, it was never possible to forecast which side of her impetuous nature would hold the balance of power at any given moment.

Adrianne's parents lived in the city only a short distance across the river, but rather than commute, Adrianne preferred to rent a room at the student residence on campus. She claimed that if you survived six months in *The Hole*, as the residence was called, you were equipped to meet anything life could throw at you.

I agreed with that assertion. Although Adrianne herself was straight, I knew that some of her friends in the residence did follow unhealthy lifestyles, which was concerning. Adrianne dismissed my "paranoia" with a wave of her hand, assuring me she could take care of herself. Still, I suspected she was at times too glib, as though her flip responses masked a private inner need hidden from view. To her credit, Adrianne did manage to spend the occasional week-end at home, even though her extracurricular activities took up the majority of her time.

Adrianne's father, as well as a member of Western's Board of Directors, was in real estate. Besides supporting a fashionable home and "ridiculously overindulged wife" (Adrianne's description, not mine), Mr. Eaton, playfully titled *His Bucksworth* by Adrianne, was able to provide living expenses for both Adrianne and Warren, who also stayed on campus.

While well known to all those involved in civic affairs, I knew very little of Mrs. Eaton. I had, of course, met her. She was most often seen through the window of her car when she came to pick up Adrianne for an afternoon of shopping in town. Other than that, Adrianne didn't spend a lot of time with either of her parents and had commented ruefully on more than one occasion that her mother had time for every little project but her family. I didn't doubt Adrianne's assertion. Even so, Mrs. Eaton was known to be generously philanthropic, and of that, both Adrianne and Warren, could be justifiably proud.

As was her habit, Adrianne came late to class. Walking in a full twenty minutes after nine, her sari draped gracefully over her arm, she reveled in the approving glances of her classmates. Her aim accomplished, she promptly discarded the guise of eastern polish, and plumped gracelessly down on her chair. Leaning forward, she placed her elbows on the table and rested her chin on her hands. Leaning on her hands was the way Adrianne normally listened to lectures. She claimed it helped her brain remain active when the lecture became inert. In actual fact, I noticed my selective friend had done much less leaning on her hands in 550 than usual.

Recognizing Adrianne, Dr. Brantwood said calmly, "Glad you could make it, Miss Eaton."

"Absolutely," Adrianne tossed back.

A quiet smile flickered across Professor Brantwood's face. For the next twenty minutes, the class listened without further interruption. Ten minutes later, Adrianne leaned over and whispered, "You can tell he showers every morning."

I didn't comment, finding it impossible to fathom the connection bathing habits had with English lectures in Adrianne's blitzkrieg mind. True to form, she enlightened me.

"I never shower in the morning," she confided, teasing the gold thread edging the blue silk. "I'm against violence too early in the day. But our Steele stand-in must relish it. He's so awake, he makes sense."

Adrianne aspired, with all the dramatic resignation of a martyr, to despise professors. I tried to convince myself that she merely aped the current blasé attitudes toward academics—that she held no real animosity toward them. In this I wasn't always successful.

Dr. Brantwood turned the last fifteen minutes of class time over to the students for an open discussion. Adrianne was quick to capitalize on the opportunity.

"Would you agree that today a liberal education is a waste of academic talent?"

Dr. Brantwood merely raised an eyebrow and nodded to the class to respond.

Mr. Saunders, who seemed to find Adrianne acceptable for more reasons than her views, agreed with her statement.

"The way I see it," he said, "university is insulated from reality."

"But reality is exactly what secondary education is all about," Mr. Stewart insisted.

"Amen, man!" Bob Davis interposed. "The reality of theory. Like we're all guinea pigs. You know it!"

The debate raged just as Adrianne hoped it would. She had a notable knack for generating off-topic discussions, and could easily sidetrack class focus to issues she wanted to discuss.

Some took sides with the system. Others were against it. Still others preferred the center ground, not wishing to have the dust of either side on their philosophies. Adrianne was not impressed with those who wouldn't commit themselves one way or the other. "Wishy Washies," as she termed them, were not her favorite people. To Adrianne, failure to take a clear stand on an issue showed a definite lack of character.

Adrianne's own style of discussion was not unique, but it was effective. The whole structure was not half as engaging to Adrianne as the beams and bolts. Passionately fond of picking up little details and building Eiffel towers with them, she would never leave an issue that interested her until every facet was explored to her satisfaction. Loving the equivocal as she did, if Adrianne had had more of a religious cast of mind, she might have been accused of casuistry. In reality, far from being concerned with how many angels could dance on the head of a pin, Adrianne didn't care how many angels danced on the whole of Canada.

As I'd heard the arguments for and against the educational system many times, my thoughts turned elsewhere. Perhaps something in the character of the new professor brought to mind Coleridge's *Kubla Khan*.

In Xanadu did Kubla Khan
A stately pleasure dome decree:
Where Alph, the sacred river, ran
Through caverns measureless to man
Down to a sunless sea.[1]

It would have been nice if the poem had been finished. I'd tried various endings of my own, but none were satisfactory. The ending had to be Coleridge's.

"Miss Collingsgate," said a cool voice. Realizing I'd missed a question directed to me, I looked up embarrassed.

"Dreaming of ibises on the Nile?" Dr. Brantwood asked. It was a rhetorical question, but something in the professor's manner struck a responsive chord.

"I was . . . thinking of *Kubla Khan*," I answered truthfully. "Wishing Coleridge could have completed it." I didn't wish to be labeled a daydreamer, but it was worse to offend someone who had come halfway.

Dr. Brantwood grimaced. "Does your fascination with Coleridge extend to his less lurid flights of fancy?"

"If you mean his acclaimed criticism of Shakespeare," I answered, feeling properly rebuffed, "yes, it does."

Satisfied that there was some literary hope for me, Dr. Brantwood directed the attention of the class to the assignments for next day.

When class was over, Adrianne was jubilant. "Way to go, Dio!" she exulted. "Clever way to end the discussion. I'm proud of you."

Misconstruing my intent, Adrianne presumed my reply to Dr. Brantwood was intended to be disruptive. I was surprised Adrianne misunderstood. That wasn't my way.

Hoping to keep her intuitive instincts at bay, I asked, "What did you think of the comments from the class?"

Adrianne kicked disdainfully at a pebble. "That Stewart," she razzed, slapping a small fist against the flat of her navy binder. "I'll bet he salutes the flag every morning and gargles "God Save The Country From The Communists" every night. He makes the John Birch Society look like an overly tolerant clambake."

"He's from an older generation," I reminded her gently. "He probably served in the war and has seen a lot of things we haven't."

"I'll bet he has. No doubt the enemy was glad he was fighting for our side."

"You don't believe in cutting anyone slack, do you?" I said, repressing a sigh. I knew I was on dangerous ground, but felt some defense of the conservative mind was needed.

"I can appreciate your desire to improve the status quo, Adrianne, but perhaps Mr. Stewart isn't interested in reform. Perhaps all he wants to do is live and let live."

"Yes. I suppose you're right," Adrianne acquiesced. She looked visibly tired, and I wanted to put my arm around her and give her a hug.

"See you tomorrow," was all I said.

"Yeah. Tomorrow," she returned.

After the first day's mix-up, Dr. Brantwood was punctuality incarnate. He began classes promptly at nine and ended exactly at ten thirty. With genuine consideration, he never ran the lecture over like many professors did when they became absorbed in a topic. As there was a scant ten minutes to make it to the next class, this very real courtesy was appreciated by all the students.

If I left the library at eight forty, I usually arrived in Arts at ten to nine. Typically, Neila, Mrs. Weiss, and Dr. Brantwood could be counted on to be there when I arrived. Adrianne insisted that Neila slept in her chair, and that if Mrs. Weiss was ever late again, it would be because all the clocks on campus but hers were wrong. Knowing Adrianne's haphazard lifestyle, I understood her discomfort around Mrs. Weiss. Always on time, Mrs. Weiss had a mind to match where nothing was ever mislaid or out of sequence. It was rumored, not unbelievably, that she had a photographic memory. Certainly she had impressive recall.

"Weiss has facts and figures starched and stacked for every occasion," Adrianne quipped. It was true; statistics were Mrs. Weiss' forte. When called upon to defend her position, she could brandish information with the effect of a lethal weapon. After graduation, Lois planned to be a high school teacher; where she would be, in all likelihood, a meritoriously efficient instructor.

Adrianne was not efficient and she wasn't punctual. The only routine she cared to follow was in vying with Janice Suffolk for last person to class. Neither Janice nor Adrianne ever arrived on time if they could help it. Outside of occasionally meeting at the door, Adrianne and Janice had little patience with each other.

If you didn't know them, it would be hard to understand their mutual coolness. Both held a hearty contempt for rules. Both were feminist, both equally disdainful of the world's injustice. Yet I couldn't help feeling that while Adrianne wanted equal rights for all, Janice desired something more than equality for herself, but that was perhaps unfair. Today, coincidentally, Adrianne and Janice were both on time.

"I see Suffolk's in," Adrianne sighed. She dropped her binder on the table and slammed down beside me. "If God meant women to have one hand groping in their bosom, he'd have given them an extra one."

Janice, the cause of Adrianne's annoyance, was reclining on her chair at the end of the table in her usual languid, cross-legged posture, her left hand alternately fondling the simulated gold button on her blouse and the pearl on the silver chain around her slender throat.

Adrianne banged her binder open, shuffling some of the loose-leaf papers into an asymmetrical heap. "Those of obvious endowments aside," she mused, her mood changing, "will you tell me how one frail child can manage all those references? I'd say from the looks of those titles that Neila's been snitching from the reserve section of the library."

I cast a quick, concerned glance in Neila's direction. Oblivious to all outside influences, Neila was hunched tensely behind a huge stack of books. It wasn't unusual for Neila to bring many books to class. Both Janice and Neila were behaving normally. The difference today was with Adrianne, who for some reason found routine behaviors aggravating.

"Ah, thank thickets! Bramblybriar to the rescue!" Adrianne swung her red clad feet onto the supporting rung of her chair and leaned on her elbows with a sigh of relief.

Just when or why Adrianne started calling Dr. Brantwood *"Bramblybriar,"* I couldn't pinpoint. I did ask her about it one day after class as we were leaving.

"You need to ask that?" she'd retorted. "You should know. You were brought up in a briar patch. Rose briars, but briars nonetheless. If this prof isn't a Bramblybriar, he certainly pretends well. He's all surprises and sharp edges. Just when you figure him out, you get your theories punctured."

Both Kumari and I laughed. "You don't like to be kept guessing?" Kumari ventured.

"No, I don't," Adrianne admitted, then added roguishly. "Be nice to keep Bramblybriar guessing, though; don't you think, Dio?" I knew better than to pick that one up.

To introduce the topic, English Literature and the Creative Process, Dr. Brantwood placed a flat print of a work by Taft on the blackboard ledge. "You might be familiar with Leonardo Taft's *Solitude of the Soul*," he stated. "It's a good example of *'relievo'*, the type commonly termed Italian Alto Relief. What you can't see in this print, is that the figure is raised from the background by half its width."

Dr. Brantwood paused for class response. It appeared no one was acquainted with the work, or if they were, they didn't care to comment.

"Yes, Dr. Brantwood continued, "as is obvious, the statue is not dressed for the senate. Don't be concerned, Miss Collingsgate. After a decade of attempting to enlighten students, the temptation to leer at statues, clothed or unclothed, is not great."

There was more than a hint of laughing patronage in Dr. Brantwood's tone. Startled that he should address his comment directly to me, I looked away, struggling to fathom his meaning.

A provocative gleam in her eyes, Adrianne leaned toward me and whispered, "Your Sunday School approach to life is showing, Di. Better shorten your skirt or be left behind."

The comment hurt. How often I'd been teased by Adrianne and taunted by others for my supposed "candy cane" morality. It was true, I did have standards. But that was my own lifestyle; I inflicted my pattern for living on no-one, and wasn't incensed against those whose idea of living the good life differed from mine. I didn't force my beliefs on others. Adrianne, of all people, should have known that. Something long repressed inside made me wish to retort, to protest the unfairness of the criticism. I raised my hand. As I'd already been executed, making some defense couldn't hurt.

"I think I understand why the statue is naked," I said boldly. "Our souls, in solitude, must be naked. In solitude, to be utterly naked is the only safety, the only truth. If we deceive ourselves with unwarranted trappings, we lie to the persons who matter most—ourselves."

There was silence in the classroom. It had been quite a speech, especially for me. I felt my face flushing and wished I'd kept my peace. Dr. Brantwood leaned back against the blackboard. Moving his head thoughtfully to one side, he looked appraisingly at me, as if about to respond.

Instead, it was Mr. Hito, the Japanese student who spoke. "Is belief," he said with careful enunciation, "Miss Collingsgate correct. True self can be met in only solitude. Public self wears shroud."

"You mean a mask," corrected Bob Davis. "Only corpses wear shrouds." A few students tittered at Davis's rude remark. Mr. Hito merely bowed his head to Davis with courteous formality.

Mrs. Buckles intervened. "I see where this is leading," she said. "The creative process, whether for poet, writer, or artist, must begin at some point in solitude."

For the first time, Dr. Brantwood granted the class a full smile. As with most people when they smile, it made him appear younger and more approachable. He nodded his head, visibly glad to have made connection with another rational mind. "Thank you, Bernice," he commended. "You have saved the day."

After class, Adrianne turned ecstatically toward me. "Can I believe my ears? Is this my Didymus—my timid armadillo—making waves? Last period you derailed the discussion. Today you're making out with the sassy back talk. What will you be doing next? Leading a student riot?"

Adrianne stopped exulting long enough to give me a warm hug. "You make me so proud! But now," she added, changing her tone, "you and Kumari go on without me. I have some serious sculling to do with Neila. She's going to drown in her own stew if someone doesn't fling her a life jacket."

Both Kumari and I breathed a sigh of relief. "Thanks, Adrianne," I said sincerely. Such an impulsive, kindly gesture was so like my effervescent friend. Although she could at times be as abrasive as sandpaper, she did care. She wanted to see the world made into a better place, and she did what she could. Neila was in for some fancy lecturing, if not outright hectoring, but with Adrianne on her case, Neila was soon going to be swinging with the best. Once Adrianne took on a project, she never gave up. Neila's fate, if not assured, was going to take a decided turn for the better.

Chapter Four

All inmost things . . . are melodious;
. . . all deep things are song.

—Thomas Carlyle: *Hero as Poet* [5]

Although the weather was mild, I was forced to stay in bed for the next few days with a severe chest cold. While Aunt Amy fussed good-naturedly, and Ginny was empathetic, I disliked having to miss classes. Most especially, I regretted missing Dr. Brantwood's class, since it might appear my absence was on account of his comments.

The second day I was away, Adrianne phoned confirming my misgivings. "Hi, Dia Mia," she greeted cheerily. "I thought you'd flown away to some mountain hermitage in Tibet. So did Brambly-briar. He asked me where you were. So where are you and why?"

"Nothing serious, Adrianne," I assured her. "Just a cold."

"What're you wearing?"

"My PJs. Why do you ask?"

"Just wanted to be sure you haven't taken the orders. With your eyes, you'd make a stunning nun, but I prefer you in street clothes."

"Thanks for calling, Adrianne." I smiled and hung up the receiver. Adrianne knew I didn't miss classes unless necessary. She was only rummaging around to see what she could discover of more sensational interest. Although at times Adrianne could be overbearing, her concern was genuine.

Fortunately, the weather continued to be warm for the next few days, enabling me to spend the sunny afternoons in the garden. It was wonderful just being outside. Just as the home was Ginny's domain, the garden was Father's. Roses were the only flower Father cultivated, but they were of variety and abundance to attract even a disinterested eye. Hybrid tea, polyantha, floribunda, miniature, and fairy roses—Father included them all. I had to agree with Adrianne on that point. I had grown up in a rose arbor.

The afternoon sun was warm on my face. Content, sitting on rock bench by the pool, I allowed myself the pleasure of simply musing. The life of a student suited me, just as the roses did the garden. Studies were my natural habitat, but today I was happy to be out in the midst of the still abundant floral loveliness.

Styled in the classic design, the garden's charm depended on perfect balance, purposefully structured by two formal pergolas, covered in season with yellow Elegance roses. One pergola arched boldly on either side of the pool, the sides of which were banked with polished flat rocks. The cobblestones of a matching walk led from the gate into two branching arms that reached around the pool in a circling sweep to the front steps. In the center of the pool, on the raised mound of earth, a stunning white Innocence rose presided alone. Surrounded only by her own reflection on the water, the Innocence was a dazzling queen on a natural throne.

As I admired the white rose reigning unchallenged on her central dais, a disturbing feeling of likeness came over me. Was I like this icy rose? Did I separate myself from life—from others—by a gulf no one could pass over? Was it more important to seek perfection than to know the communion of fellow travelers? I hoped that wasn't true. Collingsgate was far from being a remote outpost. It hosted many visitors in all seasons. Friends were always welcome.

Feeling expansive, I looked toward the university. Today, it was tempting to believe in Ginny's theory that people were really roses walking around. Some had thorns, some didn't; some were more showy, but all had beauty. Before today, I'd never seen much similarity between people and roses. Was it possible you had to know both species well to appreciate them? Like Dr. Brantwood? This I didn't doubt, but not wishing to focus on that subject, I turned my attention once again to the garden.

The China Mermaids, growing by the bench, were Ginny's favorite roses; although, Ginny loved all the roses, giving each one a personalized name. Mostly she named them after family and friends, including her canary Carlyle—the Golden Glow. The 'Adrianne' rose was the cerise Caprice, which did describe her rather deftly.

Ginny's rose was, of course, the China Mermaid, playfully dubbed "Chin Me" by Father. Mother's rose was the fragrant Zephirin Drouhin, but in truth, every rose Father planted was Mother's rose. She, like Ginny, loved them all. The flower Ginny named for Father was the Buccaneer. Privately, I thought the Masquerade floribunda was more his style.

The designated 'Diana' rose was the flame-red Heart's Desire, which wouldn't have been my choice, preferring a less showy flower for a namesake. Ginny knew my feelings, but wasn't perturbed. One day, in a playful mood, she even named a rose for my future knight, whoever he might be. She chose the Black Prince. The Black Prince wasn't really black but rather wine-red, deep as blood fire. I had to admit it was a captivating rose, especially when seen next to the white Innocence.

Dear Ginny. Her domain was larger than the house. Why hadn't I seen it before? She was here in the garden in every rose she named. The sweet memory of the day Ginny came up with her plan to name the flowers wrapped around me. She was eleven; it was a year after Mother's passing. Marching into Father's study, small hands resolutely on her hips in a defiant pose, Ginny had said firmly, "The famous people in my family will have roses named after them." Ginny was, as Father noted, "incurably romantic."

This romanticism extended to the naming of the Blue Spruce which Great Grandfather William had planted around the property. As there was no record of the trees being named, Ginny had cheerfully corrected that oversight. Coming into Collingsgate you would see Richard and Carolynne, Grandfather and Grandmother Blue Spruce, stalwartly guarding opposite ends of the east-west line of trees. Richard and Carolynne were the tallest, but all the trees had achieved considerable height. Thankfully, they were far enough from the house not to impede the view, their towering strength protecting rather than confining.

A feeling of warm gratitude swept through me. I felt thankful to have been born into this independent, strong-willed family. Through no effort or virtue of my own, I was the recipient of much love and blessed to live in a home of considerable beauty. I looked past the garden to the path that led north to the university.

Thinking of the university brought me back to my studies. Enough daydreaming for one day. Time to get to work on my presentation of Spenser's epic poem *The Faerie Queene*. It would need to be convincing. The portrayal of Queen Elizabeth I as Gloriana, and King Arthur as Magnificence, the 'complete man,' fascinated me. Nevertheless, being aware that the central thesis of the poem—the moral life—was not greatly extolled in our worldly-wise society, I had a foreboding my report would be scrutinized meticulously.

Chapter Five

And I have felt
A presence that disturbs me with the joy
Of elevated thoughts; a sense sublime
Of something far more deeply interfused

—William Wordsworth: *Tinturn Abbey*[6]

A few days after Adrianne phoned, I returned to classes. In English 550, Dr. Brantwood's lecture focused on the Romantic poets: Wordsworth, Coleridge, Shelley, Byron, and Keats. The topic was the "Poetic Vision". Midway through the lecture, Adrianne raised her hand.

"Everyone knows the 'landscape magnificent' affected Wordsworth deeply, but isn't it also true that Wordsworth glorified nature?"

"How do you mean?" Dr. Brantwood responded with interest.

"He embellished nature with his poetic vision," Adrianne replied.

"You suggest Wordsworth over-romanticized the real thing?" Dr. Brantwood asked pleasantly. "Does anyone agree? Was Wordsworth more imposing than imposed upon?"

"As the name of Wordworth's initial romantic work, *Lyrical Ballads*, suggests," Harris interjected without waiting to be recognized, "his view of nature is lyrical. It's purposefully colored—intentionally romantic."

"Your ball, Miss Eaton," Dr. Brantwood returned. "Does Wordsworth's 'emotion recollected in tranquility' stand up to scrutiny? Does Wordsworth enhance nature, or is he describing the real thing?"

"Given that Wordsworth saw poets as extraordinary men with extraordinary perception, he possibly thought he was describing the real thing," Adrianne replied, graciously conceding.

"The point being," Mrs. Weiss added, "to enable ordinary men to appreciate the beauty they might otherwise miss."

Dr. Brantwood nodded, thoughtfully looking at the class. Swiftly placing his notes in his briefcase, he directed the students to use the remaining time to describe from memory a natural scene in the vicinity of campus. We were to record only what we could factually remember of the scene and not to fantasize upon the reality in mind; the idea being to describe some part of the landscape as one might for a blind person. We were to conclude with the relationship this 'segment of nature' had to life. What was to be learned from nature? It was a novel assignment; however, the class complied without a fuss.

On my route to the university, the river wound abruptly around a bend. Without warning, the footpath that ran parallel to the water's edge cut ten or more feet straight into the river. If you didn't know the precipice was there, you might stumble down it into the swiftly moving water. The cut bank terminating the path was the result of a thunderstorm. A deluge of water had overburdened the small stream running down from the hills to join the river and sheared away the bank, leaving a potentially dangerous surprise for anyone not familiar with the change.

The recent slide, exposing raw torn earth wouldn't be the most popular choice for a living-room wall, having neither pastoral charm nor natural nobility. Not large enough to be awe inspiring, it was only a cliff of ragged, brown earth with a scarred, plain face. Nevertheless, its simplicity stood out in my mind, so I decided to attempt it. I did have the advantage of knowing the area well, as it was downriver from a favorite spot where I often went to restore my spirits after a hectic day of studies. To me, the eroded piece of earth was an example of the changeability of the natural world;

its violent birth symbolic of the impermanence and fragility of life, where nature and nature's God alone continue.

I was pleased with my choice, as the jagged cut bank certainly had relevance to real life. Landforms change; rivers cut new channels; level fields are raped of their topsoil, leaving barren wastelands; mountains are worn down to the sea and valleys raised. With the passage of the seasons and years, the entire landscape shapes anew, each stage only a temporary moment in the ever-ongoing cycle.

The following day, Dr. Brantwood returned our assignments. Coming to mine, he placed it on the table in front of me. Contrasted against the dark wood, the paper looked sickly pale. As if assessing my resilience, the professor quietly observed me for a moment, then commented in a calm voice. "You write like an idealistic freshman, Miss Collingsgate. That everything changes isn't the most original theme. It's been doing that since Eve first lusted after the forbidden fruit."

The double criticism was overpowering, and the words stung. After four years I was used to professors' acid remarks, but today Dr. Brantwood's casual indictment burned deep.

While I chafed inwardly, Dr. Brantwood calmly continued returning student papers. Heartsick, I couldn't even open mine to see my mark. Somehow, although I knew my face was flushed, I kept my composure. It would do no good to publicly advertise that the professor's words had hit their mark.

At ten thirty the period buzzer sounded reprieve. Gathering my books quickly, I rose to leave, and although still mortified, I did manage to keep my shoulders straight as I strode from the classroom. At the door, Dr. Brantwood nodded his head congenially and said quietly, "Good morning, Miss Collingsgate."

Pausing in brief amazement, I lifted my eyes to his. The class was finished, and as I knew myself to be in some disdain, the greeting was surprising. Good morning was something offered at a beginning, not an end.

Once out of earshot of the classroom, Adrianne grabbed my arm. "Hey, Deny Dee. What did I tell you?" she gloated. "Bramblybriar is paying attention to you. Beware huntress. He has a "lean and hungry"[7] look!"

I was in no mood for Adrianne's imaginative speculations. "What are you jabbering about?" I said crossly. "Didn't you hear the drumming I got in front of the whole class?"

"Sure I did. But do you think he'd dish it out if he didn't think you could take it?"

"Perhaps. But what does that have to do with his hungry look, Shakespearean or otherwise?"

"Diana," Adrianne said softly, "Profs—gods as they appear to you—have blood, not the milk of all virtue, flowing in their veins."

"You suspect they're human?"

"Au entire. Especially this one."

When I said nothing, Adrianne inquired coyly, "Have you ever seen a shepherd in wolf's clothing?"

"What are you chattering about now?" I was nearing the end of my patience.

"Nothing. Except there was one watching you last period. Quite intently too, had you cared to notice."

"Adrianne! I do wish you'd stick to facts and not impose your lyrical lunacy on my life. First a god, now a shepherd disguised as a wolf. What kind of mixed-up persona is that?"

"You can pooh-pooh all you like," Adrianne retorted, "but if my intuition is correct, you'd be safe with the wolf, but watch out for the shepherd." Adrianne looked fixedly at me, her green eyes challenging. Not wanting to create a rift between us, I tried again.

"Adrianne," I urged, "think! I just received a resounding criticism. You heard it. Everyone heard it. While you're programming the universe, at least take into account reality."

As soon as I'd said the words, I was sorry. I hadn't meant to hurt Adrianne because I was hurt. Adrianne narrowed her eyes and looked at me disgustedly out of the slits.

"You're impossible, Diana," she said flatly, "just remember, if someone does manage to sneak past those closed doors of your mind that—"

"You told me so?" I said, throwing discretion to the wind.

"For a girl who seldom dates, you're somewhat overconfident."

"Adrianne—"

Adrianne gave a long sigh and shook her head. "I'm sorry, Di. It's only that Bramblybriar is noticeably aware of you. Oh, what's the use? See you for lunch, you saintly sandhead." Adrianne started to walk away. Halting, she turned and walked back to me, resolve on her face.

"If I were you, Diana," she advised, "I'd take a wee peek at your mark. I noticed you didn't in class. See you later."

Before I could respond, Adrianne clipped off down the hall. It was now my turn to sigh. Feeling I was inexperienced and naive, Adrianne often played the governess—a governess who expected her advice to be taken seriously. Another sigh escaped unbidden. Adrianne was more worldly-wise; this I gladly conceded. I just didn't like her manufacturing scenarios where I was the blissfully unaware leading lady. That could spell disaster.

Not to be dislodged, Adrianne's admonition refused to leave my mind. I hadn't the slightest doubt my mark would be dismal, but knew I'd have to look at it sooner or later. I only hoped I'd scored a pass. Once in my carrel in the library, I dug out my paper and slowly opened it to the back page. Transfixed, I couldn't take my eyes from the grading, staring at it with blank amazement. I'd received a full nine plus.

Written in the margin was the comment, "Nothing is ever really new, but old themes reviewed intelligently, refresh. Well Done."

Dropping my head on my hands, I tried to sort out my impressions. They didn't make sense. First I'm criticized—then I receive a top mark. The two facts didn't mesh. Wondering which to believe, I decided to retreat and go home early. Gathering my books, I quickly left.

As I walked across the center green, an incident that had occurred years before came unaccountably to mind. At the time I'd been attending Wildemere, a country school a few miles from Collingsgate. The old schoolhouse, long since demolished, now lived only in the memories of the students who'd attended. My memory was not of the school itself, but of a particular classmate, Earl Archibald.

School had been dismissed for the day. Just as I arrived home and was entering the gate, Earl galloped by on his Shetland pony yelling, "I love you!" as loudly as a nine-year-old riding horseback at break-neck speed could manage. The public profession was made all the more astonishing by the manner it was delivered. Although embarrassed, I felt more concern for Earl than for myself. He looked so insecure clinging bareback to his pony, as he raced by at that frantic pace. After his precarious ride, Earl never spoke to me again, except for once on the playground, to assure me I was the meanest, ugliest, most horrid girl in the entire school. The incident hadn't crossed my mind for years. Now, unpredictable as associations are, it was as clear to me as if it had just occurred.

"Spearing Vikings, Miss Collingsgate?" It was Professor Brantwood. Deep in recollection, I had stumbled into him. He must have been attempting to cross the sidewalk, but hadn't come into view until I jarred forcefully against him.

"It was my fault," I blurted, profoundly embarrassed for the second time in one day. "I wasn't looking."

"Of course," he agreed amiably, "ostriches are fine people, too."

"Thank you . . . that is . . . I mean thank you for giving me the first class on my paper."

"Not at all. But I don't give first class marks. You have to earn them."

"Thank you," I repeated, beginning to feel like a parrot in overdrive.

"So you said," he responded gravely.

Bending, Dr. Brantwood retrieved something on the ground. It was my pencil, which must have dropped when I crashed into him. The plain orange marker looked notably stunted in his long fingers. Noticing my agitation, he handed the pencil to me with an easy gesture.

"You have no need for anxiety, Miss Collingsgate," he said quietly. "Society was long ago pillaged of its best. What little plunder is now left to us, we give away." He stood looking at me with calm violet eyes, as if debating to ask me something. Then nodding, he turned down the walk he'd been attempting to cross before the collision.

Hastily gathering myself together, I too departed for home. While relieved by Professor Brantwood's lighthearted dismissal of the awkward incidents in the classroom and on the sidewalk, his insinuation that I approached life with my head buried in the sand was disconcerting. I wondered if Adrianne had been typing his scripts.

Equally difficult to fathom, while Dr.Brantwood's comments indicated a rather destitute view of society, he himself approached life with resolve: back straight, head erect, carriage gracefully commanding respect. He was a puzzling enigma. His disenchantment with humanity resembled the attitude of those who prefer to cop out in contempt of traditional order. Paradoxically, his acceptance of responsibility for the direction of his life, bore little similarity to the rebellious lifestyle of the directionless transient.

In spite of Dr. Brantwood's dissident views, he was impressive mentally. It was just hard to know where he stood on issues. Indeed, when I attempted to form an accurate picture of his position on things, I felt like the frog that fell back two jumps into the well for every jump taken toward the light. His mind remained closed to me, while I had the uncomfortable feeling my thoughts lay open before him, exposed and indefensible as a tadpole out of water.

Chapter Six

Hear me now, oh thou bleak and unbearable world
Thou art base and debauched as can be
And a knight with his banners all bravely unfurled
Now hurls down his gauntlet to thee.

—Joe Darion: *I Am I, Don Quixote from Man of La Mancha.*[8]

At noon the following day, I met Adrianne in SUB cafeteria for lunch. We took a table opposite the soft drinks machine next to the stairs. A location open to public scrutiny was not my preference, but there was little choice. The cafeteria was already crowded and there were few tables left, so privacy was impossible.

Clearly in high spirits, Adrianne enthusiastically munched on her hamburger and chips. Shoving a golden chip into a dab of ketchup, my observant friend surveyed my homemade salad with barely concealed distaste.

"You know, Dio," she advised sweetly, "it's dining on watercress and drinking rose dew that causes you to go staggering into people like you were 'James James Morrison's mother.' Why don't you eat a decent meal?"

Adrianne wasn't concerned with my eating habits, but I was surprised she knew of the incident with Dr. Brantwood on the sidewalk. "It was an accident," I affirmed patiently. "He was going one way, I was going the other."

"Well, Miss Die Hard, don't be surprised if he changes his direction. In case you're interested, he could have stepped aside.

He saw you coming." Adrianne looked at me with an innocently satisfied air, waiting with dramatic restraint for my reaction.

Laughing outright at the ploys of her romantic imagination, I choked on a piece of lettuce in a vain attempt to keep the laughter from sounding rude. Adrianne flipped her fork upside down on her plate and rose briskly in pretended pique. "Try a hamburger. It'll improve your eyesight." She grinned cheerfully at me, magnanimously forgiving my indiscreet outburst.

"By the way, what time is it?" she asked, hastily looking at her watch with the tiny gold hands on the small heart-shaped face. "I never buy a watch with a dial I can read. Watching time fly makes me sooo nervous."

"Twelve forty-five," I said, glancing down at my own watch with the large round face and plain silver hands.

"Great. I'm late. Which means I'm right on time. See you tomorrow, Dioptric. And watch those clandestine sidewalk mergers." To illustrate her point, Adrianne banged her chair awkwardly into place, bumped dramatically into the stair railing, and slammed pell-mell down the stairs, barely missing a group of students.

"You too," I mused softly, smiling at Addy's artful Chaplinesque exit.

Miss Eaton, the comedienne, tossed me a spirited wave from the bottom of the stairs and passed through the doors to the foyer. She was off to an election rally for Nelson Cruthers. She'd been seeing a lot of Nelson since term began and was helping to manage his campaign. Her ardor inspired admiration, but I hoped she would respect my right to secret ballot. I didn't have Adrianne's confidence in Nelson.

Adrianne didn't show up for English 550 the following morning, but absence from class wasn't unusual for her. Presumably she was working late on Nelson's campaign platform. At eleven o'clock, she met me outside SUB on her way to Ag for her zoology class, which she called *Bugs*. She fell in step beside me, her cherry-red shoes exclaiming loudly against her bright copper hair.

"What is Dutiful Di doing out of the library at only eleven bells?" she teased. "Where is your towering sense of responsibility? Gone with the old gray goose, I hope."

"Adrianne," I dared to tease back, "the last time you chided me on my study habits, it was an albatross around my neck like the 'ancient mariner.' Now, only an old gray goose?"

"Good heavens, Di! Haven't you noticed? This is the twentieth century. Things change." Adrianne gave me a roguish glance. "Now, don't be evasive. What're you doing out of your safety zone this time of day? Aren't you supposed to be nicely entombed in your study carrel at Edwards until noon?"

"It's my turn for a term paper interview with Dr. Brantwood."

"Oh, is that all? Like me to go along?"

"Your company's always welcome," I said sincerely.

"That isn't what I meant and you know it, Dimocence," she retorted, rolling her composed, cat eyes at me with saucy eloquence. "You might need someone to scream for help."

"If I'm in need, there's always Dr. Brantwood," I said calmly. "If you're right, he won't mind lending a hand."

"Diana Deity. Your attitude is definitely destructive. Puts me in mind of the *Funeral March of a Marionette*."

"I didn't know you were a fan of Hitchcock."

"I'm not. Just fond of a wooden-headed friend I know."

"Completely without strings," I assured her.

"I wonder." Adrianne looked at me solemnly, her head tilted to one side. "You know, Diana," she said thoughtfully, "life is a beautiful adventure, but you'll never get to enjoy it with your head in the sand." Her admonition given, Adrianne grinned at me in the impish, charming way of hers and went her way to Ag.

Watching her swing blithely along the walk, Wordsworth's description of Milton, "Thy soul was like a Star,"[9] sprang into my thoughts. With my friend's remarkable imprint on my mind, I continued to Dr. Brantwood's English office, which was located on south campus in the renovated home WU students fondly entitled *The Manse*.

As I walked, I mulled over Adrianne's comment. How delighted she would be if she knew how similarly she and Dr. Brantwood assessed my approach to life. It was clear they both considered me sadly uninitiated; although, it would be a toss-up which one considered that state the most dangerous.

The Manse was very old. Having been built before the turn of the century, ivy had long since covered the greater part of the orange brick and even infringed on the window space. Initially, the stately building had been an elegant and massive family residence. Years later, when housing was short during the war, the family sold it to the university to provide suites for the staff. Still later, when the staff could find accommodation elsewhere, the building was subdivided further into offices.

Situated in a lovely spot overlooking the river, I hoped The Manse would outlast the vengeance of those who could see only the leaks in the plumbing and the economic waste in heating a building with so many alcoves and high ceilings. Most especially, I hoped it would outlast those who cared nothing for its history: those who wanted to rid themselves of what was, to their eyes, only a wasting "pile of brick."

With high domed ceiling and marble flooring, the main entrance to the building thankfully still retained much of its original charm. Projecting a feeling of grandeur, it represented a style of living lost to the hurrying world. No doubt if design had permitted, the vestibule would have been divided long ago with the rest of the building, but fortunately the cost of lowering the ceiling and installing heating prohibited this disfigurement.

With the exception of the vestibule, the rest of the venerable old edifice had attained, through successive remodeling, a modern pinnacle of ugliness. I'd been in The Manse many times, either on errands for Father or fulfilling assignments of my own, but I still couldn't adjust to the desecration. Apart from the entrance, the interior of the building was a grave disappointment. It wasn't as it should have been. Remodeled into obscurity, The Manse was soulless.

I gained the first-floor landing and turned north along the second floor. Halfway down the hall, I was surprised but pleased by the sound of piano music drifting through the usually quiet corridor. The music department had offices in the newly constructed Arts Center, but none that I knew of in The Manse. Pausing, I listened with growing appreciation. The flowing melody seemed to rise out of the past when the place was loved and had a heart. In the music, the picturesque old building had for the moment found its soul again.

As the serene music continued to drift through the hall, it brought a feeling of peace. It was originating, or so I thought, from Room 12, which should have been Dr. Brantwood's office. Not wishing to leave the lovely sound, but strongly disinclined to interrupt the player, I stood entranced outside the slightly open door.

"Come in, Miss Collingsgate," a familiar baritone voice invited.

I opened the door, but didn't enter. The room greeting my eyes held me immobile, transfixed as though gazing into a seer stone. The interior of the room, accordant with The Manse as it once must have been in every detail, suited the stately exterior of the building as perfectly as fine crystal compliments heirloom silver. Leather-bound books, hand-crafted desk, carved wooden mantle with its graceful mirror, turn-of-the-century furniture; it was all there. There was even an oil painting of Jean-Francois Millet's "Angelus" hanging on the wall.

Most unexpected of all, in perfect harmony with the room, Dr. Brantwood rested easily on the piano bench, playing reflectively on a worn, but still elegant grand. The music, the room, Dr. Brantwood, the very atmosphere—all were consistent with the spirit of the vestibule. It was the embodiment of what I'd always imagined—what I'd always wished to see in the fine old building. Accepting my silent veneration, the room held out to my astonished mind, an allurement that was nothing less than mesmerizing.

Dr. Brantwood looked up from his playing, motioning with a nod for me to enter. Clearly not self-conscious at having an audience, he continued playing, his graceful fingers moving effortlessly over the ivory and ebony keys.

Moving quietly to the russet armchair indicated, I listened appreciatively as the music continued to infuse my mind with wonder. How suitably ordered everything was here. It was a place for the spirit as well as the mind, with whispers of past valor drifting in on the music to renew the present. Relaxed by the soothing harmonies, I laid my head against the tall back of the chair, the velvet upholstery on the arms fawn-soft under my fingers.

"Sleeping?" At the sound of Dr. Brantwood's voice, I opened my eyes with a start. He had stopped playing and was standing by the piano observing me, the sunlight from the window highlighting his outline. Realizing I'd committed an error in etiquette, I rose hastily.

"The music, Ketèlbey," I said apologetically. "It—"

"It sometimes puts me to sleep also," Dr. Brantwood said. "That's why I play it. He grinned boyishly. "'It knits up the ravell'd sleeve of care.'"[10]

The professor didn't seem at all offended by my lapse of courtesy, but as he leaned against the piano, there was something disturbing about his congenial manner. While wishing to clarify my response, I did not wish him to know how much his authentically accoutred office and his playing moved me.

"What I mean to say is, Ketèlbey allows more than requires. He doesn't demand; we give him our regard."

"You mean he lets you sleep more than makes you?" The intelligent eyes surveying me had splotches of green around their edges; they put me in mind of the moss sometimes scattered on the surface of a forest pond.

"Have you invested in music personally, Miss Collingsgate? Or are you merely entertained?"

"Committed," I said honestly, appreciating his phrasing. "At least, I have been since I was thirteen."

Dr. Brantwood raised an interested eyebrow. "What happened at thirteen to focus your interest?"

"In Junior symphony, I lost my place in Beethoven's *Egmont Overture* and had to fake a fair number of passages before I found my place again." A slight smile played around the professor's lips. The moss on the pond gathered, deepening to a darker hue.

"Why did you hesitate so long before entering?" he asked abruptly. "I heard you approach. You have a distinctive walk."

"I . . . I thought perhaps it was the wrong room."

"Is it?"

"No. It's the right room. I have an appointment at eleven thirty, if you still have time."

Dr. Brantwood nodded, an inviting, yet puzzling smile on his face. Almost as fast as it had appeared, the smile vanished. Walking to his desk he took the black swivel chair with an easy movement and waited for me to speak.

Finding the draft of my paper, I handed it to him, standing while he scanned the contents. When finished, he looked at me thoughtfully.

"You are fluent on paper," he said matter-of-factly, "but tell me, Miss Collingsgate, why do you always take the long way home?"

Unprepared, I blurted, "Because I like to walk by the river. I enjoy the time to myself."

"That isn't what I mean," he responded, a faint smile once more begging the corners of his mouth. "In your essays, be direct. Say what you mean. Kiss it and leave it."

Although the criticism would require a good deal of editing, Dr. Brantwood's mildly reproving praise gave me the impression of being wrapped in silk from head to toe.

"Thank you, Sir," I said, hoping the formality would dispel the illusion. Still holding my paper, Dr. Brantwood leaned back in his chair, his eyes once again expressing mild amusement.

"That 'Sir' of yours isn't particularly flattering," he said, "and it makes you sound like one of Richardson's bashful heroines." Noticing my discomfort, he added, "It would make a fitting epitaph for a tombstone; rather makes me feel like one of the permanent residents up on the hill."

The thought of Dr. Brantwood staring with disapproving, ghostly eyes at a large engraved 'Sir' on his headstone restored my composure. In spite of my nervousness, I laughed.

"It would be apt. I mean, the term suits you." It was a foolish comment. Evidently Dr. Brantwood thought so too and dropped my paper on the table.

"You suggest I'm archaic?"

"No . . . entitled to respect."

"I see," he said. "You refer to position. Caste. You're the student. I'm the professor."

"Yes. I mean . . . no. Every person has a right to honest regard, but there is established protocol, precedents to be observed." Inwardly I blanched. I meant the sentiment, but the stilted wording sounded transparently insincere.

"I see," he said affably. "Like landlord and tenant. The landlord owns the land, the tenant pays the rent—*ipso facto* the respect due." The response seemed offhanded enough, but by the slightly mocking grimace on Dr. Brantwood's face, I could plainly see he was playing with me: tempting me to participate in his game.

Baffled how to respond, I was at a loss for words. Seeing my dismay, he changed his tact. "Are you fond of Don Quixote?" he asked. Now I was bewildered.

"Cervantes was a convincing author."

"The question is," Dr. Brantwood corrected, "do you admire—like—the character Cervantes created? Do you like Don Quixote—the man himself?"

"I admire anyone who follows their dream," I admitted. "Quixote wasn't crazy by moral standards."

"I'm not contesting Quixote's sanity or standards of morality. I simply ask, irrespective of personal reality, do you like Don Quixote?"

"As much as any crusader," I evaded.

"Crusader?" Dr. Brantwood asked with a tone of surprise.

"He did crusade for the right. Didn't he?" The rhetorical question fell flat.

"I see," he said. "All these years I've admired the man. Liked him. Now I discover he was a religious fanatic." The Professor looked at me quizzically.

"No. I didn't mean crusader in that sense. Quixote's cause was to right all wrongs, not to militarize his faith."

"No? But you still don't like him?" Dr. Brantwood drew a resolute line through the eleven thirty listed on his appointment book.

Glad for an opportunity to excuse myself, I retrieved my outline and thanked the professor for his time. Dr. Brantwood didn't raise his head, but as I turned to leave, he said tersely, "Conversation, Miss Collingsgate, is a war of words. More polite perhaps, but a war nonetheless."

With inglorious swiftness, I retreated from the field. Relieved the interview was over, I had once again begun to feel in Dr. Brantwood's presence, as though my ears and eyes were very small, like those of the short-legged muskrat that burrows into the sides of foul-smelling mud banks and seems not to know when to hibernate sensibly.

Outside the room, away from the authority of the professor's puzzling personality, I felt an overwhelming physical need to run. Abandoning any pretense of decorum, I raced through the autumn afternoon like a child released from school on her first day of vacation. Breathless, but not tired, I was almost to SUB when a voice chimed out, halting my flight.

Chapter Seven

If you forgive people enough you belong to them,
and they to you . . . squatter's rights of the heart.

—James Hilton: *Time and Time Again*[11]

"**S**top, Di! Where're you off to in such a dither? Trying to break the campus sprint record?" Adrianne panted up beside me. "Such eagerness," she chided breathlessly. "You should see your witch doctor. Tell him you don't fit in this world. You're not properly depressed. Got too much energy." Adrianne could harass the feathers off a bird, but I was glad to see her.

"Hi, Adrianne. Did the meeting stir the proletariat to revolution?"

"Of course. At the stroke of midnight, we're massing to demand better coffee or our dimes back. Berkeley, California, bleed your heart out. You ain't seen nuttin' yet!"

"Better coffee sounds like a reasonable excuse for a demonstration," I conceded, going along with her.

"No, necessary. Someone may die if we're forced to drink any more dishwater." Adrianne looked at me from out of the corner of one sparkling eye.

"That reminds me, Di. Are you going to give blood? Or have you already? Hold out your finger." Adrianne caught my left hand and studied it sharply. Her hand was not three quarters the size of my own.

"Nope, not yet," she deduced. "You'd better get going before they close. They'll want your blood. It's chalk full of immunity."

"To?" I asked, foolishly taking the bait.

"People, of course. Definitely people."

"What did you think of the pad?" she asked innocently.

"Pad?"

"Bramblybriar's office, what else?"

"What you think is usually more entertaining, Adrianne." If it was one thing I could do without just now, it was commenting on my experience at The Manse.

"There you go, Hedgehog. Hiding behind your bristles, again." Adrianne clipped briskly along, her heels beating a sharp staccato rhythm on the cobblestone walk. I hoped she wasn't falling into a peeve.

"You don't show it, Adrianne," I said gently, hoping to tease her into a better mood, "but you're annoyed."

"You don't show it Di High, but you're bursting with mirth and congeniality."

"I'm sincerely glad to see you."

"What has that got to do with anything? I'm talking about communication. About sharing your mind." She leaned her back against the mailbox and looked at me seriously. "Why can't you open up? Why can't you share what you feel?"

Her eyes had that dangerous spark in them that said it would take something besides words to stall the coming storm. Searching for that elusive something, I turned and looked across campus to the river. The sky was overcast in the west, the clouds clinging closely to the feet of the mountains.

"Oh what's the use? Proud and aloof. That's my Selene. Always the remote, detached moon goddess. Why can't you be mortal like the rest of us?" Adrianne stamped her foot expressively on the curb. I glanced speculatively at her small, taut figure.

"Mortal? How so?"

Adrianne stepped defiantly in front of me. "Alive to life, Diana. Feeling. Responsive. Authentic." Adrianne's eyes flashed a challenge to respond. She always won the field in verbal contest between us, but I suspected were I ever to earnestly parry words with her, she may not like the outcome. The thought gave me little pleasure.

Realizing I wouldn't argue, Adrianne shrugged her shoulders and swung away with a smart military step, copper hair bouncing, red heels clicking. As I watched her swiftly retreating figure, the silent censorship in my heart softened. Why was I so severely reserved with those I loved most? Why couldn't I share what was in my heart?

I was sorry I couldn't respond the way Adrianne wished. Impulsively, I had a sudden longing to rush after her and tell her what she meant to me and everything else she wanted to know. Anything to ease her disappointment. But I didn't. I only stood and watched until she disappeared from sight. Stood, watched, and wished for her sake that I was different.

Proud and aloof. These criticisms were not new to me. I had known their bite as a child, suffered their ridicule in high school, and endured their antagonism in university. Now the cold insinuations, like the snakes wrapping around the legs of the Israelites, could no longer be endured. I wanted to be free of their pale visors. Wistfully, I looked at the clouds shrouding the mountains and wished there was an image of bronze to heal me.

Disinclined to enter the path where it crossed by The Manse, I followed the walk to the other side of campus and picked up the path there. The changing wind, in furtive autumn fashion, now light, now lusty, was playing an enticing game of hide and tell. Whispering in my ear with confident intimacy, it would suddenly slap my cheek, only to apologize a moment later, twining ingratiatingly about my ankles like an abject pussy.

It was all passion and fluff. Exhausted by the ravaging excitement of its own agitated motion, the wind would die down to rustle quietly through the grass. Then, gaining renewed strength, it would unfold a great wing and lift swirling clutches of leaves to flutter up the sides of the white birch trees, like small brightly colored flags. Almost as the leaves gained the lower branches, the wing would capriciously fold and let the leaves fall back to the earth. Silently empathizing with their plight, I watched them eddy and swirl around the base of the trees. The wind held no real compact with the leaves; it was its own master, owing allegiance to none.

Watching the patient, tireless dancing of the leaves, I felt a new pang of remorse.

Should I be as the leaves? They perhaps didn't view their plight as I did. Perhaps they didn't feel it a sacrifice to pay the price of community: to be nudged and jostled by their kind. Perhaps they found solace from the harassment of the wind by taking part in a larger, grander idea than themselves. After all, a tree was only made possible by the combined contribution of thousands of tiny generous leaves. Yes. Adrianne was right. She was right to urge me to be a leaf, a part of the whole of life. But how?

Having no immediate answer, I determined to think of other things. Aunt Amy's advice was to "Make hay while the sun shines." The sun was shining, so I might as well be doing as dying. Thus musing, I headed back to Edwards.

Walking to the library, the isolating differences softened. Dear Adrianne. Our first meeting came before my mind's eye as clearly as if there'd been no years in between; the memory of that remarkable encounter easing my feelings like sunlight after rain. It was the second week of classes in my freshman term at university. English lectures were held in an aging, water-stained, wind-browned structure long since removed. The old Arts building was never as beautiful as The Manse, but it did have a certain self-possessed air about its well-used halls. I remember one class in the Old Arts in particular—the first time I met Adrianne.

In Room 9, at the head of the rows of chairs, Professor Britten stood straight, his manner grimly pedantic, his commencement robes flapping helplessly about his thin legs. He always wore his black graduation robes to class even though most professors had long since abandoned the practice. On this day, as usual, Professor Britten stood rigidly at the front, reading from his notes. Never once did he raise his eyes from the page; never once did he change the intonation of his voice.

"We must give the author our complete credulity," Professor Britten intoned. "We must suspend our disbelief. Only then can the author lead us into his world. Unless we forego the intoxicating pleasures of skepticism and leave slide-rule realities behind, we cannot participate in the author's reality." The professor paid no attention to a student fussing impatiently in the back row.

"A literary work has its own reality. All that matters is that this reality is consistent within itself. The laws that prevail, or those seen to be operating within the work, should not be contradicted. What we must remember is that our everyday discernible reality is not, nor does it include, all reality. It is certainly not literary reality."

An assured voice from the restless student at the back interrupted the droning of the professor, bringing a moment of relief to most students.

"Would you say Jonathan Swift's *Gulliver's Travels* has this kind of internal literary reality, Sir?"

The question while disruptive, was apparently much more interesting to the student asking it than the chalky, emotionless words of the reedy, expressionless man at the front. Professor Britten looked up briefly from his notes.

"Who is this who presumes to edify the public?" he rebuked. If the professor's tone had changed inflection, or altered in any way from his reading voice, the pedantically styled rebuff might have stilled the simmering Adrianne. As it was, the sound of Professor Britten's response was as colorless as water in a glass—so devoid of intensity that it seemed to exclude participation by the speaker altogether. A snicker fled around the room at the woeful oddity that stood so tired of life at the head of a freshman class.

Undaunted, Adrianne responded, "It is I, Adrianne Eaton, newly baptized into the fold and devoutly *wishing* to be enlightened by your stimulating discourse."

There was an audible gasp from the other students. For a brief moment, Professor Britten focused his attention on Adrianne, then exacted swift but unimpassioned justice.

"If you would be so kind to leave the class, Miss Eaton. We will attempt to survive without you."

Adrianne had shrugged and left, swaggering across the floor as jaunty as a horse in a show ring. It's doubtful Professor Britten noticed her stylish exit; he being—by the time Adrianne reached the door—already on the third sentence of his notes since the interruption.

At the end of the period, Adrianne catapulted into my life. She was standing with her hands shoved into the pockets of her smart, navy blue jacket, gazing indifferently at the announcements on the tack board by the side exit. Her red leather shoes were tapping briskly against the old baseboard. Knowing only that in Adrianne's situation I'd have been mortified, I walked toward her, hopeful of offering some consolation. Belatedly realizing she might consider my approach an intrusion, I hesitated. Before I could retreat, Adrianne turned toward me. As she did, it struck me as curious that the sunlight through the small east window illuminated Adrianne's left side only. Her other side remained shadowed in the relative darkness of the hall.

"Hello, Diana," she said nonchalantly. "How are you today? Shame to waste such a beautiful morning in this dingy, anti-Republican cave, eh?"

Totally taken by surprise, I stared blankly at her.

"I know," she laughed. "Let's go dig up good old Socrates and start living the 'examined life!'"[12] If Adrianne meant to derail me, she accomplished her aim.

"I was going to introduce myself," I explained. "How did you know my name?"

Adrianne smiled, her almond eyes brimming with mystery.

"Madame Mata Hari knows all, sees all." She laughed infectiously. "Actually I saw your name on your admittance card. You placed yours on the table just ahead of mine." Adrianne took my arm. "Confidentially, I was noticing you," she disclosed. "You looked concerned about something. Anything on your mind?" Adrianne's perfect poise was amazing. I had intended to cheer her up, and she was inquiring into my attitude.

"I was—"

"Embarrassed?" Adrianne grinned, supplying the word without offense. "Don't shed another calorie over it. Next time you feel embarrassed, say so." Although this was our first meeting, Adrianne was completely at ease. Even more surprising, it was apparent she was playing with me—testing my intelligence, evaluating my resilience.

"You have a class right away?" she inquired cheerfully.

"No. My next class is in the Ed building at ten."

"Good. Mine too. I'll walk you there. We can share our false impressions."

"Share our what?"

"Oh, you know, our misconceptions about ourselves. Get acquainted. You tell me who you think you are, and I'll tell you who I'm not." Filled with wonder at the unconventional soul addressing me, I laughed in unexpected release.

"That's better!" Adrianne chuckled. "So now we know you can laugh. If you can walk at the same time, we should both get to the next class before anyone misses us." She took my arm, and together we walked down the steps and headed toward Ed.

Once outside, Adrianne said seriously, "You look better out here. I was almost afraid you were going to be ill in that antiquated mausoleum. What a ghoul that prof has become. Presides like a judge over the dead." I couldn't help laughing again.

"You draw quite a descriptive portrait."

"I keep my eyes open."

It was clear she did. Altogether, Miss Adrianne Eaton seemed a well-adjusted, thoroughly adaptable individual and nobody's fool. Seeing my respectful glance, it was Adrianne's turn to laugh.

"Actually, I'm a good cosmetician," she said modestly. "I don't paint people. They paint themselves. I only touch them up."

"You know," she said, "I've half a notion to insert a page of *Tom Jones* into the good old boy's notes. Bet he'd read the whole page and not bat an eye. And that old building—quite the eyesore, eh? Looks like it was there before they invented haunted castles."

Twenty minutes with Adrianne and she had completely captured my interest. I had the feeling that if I looked on the bottom of her left heel, I'd find a quality craftsmanship stamp. Miss Eaton made a large impression; hers was a most uncommon mentality. Vivid and quick, candid without being coarse, she inspired my admiration and won my confidence. Little did I know, then, how dearly she would get under my skin.

"I noticed you staring out the window in class," she coaxed. "And now you're staring at your feet? Afraid someone will trip over your big brown eyes?"

We laughed together. I no longer had any fears for Adrianne. She could take care of herself. It would take more than academic indifference to crush her vibrant personality.

"Good!" she cheered. "Laughing looks good on you. Hey, do ya ever get the feeling you'd like to be a kid again?"

"Not usually. Why?"

"See that pile of leaves over there?" I nodded.

"Let's strip and leap in!" Noting my quiet dismissal of the idea, Adrianne shook a tiny index finger at me with unsquelched enthusiasm. "Okay, my lady. If nude leaf leaping's too seditious for you, we'll leave our smiles on. Come on, unbend. You look like you're about to order in a new dispensation."

Adrianne shed books, purse, and shoes and splashed rambunctiously into the middle of the newly raked pile of leaves, tossing bright colors in every direction. With her hair reflecting the sunlight in swirling pools of color, she could have been a forest sprite gone mad with the intoxication of the season. Watching her enjoy herself, I thought how gleefully Shakespeare's Puck would applaud her insurrection.

A group of students stopped to watch Adrianne's antics, vicariously enjoying her harmless indulgence. "Hi there, Yellow Jacket," a tall blond boy in a green Commerce sweater teased. "Be good now, or you won't get any nectar."

Adrianne tilted her head to one side like a perky spaniel. "My dear ignorance," she said with bored sophistication, "I drink only wine."

Chapter Eight

To go straight on like field mice through the elephant's toes
or else to go back and live out the rest of this
the littlest of our lives, itching.

—Walter de la Mare: *The Three Mulla Mulgars*[13]

The following day the morning broke swiftly in the east, flowing down upon the land with the vigor of a young colt. Offering atonement for the previous day's clouds, the dawn was unusually bright. I looked out my bedroom window in Collingsgate toward the northwest. The view brought a smile to my heart. Only the dawn could rise in such splendor and make such effulgent, rapturous promises for the day. Whether it had a mind to keep the promises or break them, didn't deter the sunrise from making a swashbuckling beginning. Flourish or decline, the rest of the day would always have the promise of that beginning.

I dressed quickly in a brown pleated skirt and beige sweater. Aunt Amy and Ginny weren't up yet; Father had already left for the university. He arose with the birds—spring, summer, fall, and winter. After a glass of milk and a piece of toast, I gathered my books and purse and put on my brown topcoat. Outside, the crisp morning air tingled with the vitality of the day's glorious awakening. As I walked, the birds chirruped a chorus of cheery concern, urging the world to get swiftly to its business without delay.

At the university there were, as usual, only a few eager students up and about. While it was barely quarter to six, Adrianne was suddenly at my side. Appearing without warning was her trademark, but this morning she didn't return my smile of greeting, appearing preoccupied with the cobblestone walk. As not speaking was abnormal for Adrianne, I didn't interrupt such a pointedly philosophical silence.

Recovering from her reverie, Adrianne reproved softly, "You'd make a wonderful Othello, Di." Adrianne wasn't joking. My reply would have to be tactful.

"That makes you . . . Desdemona?"

"Exactly." Adrianne relaxed and shot me a sisterly good-morning smile. It was all right. She was again commander of the field. She would explain.

"People should verbalize their grievances. Say what's eating them. Give others a fighting chance to break even. No one likes to be suffocated without a trial." So that was it. Adrianne was apologizing for her temper on the day before.

Smiling, I said gently, "You're forgiven, Miss Eaton. Please forgive me, also." I meant it sincerely. I wanted Adrianne to know I did care. Adrianne pressed her head against my shoulder. The touch was light, but I felt it in my heart long after.

"Thanks, Di," she said warmly.

Apologies made and accepted, Adrianne announced, "Woman, am I bugged." Seeing my concern, she explained. "Not at you. It's these paralyzing pedants that get paid to harrow up our souls with their misdirected minds."

"Professors?"

"Who else? One period with their mutated mentalities and my head feels like a community ashtray. My eyelids get calluses looking at them. They're so vulgarly plebeian." Adrianne kicked at a stone with commercial disrespect.

"I don't know why I let them irritate me," she continued. "Everyone knows professors are the leftovers from the worthwhile professions. They can't cut it in other fields, so they take their frustration out on students. They fail and we suffer." It was obvious Adrianne's classes had not gone well. Miss Eaton so seldom needed bolstering that when she did, it was serious. Diplomacy was required.

"We could do without them," I ventured to empathize. I'd heard the complaint against professors before, but today what Adrianne needed was understanding, not a lecture.

"Yes," she agreed, "we could. Except for one, perhaps." She eyed me mischievously. "Well? Aren't you the least bit curious? Wouldn't you like to know which one?"

"Yes, of course," I replied, trying to keep tempo with the importance of the revelation about to be made.

"The Bramblybriar!"

I looked up sharply. Adrianne was pleased with my surprise. Savoring her success, she prodded, "You like to hear him complimented. Don't you, Di?"

"If you like," I said evenly. This new obsession of Adrianne's was becoming tiresome.

"Oh, don't be evasive, Diana. Anyway, I don't blame you. He's young. He's good looking. He's semi-intelligent." She winked wickedly at me. "He's also a prof, but hey! Three out of four isn't bad."

"Intelligent? In spite of the fact he doesn't have red hair? How can this be?"

Adrianne shook her head. "Diaphanous," she sighed, "it's simply not possible to hold an intelligent conversation with you." To ensure her comment wouldn't be taken as a criticism, she gave me an affectionate hug. "And now," she said, shooting a glance at my watch, "I've got to miss the only class worth attending and go do penance writing a psych paper."

"What's your topic?" Irrationally, I hoped for a sane reply.

"The subliminal approach to consciousness," came the swift retort. "My best friend's a master at it." Ignoring my attempt to look shocked, Adrianne gave one further admonition.

"Look me up when you decide what you're doing on this planet, Dios. In the meantime, consider this: all brilliant men—professors included—are cruel, ruthless, and despotic. So go easy on the dedication." Laughing eyes sparkling with restored confidence, Adrianne sauced her head at me and walked jauntily away toward the Ed building.

Today, Adrianne's high manner didn't worry me. She liked to make the last comment smart to help me remember her when she was gone. One thing was certain: she wasn't upset, having learned in the brief inquisition possibly more than I knew myself. In respect to her feminine curiosity, Adrianne could be as dogmatic as anyone on campus.

To Adrianne, university was not an education. It was a test of endurance that forced students to submit to intellectual sterilization. The object of attending university, far from increasing mental acuity, was to produce non-thinking, compliant cogs; useful only to keep the rusty wheel of the status quo clanking along. About the only good universities did was placate the unthinking majority with a backward progress. Like a dog dragging garbage down the street, universities—from Adrianne's viewpoint—were laden with useless traditional baggage. And tradition, from her perspective, could rot.

With these opinions, it was natural that Adrianne was a strong supporter of the student power movement. Not surprisingly, she urged me to attend the rallies and meetings with her. Fiercely indignant over injustices supposed and real in the classroom, Adrianne felt professors were ninety nine per cent dispensable.

Personally, I doubted that returning to the medieval practice of students hiring their own private tutors would be an improvement. A good teacher was an advantage, but even without one the case was never hopeless. Where a professor failed, the books on the library shelves sufficed. I did, however, find myself forced to agree with Adrianne on one point. Dr. Brantwood was an exceptional instructor. Dangerously astute, he held one's attention. Realizing it unwise to pursue this trend of thought, I shook off my reveries and headed for the Phys Ed building for my morning swim.

Chapter Nine

The foolish have no range in their scale . . .
What is not good they call the worst
and what is not hateful, they call the best.

—Ralph Waldo Emerson: *Addresses and Lectures*[14]

"**H**i, ostrich."

I looked up from my carrel in Edwards with a smile, knowing Adrianne would be leaning against the side. She borrowed a chair from another carrel and shoved it over against my desk.

"I wondered why you missed the meeting," Adrianne said, straddling the chair and leaning her chin on the metal back. "Now I see why. You're up here with your first love as usual." She reached over and flicked through a text on my desk, her eyes disdainful as a cat eyeing a piece of spoiled meat.

"You know, Di," she warned, "if you hide in here any longer today, you'll sprout whiskers and little moley eyes."

Hoping to avoid another lecture on my lifestyle, I laid down my pen. "What did you learn at the rally?" I asked.

Adrianne kicked energetically at the rung of her chair. "There, see what I mean? You think nothing's important unless you can learn something from it. Honestly, your attitude isn't normal. In a hundred years we'll both be dead and buried. Can't you see them exhuming your grave to build a super highway, only to discover one sly little pearl?"

"You mean the type of irritating thing you'd find in a mollusk."

"Yes. Irritating. What good will all this study do, then?" Adrianne shook her head, briskly willing away my flagrant waste of time. "Keep this up and you'll wind up an airy pearl of wisdom, floating around the universe interfering with someone's fun."

I laughed helplessly and leaned my head on my hands. It was obvious Adrianne wouldn't be dissuaded today. "Okay. Let's go," I acquiesced. "We can visit outside."

Gathering my books, we walked together to the elevator. The down arrow above the elevator door turned green. A Pakistani student wearing a turban and holding an armload of books got on the lift after us. He was completely unaware that he had just entered terrorist territory, and I hoped Adrianne wouldn't embarrass the reserved gentleman. She had a passion for striking up conversations in elevators with strangers. It didn't matter if they were men or women, young or old, native or foreign; neither race nor age nor gender could deter Adrianne. As long as they were on the elevator, they were fair game. While it was possibly my own timidity, discussing with a perfect stranger whatever Adrianne happened to pull out of her hat wasn't my idea of a fun way to spend time. Today, for some kindly reason, known only to the Pakistani's guardian angel, Adrianne allowed the fortunate man to stand uncontested on his side of the elevator. Without the headpiece, he would be nearly the same height as Adrianne. Furtively, I wondered if his fighting spirit was as tall.

The clear plastic letter M lit up. I followed Adrianne out of the elevator to the library door, noting uneasily that her face wore a professionally benign expression. That could mean only one thing: Adrianne, the competent social worker, was about to take charge.

"Guess where I was before the student meeting?" she asked.

"Swimming?" Even Adrianne's haphazard schedule had some routine.

"Right. You should come. Everybody and his dog is there."

"You mean Mr. Stewart's Labradors?"

"Good guess, Di, but not this time. You know what I mean. The pool's crawling. I can't entertain everyone myself. So dump the studies for once and come help. You're too serious. Unwind. Relax. Warren's coming. He'll talk to you, if no one else has the courage."

"I do relax," I said, more out of desperation than defense. "And you know I swim every morning."

"Oh, sure. Every morning at the unlikely hour of six bells. Who're you going to meet at that ungracious time of day? A water beetle?"

"Likely not in a chlorinated pool."

"There. You see?" Adrianne chuckled. "Water too early in the day has ruined your sense of humor. Come on, Di. These books will pickle you. You've got to circulate or—"

"Or be left behind. Okay, okay. I'll come. If only to keep us friends."

Adrianne had won her point; a fact she didn't let deter her from further admonition.

"Didillo," she said as we neared the Phys Ed building, "do you still wear that ancient black coverall you call a swim suit? Hmm. I see by your silence you do." Adrianne shook her head and energetically attacked the steps.

"Give it to your worst enemy," she directed.

"Who would that be?" I said under my breath. I was beginning to feel over-managed. My clothes always distressed Adrianne. They weren't 'now' enough to suit her taste. No miniskirts, no flamboyant colors. Adrianne had a new swimsuit four times a year, her current mauve two-piece suit modern in every aspect.

There were, as Adrianne predicted, a sizable number of students in the pool. The congestion made me uneasy. Preferring a quick dip in the quiet of the morning, I wasn't in the habit of swimming with large groups at this time of day. My motivation was exercise, not socializing. Although the water in the L-shaped pool was held at the regulation temperature at all times, this afternoon it felt tepid and thick. Ignoring my discomfort, I swam over to the steps at the shallow end where Adrianne was easing into the water.

"Good heavens, Di," she gasped. "Do you know what you just did?"

I shook my head.

"You just ignored two cardinal swim rules. Get wet slowly and never leap into uncharted waters. For a girl who never walks on the wrong side of the road, you're doing all right. Do you always dive in like that?"

"Well, yes," I admitted, relieved that was all it was. "I did shower."

Adrianne didn't hear my excuse. She was standing waist-deep in the water, her hands on her hips, staring fiercely across the pool at a group of students doing laps together. Heading the group were Warren and Janice, swimming side by side.

"Looks like Suffocating Suffolk's beat you to it, Diana," Adrianne chaffed. "Come on. Let's go. It's boogie time!"

Not waiting for my reply, Adrianne struck out across the pool. I watched her in admiration. She was an excellent swimmer—strong and fast. Both she and Warren had received their lifeguard certification while still in high school. Coincidentally, it appeared Janice was an equally good swimmer. I understood Adrianne's consternation. It was perhaps more for Janice's marine ability, than the allure of her leopard bikini, that Warren, who openly admired good swimmers, was in need of a sister's protection.

Still, I lingered where I was. For one reason or another, Janice was attracting the interest of many others in the pool besides Warren. While I didn't begrudge Janice the admiration rightly her due, wisdom predicated staying out of the way. No use stirring the pot needlessly. If only I'd stayed in the library. Books never laid unwarranted expectations on anyone.

To ease my tension, I swam across the short end of the pool. I was feeling notably out of place, almost as if the surroundings were entirely new. A sensation akin to the quiet panic that must engulf a hermit who is suddenly enveloped by crowds threatened to swallow me. The hands of the pool clock contorted into a knowing grimace; the smirking clock knew I didn't belong. Time was against me. I was attempting to gain admission to an age that didn't appreciate individual differences, only the more popular forms of nonconformity.

Tired more from the grimness of my thoughts than the short swim, I crossed my arms and rested my head on the cement lip of the pool, but my reprieve was short lived. Experiencing the common sensation of being watched, I turned my head and looked up into the calm eyes of Dr. Brantwood. Unexpectedly meeting my English professor's cool gaze galvanized me into action. Slipping back into the water, I swam for the exit closest to the ladies' locker room.

My retreat wasn't a conscious decision. It was as involuntary as the blinking of an eyelid, or the reflex of a knee that's been tapped with a doctor's mallet. However inglorious, it was a natural response. Assuredly, it was the complete surprise of the brief confrontation—not the man himself—that motivated my flight. Or so I told myself.

In the seclusion of a corner shower, I undid my swim hat. Vexed with my behavior, I hoped Dr. Brantwood didn't think my hasty exit was intended rudeness. Incivility was not a quality I admired. Trying to reorder my thoughts, I concentrated on the relief afforded by the water pounding mercifully on my forehead and cheeks. The pelting water always felt good after a swim, but today it did little more than momentarily ease my embarrassment. Being embarrassed was becoming an all-too-frequent habit around Dr. Brantwood.

How I wished I hadn't yielded to Adrianne's enticing and tended to my own affairs. There was nothing for it now but to turn off the faucet and hand in my number. Collecting my books and purse from my locker, I placed them on the bench beside my wet swimsuit. Just as I was about to wring the water from my suit, Adrianne stormed up, still dripping from the pool. Snatching my suit, she wrung it fiercely. Somewhat calmed by her exertion, she slung the limp black mass over the hook in my locker.

"What possessed you into making like the Rabbit Express? I chased her away. Or was I supposed to clear the whole pool?" Adrianne slammed my locker door shut with a defiant kick of her small foot. The kick left a dripping white imprint on the army-green door.

"Oh, never mind," she sighed. "Wait. I'll be dressed in five."

Adrianne disappeared down the aisle that housed her locker. The print of her dainty foot was still visible on the door; but thankfully, Adrianne wasn't really upset. That was a relief. Grateful that she wasn't hurt, I felt remorse that I didn't, as she so often urged, integrate more gracefully.

The sound of Adrianne's locker door banging shut was my cue that she was ready to associate with me again. We left the locker room and walked up the stairs to the main floor. Flanking the foyer, double glass doors stood ready to accommodate an individual or an entire track team. Walking pertly across the landing, Adrianne nodded briskly to a figure passing on the far side of the doors. It was Dr. Brantwood riding a bicycle.

"So Bramblybriar rides a bike," Adrianne mused. "Just like everyone else. Wouldn't you know it?"

"It's always good exercise." I suggested hopefully.

"Yes, but not especially daring. Be more entertaining if he came to class in a balloon or commuted by dog team. Don't you think, Dio?"

"Perhaps Dr. Brantwood doesn't feel a need to be different. Perhaps he just wants to exercise."

Adrianne shook her head. "If he has such a penchant for the ordinary," she grinned, "what makes him so popular as a prof? And don't tell me it's that silly green tie he always wears."

"Adrianne," I appealed, "I don't know! What do you want me to say? He's a real meltdown!" It was a ridiculous description, but it seemed to please my friend.

"Way to go, Dio," she said. "He's a good swimmer, too. Strong."

"I didn't see him swim," I admitted, "but he does look the part." The words slipped out unbidden. Arising from an unconscious approbation, they were said before they could be checked.

Adrianne gave me an exultant high five. "Wow!" she exclaimed, swinging her purse over her shoulder. "An introvert with eyes. I'm proud of you, Di. Of course," she added, her eyes beaming, "Warren has twice the shoulders. But Brambly's okay for a prof."

Adrianne swung happily along beside me. There was a genuine feeling of closeness, a harmonious concord between us. As I yielded to Adrianne's elation, I was glad for my mental negligence. Rejoicing over my amazing sociability, Adrianne asked, "How old would you say he is?"

"Somewhere between thirty and forty-five."

"Hmm," Adrianne sighed, the brightness fading from her face, the cohesive feeling between us instantly ruptured. Inwardly I kicked myself. I hadn't meant to be evasive, nor was I attempting to be difficult. I truly didn't know Dr. Brantwood's age. With that mass of unruly hair, always tumbled across his forehead, he looked young, but his dignified bearing made him seem much older.

I looked up to find Adrianne leaning against the base of the lamppost at the turn-off to students' res. She was resigned, but smiling.

"No matter, Di," she soothed. "I don't mind if your favorite sport is dodge ball. You'll always be my favorite armadillo." She turned to go. "Don't forget to phone me when you turn in," she reminded softly. Looking sweetly over her shoulder at me, she added, "And in case you're interested in my opinion, my guess is under thirty-five."

I nodded, strangely pleased with her estimate. Nevertheless, the moment was passed. It would be fruitless to plead the case after the verdict was given. Subterfuge or imprudence, now was not the time for telling.

Chapter Ten

The lunatic, the lover, and the poet
Are of imagination, all compact.[15]

—William Shakespeare, *A Midsummer Night's Dream*

I looked up from my desk to the clock on the wall and allowed my eyes a moment to adjust to the dim light.

It was eleven o'clock—the end of the working day for me, the beginning for Adrianne. Stretching cramped muscles, I pushed my chair back, rose, and crossed the few steps to the easy chair beside the phone. Relaxing in the chair's spacious comfort, I dialed Adrianne and settled back to rest and count the rings. On the twenty-seventh, a voice on the other end of the line answered: groggy, irritable, and sarcastic.

"If you can't get to sleep, Di, try counting dull lectures instead of waking innocent children."

"Good morning, Adrianne."

Unperturbed, I hung up softly. Experience had taught me not to be offended by Adrianne's irascibility upon waking, but I knew better than to try to talk to her on the eve of a paper. Tomorrow morning, after an all-night session, Adrianne would rip into class just before closing buzzer and plump another first-class term paper down on Dr. Brantwood's desk. Adrianne vowed it was easier to concentrate at night without the disturbing noises and demands of the day. If the excellence of her papers was a testimony, she was right.

I couldn't myself see anything gained by cramming, but Adrianne, having no such inhibiting mindset, did produce.

I wondered what music Adrianne would be listening to tonight. Her favorite singer was Elvis, of whom she had a full-length poster tacked to the back of her door, but she would probably listen to the Beatles; she noted they made concentration easier. Adrianne never wrote papers without music blaring. So much for eliminating distracting noises.

I went to the window and drew aside the curtains. Pausing, I looked out over the river valley toward the lights of the university. The russet satin of the curtains was soft and cool in my hand and seemed to transmute by some kind of mystic alchemy into the tangible reality of the imperturbable campus lights. It was as if I could both see and feel their tranquil radiance.

The lights, so calmly presiding over the distant campus, were mainly from the students' residences, where there was little quiet day or night. I sometimes wondered how Adrianne slept at all. It was all I could do to walk through the noisy hubbub. Serenely unconcerned by the reveling, the lights evidenced the unflagging energy of the students. It was perhaps precisely for the industry they represented, rather than their ethereal quality, that campus lights held an appeal for me. They represented the life of the mind.

I looked into the sky ; it was a starry night. The distant stars, not to be outdone by the nearer lights of the campus, shone steadfastly. Lines from Robert Frost's "Choose Something Like a Star" drifted lazily through my mind. "To be . . . taciturn, in your reserve, is not allowed."[16] Not this night. This night the stars were not taciturn; they didn't burn alone. Tonight the stars in the heavens and the lights on the campus were one. Even as I stood watching, they seemed to coalesce, each forming a separate but harmonious half of a beautiful symmetry. The stars for their part gave radiant testimony of the fundamental order of the universe, and the lights of the university honored that testimony on earth.

Again, words from Frost entered my mind. ". . . Choose something like a star, to stay our minds on and be staid."[17] For a precious, awe-filled moment, I felt the communion between earth and heaven, a communion I was part of. Not wishing to close the curtains, nor yet lose the gentle feeling of belonging, I left the drapes open and lay gazing out the window at the stars until I fell asleep.

At twenty to eight the following morning, I opened the door of Room 39 and walked to the desk by the window to hand in my term paper. Neila was the only other person in the room. As she appeared to be busy with some corrections on her own paper, I didn't interrupt her with conversation. After placing my paper on the desk, I took my usual chair at the table and began arranging my clipboard for the day's notes. As I was filing the last section, the door opened and Adrianne bounced into the room.

"Hi, Dianthus," she greeted effusively. "You look surprised. Clichés about the building of Rome to the contrary, here I am!"

"So I notice," I smiled, glad her long night of furious composing had been successful.

"Good. I notice you're here, too. Well, here goes!" Walking smartly to the desk, she placed her report squarely on top of mine. It was apparent she felt confident about her work.

Adrianne glanced critically at the two starkly white papers on the dark old desk. "They look like pitiful offerings to some stern deity," she lamented with designed angst. "Do you suppose the sacrifices will require bloodletting?"

Shaking my head at Adrianne's persistent sophistication, I pulled out a chair for her. Instead of seating herself, she kicked at the rung with the toe of her shoe. "You've forgotten," she reminded me sweetly. "This is the day we neglect men's souls in favor of their less noble residue. It's *Bones* day."

I had indeed forgotten. Adrianne had taken anthropology as a home study and scheduled the once-monthly class the same time as English 550. Dutifully, I placed my books on the table and reached for my purse. Catching up with Adrianne halfway down the hall, I asked where her class was held.

"Two levels straight down," she said, pointing dramatically through the floor as though indicating hell itself. "Room AA in the basement. Used to be some janitor's cubby hole."

"Oh?"

"Yes, indeed. It's where the support staff take their victims." She looked around cautiously. "Before they torture them, by forcing them to drink coffee from The Pit." Adrianne rolled her eyes, content she'd momentarily caught me off guard.

"Great," I said laughing. "I'll walk you down."

Nodding, my friend clipped briskly down the stairs, taking care to smack her small feet noisily on each step. When I caught up with her on the landing, she said thoughtfully, "I see Neila still gets to class early."

"Yes, she does. She was there when I came. She usually is. Have you had any success studying with her?"

"Not a whole lot."

I remained quiet, knowing it was hard for Adrianne to admit defeat on any front.

"Do you notice the way Neila chews her hair?" Adrianne asked. "She reminds me of a cat I once had. Chewed his fur something fierce. Good old fuzzy face. He died of fur balls in his stomach. Do you think we better warn her?"

I drew in my breath. Adrianne did like Neila; that was understood. She'd been spending more time with her than she had to spare. In all fairness, it was sadly evident Neila's undue concern over her studies deprived her of the delight she might find in university. Without conscious intent, Neila communicated her excess tension to her classmates, often making it uncomfortable for others as well as herself.

"I think the problem," Adrianne continued speculatively, "is Neila's too skinny." Adrianne eyed me as if I were the miscreant in need of calories. Seeing my frown, she amended, "No. The real problem is proximity."

"To?"

"To that pipe factory that sits next to her. It's the rich that cause pollution. The poor can't afford it. Which reminds me. Suffering Suffolk must own a perfume business. The air around her is more concentrated than Grandma's lye soap."

I smiled, but more at Adrianne's masterfully disorganized context than her chagrin over Janice's taste in perfume.

Outside the door of Room AA, Adrianne leaned against the wall and rifled through a jumble of papers. As a rule, she didn't take notes, considering copying others' "misguided assertions" a senseless waste of time. The exception to her rule was English 550. Finding what she was searching for among the disarray of loose sheets, she handed me a white envelope.

"Wonder if you'd slip this carbon under your notes?" she asked sweetly. "Bramblybriar's too good to miss, but no prof's worth getting writer's cramp over."

Shaking my head at the inventive soul handing me the carbon, I accepted the envelope. One had to admire Adrianne's ability to avoid the tedium of routine work.

"That clunky Xerox on main is broken down again," she said. "And I refuse to use the one in Ed. It always has line-ups three term papers long. You don't mind?" Unsurpassed in the art of commando tactics, Adrianne would always be Adrianne. Smiling, I walked back to class alone.

Mr. Stewart's Labradors, their doleful brown eyes staring wistfully at the door, were sitting on their haunches outside Room 39 when I returned. The dogs often accompanied Mr. Stewart to class, waiting impatiently but loyally outside the door until he reappeared. Both dogs were well behaved and warmly attached to their master. Mr. Stewart readily returned their devotion, the inflection in his voice evidencing his love whenever he spoke of them. He had confided to Neila, "A Labrador's not just a dog. He's a true friend and must be treated like a friend."

When they attended Mr. Stewart to class, Mike and Mart could be heard pacing quietly up and down the hall as they waited for their master. The presence of the beautiful, golden-brown animals was something of a novelty. Indeed, the uniqueness of having dogs attending weekly classes on the third floor of Arts wasn't lost on either staff or students, most of whom visibly appreciated the informality.

I held out my hand for the dogs to sniff. Satisfied of my harmlessness, they allowed me to give them a rub behind the ears. The pat aggravated Mike's impatience for his master, and he lifted off his haunches and padded down the hall. Mart, the smaller of the two dogs, received the pat more sociably and allowed me to stroke his back before he too strode after Mike. I entered Room 39 and took my seat. It was still a few minutes until class started. Mr. Stewart was seated, as usual, beside Neila Connaught.

Mr. Stewart, "Jack" to his friends, was a well-to-do businessman who owned his own contracting firm. He was economically secure and could afford to devote his leisure time to study. Having no need to get ahead financially through education, Mr. Stewart, though well into his sixties, was relaxed and at ease in the classroom. He was at university because he wanted to be.

A man of habit, as well as conviction, Mr. Stewart always sat next to Neila. After seating himself, he would draw his pipe out of his left pocket and his tobacco out of his right pocket. Methodically, he would fill, but never light the pipe. To finish the recital, he would open the bottom two buttons of his tweed jacket, and settle back in his chair to enjoy a smokeless chat with Neila.

Neila would bring the conversation around to exams, and while Mr. Stewart's responses were kindly, they did seem to escalate Neila's anxiety. Perhaps as Adrianne intimated, it would be a greater kindness to separate them. Adrianne was suspicious of Mr. Stewart. She couldn't rationalize his apparent intelligence with his approbation of the educational system. To Adrianne, Western University was an intellectual desert. Yet here was Mr. Stewart happily ensconced amidst the "sand dunes of sterility" apparently quite content.

While I didn't like to disagree with Adrianne, I couldn't share her feelings toward Mr. Stewart. As his frequency in Edwards attested, he was a serious student, who put many diligent hours into his studies. But Adrianne was right on one thing. Without personal incentive, the university gave a meager dole in learning, barely enough for subsistence.

The door opened and Dr. Brantwood entered. Promptly at nine, the discussion on "Courtly Love" commenced. I was interested in hearing what the professor would have to say, as I suspected some students might be hostile to the oft' derided hypocritical aspects of courtly love.

Dr. Brantwood began. "That there was a discrepancy between the ideal and the practice of courtly love in the days of knight errantry was a given. Courtly love was a relationship largely outside of marriage. It had, as C. S. Lewis outlines in his *Allegory of Love,* at least three qualities: 'humility, courtesy, and adultery.'[18] Nevertheless, it was a process intended to modify, if not subdue, the passions of the young knights. Modeled on feudal relationships, courtly love was designed to protect virtuous maidens from being unduly molested, and ensure that the sad experiences of Chaucer's 'Wife of Bath', not become the norm. Castiglione in Book IV of *The Courtier* adapts Plato's *Symposium* to produce a dialogue on love."

Dr. Brantwood paused, then asked the students, "Do you think Bembo's process of developing wit, pureness, and passion in *The Courtier* is realistic?"

Harris responded, "Being a scholar, soldier, and perfect lover myself, I'd say it's realistic—given the right incentives."

"You style yourself a courtier, Harris?" Dr. Brantwood asked, a slightly dangerous tone in his voice.

"I admire the process and the result," Harris affirmed, shaking his bulky head and focusing on Janice, who appeared to approve the attention and the implication.

"Courtly love was not designed to be a ticket to extramarital license," Mrs. Weiss interjected firmly. "'Courtly love developed because the ladies in the French courts wanted to hear of something besides the heroic exploits of the knights. The ladies wanted stories that featured women. Realizing this, the French troubadours developed courtly love or *amour courtois,* in which the knight pledges his fealty to his liege Lord and his undying obedience, service, and love to his lady. The medieval lady controlled the relationship, and so played a leading role.'"[19] Mrs. Weiss cast a disapproving glance at Harris and Bob.

"You need to read *The Chivalric Ideal* by Diaz Gomez," she advised them primly. "The knight was 'virtuous, just, and courageous.'"[20] "Exactly," Mr. Stewart agreed. "Courtly love began as a process to mold the character. The knight's love for his lady inspired him to great

deeds. He had faith in God and charity for others. Courtly love enno-
bles the whole man: the scholar, the soldier, and the courtier."

I was grateful for both Mrs. Weiss' and Mr. Stewart's defense of
the positive aspects of courtly love, but my relief was short lived.

Without warning, Dr. Brantwood asked, "What do you make of
Bembo's statement, 'Love is nothing else but a certain coveting to
enjoy beauty,'[21] Miss Collingsgate?"

"I . . . think Bembo's idea of love was to covet the good."

"In what way?"

"Bembo equated beauty with goodness. To Bembo what is beautiful is good."

"And is it?" Dr. Brantwood pressed, a half smile on his intelligent
features. Frantically groping for an answer, I was thankful to Harris
for intervening, even though I disagreed with his view.

"If they are, if beauty and goodness are the same thing, then
the writers of *Tom Jones*, *Vanity Fair*, *Moll Flanders*, and most of the
post romantic authors are out of touch with reality," Harris said.
"Writers today are wiser. They don't pretend that what appears
beautiful is always good."

"Which means?" Dr. Brantwood questioned.

"Beauty and goodness are two different things. To love beauty
doesn't necessarily mean to love good."

"Then you would concur with Leacock, Harris," Dr. Brantwood
said, the hint of an ironic smile in his voice, "that Guido the Ghim-
let of Gent's love was indeed rare: 'that pure and divine type found
only in the middle ages.'"[22] His quick retort met with laughing
agreement from the class.

Kumari gave me a quick glance of quiet support. I was grateful
that Adrianne had chosen to miss class. She would, no doubt, have
made more than one conjecture about the questions addressed to
me. When the time rolled around to ten thirty, I was ready and
relieved to leave English 550 for another day.

Chapter Eleven

Hands, do what you're bid:
Bring the balloon of the mind
That bellies and drags in the wind
Into its narrow shed.

—William Butler Yeats: *The Wild Swans at Coole* [23]

It was Monday morning. The students were assembled in Room 39, waiting for class to begin. At twenty after nine, Dr. Brantwood had still not arrived which was puzzling, as it wasn't his habit to be late, or to miss a class without notifying students in advance. In other courses, if the professor were this tardy, most students would leave. In English 550, even at nine thirty, the students remained in their places.

At nine thirty-five, Harris looked at the clock and quipped, "It appears professors are paid by the head count and not by the hour." The class laughed at the backhanded compliment to the absent professor.

"Now you're hep. It's only teachers who get paid by the hour," Bob Davis sniped. "Otherwise they'd never know when to quit."

"I agree there's a difference between professing and teaching," Mr. Stewart said. "It depends on your definition."

"A teacher is," Harris interjected, "someone who thinks he has to say what no one needs to know and no one wants to hear." Bob threw Harris a sly grin.

"Cats, that's yesterday's news," he said. "Today teachers know where it's at. They've finally caught up with what everyone else has forgotten."

"I doubt that very much," countered Mr. Stewart. "If students know so much, they're paying a whole lot of money to have it repeated."

Adrianne leaned forward and gave the combatants her amused attention. She was enjoying the ground fire, especially since it was the teaching profession being roasted. Even Neila had to smile at Stewart's retort. It noticeably diffused the tension.

"So what's your take, Mrs. Wisewoman?" Bob asked, emphasizing the *wise*. "You buy into teachers havin' all the answers?" The question was an obvious goad.

"No, Bob, I don't," Lois replied. "Teachers don't have all the answers, just the correct ones."

It was a quick comeback, but didn't seem to convince Bob or Harris.

"That is the bottom line, isn't it?" said Harris. "It's their road or no road."

Bernice Buckles spoke. "Surely the majority of educators are tolerant of others' opinions."

"Not in my experience," Davis shot back.

"Then why are you here, Bob?" Mr. Stewart asked. "You aren't a registered student."

"Like, lay it on me, man. Good point. Know what I mean?"

Adrianne laughed. Today, she enjoyed Bob's rudeness. Mr. Hito, who'd been quietly listening, now raised one hand in a motion of calm.

"We perhaps here cling to old teaching view. Ideas change. Now teacher is helper."

"I believe the term is *facilitator*," Lois advised helpfully.

Not to be bulldozed by semantics, Harris retorted, "Facilitator for what?"

"Kiddies, we just been there," Bob groaned. "For learning what the big boys decide. You better believe it!"

"Someone has to take charge," Lois reasoned. "I agree with Carlyle, that there's no advantage in the 'collective wisdom of individual ignorance.'"[24]

"See whatcha mean, Babe," Bob said. "No point letting the ignorant direct the ignorant." He gave Lois a cheeky wink.

"Granted. It's possible each man could direct himself. But to where?" Mr. Stewart questioned. It was the second time that question had been asked, first by Harris, now by Mr. Stewart. Davis shrugged.

"To everywhere, man. Not where someone else tells him to go."

"You're talking nonsense," Mr. Stewart objected, drawing on his unlit pipe with dignified control.

"No, he's not." Harris interposed. "The issue here is self-direction. Personal responsibility for our own education."

"You think everyone should direct their own education?" Neila asked pensively, her astonishment showing.

"There are no absolutes," Harris grinned, giving Neila a dismissive glance. "When necessary, allowances can be made."

"By which you mean?" Mrs. Weiss countered, adroitly picking up the subtle slur on Neila's competence.

"That should be obvious. Direct yourself. Chart your own course."

"Like you said it, Harris Baby. There ain't no yellow brick road leading to the Emerald City," Davis drawled. "And there ain't no royal wizard gonna pull my strings."

"Wait a minute," Mr. Stewart interjected. "Respect for other's knowledge—trusting their judgment—doesn't make someone a puppet." It was obvious Mr. Stewart was losing patience with the banal banter.

"It seems appear," said Mr. Hito, choosing his words carefully, "Person bold to believe knowing things they do not know, is real puppet. Manipulates self."

I decided to leave. Noticing my intent, Adrianne laid a restraining hand on my arm. "Don't retreat, Di," she whispered. "This is just getting off the ground. Stick around. You should see some real action shortly."

"Oh baby, ya' know what they say," Davis goaded, "get yourself an Ed degree and be a puppet, too!" He looked pointedly at Mrs. Weiss. Was there respect under his mocking?

"Which means?" Lois asked, her poise unruffled.

"Like all teachers jump to the system. What's good for Daddy-O is good for all."

"Oh, is that all," Mrs. Weiss said dismissively. "You've been reading too many Al Capp comic strips, Bob. 'What's good for General Bullmoose is good for the U.S.A.'[25] may work in Dogpatch, but doesn't apply here."

"Like you sayin' ah'm a hillbilly?" Davis seemed oddly hurt.

"No. You're saying you're a hillbilly," Mrs. Weiss returned sweetly. She was smiling, but her manner was that of someone dusting off unwanted cookie crumbs.

Making himself the stopgap between the two, Mr. Hito eased the tension. With his polite formality and sincere desire to master English in all its deviant grammatical forms, he could say what others of less devout intent could not say.

"Does not one side accuse other side for what both know least and fear most?" Bob Davis ignored Aki's comment.

"Like the way I see it, what's good for the system isn't good for the serfs."

"So who's a serf?" Mr. Stewart objected.

"We all are," Harris said. "We're all serfs—if we let the establishment call the shots without our input."

Mr. Hito bowed his head briefly to Harris. "I agree. You have point. We must push back—some. All must argue in education to keep free."

"Now you're cool." Davis applauded, putting his hands together and bowing back to Hito. "Down with rigid curriculums, down with those who enforce them. Oh yeah, Baby, down with the whole bricked-in business."

"Educators don't set the curriculums," Mrs. Weiss said. "The needs of the student populace determine what will be taught."

Davis shrugged. "Like teachers teach what they're told, so it's the same thing."

"You're asking teachers to fight the system, Bob?" Mr. Stewart asked, his disbelief registering in his voice.

"That's the scene."

"And how's this to be done?"

"Easy. Just don't go along with it."

"And be out of a job?" Mrs. Weiss said, her tone emphasizing the moral lassitude in that approach.

"So? Pioneering's a rugged life. Ask any hillbilly!" Davis reminded her slyly.

I noticed Harris look thoughtfully at Davis. Harris expressed many of the same sentiments as the younger man lounging laconically on his chair, but there was a difference between the two. It was the difference of choosing and being chosen. Harris held his pragmatic, reformist ideology. It didn't hold him. Davis, on the other hand, appeared more 'governed by' than governing. To Davis, it had to be a feel-good world. No wonder he feared being a puppet. At that moment of realization, I felt an increase in empathy for Bob. We all, it seems, have our personal dragons to fight. I turned with newly awakened interest back to the discussion in progress.

"The world is changing. Educators need to keep pace," Harris was saying.

"Right On, "Davis agreed snidely. "Time to get the lead out, teachers. Get a move on, 'cause the parade's passed you by."

"This is nonsense!" Mr. Stewart said. "Teacher and institution bashing makes no sense. We're all here to learn what we can, do what we can, be what we can. We can make the best use of the resources available, or we can complain we've been cheated. If you're looking for a fraud, go look in the mirror." The stillness that followed Mr. Stewart's declamation was palpable. This time it was Harris, not Mr. Hito, who restored order.

"I doubt," he said firmly, "anyone would disagree that it's wise to do the best with what we've got. But Bob has a point. Education under our present system isn't functioning to capacity. It's in many ways failing. Educators can't afford to become so entrenched in the past that they ignore the present. Students need to be pro-active. We must all defend our freedom to reform—to change."

Unwilling to let the point pass, Mr. Stewart insisted, "Too much freedom to reform will result in social chaos." Having held her peace long enough, Mrs. Weiss took the floor.

"Surely the system has problems. Every system does. Charles Dickens recognized abuses and deficiencies in the system over a hundred years ago. That's why he created 'Gradgrind' in *Hard Times*. Gradgrind was nasty, but today that kind of narrow-minded instructor no longer exists."

She paused long enough to impale Davis with a cool glance. "We need to recognize past excellence, or future innovations will mean very little. The work of men like Johann Pestalozzi, who emphasized lessons derived from children's experience, needs to be fairly evaluated."

Bernie Buckles backed her up. "Lois has a point. Civilization is complex. Our educational traditions have roots that go back to the Greek and Roman societies. We can reform, but let's not devastate."

"Exactly," Lois said. "Do we want to build up or tear down?"

"Very wise," Mr. Hito agreed. "But believe all have error. All play wife of fish. Suggest best thoughts are distilled, drop in time."

"Now yur talkin' my language, Man," Davis effused. "I dig my distillates all ninety proof!"

The students laughed, their camaraderie restored. Lois Weiss ended the debate with the last word.

"To reform with any success, we need to start with ourselves. Assess our own motivations. Education today may not provide all the answers to societies' problems, but whatever the supposed failings of the system, it's our responsibility to keep it running, not destroy it. I personally believe A. N. Whitehead was right when he said 'the art of progress is to preserve order amid change.' "[26] Having had her say, she walked serenely to the stairs and left. In groups of twos and threes, so did the other students.

Only Adrianne and I remained. My friend looked closely at me, assessing my response. In truth, I admired Lois's courage and her convictions.

"So what do you think of the shoot out, Di? Sorry you stayed?"

"No," I admitted, "but it was kind of rough."

"You mean on teachers?"

"Yes. And on each other, too."

"You know, with the exceptions of your wily Father and Bramblybriar, most teachers and professors could use a little dynamite set under them. Do them good."

"Is it really that bad?"

"Bad? Diaphanous! Do you live on this planet?"

"Last time I looked."

"Well, look again. You know why students become teachers. You know it's the easiest route to follow academically."

"So I've heard," I acquiesced, trying to keep the coldness I felt out of my voice. Adrianne looked at me sharply, danger in her gaze.

"And you heard right. Let's face it. Anyone with an IQ higher than a chipmunk's goes to a faculty other than education."

A ring of shame encircled me at Adrianne's callous indictment. Lois Weiss was keenly intelligent. I nodded curtly to Adrianne, excused myself, and quickly left.

Chapter Twelve

. . . Be not simply good; be good for something.[27]

—Henry David Thoreau

Tuesday, Dr. Brantwood returned. Although a few of the students tried to quiz him on his absence, he gave no explanation. It was uncharacteristic of the professor to miss class without so much as an apology. Whether it was because of his mysterious absence, or the fact that he refused to be badgered on the point, the class was for the period united in a sense of wonder.

The lecture was on the works of Alfred Lord Tennyson and his faith in man's eventual progress (the lesser faith) through love (the greater principle) as the ultimate reality in life. To introduce the poetic concept of the refining influence of love, Dr. Brantwood wrote on the board a provocative quote by Michel de Ghelderode, the Belgian dramatist:

> *He is the poet . . . unfit for anything except love, friendship and ardor—a failure, therefore, in our utilitarian age which pushes out onto the fringe everything that is unproductive, that does not pay dividends. A useless mouth to feed.*[28]

"If a poet, if any man, be 'fit for love,' is he a 'useless mouth to feed?'" Dr. Brantwood asked. "Consider Lord Tennyson's poetic vision that love is the key to progress, the soul of the world. In *In Memoriam*, Tennyson writes, 'Ring in the love of truth and right,

Ring in the common love of good.' Making a more definitive state-ment, Tennyson personifies love:

The love that rose on stronger wings,
Unpalsied when he met with Death
Is comrade of the lesser faith
That sees the course of human things.[29]

Time seemed to disappear as I lost myself in the delight of Dr. Brantwood's lecture. Suddenly, the period buzzer ending class jarred me back to the present. Adrianne placed her small foot on the rung of my chair, restraining my departure. I nodded goodbye to Kumari, knowing it would be best to wait and see what Adri-anne had on her mind.

"You're too self-controlled, Die-Cast," she advised maternally, with just enough weight of reproach to engage my guilt.

"I can't very well discourse while the prof's lecturing," I defended, wondering what I'd done now.

"Don't mean that. The good-Sam thing to do when someone hits you is to hit them back twice as hard."

If I thought this was perverting the golden rule, I knew when to keep my peace. I did venture to ask, "Why would that be?"

"If you refuse to respond when you're attacked, you force your opponent to look foolish—overly aggressive."

"I'm not sure I follow you," I said honestly. "Have I been attacked?"

Adrianne granted me her most disarming, 'how obtuse' grimace and went on. "Look. How'd you feel if you were sparring in the ring with someone who refused to throw a punch back at you?"

I sighed inwardly. First Dr. Brantwood and now Adrianne. "So you think conversation is a duel, a boxing match with words?"

"What else?" Adrianne confirmed. "You think the students were hard on each other yesterday? Come with me. I want to show you what goes on after Cosmos 550 while you're closeted in Edwards. Help you lighten up."

There was no point saying no. When Adrianne was on her favorite subject of my need to keep pace, I knew better than to argue. How many times had Adrianne advised, "You can't just stow away in life. You've got to climb up the rigging and see the view from the crow's nest." *And perk up my Emily Post in social skirmishing* while I'm at it, I thought with annoyance.

Adrianne stood by the class door, resolutely daring me to defy her. "Well? Are you coming or not?"

"Yes," I complied, more in self-defense than interest. "I'm coming."

When my friend looked at me that way, it reminded me of a sparrow hawk in full dive. I would have smiled, had not Adrianne been so seriously in earnest.

In The Pit, a number of students from 550, as well as two I didn't recognize, were seated around two coffee tables in the southwest corner of the lounge. As if gathering to hash over issues was the accepted thing to do after class, those present seemed relaxed and in congenial moods. From the window side there was Mr. Stewart, Lois Weiss, Bernie Buckles, Aki Hito, Bob Davis, Harris Saunders, and the two unfamiliar students. As the chairs circled the tables, Harris was actually seated next to his verbal sparring opponent, Mr. Stewart.

Adrianne casually greeted the group. "Hi everyone. Look who I rescued from the 'Save Your Soul Bin' in the library." Knowing she didn't mean any harm, I nodded a resigned hello, hoping I wouldn't be baited into an argument just to see who had the strongest bite.

As there was only one chair empty, Mr. Stewart kindly offered me his and went in search of another. Mr. Stewart's Labradors, Mike and Mart, were as usual, keeping silent vigil a few feet away. Whenever Jack moved, the dogs would tense up and wait for the command to follow.

"It's no wonder Stew makes Neila nervous," Adrianne whispered under her breath. "His dogs are strung even tighter than she is." Adrianne paused, meeting Mart's eyes with a challenging glance of her own green orbs.

"Stew is possibly much too stable," she added dryly. "He's so certain, so cut and dried, he gives everyone else the jitters." Grinning, she turned her attention back to the members of the group who were chatting amiably with each other.

"As I was saying," Harris said, taking charge, "the university springboard has lost its bounce." Harris's head, covered with bulky, bronze-colored hair, resembled the shape of a lion. From under this dense mane, Harris waited catlike for a rebuttal. However, it wasn't Mr. Stewart, but Bob Davis who leapt eagerly into the fray.

"Uh . . . like who believes a degree opens any doors? I don't see no fame, money, or power knockin' on my door. Like ya know, there's no groovin' use for most of the stuff they dish out in this flippin' factory."

I drew in my breath involuntarily. Bob was once again skating on thin ice.

"A degree isn't intended to supply fame, money, or power, Bob," said Mr. Stewart. "The role of the university is to educate, not train for a vocation."

"If that's true, what's an education for?" Bernie asked, looking past Mr. Stewart to her freewheeling classmate, sprawled indifferently on his chair.

"Duh. For the mind, did someone say?" Davis drawled, yawning.

"If so, it's failing in your case," Harris joked, pushing Davis's chair with a friendly nudge. Bob shrugged and gave a thumbs-up to Harris. Behind the mask of Harris's wild appearance, there seemed to be honest concern for the plight of the institutional ladder he would see pillaged of its rungs.

"Why's it necessary to have one purpose for everyone?" Bernie questioned. "I thought we agreed we should all set our own goals."

"Could explain why there's so many Arts students, eh Diana?" Bob taunted. I didn't reply, not wishing to be drawn into the line of fire. Seeing my reluctance, Mr. Stewart stepped into the breach.

"Are you suggesting Arts students are less goal directed than other students wandering around campus, Bob?"

"Not all," Davis said, "only the ones I've met." The two students in Davis's company laughed. While I could feel my face burning, I didn't respond to Bob's comment. But I did wonder how far he would go. First the Education faculty and now Arts had come under his abrasive wit. Thankfully, Bernie rerouted the conversation.

"Maybe Bob has a point about power. Should that be a goal of education?" Harris leaned forward and nodded his shaggy head.

"Everyone needs power. If not by education, then by other means."

"Including revolution?" Mr. Stewart asked.

Harris laughed. "Especially revolution."

"Hear! Hear! Supremacy by peace, but preferably by war," Davis quipped.

"There are only two groups," Harris said, shooting Davis a feral glance from under massive eyebrows. "The intimidators and the intimidated."

I looked from Harris to Bob. Both men held similar opinions; this was clear. It was in their attitudes that they differed. Harris was, behind his banter, a serious student. Davis' flippant schoolboy sarcasm was bandied as much for laughs as for relevance. If I had to choose the more dangerous of the two, it would easily be Harris. Yet they were agreed on one thing. They both enjoyed the rivalry of a good verbal free-for-all. More hard to understand, they liked each other.

Mr. Hito looked up from his musings over his coffee. "I believe we here have," he said with careful enunciation, "talk with no meeting of mind." He paused, carefully considering his next words. The others assembled waited empathetically for him to continue.

"We do not each other understand," he said, "because we have not same experience."

"Why do you think this, Aki?" Mr. Stewart asked.

"Interest of self prevents us to see good in ideas of those with interest other self," Aki explained, rotating the Styrofoam coffee cup in his hands.

"Don't tell me one of you Mitsubishi guys is putting down specialization," Davis retorted, jerking his arm to scratch his back. "That'd be a nice setback for automobiles, airplanes, steamships, and World War II bombers."

"In manufacture, no. In discussion, yes," Aki clarified politely, carefully placing his coffee cup on the table. "In discussing to be agreement, must be found common ground."

"This sounds right," agreed Bernie. "Specialists do tend to teeter on their own expertise. Overspecialization could lead to conflict of interest."

"So, like man—"

"Woman," Harris corrected.

"Whoever," Davis said, unconcerned about a social *faux pas.* "Talk is talk. Who cares who agrees."

"Fair," Harris conceded, "but perhaps there should be common ground for disagreement." Appreciating his wit, the class relaxed laughing.

"I see your point," Mr. Stewart said, for once supporting Harris's view. "Verbal supremacy is pointless unless the context is mutually understood."

"Which means what?" Davis shot back.

"If you don't know what you're talking about, keep quiet," Mr. Stewart said flatly.

Lois Weiss, who'd been listening, but not taking part, intervened. "You may be right, but this discussion has wandered off track. I believe we were discussing the role of the university. Should a university education develop the mind, or prepare for a vocation? I believe it does both. And that's exactly what the faculties of science and education achieve."

"Amen," Bernie said. "Also medicine and engineering. It would be a sad indictment to suggest these graduates can't use their minds, or that their disciplines have no practical application."

"Which still leaves out Arts students, eh Diana?" Bob goaded slyly.

"It would certainly leave you out, Bob, as you have no faculty," Adrianne returned, fixing Bob with a cold glance. The students guffawed, and while I appreciated Adrianne's defense, I wondered if her remark served any useful purpose. I knew how it felt to be alienated, and didn't like to see another human being suffer the same torment, even if he did bring it upon himself.

As it was time for our next class, Adrianne and I excused ourselves. Walking up the stairs to the main floor, I noted the narrow guard railing with new perspective. It seemed to yoke the individual steps together with a compassionless embrace. Disturbed, I took my hand off the railing, feeling almost a sense of pity for the dumbly bound steps.

"You know," Adrianne remarked when we reached the main landing, "I like Aki Hito. He makes sense. But the more I hear Davis, the more I appreciate that to generalize is to be a fool."

I knew Adrianne didn't mean to be cruel, but sometimes her comments could cut to the core. Attempting to change pace, I asked, "So what's Warren doing these days?" It was the wrong topic to bring up.

"Jogging his brains loose with Janice and Jingle Bells, most likely," Adrianne fumed in obvious pique. "They—"

"Whatever happened to Daphne?" I interrupted, hoping to keep the conversation polite. "She hasn't been in 550 since the first week."

"Jingle Bells? She had a conflict with classes and had to drop out."

Just as I was breathing a sigh of relief that Adrianne had been rerouted, she added, "In the meantime, Janice and her have become chums, and that means double trouble for Warren."

"They're ganging up on him you mean?"

"Ha!" Adrianne huffed. "It would take more than those two to make a gang."

"Or ride a bicycle," I mused.

"Di Nicely, you surprise me. Isn't that a somewhat Brambly topic for you?" Adrianne gave me a thoughtful glance. "Want to celebrate the meeting of our minds?" she asked innocently.

"Yes . . . I guess so. That is . . . what do you have in mind?"

"Nothing too seditious. Let's go sing ribald songs under Dean Patterson's window." Having achieved her aim to surprise me, Adrianne blew me an airy kiss. "See you tomorrow, Deity." Still grinning, she waved and headed to the Ag building for her Bugs class.

I watched her walk jauntily away as I had so many times before. While Adrianne had no fear of speaking her mind, it puzzled me why she didn't participate more than she did in class discussions. When I asked her why, she'd replied, "Because the others can find their way to the devil without my help." Knowing I'd never unravel that statement, I headed for my own class in St. Mark's.

Chapter Thirteen

Not in vain the distance beacons. Forward, forward let us range.
Let the great world spin forever down the ringing grooves of change.

—Alfred, Lord Tennyson, *Locksley Hall* [30]

It was the final week in October. Classes had been in session for almost two months. Today Lois Weiss was presenting her paper. Last class Adrianne had given a brilliant dissertation on Percy Bysshe Shelley's *Prometheus Unbound*. Addy's choice was understandable as Shelley, like Adrianne, was a passionate reformer.

Lois chose Bunyan's *Pilgrim's Progress* for her review. True to character, she presented it in a direct and analytical manner. Only those who felt allegories shouldn't be nailed rigid were disappointed. As it was, Mrs. Weiss's logical conclusions allowed little room for dissent. Following her presentation, the discussion wandered off topic to conjecturing on man's highest achievement. Adrianne, immediately captivated, announced her view.

"The highest achievement would be an educational system able to unite mankind, do away with injustice, and eradicate needless human suffering."

"Hasn't this been man's dream since Aristotle first proposed it?" Mr. Stewart asked.

"*'Education, properly conceived, will eliminate evil and unite all people for good?'*" [31]

"It may have been, but it's been poorly applied," Adrianne retorted. "A blacksmith that couldn't shoe a horse any better than we provide our universities would be out of business."

"You'd have our glorious Alma Mater wear horseshoes in the jet age, Miss Eaton?" Harris said, pretending to misunderstand Adrianne's picturesque comparison. Janice let a languid smile spread over her beautiful face. Dr. Brantwood, who'd been leaning against the board, sat down with interest on the edge of his desk.

"No," he said, dusting chalk from his fingers. "Let's not be hasty and derail the topic before we've got a load on. "With regard to *Pilgrim's Progress*, what's your opinion, Mrs. Weiss? Did Bunyan have a particular perspective toward human achievement?"

"If you mean the question of progress through education that Adrianne has raised, I don't think that was Bunyan's point. He was describing a journey—a pilgrimage—the end of which was spiritual peace."

"Experience is a competent teacher," Harris said, directing his gaze to Mr. Stewart, who was staunchly smoking on his empty pipe. "But Adrianne's point is well taken. What does education offer today? We do still run a one-horse system. Academia needs to grow up—to come of age."

"How do we do this?" Mr. Stewart asked.

"By changing from the inside. Change must come from the inside. Academics and philosophers can theorize, but change has to come from the people in the trenches, the people doing the fighting. Teachers can assist that change." Mr. Harris shot a sharp glance at Dr. Brantwood. "Or they can flog a dead horse."

Dr. Brantwood swung his leg idly away from the side of his desk. "I stand corrected, Harris," he said affably. "Here I've been laboring under the mistaken impression that the Age of Enlightenment had already occurred. Perhaps as Dicken's *M'Choakumchild* illustrates, 'If I had learned less, I could teach more.'"[32] The class clapped their enjoyment of the professor getting the upper hand.

"I believe you're right, Dr. Brantwood," Mrs. Weiss said. "It's our ignorance we need to enlighten. History has already been where we're trying to go. There's already been change for the better."

"How so, Lois?" Harris questioned.

"Just as Hegel went beyond Aristotle's 'magnanimous man,' thinkers today, like Alfred North Whitehead, have gone beyond both."

"I agree, Lois," Bernie said, entering the conversation. "Progress has been made, but wasn't it Jean-Jacques Rousseau who really energized the Age of Enlightenment?"

"How'd he do that?" Mr. Stewart asked skeptically.

"By realizing evil is the result of poor management socially, not man's inherent badness," Harris enthused, answering for Bernice.

Dr. Brantwood nodded. *"'Vices belong less to man than to man badly governed. Govern properly and you have Utopia.'"*[33] His voice held a note of irony.

"Yes," Harris agreed, invigorated. "Reform through wise social engineering."

"But that reform came through political means rather than educational," Adrianne objected, voicing the question in my mind.

"Right!" Mrs. Weiss confirmed. "Look what Marxism, based on Rousseau's theories, accomplished. Millions were murdered. Extermination is an odd way to bring about man's best good. Neither does it speak well for government intervention. Education of the masses wasn't the objective. The masses were brainwashed as they always are under totalitarian regimes."

"Lady, you know it! The point you dig," Davis said, grinning widely, evidently much pleased with Lois's unexpected insight. "Education today is brainwashing, just like always."

"Nonsense," Mr. Stewart said. "Marxism, however brilliant, was an experiment that failed. It's not a viable model for education worth discussing."

During this heated exchange, Dr. Brantwood had remained seated on the edge of the desk, partly facing the student group, partly facing the windows. It would be difficult to tell from his detached expression which scene held the balance of his interest. I wondered if he wished for more in the discussion.

Focusing his attention inside the classroom, the professor got up from the desk and walked to the table, decisively taking a chair directly opposite my own. His action could not, even by the most sensitive, be interpreted as hostile. Even so, I knew that whether I willed it or not, I was going to be drawn once again into the discussion.

As intuition predicted, Dr. Brantwood's words were directed to me. There wasn't the shadow of a smile on his face. With an engaging glance, he asked with probing directness. "Miss Collingsgate, you reported on Spenser's *Faerie Queene*. Surely this indicates an opinion on human achievement?"

Though anticipating the question, I was surprised by the professor's serious manner. Uneasy, I tried to fathom why he would pursue such an ambiguous topic so far. Apprehending he must have been expecting me to respond with Spenser's view of *the moral life,* I attempted to divert his focus.

"The highest achievement would be for one mind to gain admission to another."

"That sounds difficult. How is this to be done?" Dr. Brantwood smiled, his tone less intense, but more unnerving in its playful mode than was his serious tone of the moment before.

"Perhaps through empathy," I ventured. "Empathy has the ability to transport us out of ourselves—to remove barriers." Feeling my muscles tensing, I willed myself to relax.

Dr. Brantwood looked at me with amused disbelief, all seriousness dispelled. He leaned back in his chair, his manner ensuring his words wouldn't be construed as a private confidence.

"If another's mind were transported beyond the physical body, Miss Collingsgate," he said, "I assure you, it would never meet with mine."

The class laughter provided a welcome buffer. Wishing to put an end to the interchange, I searched for something to say to divert the professor.

"What do you think is the highest achievement, Dr. Brantwood?"

Not entertained by the stratagem, he replied tersely, "I see you're not a relativist." As he spoke, the professor's tone put me in mind of an egg-hunting fox that well knows a quail's protective ploy when he sees it.

Dr. Brantwood did not further address me. In this, I felt his disappointment as keenly as if he'd shaken his finger at me. Unable to resolve the blow to my pride, my mind wandered.

In high school, the teacher I admired most, Dr. Mehue, was a relativist. I had since wondered why I emulated him, as at the time, I didn't understand relativism in the least. Indeed, for some years my memory of this teacher was strongly connected with a feeling of total ineptitude. This was the result of Dr. Mehue lending me a book of poems he'd written. At the time, I was eager to accept the book. Immediately upon arriving home from school, I began to read the poems. To my astonishment, I quickly realized I didn't understand them at all. Later, in some perplexity, I humbly returned Dr. Mehue's book.

Before I could excuse myself to leave, Dr. Mehue asked, "Which poem did you like the best, Diana?"

Unprepared for the question, I walked into the trap. Hastily selecting a poem, I presented, as lucidly as possible, the reasons why this particular poem was endowed with special merit. To all I had to say, Dr. Mehue listened politely. When I had exhausted my rash discourse, he asked, "Would you like to keep the book longer, Diana?"

I was stunned. The poem chosen was one of the few I thought I understood. Although I didn't understand exactly how, I knew I'd been discovered, and the recognition left a lingering uneasiness. It wasn't until the second year of university that Dr. Mehue's question bore fruit, and I began, at least in part, to understand relativism. I remember the moment of enlightenment well.

The sociology class I was enrolled in was discussing the development of identical twins, brought up under acutely different circumstances. One twin, loved and cared for, became a productive scientist. The other twin, isolated for the first six weeks of his life in a dark room, didn't develop beyond the mentality of a five-year-old. Here was the answer. In relativism, truth changes to fit the circumstance. It is dependent—relative to many other factors.

Since this incident, I had rejected relativism as a personal belief structure. To my thinking, the evidence for eternal, absolute truth was more persuasive. Even so, my experience had given me some understanding of the logic of those who refuse to view truth as stable and enduring.

"Hey, Dilosophy! Class is over." Adrianne was waiting impatiently by my chair, her books in her arms. I flinched at being caught daydreaming and quickly put my own books in order. Most of the other students, and even Dr. Brantwood, had already left the classroom. As I retrieved my white cardigan and purse, Adrianne banged my chair into place with a staunch kick of her small foot. She was still annoyed with Janice for her smugness in class.

"No circumstance, no idealism, no misdirected sense of compassion, could make me offer Janice a pass to my mind," she declared vehemently.

"Nor perfect educational system, either?"

"What are you chattering about?" Adrianne chided. "You know I'm talking about good sense, not institutional dogma."

"But you do dream of an educational design that will benefit everyone?" The question was asked more out of respect for Adrianne's views than a desire to continue the topic; I wanted to distract her to more positive ground.

Adrianne slapped a small fist smartly against her blue binder. "You're right," she agreed, with a rueful laugh. "Nothing could accommodate Janice." Adrianne gave me her sweetest, most placating smile. "You know I don't go along with mental programming. That's exactly what we've got to fight. We may not be getting brainwashed, but we're not doing our minds any service either." Addy kicked disconsolately at a loose piece of paper lying previously uncontested in the hall.

"A student might as well sit in her mother's automatic dishwasher as attend this mass butter churning some call an education," she finished undefeated.

Not waiting for an answer, my irrepressible friend saluted with military briskness and paced out the door like a winning trotting horse, determined to keep in step and yet ahead of the race. Sincerity shouted from every clip of her red heels on the cobblestone pavement.

I continued to my next class alone. Perversely, I couldn't keep my thoughts from straying back to Dr. Brantwood's comment, "I see you are not a relativist." His words sawed against my mind with an almost savage vigor that wouldn't be dispelled. It was as if he'd been intending to find me out—to challenge me personally. It was only a passing comment and nothing to be disturbed about. Yet it persisted, tempting me to resolve it with some admissible rationalization. There was none. I was almost to my next class, and still I hadn't come to terms with that one small flagellating statement.

I was suddenly lonely for someone who thought as I did; someone who could share my enthusiasm for study; someone who wouldn't scoff at my traditional values. Unable to free myself from my unsettling feelings, I wandered into the courtyard at the rear of the Arts building and took a bench nestled close into the wall of the adjoining theater. I didn't usually spend time extravagantly, but today I needed some space to clear my mind. I had always known clearly where I stood. *Now I wasn't sure.*

The green wooden bench faced an open plaza of rock and flowers. While students passed the area from time to time, it was enough out of the way of the main thoroughfare to be peaceful. I put my books on the bench beside me and leaned back against the weathered wall of the theater. The gentle rays of the sun fell full upon my face, and the wind blew soft and refreshing against my cheek. Determined not to fret, I allowed my eyes to wander idly over the flowers growing faithfully among the carefully placed rocks. After a time, the courtyard and the rockery flowers lost their separate identities and coalesced into one lovely whole. My eyes closed and I relaxed, grateful for the reprieve of a few quiet moments.

Chapter Fourteen

Where do you come from?
From another planet, sir.

—Antoine de Saint-Exupéry: *The Little Prince*[34]

For the moment, I was content within the sheltering peace of the courtyard. Without warning, a familiar voice speaking my name violated the stillness, dispelling the calm as effectively as a crowing rooster dispels the quiet sanctity of the night.

"Miss Collingsgate. Out admiring nature's beauty, and wondering how men can be born in sin, let alone deny God?"

Dr. Brantwood stood not more than three feet away, a wry smile on his face.

Surprised, I bolted off the bench and nearly stumbled into him. Fortunately, on this occasion, he stepped aside in time, allowing me to sit back down with relative composure. Unperturbed, this unpredictable man leaned against the theater wall and looked with detached objectivity over the river valley, his arms folded in front of him like a careless Buddha.

Although he didn't look at me, I felt keenly self-conscious, almost as if I was diminishing in size, and would soon slip between the lathes on the bench. Oblivious to my *Alice in Wonderland* feeling of being out of proportion, Dr. Brantwood revised his question.

"I suppose you believe there are no true atheists? That when a man dies, he will confess his error?"

"I don't believe in deathbed repentance," I forced myself to say evenly. "If a man lives as an atheist, he dies as one."

"That has a mercenary ring," Dr. Brantwood replied, with surprised interest. "Don't you promulgate the mercy of God?" I blanched.

"I understood you to ask if I thought there are sincere non-believers, not whether God will forgive them for it." Catching the contrition in Dr. Brantwood's eyes, I added, "I believe in the mercy of God, and I believe there are honest atheists. That's all I can say."

Dr. Brantwood closed his lips in a tight line. Taking his gaze from the river, he looked searchingly at me.

"That is fussy," he said. His tone approximated the same slight respect one might feel for an overly meticulous housekeeper, whose narrow zeal for cleanliness dooms her to squander her life searching for hairs on the rug with a magnifying glass.

"Perhaps. But I am not," I defended. Fussy was too near to "fake."

"How are you not fussy?" Dr. Brantwood prodded, a hint of a smile in his eyes.

"We were asked to write a novel in third year as a term assignment. It—"

"You mean to say there are no fussy novel writers?" he interrupted in open disbelief.

"No. I mean the writing engrossed me so entirely, I couldn't stop. I wrote every spare minute—through all my other classes and even through Sunday worship service."

"During prayers, did you close your eyes?"

"Yes, of course." The truth slipped out unbidden.

"That is worse than fussy," Dr. Brantwood said mildly. "That is committed." There was a surprising gentleness in his voice. It prompted me to return the quasi-compliment.

"Like you?" I caught myself just in time to prevent adding the *Sir.*"

Dr. Brantwood laughed, a mellow sound that precluded irritation.

As with all his moods, Dr. Brantwood's congeniality was short lived and ended abruptly with a change of topic. It was odd, but rather than enervate his mental vigor, his unpredictable nature seemed to energize his personality.

"Why don't you speak up more in class?" Dr. Brantwood asked, plainly interested.

The question, though justified, caught me off guard. *Why indeed? How could I respond?* I thought of my eloquent classmates whose certainty formed a solid, unbroken front against traditional morality. In class, my views would be helpless butterflies tossed out on cold winds of disparagement.

"You don't admire the vulgar process of haggling in the forum?" Dr. Brantwood prodded.

"No. I mean yes. I would participate but—"

"But what?"

"All right." I said, driven to defense. "Critical analysis can be destructive."

"You think it's wrong to ask questions?" There was a tone of wounded disbelief in his voice. His directness riveted my gaze to his.

"No," I said. "Questions are good. We should ask questions. I just can't feel a noble deed is done when truth is lost in the process."

"Is that what happens, do you think?" Dr. Brantwood looked at me reflectively.

"Discussion is good to a point," I hedged.

"And what would that point be, Miss Collingsgate?"

Helplessly, I looked at this baffling instructor. He seemed intent to push me mercilessly. How could I help him understand my views? How could I tell him that it was living waters I desired, not the stagnant pools of modern vanity.

Dr. Brantwood remained leaning patiently against the wall, waiting for my reply. Still I hesitated. *What could I say?* Nothing, given the precariousness of my solitary views. I began gathering my books to leave.

Dr. Brantwood was not so easily dissuaded. Seating himself on the opposite end of the bench, he pointedly arrested my exit by picking up one of my books.

"*Theme and Image: An Anthology,*" he said. Turning the book over in his graceful hands, he flipped deftly through the pages while scanning the contents, then looked up with a reproving glance. "You haven't read the texts?"

"Yes, I have."

"Obviously."

"No, not obviously. Carefully. A person can't . . . What's to be gained by ramming paper ships into a wall?"

"Why don't you ram a few and see?"

I shook my head in wonder. *What did he want to know?*

"Man isn't entirely calculating," I offered cautiously. "He does not—cannot—depend on reason alone."

"Agreed," Dr. Brantwood concurred unexpectedly, a tinge of regret in his voice. "Unfortunately, the mind is seldom developed to the extent it can successfully tyrannize over man's other capacities." He looked at me with thoughtful eyes, his lips begging a rueful smile.

"This is not you certainly," he said. He still did not understand.

"I do think," I said defensively. "But . . ." *What could I say?* I felt as vulnerable as a first-year freshman hauled into the Dean's office for some vilely exaggerated misdemeanor. I forced my gaze to meet Dr. Brantwood's.

"It's what I meant in class by *transport,*" I explained, feigning confidence. "I didn't mean dematerialized like a ghost: shapeless, amorphous, without quality or character." In spite of the boldness of my exposition, inside I felt like a waif cast adrift on the sea.

"Go on," Dr. Brantwood urged smiling.

"Man is tripartite: mind, body, and spirit. The mind governs the body, but the spirit rules the mind. It is when we sense another's spiritual self through the expressions of the mind, that true communion—one mind meeting another—occurs." I paused, out of breath. It had been, for me, a long speech.

Not satisfied with the convoluted explanation, Dr. Brantwood asked skeptically, "Mind, body, spirit? You refer to the 'ghost in the machine' concepts similar to Buckminster Fuller's *Phantom Captain?*"

"Something like," I assented, assuming an English professor would have studied numerous philosophies regarding the nature of man.

"You fancy all three parts are separate? Can the body, the mind, and the spirit function independently? Unrestricted?

"Yes and no. People who suffer severe brain damage can still live, if only in a vegetative state."

"That's not what I meant," he said gravely. "I meant in your trichotomy. Which takes precedence? The desires of the mind, the spirit, or the body?"

"None of them totally." Something warned me the castaway waif was about to sink beneath the waves.

"How so?"

"Proper balance requires the body be governed by the intelligence, as the mind is governed by the spirit." It was a comment destined for rebuttal.

"That's a fancy description of conscience," Dr. Brantwood said. "Surely the body only seeks its best good?"

"Some believe so," I said.

"Do you?"

"No."

"Ah, yes. Of course. Original sin. That's it, isn't it? Man is evil from birth." Dr. Brantwood replaced my book with a resigned movement. His provoking sureness stung me to respond.

"No," I said. "Man is innocent from birth."

"In your case, surely. But what about the rest of us?" There was more than a hint of laughter in his eyes. I tried again.

"When physical desires govern the mind, the spirit is also overcome. When this happens man becomes carnally minded, a slave. He loses his freedom." I hesitated. My explanation was unconvincing. Still at sea, with only flimsy words for my raft, the relentless waves of the ocean were closing over my head.

"Go on," Dr. Brantwood urged.

"A person governed by physical passions is chained to the rack of his body's incessant demands. If the body rules, mind and spirit are captured like rats aboard a sinking ship."

"I see," he said. "The solution would be for the rats, as you colorfully term the mind and spirit, to run the ship."

"Something like that," I admitted, unsure of his destination.

"That would be an advantage," he mused, giving me a provocative sideways glance. Heedlessly, I walked into the trap.

"How so?"

"When a storm rages, with the rats at the helm, they can jump ship, happily drown themselves, and leave the body in peace."

Dr. Brantwood's bizarre proposal made me blink. Still, considering my ridiculous analogy, I had to admit he had every right to his ironic conclusions. Having drowned twice, I floundered to the shore. It was a retreat made bitter by the memory of my pompous denigration of the *stagnant pools of modern vanity*. I certainly had enough vanity and more to spare, if I dared bandy word swords with this particular professor.

While wishing ardently that I'd gone to the library, instead of whiling away valuable time on a public bench, it was purely by chance that I looked fleetingly into Dr. Brantwood's eyes. He didn't appear uncomfortable. Indeed, from the amused awareness of his look, I had the distressing feeling that as my discomfort grew, he became more relaxed.

With an incorrigible lack of concern, Dr. Brantwood leaned back, stretched his legs, and allowed his arm to fall informally on the top of the bench. The only part of him that didn't appear completely at ease was his long fingers, which tapped away on the bench back, a few scant inches from my shoulder. Gazing at the water-colored strawflowers growing in among the rocks, he smiled.

"You're right," he said appreciatively. "It is a beautiful day. The morning sunlight is renewing." He paused, then added reflectively, "Almost makes a case for reincarnation."

"Certainly for life after death," I evaded, wishing I was anywhere but on this bench discussing religion with a professor I hardly knew.

"Life on this earth?" Dr. Brantwood asked, exhaling the air from his throat in a dry laugh.

"It's hard—"

"I'll rephrase the question," he interjected. "Do you believe you will live after death on Earth? The very earth upon which we are now discoursing so pleasantly?"

"Hopefully," I replied, not at all sure I concurred with the *discoursing pleasantly* part.

"Depending on?"

"God's judgment."

Dr. Brantwood's look of contented reverie departed abruptly, the jovial tone fading from his voice. Straightening his back, he took his arm down, and looked across the river.

"So you blame God, like all devout puritans. "His astounding statement was not a question.

"I meant," I faltered, "God's commands must be obeyed; this is how we earn, through grace, our place in the next life."

"You merely sharpen the old saw. Surely you can come up with something more original? Salvation by adjudicated merit is speculative."

"Everyone will live after death," I clarified. "The question is where and under what conditions."

"Of course. Heaven or Hell."

"There could be an infinity of heavens."

"And a multitude of hells?"

Not wishing to pursue this line of thought I suggested, "Earth was a Garden of Eden once. It could be so again."

"To which state of innocence you would gratefully return. Or is it that you've never left?" His words sent a shock into my mind.

"I was referring to the idea generally," I amended. "To the future condition of the earth."

"Exactly. But why wait for a future Eden? It must be possible to create our own paradise while in the flesh."

"Through knowledge, perhaps."

"If that's the key, there's a fine line between gods and devils," he said acidly. Dr. Brantwood's expression was composed, his eyes not unkind, but the firm line of his mouth indicated he wasn't dallying with words. Irrationally, I felt a thrill of excitement.

"I suppose man is an able candidate for both positions," I hazarded.

Dr. Brantwood's easy laughter gave me that feeling of being wrapped in silk again.

"What I meant," I said, not wishing to appear cynical, "is that with knowledge we have a greater chance of success in life."

"Why would that be?" Dr. Brantwood asked, his smile fading.

"Knowledge, added to experience, provides the wisdom that gives us the insight we need to avoid the obstacles that hinder progress." The pedantic explanation fell flat.

Dr. Brantwood looked at me the way a medical researcher might scrutinize the white skull of a departed, not-entirely-sane colleague on the dissection table. I winced inwardly. He was not to be dissuaded; there was to be no reprieve. Whether I willed it or not, it was clearly his intent to discuss religion with me. Even for friends, this would be a difficult topic. Something told me this was exactly the professor's objective. He was forcing me to commit myself, to speak my mind by employing my own faith-based emotions against me. His ploy was effective.

I felt the mental stress much the same as a long-distance runner feels the strain on tasked muscles. My hands had become gripped in tight communion, and my forehead, as well as my hands, felt cold and moist. I was even biting my bottom lip, a nervous reaction I'd not had since childhood. Dr. Brantwood, sensing the success of his stratagem, was in no mind to squander his advantage. What he expected of me I couldn't discern, but what he thought of my traditional beliefs was all too clear.

Seeming completely at ease, my enigmatic instructor continued absently tapping his fingers against the back of the bench. It occurred to me that not once during the whole of our conversation had I noticed any students passing. The courtyard was out of the way, but for those going to the Arts Theater, this was the only route. Also, to my wonder, the wind had gained strength and was blowing the strawflowers with punctilious bows and curtsies against the rocks. My hair which had come undone, blew in confused disorder about my face.

Unmindful of the wind, Dr. Brantwood leaned forward and rested his elbows on his knees, his fingers meeting in a tent shape. This characteristic habit of his made him seem older than his years, like an ancient sage taking meditative counsel with the inner man. Incongruently, as he sat tapping his fingers together, his focus with his thoughts, the image of rich, green moss growing on the north side of trees came to mind.

Feeling my glance, Dr. Brantwood looked up. There was a serious light in his eyes, and for the first time in the discussion, he made a statement that was neither a question nor a critique of my words.

"Success and progress aren't the same thing. Success—more often the illusion of success—is bestowed by the world. It is men or women individually," Dr. Brantwood said, briefly glancing in my direction, "who determine progress." Taken out of context, the sentiment might have sounded bitter. Coming from Dr. Brantwood, there was a note of optimism.

"Then we don't all rise or fall together," I said, more out of respect for the opinion expressed, than any desire to prove my alertness.

Dr. Brantwood impatiently brushed his hair from his forehead and rose quickly to his feet. Bending forward, he picked up my books and handed them to me.

"What have you to do with the masses, in any event, Miss Collingsgate?" he said, with a note of finality. His glance swept briefly over my head as he nodded good day; then he turned and walked away. A moment later he disappeared into the dark interior of the Arts building.

I was again alone on my bench, but the quiet arbor had lost its restorative charm. I was confused. *What had the discussion with Dr. Brantwood proven?* I drew my sweater around my shoulders, attempting to shut out the gusts of apprehension buffeting my mind; but as I left the arbor, I could see the defeated figure of Richard III huddled on Bosworth Field.

Halfway to the library, Adrianne met me. "Diana! Are you ill?" she inquired, all motherly concern. I shook my head, attempting a smile.

"I'm glad you don't think so," she said brightly, "because you look like a knight whose best suit of armor has just been drilled full of holes."

Chapter Fifteen

We are put on Earth a little space,
That we may endure the beams of love.

—William Blake: *Songs of Innocence* [35]

I walked home along the river route. The wild geese were flying in a victory formation overhead. Passing the pungent scent of the pines and coming into the garden, I spotted Father. He was turning over the ground, getting his roses ready for winter. Roses need constant care; they are demanding flowers. Seeing me, Father leaned on his shovel and smiled hello.

"So what lovely hedonistic philosophy did you learn today, dotter?"

"The usual," I said, returning his smile. "Man is autonomous. He has no need for God. In fact, God most probably doesn't exist."

Father simulated a look of stunned amazement. "You don't say? You mean to tell me, in spite of flights into space, man still thinks he's the center of the universe?"

"That's about it," I said ruefully. "Man's reason reigns supreme in the cosmos."

"What will they think of next?" Dad chuckled.

Father liked to take pokes at the secular philosophies academics offered as answers to man's basic questions. Even more, he liked to keep a spot check on me to ensure I wasn't buying into them. Father well knew the latent power—the dangerous potential—of the academic mind to dig so fast and furiously on a topic that the truth could be buried. It wasn't intentional perversion. No intelligent person means to warp the truth, it just turns out that way. In recognition of this, Father wanted me to keep my wits about me—to develop my mind, but not to lose my soul.

Having found out what he wanted to know, he advised, "The Jinn is having a guest over for dinner. Perhaps she could use your help."

The Jinn is what Father called Ginny when she was in an organizational flurry, ordering everyone around and generally getting things done in rare form. Nodding, I followed the rose-lined path around to the side of the house. As I entered the kitchen, the delicious aroma of baking chicken reminded me I'd skipped lunch.

Ginny had an LP of Perry Como playing. Perry's soothing, mellow voice filled the room with the strains of "Hot Diggity Dog Ziggity."[36] Ginny was a modern. She loved the Everly Brothers, Peter Paul and Mary, Karen Carpenter, and Joan Baez, but she also enjoyed listening to more seasoned singers. When she listened to Perry Como, I knew she was missing Mother. Perry Como was Mother's favorite singer. Wistfully, I wondered who Mother listened to now that she was in the spirit world. Brushing the unanswerable question aside, I geared for combat.

"Hi, Diddi," Ginny greeted. "You're just in time. Grab the potato masher, will you?"

"Will do. Right after I hang up my sweater and give Aunt Amy a hug."

"Have a nice day at the uni?" Aunt Amy asked.

"Yes." I knew better than to go into details with Aunt Amy. If there was a person in our family who firmly believed university was an intellectual oasis—a mecca for the pure in mind—it was Aunt Amy. I didn't want to dispel her illusions.

Mashing the potatoes, I could hear that Mother and Ginny weren't the only ones with a fondness for Mr. Como. Carlyle was singing up a racket, as only a spoiled canary can do when he is perfectly happy with himself and his retainers. Aunt Amy was noticing it, too.

"Do you think we could shut off the music or the bird, Ginny?" she asked, wiping her apron tail over her heated forehead. "There's enough noise in here to raise the dead."

"Sure," Ginny said sweetly. "Neal should be here soon. He prefers Vivaldi."

"Neal is coming to supper? The boy you asked me if I knew?"

"Yes, he is. Isn't that great? He and Dad are working on a project together. Neal is Dad's history assistant. Needs the job to earn money for his law courses."

"Then Neal is Father's guest? I thought Dad said you were having a guest for supper." The Jinn gave me an ingenuous smile.

"He's both. He works for Poppa, and I invited him."

"Oh!"

"Diana," Ginny urged, "I can't find that baroque recording of Poppa's. Would you please run up to his study and see if he's hidden it there?"

"Yes'm," I complied.

I was glad for a reprieve from the bustle of the kitchen. Heading up the stairs, I smiled to myself. Ginny managed the home with such cool efficiency, you had to admire her skill. Entering Father's study, I caught the scent of his musk aftershave lotion which always seemed to permeate the room with a sense of stability. Perhaps that was part of the reason I liked the study.

On Father's desk was a worn copy of Josephus. How Dad loved the writings of Josephus. Almost as much as I, in those years of childhood, loved the Uncle Remus stories of Brer Rabbit and Brer Fox. Finding the requested recording of Vivaldi, I returned to the kitchen.

"Thanks, Diddi," Ginny grinned. "Now could you get a move on your beautiful self and get that cabbage shredded?"

I smiled assent.

Ginny herself was beginning to move like a White Tornado. A *White Tornado* is how Father described Ginny when she was on one of her cleaning campaigns. Between Ginny and Aunt Amy, cleanliness was not next to godliness—it was first. I was glad to be able to shred the cabbage out of the way.

"Amy Mom," Ginny called over her shoulder, "could we have one of your yummy jars of peaches for dessert? To go with the coconut cake?" Ginny always called Aunt Amy *Amy Mom*, even when she didn't want special favors. The title was to honor Aunt Amy who loved Ginny as she had her own little daughter who had died in infancy.

Promptly at quarter to six, the dinner was ready and the table set.

"Diana," Ginny directed, looking at the clock, "will you please retrieve Poppa from his beloved rose pond? He's probably up to his gills in mud."

I exited the house in search of Father. Finding him at the far southern corner of the rose garden, I informed him of the summons. He nodded grinning and I headed back to the house.

As I passed the walk where it split before the pool, I was surprised to see that the *Black Prince* was still in bloom. A beautiful deep mahogany flower had opened and reigned dark and lustrous on the rose bush by the gate. Most of the roses had ceased blooming in preparation for winter dormancy, so this late bloom was unusual. I walked over and bent down to smell the flower. Its subtle fragrance was not without appeal. *My unknown knight to be*, I thought. He would be a mystery. Of this I was sure.

At a few minutes before six, Father was presentable and supper was ready. Ginny fussed over a pickle tray, while Aunt Amy took time to rest in the rocker by Carlyle's cage.

"Diddi," Ginny asked, "don't you think Neal has the most intelligent eyes?" The question was typical of Ginny. She never made any effort to veil her thoughts or hide her feelings. To Ginny, what she felt was what she said. Giving her the credit due, what others saw was what they got.

"I don't know," I said honestly, "I've never been close enough to Neal to see his eyes." A fleeting image of Dr. Brantwood's own perceptive eyes—now hazel, now violet—stole uninvited through my mind. Enough of that! I said to myself.

"Neal already has an economics degree." Ginny chatted on. "Isn't that impressive?"

"If he's studying law, he would need to have a first degree," I said. Ginny frowned.

Realizing my comment had dampened her delight, I added, "But yes. It's impressive."

At exactly one minute to six the doorbell rang, and Ginny ran to welcome Neal. She was dressed in her favorite blouse with shell-pink roses to compliment her blue pleated skirt. She did look lovely. After introductions, we gathered in the dining room around the table. Immediately following the blessing on the food, Father corralled Neal.

"Do you think there's any hope of the cold war warming up?" Dad was not against politics at supper. Tonight, it was clearly his aim to bring out the heavy artillery before the guest suspected an ambush.

"I certainly hope not, Dr. Collingsgate," Neal replied. "I think the cold war hit its peak in the fifties, between Khrushchev and Kennedy. Now the conflict is not between communist and democratic ideologies. It's between those who would internationalize for peace and those who would strengthen their national sphere-of-influence by stockpiling arsenals for a wonderful defense. Today, the cold war is over the question of how to maintain peace."

This was the correct answer. Satisfied, Father nodded. Father had served in the Second World War as ship's joiner in the Navy. He had been stationed at Halifax and so had not seen combat action. Even so, war was anathema to Dad: a totally senseless waste of life and resources. He never wanted to hear of another war. Unfortunately, that was not to be with the Korean War, and then the war in Vietnam.

"You agree with Arthur Schlesinger Jr., that the conflict for peace is nationalism versus internationalism?" Father asked, mollified that Neal was a thinking man.

"Yes," Neal said, "but I sympathize more closely with your educational anthropologist George Spindler. The real cold war split is how to obtain global peace today. It's basically between those who hold 'traditional' and those who hold 'emergent' values." Neal was talking Dad's language. Father leaned forward and earnestly scrutinized the young man seated calmly beside his daughter. If Neal had intended to make a great impression at dinner, he was going about it in the right way.

"And how would traditional and emergent values compare?" Professor Collingsgate asked, a look of craftiness on his face, as he leaned back and stuck his hands into the sides of his gray vest. For Ginny's sake, I hoped Neal wouldn't muff his lines. Neal laid his fork down and took a sip from his juice. He appeared to know the importance his next words would carry.

"Traditional values would have their basis in morality, the work ethic, and autonomy. Emergent values would be based on moral relativity, a live-for-today philosophy, and conformity. Traditionalists embrace the sphere-of-influence theory. Emergentists applaud internationalism, but that's possibly a simplistic generality. Patriotism shouldn't be confined to one camp or the other."

"Now you're cooking with gas!" Father said, taking his hands out of his vest in a sign of approval and nodding his head vigorously. "A good summation. Spindler's nailed it. 'The traditionalist views the emergentist as spineless, and weak-headed, if not downright immoral.'"[37]

"Yes," Neal concurred, visibly relaxing. "'And the emergentist regards the traditionalist as selfish, and compulsively paranoid.'"[38]

Father ignored Aunt Amy's snort of objection. Aunt Amy was nothing if not terrifyingly traditional. She might even be safely accused of traditional extremism. To Aunt Amy, what was good for one was good for all. If she was cold, you had to put your sweater on. It was easy to suspect Aunt Amy made Mephistopheles fold his paws and say his prayers each evening. The picture brought an involuntary smile to my lips. Returning to the conversation, I noted Father had not yet depleted his store of ammunition.

"The bottle neck in the strictly national 'God preserve us by-our-boundaries'[39] viewpoint is the leaders," Father said, charging full steam ahead into his best expository mode. "We are reaping the benefit of Henry Winthrop's *Sheltered Generation*. In Canada, the true-blue land grabbers are not the French or the English; they are those who would preserve their political power, their economic gains at any price; those who would keep the 'holy fires of their indignation burning because they fear the loss of personal sovereignty.' "[40] Father paused and buttered a roll, keeping an eye on Neal for his reaction.

"I believe in traditional values," Dad continued. "Don't get me wrong. But it's time we all started believing in Columbus as well. The earth is round. It is a globe. What's good for the 'Hew Hess Hay' may not be good for the world."

"I agree," Neal said. "Leaders who are alienated, isolated from a sense of social responsibility, only widen the gap between leadership and society. Nationalists determined to protect their sphere-of-influence and internationalists determined to break down traditional mores, face off in what amounts to deadly political bickering."

Aunt Amy, who'd held her peace long enough, wiped her mouth on her napkin and recited one of her favorite quotes:

The bigger fleas have lesser fleas
Upon their backs to bite them
The lesser fleas have lesser fleas
And on to infinitum! [11]

Father ignored the axiom, having heard it many times before. "So what kinds of values do you think the American and Canadian governments espouse today, Neal?"

Once again, Neal laid down his fork. "My opinion is Pierre Eliot Trudeau's government holds emergent values. Lyndon B's is a return to the traditional, but with emergent social policies." Neal paused thoughtfully. "I was just beginning university in 1963, the year President Kennedy was assassinated. Lyndon B. Johnson is a good president, but I don't think he has Kennedy's impact."

"Humph," Father said, "you can't fight poverty by instituting more social programs which increase the dole. If President Johnson really wants to mount a war on poverty, he needs to stop telling poverty-stricken people they're victims of the system and can't do anything to help themselves."

Father poured himself a glass of sour cherry juice and continued, "If you're going to succeed in life, you've got to do more than float downstream. You've got to jump in and swim against the current."

Knowing when to change the topic, Neal observed, "The picture over the sideboard of the hands carving the apple is interesting. Do the hands belong to a family member?"

"Yes," Ginny responded, eager to participate in the conversation. "It's a painting of Grandmother Carolynne's hands. She never liked it, but Father says he'd know those hands anywhere."

"They're small, but they do look efficient," Neal agreed, casting an appreciative glance at Ginny's own dainty hands, which were busily engaged in heaping a second helping of potatoes and meat onto Neal's plate. Father glanced over at Ginny.

"Virginia. Perhaps our guest doesn't know force feeding is the rule at Collingsgate."

Ginny gave Dad a 'talk-all-you-like' look and went right on heaping Neal's plate.

"I really appreciate the fine supper, Mrs. Collingsgate," Neal said, addressing Aunt Amy. "Your baked chicken is excellent. And the rolls are the best I've had in years."

"I'm not Mrs. Collingsgate," Aunt Amy said firmly. "I'm against robbing the cradle. And Ginny did most of the cooking." In spite of her vigorous disclaimer, Aunt Amy was pleased with the compliment to her protégé. A contented flush added color to her lined but loving face.

"Mother died some years ago," Ginny explained. "Aunt Amy is Mom's oldest sister. She was living alone, so we coerced her into living with us."

In truth, there was little coercing. Aunt Amy had always been devoted to Ginny. From the first time Mother had given her the wee baby to hold, it was instant love. Since then, the bonds of mutual affection had grown stronger year by year.

"I'm sorry to hear your wife passed away," Neal said to Father.

"Yes. Thank you," Dad replied. "Don't know why she had to do it, but she was determined. You can't do a thing with these Collingsgate women, once they get their minds set. If one of them gets a notion into her head, neither the Vatican, nor the Twelve Apostles, nor St. Peter himself could change her mind."

If Neal was surprised at this odd reply, he didn't show it. He did seem to have nice manners, as well as intelligence.

"What was her name?" he asked, smiling.

"Elizabeth Kathleen," Father replied. "We were married in the temple, so I'm bound to catch up with her sooner or later. She's mine and I aim to keep her."

I smiled. Father was telling Neal that the Collingsgate men married for keeps. It was Dad's way of letting prospective suitors know the way the cards were stacked.

"I intend to be married in the temple, also," Neal affirmed. This was a surprise. I hadn't known Neal was a Latter-day Saint.

Ginny apparently did, for she chimed in, "Neal went to Barbados for his mission, Diana. Isn't that exotic?"

"Actually it wasn't all that exotic," Neal said with a good-natured grin, "but it was rewarding. Many of the people live in abject poverty. The tourist industry is for those who have money. Most of the natives have very little, but they're humble, good people and I grew to love them."

By the time the preserved peaches and coconut cake were served, Neal was well acquainted with our family and we with his. He'd grown up in Eastern Canada. In fact, his parents still lived in Brampton, Ontario. Neal had wanted to see more of the country and so he had come west in 1964. He would return east when it came time to article—possibly complete his studies at McGill.

After supper, Neal headed back across the river to his rented room, and we dispersed to our various chores for the evening. Ginny went to the rocker. Getting out her guitar, she began singing a new song, "Jet Plane," written by John Denver and sung by Peter, Paul, and Mary. It seemed a plaintive song, after the lively congenial company of the evening, but I expected Ginny was tired from all her work.

As I listened to the words, love welled up in my heart. I couldn't imagine what life would be like if Ginny packed and left. We'd all possibly make do, but I knew we wouldn't like it.

Chores for the day over and assignments prepared, I got into bed and pulled one of Aunt Amy's afghans snugly around my shoulders. Feeling reminiscent, I looked over at Mother's picture.

Mother was an inch shorter than Ginny, but while Mother may have been diminutive, Father never referred to his wife by anything but her full title—Elizabeth Kathleen. When I grew old enough to appreciate the contradiction between this stiffly formal appellation and the dainty, joyful lady that was my Mother, I was quietly amused. How often had Father's generous wit evoked a well of insight into both their natures.

Unable to sleep, I lay awake remembering. The spring Mother died was not without joy. Elizabeth Kathleen had a spirit to match her name. Two days before her death, she'd sat propped round with her favorite gold satin pillows on the sofa in the living room, talking to Father as animatedly as her condition allowed. Father sat close by in his chair, some papers in his lap, half-listening, half-intent on his marking. Mother was content.

Teasing Dad, Mother said pertly, "William Wallace! Here it's spring exams, and with no time to perpetrate verbal atrocities on us mere mortals, you're almost human. And what do I do? I go tripping off to pleasant pastures elsewhere. What a thing to do. Go and leave you now that you're so busy." Resting from the exertion of her energetic tirade against herself, Mother shook her head in mock angst.

Father smiled gently and looked up briefly from his papers. Leaning toward Mother, he reached out a long arm and tenderly ruffled the silky waves of her soft blond hair. For the seventieth time, he explained that when Mother helped him with his marking, he always had twice the work. Mother had snorted indignantly at his retort, but when he gave her a second glance of mock severity, she rewarded him with a good-humored laugh. Elizabeth Kathleen was not easily deluded, her laughter flowing freely when she knew she pleased Father. His aching heart must have lightened at the sound.

Hand still on the head of the woman he loved, I could hear him saying with contrived sternness, "Baby's hair. Nothing but baby's hair. The wife of the eminent Dr. Collingsgate has baby's hair." In return, Mother had glowered back at him with the expected retaliatory fierceness; whereupon, she was satisfactorily rewarded for her part in the charade with a fond cuffing under the chin and a warm low laugh.

Dad's laugh was always comforting. It spoke more eloquently than words of his love for Mother. In front of others, he never embraced Mother with more than friendly off-handedness; but we knew of the deep bond between husband and wife: the abiding love that went beyond surface show to the inner reaches of their souls.

Yes, Mother had gone from our mortal vision, but her gentle, loving spirit lived on in her daughter Ginny and in her husband's and all our hearts. Even on the day of Mother's funeral, our intense grief at parting was moderated. It was as if Mother had bequeathed us her delight in living. Even Father's intimate sorrow was only revealed by an urgent impatience to get home quickly after the service. He didn't stay for the family dinner, excusing himself with the explanation that he feared Elizabeth Kathleen's spirit would be up in the study, trying to help with his marking and creating a truly magnificent disorder.

Chapter Sixteen

He who can look on the loveliness of the world and share its sorrow
and realize something of the wonder of both
is in immediate contact with divine things
and has got as near to God's secret as anyone can get.

—Oscar Wilde: *A Test of Friendship*[12]

In The Pit, Harris Saunders had the floor. He was recounting a recent dream, his shaggy head bent forward, a half cigarette in his fingers. The usual group of students was present from 550—individual differences suspended as students listened to Harris's remarkable account in interested community. Not wishing to intrude, I stood by the milk dispenser listening quietly as Harris talked.

"Exiled from Earth, I'd been without food and short on water for nearly five days. On the sixth day an uncharted planet came before the scanner of my tiny spaceship. Seen through the finder, the planet was ethereal in its beauty. The entire surface was crisscrossed with what looked like brilliant rainbows.

Although the planet was unfamiliar, I was too weak to continue further, so I decided to attempt a landing in the hopes of finding food and water, or perish in the attempt. All went well until just before touch down, when a blinding flash of silver-blue light prevented me from seeing the dials on my landing instrument. Without visual control, I crashed into the surface and was knocked unconscious.

When I came to, I crawled from the wreckage of my mangled ship, surprised to find myself upon one of the radiant arcs I'd observed from the air. The rainbow appeared to be a type of plastic highway constructed hundreds of feet above the true surface of the planet. The material of the highway resembled the crystal of rare gems, reflecting emerald, sapphire, and ruby coloration intermingled. About the width of a two-lane highway on Earth, these crystalline roads surrounded the planet in great jeweled arcs, allowing only small triangles of space between each intersecting arm."

Harris drew on his cigarette and continued. "As I stood marveling upon the highway, I saw a silver-blue light approaching from the distance. Turning my head to shield my eyes, I crouched behind the wreckage of my spaceship and looked cautiously to the side of the advancing light. The light was not steady, emitting rays periodically in piercing shafts. When the light came closer, I made out the form of a slender creature that sparkled with diamond brilliance in the exact center of the light. Strangely, the beautiful being paid me no notice, heedlessly passing by along the jewel roadway. As time dragged by, other ethereal beings, always surrounded by the crystal-silver light, approached, but they too passed on without heed to my plight.

By this time I was on the brink of death from lack of food and was too parched with thirst to shout. In my critical condition, I watched helplessly as the beings passed. Having the appearance of great intelligence, these resplendent personages were entirely without regard for my welfare. None stopped to inquire about my presence or care for my needs.

As the hours passed, I was left without care or shelter under the searing rays of a sun that threatened to fill the whole sky with broiler heat. Approaching delirium, I began to form a theory. It seemed to me these light creatures lived on these jewel highways for one of two reasons: either the planet surface was unfit for habitation, or they found life there degrading. Consequently, as they apparently had no need for food or shelter, they'd erected these roadways.

Finally, when the intense rays of the sun became unbearable, I dragged myself to the edge of the highway and flung myself over the side, certain of quick destruction on the planet floor below. To my surprise, instead of falling in a fiery pit or on sharp rocks, I landed without pain or injury on a warm, furry creature. Defensively, I shied away, using what strength was left to cover my face, so I might not see the animal's veracious jaws descend upon me. To my amazement, the loathsome creature began immediately to care for me. At first, I was supplied with a milky liquid from the animal's own body. Later, when I could take more solid food, I was given a fibrous root that tasted not unlike a parsnip. The food was plain, but it was not bitter and replenished my strength in a remarkably short time.

As I regained my strength, I realized there were many of these furry creatures abounding on the forested surface of the planet. Numbers didn't increase their beauty, but it was clear they meant me no harm and would see that I was well provided. For speech, they made a clicking sound with their large red tongues and teeth. Eventually, I began to gain a rudimentary understanding of their simple language. The foliage of the gnarled trees filtered out the more severe rays of the sun, so that when my skin healed from the painful blisters, I found life, if not pleasant, at least endurable among the kindly, misshapen creatures." Harris ceased speaking and waited for the others to comment.

"Does this remind you of anything, Miss Collingsgate?" It was Dr. Brantwood. Apparently he, too, had been listening to Harris's strange account. For a second our eyes met. I felt as though a slender length of finely spun hazel wire connected Dr. Brantwood's mind to mine.

"Perhaps H. G. Well's *War of the Worlds*, or the Houyhnhnms and Yahoos in *Gulliver's Travels*," I said, reluctant to admit I saw more in the tale. A brief smile graced the corners of Dr. Brantwood's mouth. He turned without comment to hear what the group had to say.

"The dream is like to be both Wells and Swift," agreed Aki Hito politely, rotating his coffee cup slowly in his thin hands. "But with most respect to your thought, Miss Diana, I think we here have something more." The students assembled in The Pit waited expectantly, curious to hear what else Mr. Hito could see. His words dispelled their wonder.

"It would seem beautiful persons living coldly on rainbows, with no concerns for sufferings of traveler, were mirages."

A vast disappointment, surging like a tidal wave, swept across my mind. Nodding to Mr. Hito, I collected my milk. As I left, I caught the scratchy sound of Bob Davis guffawing in merriment.

"You tell 'em, Hito Baby. Like I been sayin' all along, there ain't no wise old Head Cheese upstairs lookin' out for us kiddies. That's Sunday School for tiny tots. Like this is the real world—not some Willy Wonka chocolate factory."

Always the same criticisms, I thought sadly. Always the jab at those who believe in the caring goodness of the Infinite; always the same snide pity for those who fail to see things as they really are. Just before reaching the exit from Arts, I felt an urgent tug at my elbow.

"Wait up, Di Mouse," Adrianne panted. "I didn't know you were in The Pit listening, until I saw you fleeing for your life."

I nodded hello. There was a protective caring in Adrianne's voice. My friend was not interested in religion, but she was loyal and would come fiercely to my defense, if she felt there was a personal attack.

"It's okay," I assured her. "Most of the others didn't know I was there either, so the comments couldn't have been orchestrated for my benefit."

"Forgive who you will," Adrianne said archly. "He's an infidel. He's *the* infidel."

"Dr. Brantwood?"

"Possibly." Adrianne looked at me thoughtfully. "But not this time. I was referring to the hobgoblin himself—Bob Davis. He's obviously the mutated result of a long line of inbred orangutans." Addy scratched her armpits and drew her face into a suitably dense expression.

"Adrianne." I laughed in spite of myself. "You do come up with some endearing descriptions."

"Like man! He's so perverted! Ya know?"

"Okay, okay," I assented helplessly. "Let's forget it."

Chapter Seventeen

No matter how we live, we are condemned
to live together with ourselves.

—Hannah Arendt: *Life of the Mind* [43]

Election speeches for Student Union president and reps were scheduled for Friday. Nelson Cruthers, an acclaimed Big L liberal, was running against law student John Cairn, Keynes Houseman (commerce), and Jill Jackson (also law). If pre-election rumor was to be credited, the main race would be between Nelson Cruthers and John Cairn. It was said John was almost as far right as Nelson was left. Some felt if this was the case, it wasn't much of a choice. These students would vote for Keynes Houseman running for Reform or Jill Jackson running for Social Credit.

As Adrianne had instructed, I was outside Edwards at precisely two p.m. At precisely ten minutes past, Adrianne arrived and escorted me directly to SUB, where Nelson and John were giving their maiden speeches. By the time we arrived, the preliminaries were finished and the speeches were about to begin.

Nelson Cruthers, John Cairn, his campaign manager, and a law professor, Dr. Grant Lyman, were sitting comfortably together at a table a few feet from the speaker's platform. Keynes Houseman, Jill Jackson, and their respective campaign managers were seated at another table directly opposite. The SUB main lounge was just over half full. Campus radio was playing Glen Campbell's *Galveston*.

Adrianne motioned me to follow her to Nelson's table. I shook my head, preferring the anonymity of the audience. Adrianne sighed but left me to my own devices and took her place beside Nelson. If the posters and publicity Nelson had received prior to today was an indication, Adrianne was an able campaign manager. She could, it appeared, hold her own on any stage. She certainly didn't need backup from someone who had no real interest in campus politics. Grimacing at my self-imposed expendability, I settled back into a lounge chair by the west window and propped my books on my knees.

John spoke first. Speaking first was a challenge because it gave those speaking later a target to attack. In John's case it was a grave tactical error, due to his unfortunate reputation for unnecessary elegance, which some thought superfluous. True to form, his speech pegged him as something of a modern-day misfit by its flowery, oratorical style. Personally I much preferred hearing a fluent speaker build a blossom palace, to hearing an unimaginative man underplay the possibilities. Realizing John had reached the main thrust of his speech, I focused on his words.

"If, in attempting to change for the better, we destroy order, what is left? What is left is that the individual is isolated, cast adrift from the anchor of community. Taken to the extreme, chaos results, leaving everyone to fend for themselves."

Mockingly seconding John's plea for self-restraint, Nelson coughed a ridiculing, "Hear, hear!"

"Out of the mouths of babes," John returned swiftly. The audience snorted their appreciation of the exchange.

I looked more closely at John. His eyes held dedication. Student government was not the bad joke to this young man that it was to Nelson and to others of the more enlightened set. Intrigued by the thought, I glanced over at Nelson. He was sprawled on his chair, arms and legs in an acute paroxysm of disorder. His contempt for groveling student unions that fronted covert administrative aims was shown by his posture. To Nelson, past SU presidents were puppets; they danced to the system, nothing more. The democratic process on campus was little more than a farce that Nelson found to be more humorous than grizzly. According to Nelson, democracy in general was only a political ploy to enable capitalists to fleece the country.

I wondered how much of Nelson's platform had been formulated by Adrianne. Did she really feel so hostile toward and suspicious of administrative policies on campus? John's next words caught my attention and made me forget my doubts for the moment.

"If we lose self control and undermine the safeguards built into democratic procedures here at Western, what good will we have accomplished? We will find ourselves harmed, not benefited. Like the shortsighted slave owner that whips his slave to an untimely death, those who flail democracy in theory for the imperfections of democracy in practice, risk destroying a faithful and useful servant. To destroy that which is beneficial, be it servant or institution, is barely veiled masochism. We must preserve, not break down. The liberty we have has been bought with the blood of brave men and women—men and women who heroically died for our sakes." Pausing to take a sip of water, John continued.

"Universities cannot be isolated microcosms. They cannot be a law unto themselves. If we at Western denigrate democracy, we devalue freedom. By giving rein to irresponsible criticism, we invite despoliation of individual rights in society at large such as the world has never before experienced. Carlyle was misled. It is not 'democracy that demoralizes society;' it is society that despoils democracy. If we court disorder on campus by demeaning or bypassing established processes, we solicit reproof more devastating than the bony hand of the grim reaper."

Interrupting, Nelson Cruthers waved his own bony hand, heckling, "Death by student fees or death by speeches!"

Unruffled by the comment or the laughter, John would have continued, but Nelson interrupted a second time. "This is fine rhetoric. But we need more than high-sounding words. Everyone knows democracy, as it is reflected in student government on campus, is flawed and will rot inwardly long before it can be trampled from without."

The constituents cheered. There was stamping of feet and shouts of, "You tell 'em, Nelson." Favor was openly for the Liberal platform, whatever that was. Nelson, now standing next to John on the podium, took the opportunity to ride his success.

"The rape of student rights at Western is yesterday's history. Look around you! Do students have any real say in how things are run at this university?"

Delighted shouts of "No!" arose from the listeners. Nelson smirked and drove on.

"The student union, as it now exists, is a pawn of the system. It's time we used our brains instead of our fantasies. It's time we students actually ran student government."

What was supposed to have been separate speeches had turned into a heated debate. It was apparent Nelson played the game by his own rules. John's reply to Nelson's mob-baiting was sternly serious.

"What does such talk really gain? If we want more of a say in running things, we must show ourselves to be responsible, whether on campus or in society at large. If we grind due process, we grind our own bones." John took his seat. I felt a surge of compassion for him. He was eloquent. But I knew, as did others in the room, that he had lost the election. In being too honest, he must now endure the mockery of a premature defeat.

Adrianne looked at her watch and jumped off her chair with obvious agitation. She spoke to Nelson, her gestures imparting concern. I followed her into the lobby, preparing for the invective sure to follow.

Instead of a tirade, Adrianne said softly, "John's a nice person." Then, perhaps feeling she'd revealed too much, she added, "And I'd venture as brain boggling an orator as old pebbles in his mouth. What's his name? You know—Androcles? Themistocles? Empedocles?"

"Demosthenes," I supplied obediently.

"Well, whoever. Fortunately, our generation doesn't dig good oratory."

Two days later, Adrianne shoved the university paper, *The Curb and Gutter,* in front of me as I sat at my carrel in Edwards. My attention was drawn to a pair of political cartoons. The first pictured John Cairn anxiously patching a gigantic hole in a dike with chewing gum. The second showed John struggling to support his lame horse, *Governor Stewball*, on his back. The grinning, large-toothed animal was munching John's hair.

While the consensus was that John Cairn had handed the election to Nelson, a few loyal supporters attended the last campaign in SUB. I attended for Adrianne's sake. Aware that Adrianne wouldn't find my reason praiseworthy, I kept my motivation to myself. I knew I was drawing a fine line between diplomacy and dishonesty, but felt tact was the best option.

Oddly, there'd been a time when I'd found debate for debate's sake stimulating. That had been in high school. I'd even skipped class on a few occasions to attend the Benton Cup debates at the university. What Adrianne would think if she knew of my truancy was another matter. Her opinion of my 'bloodless existence' as she termed it, alternated between a strained tolerance and voluble objections.

Getting to SUB late, I found a seat and sat down. Adrianne, in her usual place at Nelson's table, waved me a saucy hello. Outside of the candidates and a scattering of loyal supporters, the lounge was nearly empty. Harboring my own ulterior motives for attending, I couldn't condemn my fellow students for their absence. I did, however, feel a pang of sympathy for those students who'd worked so hard to make this year's campaign a success.

Nelson Cruthers, dressed in blue jeans and an orange turtleneck sweater, was the first speaker. His shoulder-length hair, which kept falling in his eyes, prevented too close a look at his face. When it came to appearance, I knew a haircut, tie, and jacket could conceal as many vices as sloppiness revealed. Even so, Nelson's overly casual appearance did arouse an uncharitable feeling in me that his rejection of deportment went too far.

Not that he was without his virtues. Nelson did have a command of language, which he used as politicians do, to both persuade and evade at the same time. Indeed, he had the jargon down so pat, it was as if he'd coined it himself. Popular phraseology was clearly his forte; he knew how to fire the mob response. Yet, if only to me, he seemed more of an intellectual vagrant than a dedicated leader.

Nelson concluded his remarks and sat down, characteristically swinging his leg over the arm of his chair. It was once again John

Cairn's turn to speak, the theme of his closing speech much the same as his first: he was sincerely concerned about current trends on campus and in society. Posture erect, John spoke his principles.

"Western civilization is now living in a backwash of her once-proud ambitions. Slothful, but vain, she wallows in a slough of unsurpassed arrogance. We must stem this polluting tide of conceit and indifference, or we will awaken one sad morning to find our fine cities have sunk below the grime, without even an oil slick to mark their passing."

Shouts of "rubbish" and "can it, Cairn" prevented John from continuing further. A tall, dark-haired student wearing an engineer's jacket jeered, "Hey, Cairn. Now tell us about the flying saucer you captured."

Undismayed, John answered coolly, "Do you mean the pink one or the blue one?"

The annoyance of the student was subsumed in the laughter of the group. To his credit, the engineer drew his legs under his chair and thumped good-naturedly on the table with his fist.

A girl in western attire with straight, straw-colored hair, rose and faced the platform with bold assurance. "Surely you don't believe our civilization is really on the brink of self-destruction?" she scoffed. She stood with her hands on her hips, suede boots well apart, defying John to answer. The rest of the small group waited expectantly. No doubt some hoped this ridiculous egghead from law would go back to his bench, and leave student union government to the worldly wise. But if there were those who expected John Cairn to blotch his response, they were disappointed.

"Would you deny us the pleasure of destroying ourselves, Miss?" John returned dryly.

To appreciative snickers, the student shrugged and stepped back to her chair. It was apparent John knew when *not* to take a question seriously. It was Nelson who saved face for the opposition.

"Only if we have to depend on the Bomark Missiles," he said shrewdly.

It was a standoff. Neither side had gained. Standing tall behind the platform, John shook his head. With notes in hand, he looked over the heads of those in the room to the back window of the lounge. Through the window, instead of trees and the cobbled stone of the walk, he seemed to be seeing some tragic, destined rendezvous in time.

Quietly, he said, "I only state what every intelligent person must know. Either we go forward or backward. We choose self-control or indulgence. Responsible freedom or captivity."

The group clapped with mocking slowness, snidely conveying their opinion of this irrational, out-of-touch young man. I watched John take his chair, his disappointment veiled by the natural dignity of his character.

Gathering my belongings, I left the lounge and walked down to the basement of SUB where the campus bookstore was located. Adrianne would be a few minutes, arranging last minute details for the voting next day, and I needed a refill for my pen and a pack of typewriter paper.

Passing the rows of English texts, I caught sight of Kumari Nagarsenker an aisle away in the philosophy section. Thinking I would like to say hello, I impulsively turned in her direction. Rounding the corner, I was surprised to see another familiar figure browsing through the books. It was Dr. Brantwood. Certainly it was a logical place for him to be, but I hadn't forgotten my recent encounter with him, and the bookstore was no place for controversy. Deciding to speak with Kumari later, I returned the way I had come.

Waiting for the clerk to ring up the purchases of the two students ahead of me, I gazed absently at the rows of stick pens on the counter by the till. *Was I like a stick pen? Stiff and unyielding?* Having no answer, I turned my attention to a rack of postcards, but instead of seeing the cards, I saw the serious, bent head in the philosophy section.

Strangely, the mental image of Dr. Brantwood searching intently through the books brought back another image, that of John Cairn standing at the podium, notes in hand, idealism in his eyes. Other than being slim, there was little physical resemblance between the two. John Cairn was of the blond, blue-eyed Scandinavian stock; Dr. Brantwood's appearance didn't declare his national origin. It wasn't physical similarity that held these two images side by side in my mind.

The student ahead of me spread a number of drafting nibs on the counter for the clerk to count. As he did, I noticed for the first time that he had only one arm. Recognizing the student's disability, I involuntarily turned away, briefly closing my eyes. When I again opened them, it was to find myself looking into the quiet countenance of Professor Brantwood. His straightforward glance was neither sympathetic nor critical. I nodded and turned back to the counter, handing the clerk my paper and cartridge. After paying the sales girl the two dollars and sixty-five cents, I promptly left.

Adrianne met me at the door of the lounge. From there we walked to the main entrance without speaking, each lost in personal thoughts. At the inner doors, we passed the girl and the engineering student who'd questioned John Cairn earlier at the rally.

"Never trust a religious politician," the engineer was saying to his companion. "Noah Cairn is probably in the umbrella business." The girl laughed, and the two walked complacently away together.

"No doubt he thinks the Pope should ask his permission to breathe," Adrianne chaffed. It was obvious she didn't enjoy the sarcasm. I knew she was still a strong supporter of Nelson's platform, but the last few days had clearly wrought a transformation in her opinion of the conservative viewpoint. I wondered if she might view her erstwhile opponent with new regard.

Arriving at Admin, Adrianne stood disconsolately on the SUB steps above me. The late afternoon sun, only partially showing beyond a puffy autumn cloud, shone gently on her copper hair, while a determined gust of wind tugged and pushed at her plaid skirt, as if trying to tease her out of her pensive mood. Oblivious to the charm of the afternoon, Addy's expression remained unchanged.

"You'd make a good artist's study," I said, awed by the intentness of the small frame silhouetted against the sky.

"Something surreal by Salvador Dali, no doubt," she tossed back, more like her usual self.

"At least Vincent van Gogh," I accorded, smiling.

Relaxing, Adrianne pranced down the steps. Walking beside me on the level, she was again the Adrianne I knew: confident and undismayed. Outside the main entrance to Edwards, Adrianne leaned back against the center beam between the two doors and scrutinized the students bustling up the walk. Her reverie over, at least for the moment, she spoke, her voice sounding faintly weary.

"Maybe it's possible to be 'too hep.' Maybe being totally in sync with contemporary thought isn't everything."

I didn't reply, but my heart went out to her. Standing immobile in front of the towering eight-story building, Adrianne looked, for the first time since I'd known her, almost defeated. It made me want to put my arm around her and say something consoling, but I knew she wouldn't appreciate it. Adrianne didn't like to be mollycoddled. So I looked away and asked a strictly conversational question that wouldn't betray her trust or feelings.

"Think the engineers will release the Ed Queen in time to attend the Harvest Ball?" It was an idle question on a subject that held no interest for me, but it roused Adrianne from her despondency.

Her good spirits restored, she banged the library door open. Graciously holding the door for me, she quipped, "The question should be, can the Ed Queen be revived in time for the ball? I understand it's stupefyingly stuffy being held for ransom in an engineer's locker, especially with the engineer in it."

Adrianne put her arm around me and ushered the way up the stairs through the turnstile. As we walked past the "Quiet Please" sign, Adrianne took special care to ensure her shoes made the loudest clicking sounds possible.

Chapter Eighteen

Liberty is telling people what they do not want to hear.

—George Orwell: *The Animal Farm*[11]

Nelson Cruthers was elected Student Union president. No one was surprised. It was, however, interesting to learn how close the polls were. John Cairn had evidently impressed more people than Adrianne.

The Saturday following elections, Adrianne and Warren drove out to Collingsgate. Normally, Adrianne's jam-packed schedule allowed little time for visiting. When she did visit, Aunt Amy, who thought highly of both Eaton twins, always welcomed her warmly.

From my upstairs window, I watched Warren's red sports car approach. Warren handled the svelte little car with the sure pride of ownership. He'd earned the money for his BMW working summers, and he valued his investment too highly to drive carelessly. Anticipating their visit, I walked down the stairs to meet them. They were already in the kitchen talking to Ginny and Aunt Amy by the time I got there. Adrianne needed no community of shared interest to enable her to hold a conversation. She could elicit a response from a stone.

Today the topic up for animated discussion was afghans. Adrianne couldn't help but score on this one. Aunt Amy did beautiful crocheting and was always pleased with others' interest in her work. Ginny, who was as proud of the afghans as Aunt Amy, drew Adrianne into the family room to view the latest masterpiece under construction.

Warren remained in the kitchen. Leaning against the cupboard, he whistled softly to Carlyle. In response, the lively little bird hopped excitedly around its silver cage. Delighted with the attention, it lifted its feathers and gave a melodic trill.

Carlyle had been in the family since Ginny's fifteenth birthday. The prized warbler couldn't have found a more devoted owner, and he ruled his roost with imperial majesty. Capricious as always, Carlyle soon decided his cuttlebone was more to his liking than Warren's proffered finger and blithely returned to his own concerns.

"Don't feel rejected, Warren," I said. "You seem to have impressed Carlyle more in one minute than I have in two and a half years."

"I can't believe that," Warren replied, smiling. Warren had a talent for making others feel good. I hadn't seen a lot of Warren, our association being the result of my friendship with Adrianne. For the little I knew him, I enjoyed his company. On occasion, I even had the feeling that there'd never been a time when I didn't know Warren.

Remembering Warren was interested in biology, I invited him to Father's study to see his collection of roots. A root collection wasn't a usual thing, but Father claimed more could be learned about a plant from its root than from any other part.

Father met us at the study door. He was dressed in his favorite seasons old corduroy jacket, currently wearing through its second set of elbow patches; which shabby relic Ginny hid at every opportunity. Even as she hid it, she knew Father would eventually discover it and cart it out to wear. Hiding and finding the jacket was a game between them.

I left Warren in the study with Father and returned downstairs to join the women. The owl clock hanging in the stairwell watched me pass. Its wise owl eyes seemed to be considering some important matter that I'd missed, but sphinx-like, it jealously guarded the knowledge it withheld.

Adrianne met me at the bottom of the stairs. Standing squarely in front of me, cherry red shoes planted firmly on the wine carpet, she appraised me critically. Disappointment registered in her expression.

"What did you do that for?" she asked cryptically.

"Do what?"

"Chase Warren into the study. Do you want to be the only grad not at the Harvest Ball?"

"Am I going to the Harvest Ball?"

"Ask Warren."

"Right now?"

Adrianne sighed dramatically. "Forget it. No use swimming upstream."

Ginny came up behind Adrianne. Shaking a dainty finger at me, she put her arm around Addy's waist and with sisterly insight escorted her into the family room.

"Tell the men hot cinnamon buns will be served in the kitchen in exactly five minutes," Ginny said over her shoulder.

I watched them walk away together; they were well matched. It was interesting that my two closest friends were so similar in size, poise, and personality. The thought occurred to me that they would both make able generals. Charmed, I smiled at the picture of Adrianne and Ginny happily ordering around divisions of soldiers to their hearts' content.

Chapter Nineteen

To a world too prone to be prosaic,
I bring my own panacea.

—Robert Wright & George Forrest, *Kismet* [45]

The week flew swiftly by. It was Friday afternoon. Time to drop by Father's office and see if he needed any errands run before I left campus for the day. Father's office was on the third floor of the Ed building, facing west toward his revered mountains.

Friday night was marking night. Dad usually didn't come home until late on Friday, preferring to finish up his work at the university and then remain at Collingsgate on Saturdays. While this would have been difficult for some, Father had the seniority and full professorship to do what he liked. This didn't mean he squandered time. Between teaching, publishing, gardening, and his church duties, he had a challenging schedule. All things considered, Father didn't have a lot of time to himself and his own pursuits.

Halfway to Dad's office, I bumped into Adrianne and Warren.

"So where're you off to, Diddi?" Adrianne asked.

Knowing Adrianne knew full well where I was going, I recklessly made up the first thing that popped into my head. "I'm taking a short cut to The Manse to see what I can stir up."

"Great," Adrianne approved. "Where there's hair to be raised, preferably dark brown, count me in. Warren and I will come along and back you up. Won't we, Warren?" Adrianne tossed a look at Warren that meant they would. He grinned affectionately.

"Sure, sis. Whatever you say." Turning toward me, Warren gave me a quick wink.

"I hear the English 550 prof has it in for you."

"He does? What makes you say that?"

"I've heard rumors that you do your own thinking."

"Thanks, Warren," I said, touched by the unexpected praise.

"Now that we've got that settled," Adrianne chimed in, "let's boogie on to The Manse." She was determined to call my bluff.

As there was nothing else I could do, I backed down. "Adrianne. You know I stop by Father's study to see what he needs every Friday. Today's no different. I was being facetious."

"Diana, my darling, you are never facetious. Hidden underneath that gorgeous hide of yours is sheer sincerity. So, let's get this show on the road. I'm for raising some eyebrows at The Manse."

"Warren," I remonstrated, "I wasn't going to The Manse."

"Actually, I'd like to speak to Professor Collingsgate myself," Warren said, adroitly picking up his cue and intervening. "Need to ask him some questions about my history paper."

I breathed an inward sigh of relief. Adrianne eyed me skeptically, but gave in with grace. She was genuinely fond of Warren. In spite of her bossing, she was as close to him as someone could be close to a one and only twin sibling.

"If that's the case," she said, "I'll trundle back to The Hole and get some shut-eye before Dianne comes. It's girls' night out on the town." Adrianne always called her mother by her Christian name, Dianne. Just why, I never knew.

"Where are you and Dianne going tonight?" I asked.

"The usual. We'll shop, have supper, take in a show. There's one playing with Sandy Dennis called *Sweet November* that sounds upbeat. Either that or *The Pink Panther* with Peter Sellers. I think *Breakfast at Tiffany's* with Audrey Hepburn and *The Sound of Music* with Julie Andrews are still running, so there's a good selection. Maybe we'll see them all. Have fun at Riki's Grotto."

Adrianne gave me a curious glance. "And see you Monday bright and early in Brambly's briar patch."

Pirouetting on her heel, she saluted a snappy goodbye and was gone. For some reason, I felt a cold premonition, a half-formed fear that Adrianne would evaporate into thin air like the morning dew, but that was illogical and as Warren and I continued together to Father's office, I put it from my mind,

"I hope you know Adrianne really likes your father," Warren said. "Sis has a name for everyone and everything."

"So I've noticed," I said, smiling. "*Riki Tiki Tavi* seems to suit Father as well as anything." I was touched by Warren's sensitivity for my feelings.

"Yes," he said, "Addy insists Prof Riki is a mongoose who always gets his student. Are you going to the Harvest Ball, Diana?" The question didn't totally surprise me, considering Adrianne's comment on Saturday, but even so, I hadn't expected Warren to bring it up.

"Hadn't planned on it," I said truthfully. Warren nodded.

After a pause, he offered, "They're having the Rockets. Live band and all."

"Oh. Are you taking Janice?"

Warren grinned. "Hadn't planned on it."

I nodded and we continued in silence to the Ed building. When we got there, Dad was listening to his favorite recording of *Kismet* with Richard Kiley and marking up a storm. Dad had wildly diversified taste in music. *Kismet* had been a favorite of Mother's, too, both Charles Lederer's book and the screenplay before the musical appeared in 1953. I suspected Father listened to *Kismet* when he was most missing his Elizabeth Kathleen.

The door of his study was open. Absorbed in his marking, one hand in the can of peanuts always on his desk, Father didn't see us approach. Dad's office wasn't as large as Dr. Brantwood's suite in The Manse, but it was spacious enough. The impression of smallness was perhaps due to the mountains of books stacked everywhere.

The generalized disorder in Dad's study had frequently driven Mother to all night cleaning orgies. Father allowed her "fussy frumiousness," as he termed her need for order, but only if she cleaned at night when he didn't need the office. Unfortunately, since Mother's passing, the stacks of books had grown steadily and disorder abounded.

Even so, his university study was the one place Father would not allow The Jinn's tampering. Not to take her exile lying down, whenever Father misplaced this or that, which he did with dependable frequency, Ginny would remind him that it was probably buried under pile B in section Z of that dismal grotto he called his campus office. The term had stuck. Ever after, Father's office was called, with affection or disdain, depending on your point of view, *The Grotto.*

Father looked up from his marking. Seeing Warren and I standing in the doorway, he turned the recording of *Kismet* down and addressed Warren.

"Young man, I see you've taken up with the campus riff-raff! Do you want your grades to reflect the company you keep?"

"I certainly hope so, Sir."

Father's mouth curved in a satisfied smile. He delighted in testing the mettle of his pupils.

"Hi, Dad," I said. "Warren would like to discuss his paper with you. So, if you have errands for me, I'll leave you both in peace."

"I do," Father grunted. "Would you shimmy up the SUB flagpole and get some intellectual fervor going on campus?"

I smiled. Dad was always looking for ways to fuel student interest in their studies, but this was a new way to ignite the academic fires.

"I doubt if anyone would salute," I said. "However, John Cairn and Nelson Cruthers did start a small brush fire in SUB. The election speeches this year were quite heated."

"John Cairn running, eh? I know him. Good man. So who won?"

"Nelson Cruthers. Adrianne managed his campaign."

"You don't say?" Father looked up with interest, rubbing his head thoughtfully. His eyes showed a hint of a twinkle.

"Don't suppose your friend Adrianne could give us a hand with that rapscallion Jinn? She's gone and hid my lovely jacket again. Can't understand her animosity to such a valuable article."

I looked helplessly at Warren. To call the jacket 'valuable' was pushing the limits of even the most creative imagination.

"Ginny hides Dad's old coat," I started to explain. "That is, she—"

"Has a tidy streak," Warren finished, smiling. It was clear Warren had silently appraised Dad's office and understood Ginny's viewpoint.

"If you're going to gang up on me, you'd better get going," Father said, peeved. "Those grad diplomas need to be delivered to Dean Patterson's office. They're all signed and ready to go." Dad's office may have been in sartorial disarray, but he was never careless in his duty.

"Will do," I said. "Have a good time, you two." Nodding to Warren, I collected the papers and left.

Walking toward the Dean's office, it crossed my mind that unlike many other students, Warren didn't find Father overly perturbing. Indeed, at least on that point, Warren appeared as resilient as Adrianne and I wondered if he didn't share his sister's flair for coping with the unexpected. Warren's notable composure gave me a warm feeling of satisfaction. Perhaps Adrianne needn't worry about Janice after all. If Warren wanted to become involved with Janice, he would. If he didn't, I now doubted that Janice's wiles wouldn't entice him to change his mind. It was possible that Warren was as strong in his way as Adrianne was in hers.

I found this strangely gratifying. It was pleasant to know Father's "onion" theory of personality wouldn't disconcert Warren. Father was convinced if you peeled off the rough outer layers of people, you'd find the true gold within. Failing that, you'd find an onion. I smiled. Warren didn't need to be peeled to reveal his worth. He was what he was.

Chapter Twenty

Deign on the passing world to turn thine eyes,
And pause a while from learning to be wise.

—Samuel Johnson: *The Vanity of Human Wishes*[16]

That Sunday after service, Neal was again invited for dinner. Stirring up the duff for the roast in her best form, The Jinn advised us that Neal was coming to supper to save his law career.

"Why is that?" I asked, intrigued.

"Because of too many peanut butter sandwiches."

"And?" I couldn't wait to hear the salient connection between peanut butter and Neal's future in corporate law.

"And tomorrow he writes an important final," Ginny emphasized, her tone precluding further denseness on my part. "*And* he needs proper nourishment to think clearly."

Aunt Amy looked up from making the salad. She had that knowing smile that said, "Ask a silly question, get a silly answer." Paraphrased, the look meant "set the table."

"No. Not those old plates today, Diddi. This is Sunday."

"That's what I thought," I said quietly under my breath. "Christmas must have snuck up on me unawares." Out loud I confirmed, "Okay. I'll put on the good china."

Mephistopheles twined around my ankles, begging for a scratch. "You know some things, don't you, Meph? You're not deceived, you sly, scoffing old cat!"

Neal arrived on time in his green Plymouth. It was a modest car, quietly indicative of Neal's good sense. We didn't use the term common sense at Collingsgate; although, it was possible Neal had plenty of that as well. At least we didn't say common sense when Father was around. It would set him off mourning the lack of anything 'common' about sense. Obviously, if sense were common, more people would have it.

Neal was ushered into the kitchen. Summarily, I was dispatched to give Father notice to come at once. When I entered the study, Dad was reclining back in his chair, his feet propped on his desk, reading Hugh Nibley's, *The World and the Prophets*.

"Wrap your luffly head around this, Diana," he said, in one of his rare, serious moods. Dad began to read, ". . . 'conventional Christian doctrine . . . is . . . a solid and imposing dike to keep out the sea—to shut off the sight and even the memory of the sea which the Christian soul should be exploring.' "[47]

Father finished reading and waited with a what-do-you-make-of-this expression. It was my cue.

"It's possibly what makes the restored gospel unique," I said.

"How so?"

"Ours is a literal gospel. 'We believe in the same organization that existed in the Primitive Church, namely, apostles, prophets, pastors, teachers, evangelists, and so forth.' "[48]

"Don't tell me you still believe the *Articles of Faith*?" Father teased, losing his serious tone. "Ahm amazed thet with all yur fancy larnin', ya kin still reemembir thim." Father would indulge in the "lecherous pursuit of the fiendish vernacular," as Ginny put it.

"Yes, Dad, I do."

"That's good," he said, appeased I wasn't apostate. As with most discussions Father instigated, this one had been designed with an objective in mind. Closing the book, he got to his feet.

"We'd best go down to dinner, or The Jinn dervish will be whirling up here redefining the weather." He paused just before the landing. "He's right. Nibley's right. Literalism may not be currently popular dogma, but thank heavens for the Prophet Joseph to teach us the truth."

I knew what Dad meant. 'Deconstructionism,' the rewriting of original doctrine through the devaluing of language, did occur in both religion and history, but through revelation to Joseph Smith, the Gospel of Jesus Christ of Latter-day Saints was not rewritten.

"Yes," I said. "Ours isn't a deconstructed gospel. It's the real thing."

"About time you made an appearance," Ginny scolded affectionately. Giving Father a hug, she ushered us all into the dining room. I noticed she was wearing the rose cameo necklace Mother had given her. Her blue eyes sparkled with enthusiasm as she anticipated the joy of the day with family, but I suspected it was Neal's coming that was bringing out most of her radiance.

As was his custom, as soon as grace was offered, Dad launched his first verbal missile directly at Neal.

"So does the modern legal mind favor constructing or deconstructing the law?"

"With regard to what, sir?" Neal asked sensibly.

"With regard to keeping the country fit to live in."

"Certainly old or unjust laws can be changed and new ones formulated," Neal assented." The process is rather complex." He paused, and then added, "Interestingly, it isn't always the judiciary that promulgates change. With regard to human rights, often it's the people themselves. They demand new legislation, new ways of interpreting old statutes."

"So are you saying law is the result of reason, rather than eternal principle?" Father was on one of his philosophical rampages.

Ginny gave Father her 'superlative look.' She'd had enough cerebral cockamamie for one meal. How like Mother she was. It was always Mother who brought Dad back to earth when his flights of theorizing threatened to send us all spinning into outer space. Without Mother and now Ginny, Father would probably have disappeared into some vast, bottomless ether of his own devising.

"A good meal needs someone to eat it," Ginny said sweetly. "This is also an eternal principle. I vote we have some dinner."

"I'll say amen to that," Neal said. He gave an appreciative glance at the feast spread before him.

For a while, everyone enjoyed the meal in silence. The appealing harmonies of the Tabernacle Choir filled the room, bringing a spirit of quiet contentment. After a few minutes, it was Neal who re-opened the conversation.

"Where did you meet your wife, Professor Collingsgate?"

"In the local Duck Pond," Dad said abruptly. He was still peeved over not being allowed to ruminate upon things rational at the dinner table. Neal's eyebrows raised a little.

"What he means," said Ginny, "is that they met at university. Poppa calls Western *The Duck Pond.*"

"Which it is," Father insisted. "There's at least three and one half ducks sitting right here who paddle there every day." If Neal was puzzled about the half duck, it didn't show.

"Are you planning on joining your feathered friends in the pond?" Neal asked Ginny.

"Yes," Ginny said. "Both Mother and Father went to Western, so I will, too."

For some reason, doubt crept into my mind. I pushed it firmly away; Ginny's grades were excellent. There was no reason she couldn't go to Western or anywhere else she chose.

"So what did your mother take?" Neal asked.

"She took Home Economics," Ginny answered proudly. "Mom was a great homemaker."

"And that's how she met you, Professor Collingsgate?"

"In Home Ec?" Dad said blinking, mystified how anyone could think that. Father could boil water and that was all.

"Mom needed an elective course to fill out her program, so she opted for history," Ginny explained. "Dad just happened to be young, available, and teaching the class."

"So you married one of your students?" From someone else, the comment may have sounded rude, but coming from Neal, it didn't seem to push the limits of good manners.

"Had to," Father replied, with typical William Wallace logic. "Not much else to do with her. Elizabeth Kathleen was a dreadful scholar. She'd never have made an archivist. Way too tidy."

"Dad is teasing," Ginny cut in, giving Father a saucy grin. "Mom did well in history." Neal's smile indicated he thought she had too.

"Now Jinn," Father objected. "You know a man has got to have standards. I couldn't let yer ma run around loose and become a menace to society."

"Oh Poppa! Just like the returned missionaries are a menace," Ginny snorted. Ginny never could understand her favorite Poppa's need to flavor the facts with fiction.

Turning to me, Neal asked, "Do you take Institute, Diana?"

"Yes," I said. "Wednesday night. And you?"

"Tuesday morning. So that's why I've never seen you there." It did explain why he hadn't seen me on Tuesdays, but I knew it didn't explain my absence from social functions.

"Not exactly," I admitted. "I attend church with my family at the Whyte Avenue Chapel. Other than that, studies and symphony don't leave me much time."

"Diddi's not antisocial," Ginny said, coming to my defense, even though I hadn't been attacked. "She just likes to study. She's going to graduate *summa cum laude.*"

"Never count your chickens before they're hatched," Aunt Amy cautioned. I nodded, but smiled at Ginny, appreciating her vote of confidence.

"Aunt Amy's right," I assented. "We all just plug along and do the best we can. Do you enjoy the Institute, Neal?"

"Yes. It's a great place. The director, Wayne Nyman, is a good instructor. Wouldn't you say?" Neal was politely including me in the conversation. It was nice of him, but I knew he would much rather talk to Dad or Ginny. Thankfully, Aunt Amy intervened.

"We all have to make hay while the sun shines," she said. "I enjoy my class at the Tute. We're studying Church Doctrine and Talmage's, *Jesus the Christ.*"

"So you attend university?" Neal asked. "You're a student, too?"

"I don't know that taking one class makes me a student," Aunt Amy said. "But, yes, I take a course from Dr. Collingsgate. It qualifies me to take Institute, so long as I behave."

Neal nodded, his expression reflecting his appreciation for Aunt Amy's skill with a snappy come back.

Dessert was strawberries and shortcake, but by the time Ginny had finished refilling Neal's bowl for the third time, he was ready for a reprieve.

"Why don't we go into the family room?" Aunt Amy suggested, coming to Neal's aid. "There's no time like the present."

No sooner were we seated in the family room then Mephistopheles jumped up on Aunt Amy's lap and glowered at Neal through suspicious green eyes.

"Meph is jealously territorial," Ginny explained.

"Guarding his domain, is he?"

Ginny chuckled. "Yes. He's afraid you'll jump up on Amy Mom's lap, too."

Everyone laughed at the thought of Neal, who was at least six-foot two and a good 165 pounds, perched and purring on Aunt Amy's lap. Aunt Amy was only five-foot four in heels and 110 pounds soaking wet.

Having some work to do, I excused myself. Father also excused himself, lamenting that if he was going to have time to watch his favorite TV program, *Country Hoedown*, next Saturday, he'd better get the week going. That was Father, always planning well in advance. Here it was only Sunday, and he was already thinking a full seven days away. He claimed the more he got done during the week before *Country Hoedown*, the less worse he felt after.

I concurred with the worse part. I liked King Ganam's fiddling, Tommy Hunter's guitar, and Tommy Common's singing, but the rest of the program didn't appeal to me. Father loved Gordie Tapp, the host. Having eclectic tastes, Dad would listen to all styles of music. I preferred classical. While Dad also enjoyed a good symphony from time to time, he was forever warning me that listening exclusively to classical music oxidizes the brain.

Upon entering my room, I paused by the dresser to look at Mom's picture. Dear Mother. She had always been Father's most devoted disciple. Dad knew it, no matter how he masked his feelings when drawn into talking about her. Mother had a practical turn of nature, but she could keep up with a conversation. That wasn't something that could be said for everyone. Unfortunately, if you wanted to get on with Father, it was a necessary attribute. Father wasn't a great fan of meaningless chitchat.

My mind wandered. Growing up at Collingsgate, I'd become accustomed to Dad's style of discussion. I liked to listen to him and his friends talk. Those associates of Father's, who stayed long enough to get their teeth into a topic, were bound to be interesting people; while those who couldn't keep pace didn't court Father's company with any degree of enthusiasm. Father could, if he so chose, make a rattlesnake molt. Indeed, I suspected he seduced them to gather round him for just that purpose.

In the classroom, Father adopted the same tactics. He never dumped information; he was no father bird dropping food into the gaping mouths of its young. He made the students sweat for what they got, and what they got from Father was sure to be full of cockleburs.

"University is not a blooming aviary," he was fond of saying. "A duck pond, yes. But not an aviary. No drop-feeding allowed. Regurgitation forbidden." I had to admit that in this assertion, Professor Collingsgate was strictly sincere. Like Sterne's *Tristram Shandy*, Father rode his hobbyhorse—his bias for individual initiative—unflinchingly. If students couldn't or wouldn't do their own shoveling in Father's class, they didn't last long.

"You can't sit on your shovel and expect someone to dig you a well," he moralized happily.

I smiled. Father's students suffered, swore revenge, quit, started again, demanded his dismissal from staff, and burned him in dreadful effigy, but those who didn't fall by the wayside walked erect and confident from his class at the end of the course. A few even forgave him and joined the small but loyal ranks of his admirers.

Mother had been one of these. She laughingly observed that Father must have had his head in a book when she snuck up on him. She needn't have pretended. Father adored her, and she knew it. She was an older version of Ginny, accepting love freely as she gave it.

The next morning, I arose early. Coming down to the kitchen, I was surprised to see Aunt Amy also up, eating a piece of rye bread and cheese. Aunt Amy claimed eating rye bread and cheese always made her think better. Although Ginny's Amy Mom was patently fond of platitudes, I knew it was more than the 'early bird gets the worm' that motivated her to rise so early today.

"Something on your mind, Aunt Amy?" I asked.

"There should be, if there isn't," she shot back. "If you can't see your nose in front of your face, there's something wrong with your vision. It's what's on Ginny's mind that's bothering me."

"Oh. And what would that be?"

"Something bigger than Mephistopheles can deal with alone."

"I'm sure there isn't anything to worry about," I consoled, suppressing a smile. It was tempting to repeat the platitude about 'not crossing your bridges before you come to them,' but I knew better. Aunt Amy would never tolerate having her platitudes return home to the roost. She didn't like to be patronized; this I knew from experience.

"Do you see me worrying?" she retorted irascibly. "I'm not worrying; I'm thinking. 'A stitch in time saves nine.' Now skedaddle and leave me to it."

Happy to oblige, I slipped out the kitchen door.

Chapter Twenty-One

The tumult and the shouting dies;
The Captains and the Kings depart:
Still stands Thine ancient sacrifice,
An humble and a contrite heart.

—Rudyard Kipling: *The Recessional*[49]

It was November eleventh. As usual, the University Symphony Orchestra was scheduled to perform for the Remembrance Day service in Convocation Hall. Since enrolling at Western, I had played violin in the orchestra, and found it to be my element. In both its social and solitary aspects, participation in the symphony suited me, as a good orchestra, always more than the sum of its parts, transcends individual contribution. With the rising of the baton, the delight of being a needed part of a unified whole would sweep me into another world on a magic carpet of sound.

Mike Morrison, an Ag student, sat beside me. Mike was short and thickly built with sand-colored hair. When he spoke, which wasn't often, he had a pleasant bass voice. I didn't know any more personal details about Mike. We shared the same stand and played the same music, but outside of the occasional transfer of rosin from my violin case to Mike's hand, we were each content to let the music speak for us.

The répertoire for the remembrance program was well known to USO members. Because we were already familiar with Handel's *Largo in G from Xerxes,* Sibelius's *On Great Lone Hills,* and *The Pilgrim's Chorus* from Wagner's *Tannhauser,* no extra practices were scheduled beyond the regular Thursday night rehearsals.

Following the numbers by the symphony, June Lyle, a mezzo-soprano with the University Mixed Chorus, was to sing Irving Berlin's *Give Me Your Tired, Your Poor*. There would also be the expected tributes to those who fought for our freedom, the honoring of those killed in the wars, and the reading of the lists.

Unfortunately, shortly after five o'clock on the evening of the eleventh, an unprecedented deluge of rain threatened to cancel the short program. In spite of the torrential downpour, the program went forward. Neither the symphony conductor, the venerable Tom Ralston, nor the choir conductor, Dr. Herman Schmidt, were ones to concede defeat over a few drops of water. The girls in the symphony somehow managed to keep their long black skirts from becoming saturated with mud and moisture; although, anyone caught without protection for their head was sure to have very damp hair.

I had managed to get as far as the overhang of the Arts building when a virtual waterfall descended from the heavens. Pausing under the protecting ledge, I waited for a letup to make my way to Con Hall. Adrianne, running for all she was worth, pushed in beside me under the overhang.

"Great weather for us Western Ducks," she laughed, energetically shaking her plaid umbrella and sending streams of water spraying in all directions. Adrianne delighted in both the rain and Father's perverse perspective of Western.

Looking at me slyly, she added, "Today we can get as wet OUT of, as IN the Duck Pond. All in favor of cancelling classes? Motion passed. Diadem, you should have been at the last choir rehearsal. Maestro Schmidt was in rare form!"

"The maestro still claiming sopranos have egos inversely proportional to how well they sing?" The question was a throw away, which Adrianne gleefully exploited.

"Ladiez, puleeze! Ve do nyet hit ze high notes! Ve do nyet scaream! Ve zing wis our zouls!" Adrianne enjoyed mimicking her conductor, but I knew Maestro Schmidt was very much Adrianne's kind of person: intelligent, articulate, and imaginative.

The downpour eased, giving a brief respite. Conversation suspended, we made the dash to Con Hall, splashing straight through the puddles in our effort to get to shelter before the torrent began again.

Once inside, Adrianne shook off the water and went quickly to join the choir. I slipped backstage to take my place in the symphony. The symphony was usually in the orchestra pit and the choir on the stage; but today, because of the nature of the program, the symphony was to be on the stage, while the choir would be on risers.

I looked around. The gray skirts and navy blazers emblazoned with the university crest, *Quaecumque vera, (Whatsoever Things Are True)* always looked so smart on chorus members. It was much more attractive than USO concert dress of unrelenting black. The thought made me smile. For once Adrianne and I agreed on what was 'appropriate' dress. It was good she didn't know my opinion. If she had, I could hear her exclaiming in joyous disbelief.

"Happy day, Diana! Next thing you'll be demanding harem gauze and head feathers." Giving an inch with Adrianne was never wise.

At the signal from the concertmaster, Myron Maeser, symphony members began tuning their instruments. Dr. Ralston, our conductor, took his place at the podium in the center of the forty-member group, and the symphony stood for the playing of the national anthem.

From my position, fourth from the front on the aisle side, I could easily see the large bowl-shaped theater. Perhaps due to the heavy rainfall, only the main floor was occupied. The balcony, which wasn't needed, was roped off. It appeared those attending were either faculty members and their families or war veterans, for which the first three rows were reserved. The university president, Dr. N. Sloan Creighton, was there with his wife, Evelyn, and their two youngest sons. The aging chancellor, Bryan White, was also present. In addition, there was a small scattering of students and a few community residents.

Father, Ginny, and Aunt Amy, whose husband had been killed in World War II, were seated in the center aisle a few rows from the front. Neal was sitting next to Ginny. Warren and his parents sat a few benches away. Remembrance Day was one of the rare times the Eatons found time to be together as a family.

There were probably more people attending that I knew; but I didn't search them out, having caught sight of someone who prompted me to return my attention to the music score. Dr. G. L. Brantwood occupied a chair on the last row, just in front of the black uniformed usher. Shoulders straight, arms relaxed, Dr. Brantwood was also surveying the people assembled to honor the country's servicemen. For a brief interval our glances met and held.

Strangely unnerved from the short visual exchange, I attempted to focus on the music. I was glad I was holding my violin. It was comforting to feel the instrument's smooth firmness in my hand. That is, it was comforting until the thought occurred to me that the rich brown color of my violin was a close match to Dr. Brantwood's hair. *What put that into my head*, I wondered.

Thankfully, with the lifting of Dr. Ralston's baton, self-consciousness dissipated as I lost myself in the score. For the moment, it made no difference if the small audience was gathered out of duty or respect. The honor due the nation's valiant defense forces was paid in the music. When the symphony and choir had finished the *Recessional*, a war veteran, Mr. Paul Moran, dressed in an Air Force uniform and wearing a decoration of merit, stepped briskly to the podium. Group Captain Moran had a kindly face, upon which the lines of character were clearly etched. It was the face of someone whose wisdom is born of first-hand experience. I listened closely as he recited Laurence Binyon's words from *For the Fallen*. "At the going down of the sun and in the morning, We will remember them."[50]

There was a slight movement at the back of the hall. Dr. Brantwood had risen and walked quietly to the left side exit.

Following the program, Father stopped for a moment to talk to Howard Eaton. Mr. Eaton asked Father if he thought the world had learned enough from history to prevent future world wars. It was a question Father heard often.

"Possibly not," Dad replied. "Unfortunately, there are no honorary degrees in wisdom. The lessons of history are seldom conferred posthumously." Dad paused, and then added, "True wisdom may well be an ability to recognize our own folly, which few generations seem capable of doing."

"I believe it was Alfred Adler who commented, 'It's easier to fight for one's principles than to live up to them,'"[51] Neal contributed.

Father raised an eyebrow. "It's easier for the living," he humphed. "Those who've already paid the ultimate price may not agree with Mr. Adler."

Neal nodded, smiling agreement.

Wishing to get home in time to hear a CBC broadcast, Father said his good evenings and ushered his family imperatively down the aisle. As it was still raining, I decided to catch a ride with him. Neal was taking Ginny home, so she wouldn't be riding with us.

As soon as we were in the car, Aunt Amy lost no time in laying her cards on the table. She was a firm believer in getting things 'off her mind.'

"William Wallace," she directed, "you know I'm not one to pussy foot around. It's high time to take the bull by the horns with Ginny and her young man."

Father glanced appraisingly at Aunt Amy. "You think Neal should give up the bar, get a pussy cat, and become a bull fighter?"

"Humph!" Aunt Amy snorted. "You know my meaning full well, Dr. Collingsgate."

A resigned sigh escaped Father's lips. "Yes, I expect I do, Amelia," he conceded. "You want me to wave a red flag in front of Neal. But my interfering won't halt Neal's ardor, only encourage it. We're going to have to let Virginia and Neal work this out between themselves."

"But Ginny's so young."

"Virginia became a woman years ago, the day her Mother died," Father said gently. "Our Jinn girl can take care of herself."

Aunt Amy silently accepted defeat. She had spoken her peace and done what she could. I was proud of both Father and Aunt Amy. They may have looked at issues differently, but they were both motivated by the strongest ties of love; both undeniably committed to the welfare of those they cherished.

Chapter Twenty-Two

He lived very long, and thought all the time,
so that although he did not think well,
he had, generally, thought a good deal by the end of it.

—T. H. White: *The Sword in the Stone.*[52]

Two days after the Armistice program it was still raining. Few on campus escaped a soaking. For three days the rain continued steadily from a low, gray sky. Intermittently, the pelting rain would cease for a short period, but the overcast sky refused to clear or the rain clouds lift. For the most part, the heavens hugged the earth and wept steadfastly.

Pools of water formed in the hollows of the cobblestones backing Admin and also along the walks. Water stood on the dented top of the red mailbox by SUB and even on the centers of the steps. Wherever there was a slight basin in the earth or shallow indent in the cement, water collected. By the third day there were pools of water everywhere, and the campus, thoroughly scrubbed, wore a grimacing but clean face.

In a spirit of bravado, an anonymous student tacked a sign, "The Second Great Flood," on the sodden wood of the bench by Arts. The bench, with its unprotected back to the cold stone wall, now overlooked one of the larger pools on campus. Anyone wishing to enter the Arts Theater had to wade through the growing reservoir of water or balance precariously on the rocks bordering the flowers. The paper sign didn't long withstand the battering of the rain, but it lasted long enough to bring a smile to a few wet faces.

On the afternoon of the third day, Adrianne arranged to meet me in the SUB lounge at two o'clock. With no class to attend, I decided to go over early and study while I waited for her. Arriving at SUB, I stepped cautiously up the slippery wet stairs.

The interior of the lounge was painfully dark. Adding to the dismal atmosphere, the deep brown color of the furniture did little to lighten the dreariness of the day, the subdued lighting doing even less to relieve the pervading gloom.

Not wishing to succumb to melancholy, I took a chair by the west windows. I'd removed my raincoat at the door and wiped my boots, but they were still wet. Drops of water converged together in rivulets and wound their way down the boots' sides, accumulating in tiny puddles. Similar streaks of water were running down the panes of glass on the window.

Watching the droplets' lazy course, I became aware of someone approaching. It wasn't Adrianne. A very damp Professor Brantwood walked over to a chair next to mine, and for a moment he stood gazing out the water-streaked window across the sodden green. Turning toward me, he nodded pleasantly, hung his topcoat over the back of a chair, and removed a soggy hat from his head, which hat, while still dripping, he placed beside my purse on the side table.

"Sun hat," he quipped with a friendly smile.

Reluctantly I returned his smile and gazed down, in some consternation, at my rain-rumpled woolen skirt. It wasn't that I was displeased to see Dr. Brantwood; it was that I wished to avoid further difficult conversation with him. While we both held a similar interest in literature, we inhabited different worlds—different social strata.

Unaware of my uneasiness, Dr. Brantwood relaxed back in his chair, his hands resting on the chair's upholstered arms. Today his hands looked unaccountably white, almost light producing. Inadvertently noticing his fingers tapping on the soft leather, I grew further disconcerted with a feeling that I was eavesdropping. Flustered,

I reached for a book to study, but before I could grasp the targeted text, Dr. Brantwood, with a reminiscent smile, addressed me.

"Not out enjoying nature today, Miss Collingsgate? Not reveling in the 'landscape magnificent?' "[53]

I smiled foolishly. It was all I could do. He still didn't understand. And I couldn't tell him—didn't wish to tell him. I only wished to be left in peace with my books. They didn't quiz me or probe into my thoughts as did this strangely determined professor. My books were content to let me live a solitary life. Why couldn't he? I looked down, perplexed at what to say, and rested my hands on my knees.

When I didn't answer, Dr. Brantwood mused dryly, "You look desolated. So you think 'fortune is [sic] really predicated on such slender terms as these?' "[54]

Without conscious volition I replied, "'Then fate's a thing without a head; a puzzle never understood . . . .'"[55] I looked at the professor intrigued. He had referred to lines from Dad's favorite musical, *Kismet*.

"So you believe in Kismet?" Dr. Brantwood asked pleasantly.

"No, I don't. We determine our own destiny. We can't blame fate."

Dr. Brantwood's abundant brown hair fell damp and tousled on his forehead. Indifferent to his appearance, he brushed the unruly mass impatiently to the side, but it tumbled stubbornly back across his brow. Observing this pointless procedure, unbidden laughter broke through the confines of my reserve, causing Dr. Brantwood to raise a quizzical eyebrow.

"You find fate amusing?"

"No . . . no . . . I mean, your hair . . . it seems to choose its own fate."

The professor's unamused grimace dismissed that topic. In the dimly lit lounge, his eyes appeared darker than usual, the limited lighting masking any insight into his thoughts. Thinking he might well prefer to be alone, I reached for my coat. The disturbing conversation by the Arts Theater still held painful clarity, but before I could leave, Dr. Brantwood spoke.

"Do you believe in telepathy, Miss Collingsgate?" I looked at him amazed. What would he ask me next? Did I think the moon was made of daydreams?

"I refer to extra-sensory communication," he explained patiently, assuming I'd misunderstood the question. "The 'transport' to borrow your word, of 'intelligence' person to person across space."

I shook my head, no.

"Negative belief is positive proof against?"

"No."

"But you contend positive belief is proof for?"

"No. Not if you mean proof for The Infinite." Defenses on the alert, I found myself perched uncomfortably on the arm of the chair, coat over my arm. Desperately, I sought for something to say that would excuse me from further debate. I'd been here before with Dr. Brantwood and had no desire to return.

Seemingly unaware of my discomfort, Dr. Brantwood prodded, "So what does belief prove?"

"I don't suppose anymore than you that belief proves or disproves God. God does not require proving." I fervently hoped this direct answer would satisfy him. I wanted the topic closed. My belief was my belief.

"Hmm," he mused, "so what is the purpose of belief?" His tone held unabashed interest, but the startling question demanded sacrifice. Isaac was once again strapped to the altar. There was a long calumnious silence.

"Then we agree at last," he said wryly. "Belief is irrelevant." With the new taunt, my mind regained its battered equilibrium. Isaac had, after all, walked with his father down the mountain.

"With regard to the truth or falsity of a theory, yes," I said. "We agree. Belief is irrelevant. But belief is extremely relevant to the person holding the belief."

Dr. Brantwood made no response. Why did he press me so hard? What was his objective? It was almost as if he wished me to persuade him. If so, was this enigmatic professor's interest in the premises for Christian faith sincere? I didn't know, but under the continued surveillance of his solemn eyes, the contrition I felt mounted. It seemed there was no honest defense against him.

"You remind me of Father," I said in a weak attempt at reciprocity.

"Indeed? Do I know this dubiously honored person?"

Surprised by the interest in Dr. Brantwood's voice, I shook my head.

"That is, you might," I corrected, softening the equivocation as much as I dared. Father had a reputation for excellence on campus. It didn't seem right to flaunt my pride in him before his unsuspecting colleague. If Dr. Brantwood knew Professor Collingsgate, that would be enough.

When I again looked up, the slight smile had disappeared from the professor's face. Hands folded, head slightly at an angle, he surveyed me openly from under calm, straight brows. The frankness of his gaze, which appeared both puzzled and partially admiring, startled me, causing me to drop my coat. The coat fell on the floor and lay like a self-abasing servant in a prostrate heap at his feet.

Undisturbed by the nervous error, Dr. Brantwood bent easily and retrieved it for me. Holding the coat by the collar, he replaced it across my knee with relaxed facility. It felt as though a competent mother cat had just deposited her kitten on my lap. Leaning back in his chair, Dr. Brantwood said casually, "You do not remind me of anyone, Miss Collingsgate."

There was a limit to my endurance. Seeing Adrianne across the room, I arose, excused myself, and walked quickly away.

"Hold that boat, Noah!" Adrianne exclaimed, vigorously shaking the rain off. "There's enough water on campus to drown a whale."

"Yes," I agreed ruefully, "a person could get thoroughly drenched."

"So—should we get at it?" Adrianne wanted to go over her Bugs assignment with me. She had the strange idea that Father's interest in biology made me an expert in the field.

Two hours later we had finished. I wasn't convinced I was of any help, but my friend seemed satisfied. She breathed a relieved sigh and suggested we go over to The Pit for hot chocolate. I agreed and we began the walk across campus. The rain had ceased and the clouds broke apart, revealing a lovely blue sky. The evening sunlight did much to lighten both our spirits.

"So guess who's in my Bugs class, Dia Mia?"

"Who?"

"Daftsby."

"Daftsby?"

"You know, Jingle Bells. Daphne Englesby."

"You call Jingle Bells, Daftsby?" I was dumbfounded. Even after four years of first-hand experience with Adrianne's notable penchant for nicknames, it was still hard to believe she would call a fellow student 'Daftsby'.

"Yes, I do," Adrianne said. "I call Jingle Bells Daftsby because she isn't. The flippancy is a façade. Underneath Daphne is . . ." Adrianne groped for the right word. "Daphne is nice," she finished sincerely. "Really nice."

"You sound serious."

"I am. We aren't close friends, but she's a thoughtful soul, so I can't call her Jingle Bells anymore."

"Instead you call her Daftsby."

Perfectly logical, if you're Adrianne; yet I couldn't help wondering how Daphne felt, and what she might say about my charmingly perceptive friend. I hoped Daphne returned Adrianne's good opinion, as Adrianne didn't give respect lightly. One thing you could trust about Addy—she was always one hundred percent honest in her feelings about people.

Coming to Arts, we paused and watched the wind blow dripping leaves off the weeping willows by the walk. Even while sodden with moisture, the leaves quickly sailed beyond our line of vision. It seemed to affect Adrianne strangely. A look of disquiet replaced her normally confident expression.

"You know, Diana," she said pensively, "sometimes I think if I don't keep my eyes on you, you'll disappear." She looked at me seriously, her eyes holding a mute appeal. "I mean, sometimes I feel like one minute you'll be here and the next you'll be gone, like a leaf on the wind." Adrianne's words jarred into my consciousness. It had been only a short while since I'd felt the same about her.

"You can count on me, Addy," I said, reaching to be supportive. "If our friendship has lasted this long, it should endure a while longer."

"I know," she said, "but what if someday I come to find you in Edwards, and all that's left of you is a leather-bound journal entitled *Protocol For Prohibitive Personalities*?"

"Then I guess you'll have to check me out and take me home with you," I said, laughing. "Do some research." I refused to be drawn into a staged argument. Giving me an artfully wicked look, Adrianne narrowed her eyes, and smiled with faultless feline composure.

After hot chocolate we again paused outside of Arts. "Don't miss the Ark, Didillo," she advised, contemplating the deepening pools of water. "They'll want to preserve your species."

I gave her a quizzical look.

"Because you're one of a kind," she said affectionately. "Good night, Dia Mia. See you tomorrow in Cosmos 550."

"*Cosmos 550?*"

"You know, English class, where we study the moon, the stars, and even some English."

We laughed together. As I watched Adrianne depart, a rush of affection filled my heart. Knowing I was watching, my friend made sure to splash joyously through every rain puddle.

You're the one of a kind, I thought. *You're so anchored in the present, as if every minute is precious.*

As I mused on this particular trait of Adrianne's, I made my way to Edwards. It was almost four o'clock, but I needed to catch up on some work for a music class I was taking on counterpoint. It occurred to me that Professor Brantwood's idea of a good discussion was a bit like counterpoint: two or more themes running simultaneously—harmony in dissonance.

Two hours later, it was once again drizzling cold sheets of rain that threatened to freeze into ice as they fell. Out of the rain, seated in my study carrel at Edwards, I was glad to feel the warm air of the wall register blowing against my legs. In the familiar surroundings I felt revitalized.

At seven, needing a break from my studies, I rose stiffly from my wooden chair and walked to the porcelain fountain in the foyer for a drink. My eyes needing a rest as much as my limbs needed movement, I walked to the window. The rain had lessened but not subsided, and as evening drew on it was growing dark. Silhouettes of students hurrying home appeared and then faded into the twilight. Of the buildings visible, SUB looked the most somber. Recently constructed of cheerless gray cement, it had no growth of ivy to relieve the bleak austerity of its serviceable finish. Undaunted by its lack of beauty, it stood defiant in the rain.

I stretched my arms behind my back, quietly amused. Looking at the stern visage of that resolute edifice, I wondered if that was what Dr. Brantwood meant when he said I reminded him of no one else. I couldn't be that forbidding.

For a few moments, I leaned against the wall, eyes idly scanning the uncomplaining trees patiently enduring the buffeting of the rain. Whatever mistaken opinions Dr. Brantwood may have about me, he was an outstanding professor. The thought that he was as good as Father, perhaps better, had crossed my mind more than once lately.

As memories will sometimes intrude upon the present, I saw myself in childhood as a grade three student in Wildemere School. A schoolmate had unwisely jeered at Father's profession of teaching in an "old head-glue factory." In horror at hearing Father's work at university so derided, I had slapped the boy smartly on the side of his head. The outspoken critic, Calvin Colpits, went home from school that day with the memory of my reply literally ringing in his ears.

Oddly enough, when Father heard of the incident through the teacher who phoned, he didn't administer the corporal punishment I was expecting. Taking me aside, he sat me on a chair and folded his arms thoughtfully. Just when I felt I could stand his silence no longer, he spoke.

"Diana, my little Scottish Terrier. Wud ye do yer pur auld Fahther a wee service?"

I nodded vigorously. Anything to keep him from his disappointment in me.

"Do ye thin ye ken refrain noo from these battles ye are wagin'?"

Again, I nodded emphatically.

"Good," he commended. "I wuz afeared we might have ta enroll ye in a pugilist class ta better defend ma honor!" Father had paused and then given me a stern glance. "I'm glad that won't be necessary." It was a reprimand I didn't forget.

Yes. There was a similarity. Like Father, Dr. Brantwood had the ability to make his words count. He knew their individual worth and their collective bargaining power. Far from woolgathering, it was doubtful either man spoke without having a specific objective in mind. The thought made me uneasy, and I returned to my studies.

A few days later the sun returned, bringing with it a languid Indian summer to caress the earth with its welcoming warmth. Content, I devoted the declining days of November to my studies. When I was not in my carrel at the library, in classes, or music rehearsal, I walked along the river. Truly the beauty of this fall rivaled the glory of all those gone before. Almost to the very midnight of its allotted time, the season was still abundantly rich in color. Although the limbs of most birch and popular trees were now barren of leaves, the earth at their feet remained swathed in pools of browning, golden leaves.

Sometimes in the early mornings, as I walked along the dirt path to classes, I would see the occasional flock of ducks flying south. On other days, well-ordered formations of Canada geese could be seen swooping far overhead. Sightings of this grand bird were not rare, but I always felt both inspired and saddened by their passing. On one particular day, I noted a large black crow with glossy, purple-black plumage sitting high on the branch of a quaking aspen. Unaffected by the wonder of the geese passing overhead, the crow spread his ebony wings and flew indifferently in a jagged line down to the river. That was the way of life. The things that stirred one heart to rejoice would not move another to even notice.

Chapter Twenty-Three

Rhodora! If the sages ask thee why
This charm is wasted on the Earth and sky
Tell them dear that if eyes were made for seeing
Then beauty is its own excuse for being; [56]

—Ralph Waldo Emerson: *Rhodora*

"Miss Collingsgate. I see from your essay that you know your bedtime stories."

Dr. Brantwood was seated at his desk in Room 39, marking papers. The class was over. Most students had already disbanded, but I had remained behind arranging my notes. The professor hadn't looked up when he addressed me, but was obviously aware of my presence. Realizing he was waiting for a response, I rose and walked over to him. As I neared his desk, my intuition warned me too late that I should have fled with the others when the buzzer sounded.

Dr. Brantwood raised his head. "You seem to derive most of your comparisons from children's literature. Do you read any mature works?" It was the second time he'd questioned me on my reading habits this term.

"Well," he prompted," are you residing in your body today Miss Collingsgate, or has your mind jumped ship again?" Seeing he wouldn't be put off, I spoke.

"If you're referring to the quote from Antoine de Saint-Exupéry's *The Little Prince*, I fail to see your point. I believe the book was intended for a mature audience, as well as youthful readers."

"It may have been," Dr. Brantwood said, "but to illustrate the 'futility of pride' theme in Thackeray's *Vanity Fair*, with a purely fictional account of a traveler from the stars, connotes a strange juxtaposition. You have your realities confused."

"The Little Prince was prideful," I reminded him. "Until he learned to see with his heart, he couldn't see the foolish Rose's real feelings for him, just as Amelia couldn't see Dobbin's true worth in *Vanity Fair*."

Professor Brantwood put his pen down on the desk, leaned back in his chair, and looked at me quizzically. Rubbing his chin, he smiled.

"Okay. Let's enter your reality. What other fairy tales do you find relevant to man's mundane travails?"

"Lots of them."

"Such as?"

"*Puss 'n Boots, Red Riding Hood, Jack and the Beanstalk*. These may provide relevant analogies."

"Go on," he urged.

"They suggest themes of power, deception, avarice. Certainly not fare for children."

"Does this mean you'll be launching a cleanup campaign in children's lit?" There was smiling skepticism in Dr. Brantwood's tone.

"Pardon me?"

"Parents be Alerted! Jack the Giant Killer is Greedy Psychopath and Red Riding Hood Masquerades as Street Walker." I blanched at the raw description.

Noting my dismay, Dr. Brantwood added playfully, "I beg your pardon. 'Path Walker' is possibly more polite."

"Possibly not straight and narrow, in either case," I agreed. Over exhilarated, I was dangerously close to brinkmanship.

"I suspect Miss Hood is more naive than naughty," Dr. Brantwood said lightly. "Wouldn't you agree?"

"Colorful, certainly," I assented, noting the smart red line woven into Dr. Brantwood's jacket.

"Hmm," he mused, an engaging smile on his face. He seemed to delight in undermining me.

"No," I said, "I didn't mean that the color of a person's cloak: the creeds they believe, make them good or bad. I'm not blackening her character."

Dr. Brantwood's gaze rested briefly on the white cuff of my cardigan. "Of course not," he said. "But what color would *you* paint Red Riding Hood?" There was a smile in his voice, but his eyes were a serious hazel study.

"None at all. That's up to her."

"And if she had no paints? Would you lend her yours?"

"If she was pleased with the colors in my palate."

"Are you?"

The open candor of Dr. Brantwood's manner and the unexpected personal focus of his disarming question struck home. Defensively I looked away, my glance falling on the professor's ringless left hand. The sight of his fingers tapping on the mahogany wood sent a wave of awareness through me. Feeling even more foolish, I stared at the wastebasket, unable to look back at Dr. Brantwood, or retreat to my chair.

I was keenly annoyed with myself. Where was my poise? There was no reason to become embarrassed by a professor's hands. Everyone has hands. Dr. Brantwood had hands, too, it appeared. Certainly only a very dull person would deny their beauty and energy. It wasn't surprising he was a pianist of some excellence. Unable to still my unscholarly thoughts, I was in a quandary to know how to excuse myself. Why hadn't I had the good sense to leave when the leaving was good?

"Miss Collingsgate," Dr. Brantwood prompted, "are you going to spend the entire day examining the wastebasket? You won't find any giant killers in there. Only some student papers, which almost had the same effect."

My breath caught in an appreciative gasp. "You think of yourself as a giant? An ogre?"

"Do you, Miss Collingsgate?"

"Ah. . . No." Privately, I wasn't entirely sure that was the truth.

"Then you will have coffee with me?"

For the first time, I looked directly into the unself-conscious gaze of the honest eyes that surveyed me. Students and faculty socialized to a limited degree from time to time, but the idea of sharing a table with Dr. Brantwood in The Pit was ludicrous. I could hear the noisy, pointless chatter of students too close to my elbows, and see the spilled coffee on the tables, the empty wrappers not always tossed with sure aim at the baskets. The Pit was not my element; I would be a fish washed up on the beach in The Pit. If I was floundering here, I would suffocate there.

Declining as politely as possible, I walked out of the classroom. As I hurried away, I could feel Dr. Brantwood's puzzled glance. No doubt he considered me socially inept. I wasn't pleased with my own behavior, but under the circumstances, it couldn't be avoided.

Outside the sunlight welcomed me, its cheerful warmth bringing some relief. It was good to breathe the fresh air, to feel the bright hope of day outside the confines of the classroom. In the dark heart of the building, I'd begun to feel like a fugitive. In the natural world, whose only boundary was sky and earth, the restraints imposed upon my spirit by manmade structures lifted, and I felt recreated. Feeling a surge of vitality, I began to run with an exuberance not experienced since childhood. My feet felt as light as soft spring clouds and I felt as though nothing could ever enclose me again.

Thoroughly elated, I continued running. After crossing the footbridge to the south of campus, I sped across the grassy plateau and skidded down the steeply sloping embankment. The headlong scramble down the hill finally exhausted my energy, making me glad to reach the riverbank, where I dropped gratefully to a mossy place beside the water's edge.

For a time, I rested. My breath came in uneven spurts, and my cheeks felt flushed from the exertion, but it was good, almost atoning, to be by the river. Looking around the clearing, my thoughts became more composed. The place wasn't new to me; I came often. The quiet spot and I were, in fact, old friends. Possibly because of the steep climb back to the university, other students didn't often intrude, and it was unlikely that anyone else would care to frequent my sanctuary.

Alone by the river's edge, peace and solitude were my companions. Without fear of being disturbed, I could lie full length on the bank on warm days and watch the rippling water. There was a striped chipmunk and a gray squirrel that often liked to poke about in the trees at the edge of the clearing, but these friends weren't intruders. They belonged. It was their home, just as it was my refuge. United in our need for sanctuary, there was a bond between us.

Admittedly, the riverside was much wilder than the ridge above. Here there was no bench, table, or prepared lawn. A fallen tree sufficed as bench and patches of unclipped grass for table. It was better wild. In the natural setting, I wasn't an outsider but belonged as surely as the silver-breasted seagulls that flew over the river. I watched a pair of gulls wheeling overhead. Watching them circle above made me glad to be in this lovely place for what might be the last time of the season. Soon deep drifts of snow would make the hill impassible and render the retreat inaccessible.

Relaxing, I leaned back and hummed softly to myself. A silver piece of driftwood floated by on the water's surface like a small boat. Unconcerned by who might be watching, the sleek silver ship continued on its course. By the time the miniature log vessel sailed out of sight, the tightness I'd felt in the classroom was entirely gone. I could even recall the encounter with Dr. Brantwood without tensing.

When Ginny and I were little, our bedtime stories were derived from the annals of Roman history. Father had regaled us with tales of daring from the times of the first fierce Etruscan warriors to the last tormented Caesars. While I supposed I also knew enough fictitious lore to make Dr. Brantwood's accusations valid, I couldn't agree it dominated my thinking. Through father's tutoring, I knew what went on in the so-called real world.

Alerted by the snapping sound of a twig breaking, I raised my head in the direction of the noise. Instantly recognizing the familiar form, I jumped quickly to my feet. Dr. Brantwood had reached the base of the hill and was headed directly toward me. As his long strides shortened the distance between us to a few yards, my mind scrambled for an explanation of his presence, for a logical reason that would allay the near panic I felt.

With the river at my back and the only exit up the hill, there was nothing to do but wait. In the interim, I felt as stiff and awkward as a young girl at her first formal. Unaware of my agitation, Dr. Brantwood walked briskly to the fallen tree. Stopping abruptly a few feet in front of me, he shoved his insurgent hair from his forehead with a brusque, impatient motion.

"Do you always tear off like that?" he asked, clearly exasperated. "I thought you'd break your neck plunging down the hill that way." He gave me a hard, level glance, his eyes dark with displeasure.

Bewildered by his stern look, I took a surprised step backward. Seeing my astonishment, Dr. Brantwood's expression softened. Frowning, he pushed his hands into the pockets of his tan slacks and walked past me to a small rise a few feet away. His back to me, he looked out over the river.

"Yes. I can see why you come here. 'When sea-winds pierced our solitudes, I found the fresh Rhodora in the woods,'" he mused, for some unfathomable reason quoting Emerson's "Rhodora."

Turning away from the river, Dr. Brantwood walked toward me and held out his hand. Surprised, I was about to offer him mine in return, when I realized he didn't wish to take my hand, but for me to take something in his. On his outstretched palm, he held a small leather purse. The initials D.C. engraved into the smooth surface of the wallet sprang up at me.

"It fell out of your pocket when you bolted in such a hurry," he said. "I thought you might need it for the weekend."

"Th . .thank you, I stammered. You needn't have bothered coming all this way for—" I couldn't finish. Would I always feel like an immature schoolgirl in Dr. Brantwood's presence? Even so, his thoughtful gesture and his concern for my welfare revealed a new dimension of his character—a dimension that unfolded before my wondering mind like the vista of a wide, uncluttered plain.

Appearing not to notice my lapse of speech, Dr. Brantwood graciously accepted my thank you. His task completed, I expected him to leave me to the fellowship of the river, but he did not. Perversely, he dropped down on a smoothly weathered portion of the log. Leaning forward, elbows resting on his knees, he had the attitude of someone relaxing before a warm fire in anticipation of having an openhearted chat with a close friend.

I was perplexed. I was a student, not a friend: a disciple at best. In spite of Dr. Brantwood engaging me in conversation from time to time, we weren't colleagues. No matter how I emulated him, we were not on equal footing.

Confused, I glanced down at the river flowing unobtrusively in its channel close to the bank. On the gently undulating surface of the water shimmered the faint reflection of Dr. Brantwood's graceful hands folded together on his knees. Without warning, but also without passion or force, the sham over my heart was dispelled. The truth was silently revealed in that softly wavering reflection on the water.

It was not a terrifying revelation; it was gentle. It lifted me much the same as the breaking of the dawn always lifted me. Like the early arms of light embracing the earth, the truth warmed my soul. I didn't want Dr. Brantwood to leave. I wanted him to stay, never leaving this sheltered retreat—always near me. I knew then why I had loitered in class after the bell. I hadn't wanted to go while he was still there.

At what point Dr. Brantwood's existence began to personally impact my own was hard to know. Judging from the intensity of feeling now unveiled within my heart, I realized my regard for him must have been quietly growing for some time. Gradually, imperceptibly, I had come to love him.

I sank down on the flattened crown of a rock near the end of the log. The moss at my feet was the most beautiful gray-green I had ever seen. There in the natural clearing, a short distance from him, I felt I could remain always.

I wondered. Was I like the fawn that had strayed onto campus at the beginning of fall term: the one that had lost its way and wandered down from the hills into the very heart of the university? The noisy industry of campus bustle had frightened the disoriented creature so badly it had stood perfectly still, trembling on the cobblestone walk by Arts, not knowing which way to turn or run. It was later reported that one of the professors had shepherded the traumatized animal back to the wild where it belonged.

So that was why Dr. Brantwood had missed class that day. Until this moment, I hadn't connected the incident with him. Now I realized that guiding the fawn back to its home would be a natural thing for him to do. As though reading my thoughts, Dr. Brantwood spoke.

"You remind me of the fawn on campus, Miss Collingsgate."

Startled, I asked, "You would rescue me?"

"If you like," Dr. Brantwood replied mildly, looking with calm frankness into my eyes. "Are you lost?"

"No."

"In that case, you won't require my service further." The professor's rich baritone voice rose and blended with the river scene as gracefully as the wings of the gulls. He stood to leave. Numbly wishing I could ask him to stay, I nodded goodbye.

No longer hearing his footsteps crunching the dried leaves, I looked in hopes of seeing him once more before he disappeared over the brow of the hill. My heart caught; he hadn't gone. He was standing at the base of the hill where I'd first heard the twig snap under his foot a short time before, his lean form reclining lightly against the striped white bark of a birch.

Across the intervening distance, Dr. Brantwood was also observing me. Returning his gaze I stood immobile, as time dissolved. The timeless ages, the future eons were nothing. The all-encompassing present was both timeless and ageless. In it, I was held consenting.

Dr. Brantwood's questioning eyes, the fine mass of unruly hair, the intelligent mouth, and eloquent hands were delineated to my view as before one beholding a vision. He seemed a reincarnated dream that had been carelessly abandoned long ago and left to linger, patiently waiting for someone to remember it and offer fulfillment.

The long form of the vision moved. A warming smile still on his face, Dr. Brantwood turned and began climbing the hill. In that instant my reserve broke, and I hastened after him. He didn't know my heart; he must not think me rude. He must at least know I meant no incivility by my silence.

"I, that is . . . you . . . please forgive . . . ."

Dr. Brantwood smiled politely. His eyes still held their quizzical warmth, and I felt perilously near disclosing myself.

"Our forefathers must have paddled upriver to this very spot," I said, regaining control of my feelings. "Perhaps in their minds, they could see the university where it now stands."

Dr. Brantwood shot a surveying glance at the university build-ings crowning the hill in the distance and nodded assent with an amiable jerk of his head.

We climbed the hill in silence together until we reached a small plateau, halfway up the hill. From that point, the hill rose in a more determined incline. Branching off, there was a narrow footpath leading in the direction of my home. I looked at the path diverging from the upward route and knew I would not climb the rest of the hill with him. Realizing my intention, Dr. Brantwood waited until I was abreast of him on the level.

"Do you see that mountain?" he asked, pointing to a crystalline peak rising above the rest.

I nodded.

"It is glass," he said, earnestly. "A frozen dream. Look on the rim of that icy ridge. You can see the aspirations sparkle. But don't be deceived. The mountain's radiance is cold, glittering splendor. If you let it, it will steal your soul."

"Yet you challenge it," I whispered, marveling that Dr. Brant-wood would reveal so much. "You see the power in the dream—the hidden potential."

Awed, we looked together at the distant summit, which did in truth, with the sunlight reflecting off its high turrets, look as if the translucent peak—all the unfulfilled yearnings of the human heart—were indeed molded of silver-frosted glass.

"Yes. One must," he said absently. He turned back to the hill, a hint of impatience in his voice. "It's the only way."

Dr. Brantwood's words increased my amazement, but as I stood and gazed at the gleaming, snow-capped pinnacle, I knew he was right. Remote, even in its fascination, the mountain was all he said, and now I too had looked and responded to the mountain's chal-lenge. Those frozen dreams were my dreams. Those unfulfilled longings my own.

Walking home, I noticed the rolling bundles of cumulus clouds that signified the approach of winter hugging the foothills at the base of the mountains. The Indian summer had encroached upon the winter season for nearly a month, and the cold weather was long overdue. It was stolen splendor, but in trespassing the bounds of its allotted time, the lingering autumn had made the earth intensely beautiful.

Never had I felt life so abundantly. The world was animate. Color pervaded every aspect of nature, from the subdued sapphire and pearl of the sky and clouds, to the rippling purple marine of the river. The hills, often parched and brown in summer, now enjoyed rich shadings of orange, red, and gold as shrubs and bushes touched with frost yielded up their ultimate glory. I looked down the hill at the path wandering by the river. Fallen leaves of yellow-gold fluttered and whispered against the darkly grained trunks of the trees. Then, as the silently lapping water of the wind-ransomed river nudged the shore, I understood. He was the autumn.

Chapter Twenty-Four

Wise men come, wise men go
Ever promising the riddle of life to know.[57]

—Robert Wright and George Forrest: *Kismet, Sands of Time*

The ring of milky-blue spruce trees circling Collingsgate came into view around the bend of the river. There was no use pretending. It had been a total awakening and the disclosure of my heart would have a profound effect on my life. Leaning against the bristling trunk of a tall spruce, I ordered my thoughts. I seriously needed to calm myself, to still the frothy ebullience that threatened to bubble over and make foolish the truth in my heart. It would serve no purpose to parade my feelings. The heart's depths should never be put on frivolous display, even for a fond public.

Nearing the garden gate, I could see Father tying back the Camelot rose in preparation for winter. Holding long twists of brown twine in gloved hands, he was working in his beloved brown jacket on the roses to the right of the rocked pool. There was a good-sized stack of straw at his feet to use for packing around the tender stems to secure the plants from the cold. Hearing me approach, Father looked up. I took a deep breath of the musty garden air and walked to greet him.

"S'what's this I heerd 'bout yer bein' kicked outta school, an' gonna be a bum an' not able to sipport your pur auld fadder an' baby sitter?" Father's banter was always an expression of his joy in living. I answered him in kind.

"Do ye thin thet yourn faithful dotter wud do iny sich thing? An go on wi ye."

"Ach, du lieber! Is it sassy ye are me leetle gozling. An me an yer pur auld mither, God rest her soul, raized ye since ye were a wee bairn, an niver giv'd ye the back of our hand but twice, an then ony tae help ye teeth."

We both laughed—Father in pleasure at being appreciated, I in relief.

"I see you've got Robert Goulet ready for winter." Robert Goulet was the name Ginny gave the Camelot rose. Mr. Goulet had played Sir Lancelot in the screenplay, which was still a huge success.

"Yes," Dad said, "but I seriously question his knightly code of ethics."

"Goulet's or Lancelot's?"

"Sir Lancelot's, of course," Dad replied dryly. "What Mr. Goulet does is his concern."

"Oh. You mean 'courtly love'. Castiglione's *Courtier* goes into that."

"That may be. But any knight who lets his romantic impulses override his moral obligations is not courtly. He is throwing decent conduct to the wind."

"You mean if we let our hearts rule our heads, we may wind up in bed with the enemy?" While I agreed with Father's perspective, today it gave me a peculiar pleasure to shock him with an outrageous statement of my own.

Father paused, a respectful alertness in his gray-blue eyes. Thoughtfully, he replaced his red-tipped shears in his back pocket. "What have ye bin readin', mine dotter?" he asked, almost, but not quite shocked.

"Just the usual colorful metaphors in the usual unsanctified English novels," I replied, laughing.

"In that case, you'd best go whitewash yourself for supper. The Jinn will be bursting out of her bottle if we don't both hustle."

I nodded and headed through the overhanging arbor toward the house. Having a set task to do was a relief, as I needed to settle down before someone started suspecting something was different about me.

Ginny would secure the moment with her infectious delight in living. I could easily hide my euphoric feelings behind her dependable exuberance.

As if summoned by my thoughts, the appealing laughter of a young woman sounded from the kitchen. As I entered, Carlyle was preening himself on his swing, and Mephistopheles was wrapping his fluffy tail around Ginny's legs.

"Hi, Diddi," Ginny greeted. "Where have you been? I got so starved waiting for supper, I ate six of Poppa's best show roses, stem to prickle."

"You didn't!" Father roared, in pretended outrage. He had entered the kitchen behind me. Now he stamped toward Ginny. "You rapscallion! Let me at you! Just wait 'til I get my spray dust, you mealy bug you!"

Father dived at Ginny, but not before she had her laughing hands entangled in his hair. Pleased with the day and with themselves, they roughhoused from kitchen to family room. I stood alone in the kitchen, my hand resting on the back of Ginny's favorite rocker. I couldn't help feeling a pang of remorse at my separateness. Father loved all family members equally, but he was especially close to Ginny. He was her knight, forever dependable and true. Theirs was a perfect synchronicity.

Walking to the archway between kitchen and family room, I paused a moment to watch the frolic. Father had dropped exhausted from the free-for-all on the couch; whereupon, Ginny clamored onto his knee. Although mature beyond her years, as Father himself noted the night of the Armistice program, Ginny still felt Father's knee was her special domain. She would no doubt become as narrowly national as Mephistopheles if she thought the precious summit might be invaded. Attaining the guarded territory easily, Ginny jumped swiftly down.

"Poppa!" she howled. "You've been into the garlic pickles again. You terrible Poppa! Why do I make them for you?" Ginny stood a little way from Father, hands resting archly on hips, refined but 'depised' nose held resolutely in the air.

"Hmm," Father said impenitently, "Maybe you likum poli sausage better? Me teach you likum."

"You be um scalped if I catch you in them anymore today," Ginny fired back.

I left them to delight in one another and headed upstairs to wash. The finished afghan Aunt Amy had given Ginny resided proudly on the back of Father's chair in his study. The twice given treasure expressed Ginny's and Father's deep bond more eloquently than effusive antics ever could. Looking at the lovingly crafted afghan, I pondered the connecting link I might have been in the family equation.

Reaching the hall foyer, I turned toward my room. The eyes of the owl clock were strangely sympathetic. In my mind's eye, Father materialized alone and lonely without his Ginny, as he surely would be one day, and my heart ached for him. Let them play. Now was the time.

As I hung up the towel, the wistful words of Haji, the beggar poet in *Kismet*, filtered into my mind. "Lovers come, Lovers go, And all that there is to know, they know."[58] I paused, yearning to believe the lines were more than charming sentimentality, more than romantic delusion.

Chapter Twenty-Five

Come out of thyself,
Stand in the open;
Within thy heart wilt thou hear
The response of all the world.[59]

—Rabindranath Tagore: *The Sheaves, The Invitation*

In the days following the revelation by the river, I was careful to keep my feelings quietly secluded. Out of respect for Dr. Brantwood, I didn't wish upon him the encumbrance or embarrassment of an unwanted devotion. In his position he would be obliged to deem any personal interest in him by a student, a vain and frivolous attachment.

Nevertheless, as I listened each day to the English 550 lectures, and found my mental processes more and more engaged by the fineness of his mind, my appreciation for him continued to grow. With increasing difficulty, I restrained the smiles that struggled to leap ever more spontaneously from my heart to my lips when he spoke. Being in his class became a game of emotional chess with myself, in which I had to outmaneuver my own heartfelt responses. How much Adrianne, with her intuitive insight, knew of my personal feelings, I dared not guess.

As my feelings for Dr. Brantwood deepened, so my separateness from him increased. In my heightened awareness of him, I felt painfully vulnerable in his presence. While strongly desiring his association, his company was precisely what I knew I must avoid.

For both our sakes, I had to keep my distance. I had to resist the temptation to go where I knew he would be; and yet, recalcitrant as a wayward child, those were the very places I longed to be most.

In such a division of mind and heart, I watched as the waning days of November passed, taking with them the Indian Summer and the last roses in Father's garden. The faded, once-opulent petals of the Black Prince lay on the cold ground under a light snow that fell the first week in December. Lights from the students' residences burned later and later on the starry nights as students commenced serious study for the Christmas midterms and finals.

The second week in December, the first heavy snowfall descended. A myriad of snowflakes drifted down, joyfully disuniting themselves from their mother the sky. Many snowflakes, amazing in their design, fell on the river, delivering up their crystal beauty to the coal black water. On the hills, piles of intricately patterned snowlace covered the earth's cold breast with a merciful white mantle. Sacrificing self-interest, the individual snowflake's fleeting existence was redeemed by their perfection, their fragile beauty warming my heart.

So it was with Dr. Brantwood's words. When he spoke, it was as though a tiny pair of earphones located in my mind received the message, so close was the connection between his thought and my understanding. Indeed, it began to feel as though his thoughts were the creation of my own mind, as though his ideas were born in my very person.

Ever more amazed, I garnered each precious moment in English 550. Yet, even as I shepherded the moments, I realized there was an Achilles heel to Dr. Brantwood. He had an abruptness, perhaps the result of too stern self-discipline, that caused him to leave many ideas incomplete—only half molded—never to know the final touch of the crafter's hand. The mind that had the power to construct could also tear down. The hands that held the reigns of the sky chariot were human and pulsed with the temporal breath of mortality.

Whatever Dr. Brantwood's private dragons might be, his influence on the English 550 class was real. A change had been wrought. In forthrightly discussing a wide variety of topics, students were becoming more and more amenable to each other's views.

English 550 was not just another 'memorize-and-parrot-back' class. It was impossible to attend and not begin to think more broadly, to become more involved in the learning process. Whether by desire or self-defense, class members shed their conventional responses for the risk and reward of personal investment. Not that the students couldn't still be blunt or brutal, but there was less intentional cruelty about the verbal swordplay, less emotional bloodletting. For whatever reasons, English 550 had become a community.

The English 550 final was eight days away. Lecture over, there was a lull in the topic under discussion. Mr. Stewart took his pipe from his mouth and addressed Dr. Brantwood.

"I have noticed that the few readings you've assigned have tended toward atheism. If you don't mind my asking, is this a statement of your personal views?"

"You mean am I an atheist?" Dr. Brantwood returned easily.

Mr. Stewart nodded and put his smokeless pipe back in his mouth. I felt the back of my neck tingle.

"That's an unfair question," Harris interposed. "It begs the second question of whether you consider atheism ethical or unethical." Mr. Stewart looked at Harris with some surprise.

"With no offense," he said, "godlessness is a violation of principle."

"Hey, like groovy, we got a Kant cannon for a professor. Cool, Man!" Bob Davis exclaimed, coming unexpectedly to Dr. Brantwood's defense.

Dr. Brantwood smiled and nodded to Bob. Pleased, Bob gave a thumbs-up.

"In how respect, most deference to opinion, Mr. Stewart," asked Mr. Aki Hito, politely, "is no belief of God to be wrong? What is basis for this thinking?"

"The first of the Ten Commandments. 'Thou shalt love the Lord thy God'."

"But if person does not believe in God, how should this be bad? Ethics cannot be proved by laws unknown to persons, source of which is not believed."

"That's the point exactly, Aki," Harris agreed. "If you don't believe in God, you shouldn't have to justify what you do believe by God's laws. Forcing belief becomes the unethical behavior."

"You know it," Bob said. "Run your own life. Bob Davis will take care of Bob Davis."

It appeared Adrianne doubted Davis' bold assertion was so, but she didn't comment. In spite of Bob's glib secularism, it was his insecurity that struck the awareness most forcibly. In some ways he seemed more frightened than Neila.

Suddenly I knew what it was about Janice that infuriated Adrianne. Janice was subsumed in the universal, her self-assurance the result of having no independent viewpoint apart from the group. The group was her safety net, her shield from herself. Perhaps being an individual wasn't as easy as it seemed. Perhaps it was the hardest choice of all.

"What you suggest, Bob," Bernie said thoughtfully, "is that there's no source of morality outside the individual; that moral conduct is entirely relative to individual belief."

Before Bob could respond, Mr. Stewart cut in. "All morality, to be morality, originates from the same source—God. Left to their own devices, men become barbaric. This is the whole premise of Golding's *Lord of The Flies*."

"Maybe, and maybe not," Harris interjected. "What isn't true is that all atheists are immoral and all Christians moral. This we know, from the atrocities perpetrated in the name of religion, is pure myth. Golding's was an extreme view. Isolated segments of society can remain ethically viable and adhere to responsible social behavior, without some punitive external authority, some powerful watchdog governing their actions."

"Agree. Unwise to generalize too broad," Mr. Hito contributed politely. "Many religions believe in source of wisdom beside Christian God. Buddhists believe Buddha, Muslims believe Muhammad. Should not confuse God belief or no belief with lack of ethics."

During the interchange, Dr. Brantwood remained quietly leaning against the back of his chair, one arm stretched informally on his desk. He looked relaxed and unconcerned. Turning toward me, he asked with characteristic composure, "And you Miss Collingsgate? What do you think? Was Milton right? Was Satan's expulsion from Paradise a moral indiscretion?"

My throat constricted into a tight knot. Thankfully, Lois Weiss intervened, giving me time to think of a diplomatic response.

"Harris has a point," Lois said. "Belief or disbelief in a universal directing force or deity doesn't make a person moral or immoral."

"Thank you, Lois," Mr. Stewart returned. "I understand Harris's point. But does he? I didn't ask him the question, yet he seems determined to defend himself."

The class laughed. Harris, to his credit, laughed also.

"Not at all, Jack," Harris said when the laughter subsided. "I haven't had to defend myself. The converted have done that for me. "He shot Mr. Stewart a friendly grin. "The point is that morality is social, not theological. Man-made laws, not superpowers, determine human ethics. With regard to *Paradise Lost*, Professor Brantwood, Milton was a poet. He used poetical constructs, not reality, as the basis for his writing. The same is true for Golding's *Lord of the Flies*, Jack."

Once again, Dr. Brantwood intervened, remorselessly redirecting the conversation back to me. Catching the penetrating look in his eyes, I felt encapsulated, willfully entombed in a hazel universe.

"Would you agree, Miss Collingsgate? Are God's ethics only poetical constructs?"

I drew in my breath. "I believe there are eternal principles— God's ethics if you like—governing the universe," I said carefully. "I think Milton may have discovered a few of these. I also believe there are good and useful laws that serve society well. I think Golding's castaways may have discarded these."

"So God makes the laws?"

"No. He doesn't."

"No?" Dr. Brantwood asked, openly surprised by my answer. "You mean God is all powerful, but He doesn't make the laws?"

I was trapped. It was all the way now or nothing.

"No," I said firmly. "Principles of truth, like God, are eternal. They've always existed and will always continue to exist. God is the being perfectly in harmony with these principles and wishes mortals to also be in harmony. As men come to understand the nature of God, they come to understand that our laws are a reflection or application of these eternal principles."

Dr. Brantwood appeared to digest my over lengthy exposition calmly, but before he could comment, Mr. Hito spoke.

"We are here dealing with too many questions. Does God exist is different question from nature of God, which is different question from ethics of belief, which is different question from what is law, which is different question from principle of truth and how exist."

"You're right, Aki," Harris said, bowing his head deferentially to Mr. Hito. "However, the whole idea of God, and that includes his nature and or laws he may or may not enact, or be himself governed by, is irrelevant. Men, through the process of social evolution, determine morality. Belief or disbelief in God has nothing to do with the laws that keep society running."

"Let me ask you this, Harris," Lois interjected. "Just for the exercise, suppose there is a God. And suppose that by Him all principles of existence are either established or affirmed. Wouldn't that make your view of a purely human-based morality questionable?"

"Not necessarily," returned Harris. "Perhaps it's God, if he exists, who's immoral. Maybe Milton was wrong. Maybe it *was* an indiscretion for God to expel Satan from Paradise."

"Yeah, man," said Davis. "Nothing out there makes sense. We've got wars, and we've got famines, and we've got Pierre Elliott Trudeau. Like, if God exists, He's either crazy, or He don't care."

Mr. Stewart had reached his limit. "God cannot be immoral," he said. "What you're postulating is a devil."

"Well, Miss Collingsgate?" Dr. Brantwood said. "It seems Milton's Satan and Mr. Davis hold similar opinions. God, 'Sole reigning, holds the tyranny of heaven.' So what's it to be? God or Devil?"

"I believe Mr. Stewart is partially correct, Dr. Brantwood. Each person must answer honestly to himself—does God exist? There can be no avoiding this question, no middle-of-the-road defense. Either God exists, or He doesn't. We all must answer yes or no.

The question of whether God rules by merit or might, as Satan suggests in *Paradise Lost*, is a secondary issue."

"Man cannot conceive God," Dr. Brantwood said mildly, focusing his attention upon me in a way that raised my temperature considerably. "The object must pass the concept. Anselm may prove God to some, but in so doing, God is made incomprehensible. So I ask you, Miss Collingsgate, what good does it do to believe or disbelieve the existence of something man cannot by nature comprehend?"

The disarming ease with which Dr. Brantwood spoke sent an icy shiver down my spine. Bob had nailed him correctly. But was this Kantian transcendental view really what Dr. Brantwood believed? Some defense had to be made.

"Perhaps this is exactly the point, Dr. Brantwood. A priori reasoning is insufficient. A personal experience, revelation if you will, is needed."

"You may be right, Diana," Harris said. "But as neither theism nor atheism can be proved, the only tenable position left is agnosticism."

My breath caught involuntarily. Harris was nothing if not the quintessential humanist. Finding no compelling reason for belief or disbelief in either creator or created universe, he put his faith in the scientific evolution of man's reason, social philosophies, and cultural idealism.

"As one perfectionist to another," Dr. Brantwood said, "would you agree Miss Collingsgate? Is belief the *sine qua non*?"

Mercifully, before I could respond, the buzzer sounded, ending the discussion.

Once outside the classroom, Adrianne gave a relieved sigh. "I'm glad that's over. I detest getting embroiled in theology." My friend of friends paused and looked at me appraisingly with her perceptive green eyes.

"You must feel like a toasted cheese sandwich with the grilling Brantwood gave you, Di. What on earth did you do to get his back up? Something you're not telling me? Come on, confess. What did you do? Trip Brambly into his own briar patch?"

I laughed at Adrianne's outrageous spontaneity. Nevertheless, recalling the serious light in Dr. Brantwood's eyes, I was concerned.

Following class, I went directly to Edwards. Aunt Amy had packed a lovely lunch of cold fried chicken and her special whole wheat bread for me with spice cookies, but I wasn't hungry. I needed time to adjust to the closing of English 550. It wasn't this alone that distressed me. Rather it was a feeling that I'd abandoned a sacred trust. To my knowledge, Dr. Brantwood's comment on his need for perfection was the one personal admission he'd made in class about himself. It wasn't his nature to make personal revelations, and I felt responsible. It was as if I had led Dr. Brantwood into self-betrayal, as if my silence had beguiled him.

Chapter Twenty-Six

To see clearly is poetry, prophecy, and religion, all in one.[60]

—John Ruskin: *Modern Painters*

The English 550 final exam was scheduled for the Thursday before Christmas break. It was held in the regular classroom in Arts. One of the last to finish the exam, I laid my paper on the desk and turned to leave.

"Stay a moment, will you please, Miss Collingsgate?" Dr. Brant-wood asked. His tone was formal, and his manner strictly business, so I presumed he wanted to check some matter with me about course assignments. When the other students had all left, Dr. Brantwood rose from his desk and walked over to where I stood waiting for him. Stopping directly opposite, he faced me squarely, his eyes challenging.

"Would you mind explaining what you were doing during the exam, Miss Collingsgate?"

The unexpected question struck me with the force of ice water thrown in my face. Astounded, I reflexively drew back. Dr. Brantwood and I were clearly not on the same page, and I knew my reply would have to be succinct. Bewildered, I searched for an answer. There was only one answer—the truth.

"I was watching you." The feeble admission groped along the table and huddled to an untimely death. I straightened my shoulders, forcing myself to continue. "You were so intent, so earnest on your marking. You were . . . almost fierce."

"Have you ever had to mark first year papers?"

"No."

"Ever had a shotgun held to your head?"

"No!"

"Hmm." But you do know what it's like to feud with ignorance?"

"I've looked in the mirror, yes," I said, making a desperate attempt to ease the tension with some slight humor. Dr. Brantwood's welcome laughter swept me with relief.

Encouraged by the change in his manner, I suggested impulsively, "Perfection's a harsh master, but you don't quell before it. You're no slave." The unrehearsed words tumbled rashly from the wells of my admiration for this dedicated man. Dr. Brantwood looked at me tolerantly, as one might look at a small child caught with cookie crumbs on her face.

"As some young man is a slave to you?" he mused absently. "Incidentally, you've written better term papers. You've a strong penchant for courting obscurity, Miss Collingsgate."

The professional criticism following so closely on the heels of his more personal comment swarmed about my ears like bees buzzing. I struggled to fathom his line of reasoning. At once formal and sternly serious, now personal and provocatively playful, his object eluded my grasp.

"No," I amended. "You misunderstand. Please accept my apology. I'm not normally in the habit of staring. I don't intrude on privacy. That is vulgar."

"Privacy is vulgar?"

"No. Private is private. Shared is vulgar. No . . . I mean shared privacy is . . . "I was hopelessly befuddled.

"Hmm," he said, justifiably amused. "I see. If that's all, you're welcome to vulgarize privacy with me anytime, Miss Collingsgate."

I felt a flush of warmth travel across my cheeks, accompanied by a wave of awe at the elasticity of Dr. Brantwood's mind. I nodded, smiling. He gallantly held the door for me as I pressed by him into the hall. The conversation had been disconcerting at best, and yet I felt an inexplicable release.

Almost to Edwards, there was a nudge at my side as Adrianne swung into step beside me. "That has to be the most recklessly relevant redhead I've ever met," she announced. "And I'll miss him, even if he is a prof." Adrianne was glowing with the confidence that comes from writing a good exam.

Trapped into commenting, I blurted, "Redhead? His hair is brown."

"Aha! You do know who I mean," she said, pleased her ruse had worked. "As for his hair, it only looks brown. He's one of us, definitely one of us."

"I thought you distrusted any and all of the professorial species," I said, fervently hoping Adrianne wouldn't interrogate me on why I was detained.

"Oh, I do. Dreadfully. But that one is delicious." I looked cautiously at Adrianne, trying to determine if she was serious.

"He's so repressed," she continued. "They all are, of course. Horribly so. But Bramblybriar has got to be the *summum bonum* of repression. He looks positively sublimated." Cocking an innocently inquisitive eyebrow at me, Adrianne kicked amiably at a stone. "Wouldn't you love to watch Bramblybriar in liberated cinematic action?"

My breath caught. Adrianne's line of attack was dangerously close to camp. Wishing to avoid collusion, I said, "Plato and Sigmund Freud are an odd combination. The highest good and repressed desire don't exactly connect."

"Oh, I never connect anything," Adrianne sallied, grinning. "I just throw everything all in together and let the pieces lie where they fall." Adrianne eyed me coolly, the gleam of a smirk on her face.

"As I was saying before the detour," she continued coyly, offering me an inoffensive piece of red licorice, "who wants a big, hairy Sasquatch making passes at you?"

"A big hairy what?" I was honestly derailed, but Adrianne didn't buy it.

"You know what I mean. Big smelly feet and a head bricked in like a medieval dungeon doesn't a man make. Muscle and brawn isn't necessary to make the species attractive."

"I'd say Warren is very attractive. He's well-built and intelligent."

"I'm not talking about Warren and you know it. Stop bluffing! You know who I mean."

Realizing the round was lost, I silently acquiesced. Dr. Brantwood's physical attributes weren't boldly stated, but they were a fitting enhancement to his discerning mind. His was a total charm. Adrianne, whose interest was all the more tantalized by my silence, attempted a more direct approach.

"What're you hashing over in that ivy archive you call your head, my lovely armadillo? Forget something in Cosmos 550?"

"All right!" I said impulsively. "Professors can be athletic. They can be attractive like anyone else."

"Way to revolve, Dio. So there's life on your planet after all. But then who wouldn't appreciate tall, bronzed, and Brambly?"

I nodded obediently. Adrianne had won her point. It would be no use dissimulating further. She was not enraptured with Dr. Brantwood or any other professor. She was, however, extremely curious to know if I was. Now she knew.

Chapter Twenty-Seven

It is a characteristic of wisdom not to do desperate things.[61]

—Henry David Thoreau: *Walden*

Friday evening before Christmas break, I had to work late at the university photocopying. The Xerox machine in Edwards was in the foyer on the same floor as my study carrel. Except for a few students, the desk clerks, and the guard at the exit, the library was deserted. I suspected Mr. Stewart, his dogs, one solitary clerk, and myself were the only ones on the entire floor. Mr. Stewart wasn't in sight, but Mart and Mike were pacing the length of the foyer when I came out to use the Xerox at nine thirty. I'd have to work quickly as Edwards would be closing at ten. The large building was too intensely quiet, even for me, and I was glad to see the dogs.

As I worked, placing the material to be copied under the thick rubber flaps of the machine, Mart sat on his haunches by my side. He pricked his ears and lifted his paw every time the machine started and the red light came on, while Mike paced persistently back and forth at the head of the stairs. Although it was not customary to take dogs into Edwards or any other campus building, for some unknown reason, no one questioned Mike or Mart's diligent attendance on their master.

I opened the last case study from sociology and centered it carefully on the glass plate of the machine. Alerted to someone coming up the stairs, Mike padded over, ears listening. Dr. Brantwood, carrying a large stack of books in his arms, reached the top step and walked directly to the glass doors opening into the library. Opening the door with his foot, he passed through and disappeared, apparently not noticing my presence at the Xerox.

My first reaction was to leave immediately and complete the copying another day. Then, thinking I'd be finished before Dr. Brantwood returned, I stifled the urge to retreat and placed the next page on the machine. The copy machine hadn't completed its assigned task before the glass doors opened once more and Dr. Brantwood, no longer carrying books, walked sociably toward me.

As he approached, Mart stood protectively by my knee. Just why, I didn't know. The dog knew the professor and shouldn't have been nervous. More in an effort to calm my own nerves than reassure the dog, I reached down to give Mart a pat. At the same instant Dr. Brantwood also reached to bolster the dog, and our hands collided a few inches from Mart's head. For a brief second his hand closed gently over mine. Not wishing to betray my feelings, I quickly withdrew my hand and looked away from him to the silent machine. The pile of bond paper on the receiving tray appeared an inert, white lump. As yet unimprinted, it had no wisdom to share.

"You are the most quiet woman I've ever met," Dr. Brantwood said gently. "You are . . . reverent."

"Thank you," I said, wishing fervently I'd followed my inclination to leave, yet somehow glad that I'd stayed.

With his usual unpredictability, Professor Brantwood leaned against the copier and laughed. The warm full sound echoed off the walls of the foyer and enveloped me in tremulous warmth. Lips still smiling, he looked at me curiously.

"I accept your thank you, Miss Collingsgate. Although some might contend too much reverence leads to human bondage."

"I wouldn't call religion bondage," I said gravely, instantly alerted to his true intent. "There is no constraint upon me. I believe freely."

"In what? Do you serve a god or gods? Are you Orthodox or Protestant? What faith says simply, I believe?" Dr. Brantwood stood a short distance away, leaning lightly against the wall. Body straight, arms folded, head to one side, frank eyes surveying me, he was terrifyingly real. And he had the complete advantage; he held all the cards. My emotions had become inextricably involved, while he was without encumbrance. Concerned, I moved away from him toward the window. Mustering my courage, I spoke.

"I believe in the God that delivered Moses out of Egypt."

"And ordered the destruction of the Canaanites?"

"Correct."

"I see. You revere your god no matter what. You defend your one god, even if he destroys all other peoples' gods and beliefs."

I looked at him aghast. How could even Dr. Brantwood border on blasphemy so coolly? His eyes were a dark shade, but he was not discomfited.

"I don't answer for God," I said, genuinely disturbed. "God doesn't require my defense."

"And what about those who believe differently from you? What do you think of them?"

"I respect all honest beliefs and all honest people."

Dr. Brantwood stepped firmly toward me. "Respect? Respect is a worm of time. Seeking for respect destroys a sincere man and corrupts an honest nation."

"I realize you're not a Christian," I accorded, dismayed by his intensity, and yet awed by the energizing verve of the man. He ignored my attempt at conciliation.

"While you respect everyone so freely, would you give deference to a servant of the rational? Would you give equal regard to an honest heathen? Bend your knee to pagan authority?"

"I can't see how it would matter whether I did or I didn't," I said, honestly stunned. "But yes, I bow to authority. I recognize all earthly governments and magistrates."

Dr. Brantwood looked at me in measured silence. When he spoke again, his tone had lost its intensity, gaining in its stead a quiet, impersonal objectivity.

"Then you support the hypocrisy of demagogues, put totalitarians at the heads of nations, and pray for potentates and dictators. Respect? Where's the respect in elevating a chosen few to wield the whip?"

"I should have qualified my terms," I amended, realizing my error. I should have said 'just' governments and 'fair-minded' magistrates. In any event, I don't choose."

"But would you choose if you had the power, Miss Collingsgate? Would you choose one man to rule the world?" Dr. Brantwood's words, uttered with such deceptive calm, cut into my mind with chilling sharpness. I steadied my hand against the cold metal machine seeking to dispel the paralysis threatening to engulf my mind. Regaining my composure, I tried rephrasing.

"I don't make the laws; therefore, any choice of mine would be presumptive."

"But if a man chose you?" Dr. Brantwood said, looking at me quietly over the black protective shield of the Xerox machine. There was an uneasy, almost shattering stillness. Taking command of myself, I straightened my shoulders and spoke firmly.

"I should gladly honor righteous dominion till death."

"And in death, poet?"

"In death I should wait for a new life to serve."

Dr. Brantwood gave a low whistle. "And this is what you call respect?"

"Yes," I said steadily. I could be pushed, but I wouldn't be railroaded. "Yes. It's the highest form of respect. It is true reverence. What I feel for God."

"Good," he said. "In that case, mere mortals needn't be burdened with it."

I looked at Dr. Brantwood in mute concern. Moving with restless agility, he stepped back and glanced at the slender black hands on the silver face of the wall clock. It was nine forty-five. The library would close in fifteen minutes.

"Will you have coffee with me this evening, Miss Collingsgate?"

"Will I . . . ?"

"Will you have coffee with me? You do drink some form of liquid?"

"Yes," I said, "I do drink some ah. . . liquid."

"Fine. I'll meet you at the front door in ten." Dr. Brantwood nodded, smiling at me with unaffected charm. Disoriented by the quicksilver change in his mood, I wondered just what I had gotten myself into.

Twenty minutes later, Professor Brantwood politely held open the front door of his suite in The Manse. Oddly, the elegant room seemed to welcome me with an inviting friendliness. Knowing I was taking a serious chance coming here with Dr. Brantwood, I fervently hoped I wouldn't say anything revealingly foolish and willed myself to remain calm.

Dr. Brantwood took my coat with a relaxed, easy movement and hung it in the alcove behind the lounge; then placed his own brown topcoat next to mine. The cold of winter was beginning to be sincerely felt. Thoroughly chilled from the walk from Edwards to The Manse, I moved to the fireplace to warm myself, while I waited for Dr. Brantwood to return with the coffee and hot chocolate from the kitchen down the hall. The fire in the hearth was artificial, but the electric substitute, with the natural-looking logs, produced ample heat through the directed blower to give the illusion of a real fire. I watched the serrated, revolving wheel catch the red light from the hidden bulb and send it flickering and dancing though the translucent logs. Warmed by the radiated heat, it seemed oddly natural to be standing in front of Dr. Brantwood's fireplace.

Relaxing a little, my focus shifted to the desk by the window. As was usual, Dr. Brantwood's desk had books systematically arranged along the back. What captured my attention was not the books, but an impression that while the desk was unoccupied, it still embodied Dr. Brantwood's spirit, as if he were at the very moment seated there, concentrating on some invisible treatise open before him. Feeling like I was trespassing, I again shifted my gaze. This time my glance fell on the mirror presiding over the mantle. There seemed to be a sage-like quality about the mirror, as if it had the ability to record with its prudent eye the secrete inner life of all who entered into its realm.

Looking into the mirror's depths, it was almost as though I could see the lingering images of past days. What I did see was strictly in the present: Dr. Brantwood re-entering the room. My heart gave an uncontrollable leap; I would have to keep my guard up. Dr. Brantwood smiled, or his reflection in the mirror smiled. It wasn't the rare personal smile I'd come to love, but a smile such as one might offer at a tiresome formal dinner.

"Are you warm?" he asked, with the same voice quality as his smile. Something in his tone forced me to remain frozen where I stood, seeing him only in the mirror. Standing by the piano, his hand on the smoothly polished wood, Dr. Brantwood looked as he had that day by the river. Yet so much had changed since the revelation by the water's edge. The evening would require exceptional vigilance.

"What do you see, Miss Collingsgate?" he asked presently. "What do you see in the mirror?"

As usual, I was unprepared for his directness.

"I see a grand piano, a desk with treasured books, a comfortable chair—"

"You see all that, do you?" he interrupted. His voice held a hint of irony, his eyes searching mine. The intentness of his gaze made me feel as though I was as transparent to him as the logs on the hearth, as though he could discern the tender heart of my true regard secreted beneath the outward deception. Then the answer came.

It was him he wanted me to see. My eyes swept his face in the mirror. Unable to ignore the truth longer, I turned and faced him. Never in my most exultant regard for this mentally vigorous man had I imagined he might reciprocate my feelings. It was beyond my ability to accept.

"Dr. Brantwood?" I whispered, amazement flooding my mind.

Quietly he walked across the intervening distance between us and stood straight but relaxed a few handbreadths in front of me. He looked at me thoughtfully, intently scanning my face with serious, violet-toned eyes.

"You do see, do you?" he said calmly. Placing his hands on my shoulders, he gently turned me back to the mirror. My eyes answered his, but I couldn't speak.

"Do you think, Diana," he said in a voice even more gentle than his touch, "that while you see, I see nothing? You have been so resolved to live in the world by yourself, will you now allow a fellow sojourner to travel with you? Or will your inventive mind devise a new delay?" His voice was soft and so very low, his eyes a focused intensity that warmed my spirit. I felt the controlled force of his presence near me as keenly as I had ever perceived any living being. As earnestly as his hands held my shoulders, his nearness importuned my heart. I heard his words and understood their challenge. *Come, meet me. Walk halfway.*

I looked to find him, but as I again searched the depths of the mirror, I could not see him. It seemed I looked both beyond, but not as far, as the man himself, and in that boundless space where he was not, stood a marble lady with molded self-control. Her carriage was straight, her head regal, her bearing proud. If there was vast inconsistency in her serene appearance and the agitated state of her heart, it wasn't visible to the eye. Looking at the composed features of the stiff white image in the mirror, it was as though I was seeing myself for the first time—as others saw me—unapproachable and distant.

The austere mirror image surveying me was so different from the person I was inside. I knew the generosity of caring, but my coldly aloof sister in the mirror showed little compassion. She didn't give fair return for the gift she received. If there was love and gratitude in her heart, it was hidden, and remained—even to this man—a cloistered virtue.

Humbled, I turned from the mirror to Dr. Brantwood. "I'm not indifferent," I told him earnestly, my heart beseeching his.

Dr. Brantwood smiled warmly, the pressure of his hands increasing with an intensity that seemed to concentrate the whole vigor of the man into his touch. He accepted my vague response and still, the awakening touch of his hands continued, more compelling, more joyful than anything I'd ever known or experienced before.

Chapter Twenty-Eight

Which of us is not forever a stranger and alone? [62]

—Thomas Wolfe: *Look Homeward, Angel*

It was early morning. The first faint rays of winter sunlight were softly filtering through the partially drawn drapes covering the window on the east wall. My winter coat was tucked around me where I lay stiff and cramped on the lounge. I was warm, but I felt like I'd been traveling for hours over torturous terrain. I had, in fact, been on a journey in a dream.

I'd been riding a pony bareback at a fast gallop along the rim of a canyon. Below the rim, the precipitous walls dropped over a hundred feet to the canyon floor. Black boulders jutted out, banking a river that pummeled the dark sides of the jagged rocks in a vain attempt to escape the narrow canyon walls. The water thundered against the cruel rocks with such force that I could feel the icy spray on my face as I clung to the pony's slippery back. Brushing the mist from my eyes, I tangled my hands tightly in the pony's mane to keep from pitching into the canyon.

As I strove to stay on the wildly careening little horse, the reflection from the water below flashed into my eyes with blinding brilliance. The water was white as snow. No. It was whiter than snow. It was white as the glory of God. As I contemplated the whiteness, I saw emerging from the water two bleeding hands clasped together in prayer. At the sight of the two clasped hands, the searing pain in my eyes spread to my heart, and I knew where the whiteness of the water originated. The bruised and bleeding hands were glowing, radiating intense white light in all directions. I closed my eyes. Mercifully, the sound of talking shattered the scene as my dream dissolved into the regions from whence it came. I awoke to quiet voices.

"Don't teach her so well she can't forget." The voice was unfamiliar and I looked to see who spoke.

Dr. Brantwood rose from his chair by the desk and addressed the speaker. "You know the way?" Receiving a nod, Dr. Brantwood walked quietly across the room and out the door. His step was confident as always. He walked as a man walks whose mind knows no disquietude.

I looked from the door, now closed behind Dr. Brantwood, to the person who'd spoken earlier. Dr. Banescroft, of the medical faculty, was standing by the desk. A man in his mid-sixties, his stance proclaimed his efficiency. He seemed a dependably ready man, which was surprising in a person of his ample proportions. Yet in spite of the refusal of the bottom button on his jacket to close, he had an eminently respectable look and was, I knew, well liked by his colleagues.

Encountering my questioning glance, Dr. Banescroft gave me a quick professional smile, then walking to the lounge, he handed me a glass of water. Placing a skillful hand on my back, he helped me sit up and drink. His eyes, the same subdued blue as the water glass, considered me benignly.

"So, Miss Collingsgate. You caused Dr. Brantwood some concern. You're all right of course, but you'll feel a slight effect from the sedative for a while. Do you have a history of loss of consciousness?"

I shook my head, placing my feet firmly on the floor.

"Have you ever had a concussion?"

Again, I shook my head.

"Or experienced amnesia?"

I stifled a surprised gasp. Confused, I gazed at the gold band girding the stocky ring finger of Dr. Banescroft's left hand. "No. None of those," I said, determined to take charge of myself. "I'm fine, Dr. Banescroft. Thank you." The doctor's questions were compounding the extreme and utter foolishness I felt.

"One more question. Is there any record of epilepsy or convulsions in your family?"

"No."

"I thought not," he said frankly. "The human mind has many resources when faced with the unexpected. We're not always logical or predictable, or even believable in our behaviors."

Dr. Banescroft rose and lifted my coat from the lounge, his business-like manner expressing courteous but obvious impatience. I also rose. When I'd fastened my coat, he ushered me into the hall and down the stairs into the parking lot. I preceded him to a rust-colored Mercedes Benz parked next to the walk. There were other cars in the lot, but the Benz could belong only to Dr. Banescroft. They were both designed for quality and modeled for comfort.

Dr. Banescroft unlocked the car door with a squat, silver key. The morning breeze was just picking up, while the moonlight, barely breaking through the night clouds, fell in icy shafts about the maple trees that guarded the lot. It couldn't have been more than one a.m. I breathed in deeply, willing the crisp winter air to clear my head. From the side door of The Manse our footprints were etched in the newly fallen snow that covered the ground like fine white dust. On the unmarked snowy surface, the prints looked unusually stark.

"I could easily walk home," I said. Dr. Banescroft paid no attention, ushering me into the car with a brusque but kindly motion. He closed the left door and drew his red wool scarf more closely about his neck, before unlocking the door on the driver's side. Since awakening, I'd received a great many impressions, none of which were organized. As we drove past trees and houses in silence, I attempted to inflict some order on my thoughts. The events of the past hours were beginning to group into workable units when Dr. Banescroft spoke.

"I wouldn't mention this to your Father. He's very proud of you." Dr. Banescroft's tone was concerned but authoritative. I winced inwardly.

"You don't think?" I objected, mortified.

"I do not *think* anything, young woman," Dr. Banescroft interrupted firmly. "I do know you were unconscious for a short time.

As there seems to be no physical reason for your lapse, the root must be psychological. You should perhaps see a psychiatrist."

"A psychiatrist?"

"Yes. A psychiatrist," he repeated firmly. Seeing my amazement, he continued. "Your father is a valuable asset to this university. You, as his daughter, should have inherited something of his mind."

I winced again. I hadn't been reprimanded so sternly since leaving adolescence, possibly because within my own mind, I felt what Dr. Banescroft said was true.

As he continued to lecture me in his direct and forthright manner, his honesty compelled me to a vivid, albeit uncomfortable reflection upon my behavior. I did know that most instances of hysteria and associated motor neural lapses were known to afflict the physiologically naive and superstitious, but didn't occur, except perhaps rarely, among those of more sophisticated culture and education.

"But does not," I acquiesced aloud.

Dr. Banescroft looked momentarily puzzled, then raised his eyebrows in agreement. "That's correct, Miss Collingsgate," he affirmed. "One does not indulge in exhibitionism at such a fine university as Western."

"I would never make a display of my regard for Dr. Brantwood," I defended gravely.

"Nor of his for you?" he parried. "Make no mistake, Miss Collingsgate. Dr. Brantwood's stamp on your forehead would confer no higher prestige than you now have. And you would suffer from the status grubbing." I shrank inside under the unfair indictment. Dr. Banescroft's words were a gross misjudgment.

"Please don't be concerned further," I said evenly. "I'm not destitute of moral obligation to Western, nor do I abjure personal responsibility for either my actions or associations. You can't believe I have the will to trample a man of Dr. Brantwood's stature?"

Dr. Banescroft shook his head impatiently. Taking his large right hand from the wheel, he reached over and patted my own smaller hands clenched in a tight, innocuous white ball on my lap. I felt the reprimand in his kindness more keenly than in his galling advice.

"No, my dear foolish child," he said with parental, if misguided, concern, "you do not. But he does. He most certainly does."

Summarily, Dr. Banescroft deposited me at my front gate and drove on down the road, leaving me in the quiet stillness of the sleeping rose arbor. Leaning against the center pergola, now barren of vine and blossom, I turned my flushed face into the wind, thankful to be alone at last. The slender, naked arms of the Black Prince, residing watchfully on the hummock by the gate, were still tipped with frost.

Chapter Twenty-Nine

Errors, like straws, upon the surface flow;
He who would search for pearls must dive below.[63]

—John Dryden: *All For Love, Prologue*

In the days that followed before Christmas, there was little time to spend on introspection. Both love and a vast bewilderment were sequestered silently in my heart. Predictably, as the days passed without word from Dr. Brantwood, my personal anxiety grew. I could only suppose he was determined, on account of my distressing, ridiculous behavior, to put me wisely out of his mind and life. I couldn't blame him, as my conduct, though not by choice, had been less than charming. While it may at one time have been a popular past-time for naive and coquettish maidens, losing consciousness in the nineteen sixties, was a century out of style and good taste.

The first day of the Christmas break was a day of bustle and busyness. Saturday morning Ginny insisted I drive into town with her to complete the Christmas shopping, absolutely forbidding my doing one stitch of schoolwork until Christmas had been celebrated properly. Late in the afternoon, after hours of tramping through the noise and congestion in the shops and fighting for survival on the busy streets, we returned home with more parcels than even Ginny could find friends to endow. When we got home, Father met us at the door, which Ginny had lavishly decorated with holly, red rose hips, and silver bells.

"I'm glad Elizabeth Kathleen had the good sense to have only two children," Father said as he unloaded the boxes and bags from our green Chevy sedan. "If there were any more spendthrifts at Collingsgate, I'd be forced to open a chain store to keep you all in supplies."

"Mother would approve of everything we bought," Ginny chirped. "And you know you love Christmas as much as anyone, Poppa. You're just too sadistically stubborn to admit it."

"Sadistic? You shocking scapegrace! All these years I bin tryin' ta bring ya up proper like, larn ya gud ettyquette an' luffly language, an' ya malign yer pur Faather with sich backtalk. First thing after Christmas it's stomatoplasty at Dr. Bevans for you!"

Ginny laughed, set her stack of parcels on the table and gave Meph a hearty rub under the chin. "What on earth is stomatoplasty?"

"It's plastic mouth surgery. Help you keep a civil lip," Father replied, a gleam of triumph in his eyes for having bested The Jinn.

"Oh, go up to your study, you terrible Poppa. I'll let you know when you can come out—if ever," was Ginny's sassy retort. Father did as he was told. He knew when leaving was the *only* rational thing to do.

Saturday evening Adrianne and Warren came over to spend some time before they left with their parents to celebrate the Christmas season in Los Angeles. The Eatons were not practicing Christians in the sense of regular church attendance, but they did celebrate the Christmas season. Adrianne was ecstatic over the trip, mostly because she and Warren would have Dianne and His Bucksworth all to themselves for ten uninterrupted days. I was glad for my friends' chance for a family holiday and did my best not to let my inner turmoil detract from their joy.

Bouncing into the kitchen ahead of Warren, Adrianne gave me a quick hug and reached to pick up Mephistopheles. "How's my namesake today?" she asked, cuddling and stroking the purring cat. How Adrianne could credit herself with inspiring Mephistopheles' name eluded me. She may not have been perfect, but she was certainly not the habituated sinner her comment implied.

"That cat is a good judge of character," Aunt Amy responded from where she was sitting in the rocker, crocheting. "Maybe you have that in common." Aunt Amy was herself rather feline, being able to quietly surprise with her uncanny, if illogical, insight.

"Hello, Aunt Amy," Adrianne greeted warmly. "So what lucky person's going to receive your latest resplendent creation in wool?"

"Hmph," Aunt Amy retorted, not to be cajoled by flattery. "I think I'll use it as a cover for that history-hashing bird. Carlyle makes so much racket I can't hear myself think." Adrianne smiled, her shrewd eyes glinting appreciatively. She and Aunt Amy had long been social sparring partners and held mutual esteem for one another.

Adrianne walked over to Carlyle's cage and poked her finger between the bars to ruffle Carlyle's neck feathers. "Hello Thomas," she crooned. "Something tells me you and Nelson C. like to swing on the same perch."

"What was that?" I asked, unable to avoid being drawn in by Adrianne's statement.

"Put it this way. Nelson would love this democratically demoralized bird. Mr. J. Cairn, on the other hand, might have some reservations about Carlyle's fascist tendencies."

The statement teased a chuckle from Warren. "Addy's got her own views on character." Coming forward from where he'd been standing by the door, he politely extended his hand to Aunt Amy. Giving Warren's hand a hearty pump, Aunt Amy excused herself from the hubbub.

Warren handed me a package. "Santa didn't need this," he said, grinning.

"Thank you, Warren," I said. "That's very thoughtful, but I haven't. . .

"That's all right, Dio," Adrianne broke in. "Santa has more where that came from. You just have to find the right delivery service."

"Yes, I see. Thank you for the presents Adrianne, and the delivery service, Warren."

Adrianne had consented with me to restrict our gift exchange to one Christmas present. Apparently this was her inventive way of getting around our agreement.

"I told Addy you'd catch on, Diana," Warren grinned. "I'm glad you did, though, because I've a gift of my own to give you."

Now I was surprised. Two presents from Adrianne and one from Warren. What kind of conspiracy had these two redheaded rogues been plotting? Impulsively and entirely out of character, I reached up and gave Warren a quick hug of gratitude.

"Merry Christmas, Warren."

"Would you get a load of this?" Adrianne crowed. "Here it is still winter and Dionysius Iciclous is beginning to thaw. What will you do by summer, Di? Have a flash flood?"

"Wasn't thinking," I said sheepishly.

"Here's to more not thinking!" Adrianne bounded over and gave me an enthusiastic hug.

"Me too, me too!" chimed in Ginny, who'd just entered the kitchen. Jubilantly bouncing into the middle of the circle, Ginny joyously embraced everyone.

"Maybe we should skip Los Angeles for Christmas," Warren said, grinning. "Seems to be plenty of action here." How like Adrianne he was. Why had I never noticed it before this year?

When Adrianne and Warren left, I took their gifts into the living room and placed them under the tree. Intrigued, I looked at Warren's present. It was beautifully wrapped with a lemon yellow bow and hummingbird. An overwhelming feeling of gratitude for these two dear friends swept through me, easing for a moment the keen distress plaguing my mind and spirit.

On Sunday, Father, Ginny, Aunt Amy, and I attended Christmas service. There was to be a surprise this year. In happy anticipation, everyone gathered in the cultural hall behind the chapel. Spencer Dykie took his seat at the organ ready for the special service to begin. Although only a year older than Ginny, Spencer was a mature musician and took his post seriously. He'd been at Collingsgate many times, as he and Ginny had become good friends over the years.

The pageant of the birth of Christ, put on by the Primary, was beautifully done. Sister Carol Marshall portrayed the Mother Mary and the Brooks' new baby, Benny, the Holy Christ Child. Sister Marshal, with Joseph walking beside, rode up the aisle on a real donkey. Now everyone knew why we were in the gymnasium.

As the donkey plodded patiently along to the large wooden stall and manger in front, the choir caroled, *O Little Town of Bethlehem.* When Mary had dismounted and picked up her sleeping babe from the straw-filled manger, Ginny, dressed as an angel, sang *Away In a Manger.* I noticed Spencer paying strict attention to his accompaniment as she sang, and a question sprang into my mind. I hoped I was wrong for Spencer's sake. The blessed simplicity of the birth of Christ and the greatness of His gift to all men caused tears to well in the eyes of many assembled. In my heart, also, was a deep thankfulness.

Sunday afternoon the University Symphony and Chorus combined to perform Handel's *Messiah* in Con Hall. Adrianne was absent, being with her family in Los Angeles. There was a good attendance; although, if Dr. Brantwood was present, I couldn't distinguish him in the audience. During the intermission, Mike handed me a new package of rosin tied with a red ribbon.

"Keep this one for yourself," he said, smiling shyly. "I've about used up your other one." It was a kind gesture, but even more surprising than Warren's gift had been as Mike and I didn't associate outside of symphony.

Flowers of the heart, I thought, remembering the time Ginny had given Mother a beautiful new pincushion for Christmas. The red velvet pincushion still hung in Father's bedroom next to Mother and Father's picture. When Ginny brought the carefully constructed gift to Mother, all wrapped in a jumble of squashed, creased-paper layers, she'd climbed up on Mother's lap and given her a long, heart-felt hug.

"Guess what this is, Momma," Ginny said in her prettiest manner, chubby baby hands planted affectionately either side of Mother's face.

"I bet it's a present from my best baby girl," Mother said happily.

"No! T'isn't!" Ginny laughed, delighted she had outwitted Mother. "It's a flower of my heart." So it is. Out of the heart's riches, such perfect gifts proceed.

Tuesday morning dawned and with it Christmas came, bringing both jubilance and sacred reflections. As was the custom, we gathered in the living room by the Christmas tree to open our presents. Where Dr. Brantwood was and what he might be doing, I couldn't guess. Would he celebrate this sacred, special day? The question was unanswerable. I yearned to see him, to apologize, to explain—somehow. No doubt he thought me too ridiculously immature to bother with again.

"Diddi, loveliest, do pay attention. It's your turn to open a gift," Ginny urged, bringing me back to the present. She was waving a beautiful box in blue and silver wrapping under my nose. Home-made stars of cardboard, ornamented with sparkling silver glitter, were placed on the top of the box in the shape of the constellation Diana, the Huntress. Unable to restrain her eagerness longer, Ginny withdrew the gift and began unwrapping it herself.

"You go slow too fast, Diddi," she teased. "I'll atrophy waiting for you to unwrap it." There was a smile of impish delight on her lovely, unspoiled face. Small, slender hands tugged excitedly at the frosted silver ribbon that was soon heedlessly discarded. A few of the stars became unglued and fell to the floor, as Ginny undid the outer layers of paper with ruthless haste. In her ambitious demolition of the wrapping she'd so painstakingly arranged, Ginny resembled wilder ancestry than she could rightly claim. Since she'd been a very little girl, Ginny never had been able to open a present peacefully, but must always war upon it with almost barbarous enthusiasm.

The outer wrapping disposed, Ginny pushed a long, cream cardboard box toward me. Lifting the lid off the box as quickly as I could, to appease the anxious interest of the fiercely tender young heart that threatened to wreak havoc on us both in its abundance of delight, I discovered a large section of black lace. It was not an ordinary piece of lace. Removed from the box, the graceful folds of a genuine Spanish mantilla were revealed. The mantilla was of flawless perfection. It would require exceptional craftsmanship to fashion a design so intricate.

"Virginia Elizabeth . . ." Unable to express the love I felt, I fingered the exquisite gift, soft tears falling inwardly. "Where did you ever?"

"Try it on, Diddi," Ginny interrupted. "I found it when I was in Mexico with Aunt Gladys last summer. As soon as I saw it, I knew it was you. It is you exactly."

"It's you first, Ginny."

I looked past my selfless sister and the pile of presents to the green bayberry candles on the ledge of the fireplace. We had bayberry candles on the mantle every Christmas. They were Mother's favorite candles. Ginny set them out faithfully each year as a memorial. *You are the best memorial,* I thought fondly, looking at the bent head of the lovely young woman next to me.

"Would you like to hear your record, Poppa?" Ginny asked Father, who was sitting in his favorite chair, afghan around his shoulders, his beloved book, *Care and Nurture of Roses,* propped open on his lap. During December and most of January and February, Father controlled his frustration at not being able to follow his horticultural inclinations, by reading up on gardening in every book available.

Nodding to Ginny, Father closed the rose book and put his reading glasses away in the pocket of his cord jacket. Christmas was the one time of year Father could wear his favorite jacket with no fear of reproof. Father reveled in his moment of grace as the heartfelt joy of the *Star Carol,* performed by the Tabernacle Choir, filled the family room. This special Christmas recording was Ginny's gift to Father. That she gave more than she received was never more noticeable than at Christmas.

The scent of fresh pine mingling with the bayberry and the sound of the music put me in a reminiscent mind. Thirteen years past, when Ginny was a tiny four-year-old, she had left the house in a lightning storm and run into the yard. Immediately noting her absence, Father had quickly begun a search which led him eventually outside, where he found Ginny huddled in a tiny pitiful ball under a blue spruce, trembling with the intense fear that only a small child alone in a storm can know. Catching her up quickly into his protecting arms, Father carried her swiftly back into the family room. Solemnly, she had allowed Mother to take her wet clothes and wrap her in a warm dry towel, her little face reflecting a defiant courage. Placing Ginny in his big chair in front of the fire,

Father gave her a moment to think before asking her why she'd left the house during the storm when she knew it wasn't safe. Two big tears tumbled down Ginny's cheeks like liquid jewels.

"Because Johnny Brickelmire said people who were struck by lightning got smart, and I want to be smart like you." She looked at Father with wide eyes, as if that should have been understood.

"You'll have to daydream at university, Diddi," Ginny said, rousing me from my reverie. In her hands she held the present with the yellow-gold wrapping and the small, beautifully made hummingbird perched on the lip of the fat lemon bow.

I shook my head. "I'd like to enjoy Warren's present wrapped a little longer, Ginny. It's too beautiful to destroy. Besides, it will look perfect by the bayberry candles on the mantle."

"Okay," she said, smiling. "If that pleases you, Diddi. But we can't sit around in our PJs all day. Neal is coming for dinner." Ginny bounced to her feet, scooping a great pile of loose wrapping and ribbon into her arms.

"Neal seems to be coming over fairly often," I said gently. "'Do his parents know he's out with you, Cecilia?'"[61]

Ginny threw a red and gold lounge pillow at me. "Of course they know. He's written them and told them all about us. So there, smarty sitter." Ginny always called me *smarty sitter* when I got the better of her. 'Sitter' was a leftover from her toddler days when she couldn't say sister.

"Perhaps Neal should write the same letter to Father," I suggested. I was pushing. I knew it, but Virginia was my younger sister, and I felt responsible.

"I'll tell Neal to get on it," Ginny said, not the least subdued. She caught an armload of wrapping paper to her breast and twirled around the room, only to drop with a luxurious sigh in the chair Father had vacated a moment before.

Something remembered from recent not-so-pleasant conversations with Dr. Brantwood tugged at my mind. "Ginny," I asked, "what do you and Neal talk about when you're together?"

"Oh, everything. Nothing. Mostly Neal's law plans. He's going to article in the East you know."

"Yes, I know. It's been mentioned a few times."

"He mentions you, Diddi," Ginny confided, a maternal overtone in her voice. "He said you were in Poly-Sci together in third year. Said you were the quietest girl in class."

"I suppose I was." Distracted by her comment, I looked at the picture of Ginny and myself on the mantle. Was Ginny the older sister and I the younger?

"Neal graduates this spring, doesn't he?" I asked, in an attempt to stay oriented.

"The twenty-eighth of April to be exact. But today he's coming for dinner. *And* he expects homemade cinnamon buns, so it's time to get operational."

"If Neal's coming for my homemade cinnamon buns," I objected, "he's in for a huge shock." Catching the spark in a crystal-blue eye that warned me The Jinn was about to change into her alter identity as the White Tornado, I got operational, as advised. Catching the load of papers from Ginny's arms, I made my way through the clutter to the kitchen and out the back door.

The transition from the warm family room to the cold winter morning outside was abrupt. Biting cold penetrated instantly through the thin soles of my slippers as I stepped gingerly along the newly shoveled walk to the refuse cans. My blue flannelette housecoat was full length, but it did little to shield against the chilling cut of the strident winter air. The searing cold jarred into every bone, and yet I was glad to be outside. I folded my arms tightly in front of me, in a futile attempt to lock in heat; but whatever warmth was there seemed drawn away by the intensely blue mountains, rising with such impelling immensity on the horizon. They *are* glass, I thought with awe. *They are beautiful, cold, glass mountains.*

Standing outside, with the freezing wind biting into my legs and arms, I contemplated inviting Dr. Brantwood for dinner. Mocking the thought, the mountains glittered aloofly in the distance, coolly dismissing that idea. After what had ensued between us, an invitation was out of the question. While I longed to be near him, I didn't wish to put him in an uncomfortable position. It wasn't that I doubted his broad-mindedness, or thought him ungenerous. He would never deny others their joy in Christmas, but I knew he would feel out of place. Given what had transpired between us, we would both feel awkward.

As I stood there shivering in the cold, I felt for the first time the full impact of my silent devotion to this complex man. Whereas the first awakening of love had been gentle, this powerful new response Dr. Brantwood's reciprocated interest aroused was spiritually distressing. I was not in a moral quandary; we were intelligent people. It was lawful to admire, to hold in reverence in the heart. And still, as I stood quaking in the early morning cold, the blue mountains beckoning, there were many questions I could not answer.

"Diana Lynn Esther Collingsgate! Come inside this instant! You'll turn as blue as those mountains!" I turned to see The Jinn holding the door open and beckoning me urgently inside.

Obeying the summons, only too glad to be out of the numbing cold, I fled to my room and quickly dressed. Neal would arrive in two hours and there was, as Ginny directed, much to do. Laying the lovely mantilla from Ginny on the bedspread, I hoped Father would like his LP of Albinoni. Ginny had fussed over her recording of Donny and Marie Osmond, but as she knew well in advance what she was getting, the surprise was spoiled. I hadn't meant to let her in on the secret, but Ginny had her own means of interrogation and had extracted the truth. Whereupon, she'd showered me with kisses and hugs and begged to be allowed to have it early. At least I'd remained firm on that account.

Aunt Amy was spending Christmas with her brother, Dennis, and his family in Colorado. We would exchange gifts with her when she returned. Remorsefully, I wished I'd had the courage to give Dr. Brantwood the leather-bound volume of Kahlil Gibran's *The Prophet*, purchased for him on an unrestrained whim in appreciation of his teaching English 550. Sadly, there'd be no occasion to present it to him now. The thought caused a pang of regret.

Without Aunt Amy to assist The Jinn, I was assigned double duty, and the next two hours flew by in a flurry of dinner preparations. The aroma of roasting turkey, mince pie, and freshly baked cinnamon buns scented the air as Neal's car pulled into the driveway. While I didn't mean to eavesdrop, it was impossible not to notice the quick kiss of greeting Neal gave Ginny at the door under the holly. The girl that was my sister was growing into a woman at a terrific pace.

Neal had come laden with gifts, which he and Ginny quickly deposited under the tree in the living room. Just as quickly, they were back in the kitchen, and Father ushered from his study to sit down to the abundance of festive foods, Ginny had so lovingly prepared. This time, as soon as grace was offered, Neal beat Father to the draw.

"Would it be all right if I had a cinnamon bun first, Virginia? My mouth has been watering for one all day." If Neal wanted to undermine his relationship with Ginny, he was once again going about it the wrong way. Still, I wondered if The Jinn would acquiesce. She strongly disapproved of people snitching dessert before the main meal was properly enjoyed.

When Ginny cheerfully conceded by bringing a whole tray of fresh, oven-hot buns to set beside Neal's plate, I could see Father was more than a little puzzled. Gallantly, Dad decided to ignore the enigma that was woman, and launched into a discussion with Neal on the Christmas address from Queen Elizabeth. Ginny, not to be left out of the conversation on Christmas day, rerouted the topic to Neal's mission. When that had been satisfactorily discussed, Ginny changed the topic once again.

"When President McKay was in New Zealand in 1921, he attended a Hui Tau—a church conference. More than a thousand visitors were sheltered in large tents where they could listen to the conference or sleep on the beds which were set up."

"And what did President McKay make of this bed-sitting arrangement?" Father asked, raising an eyebrow in wonder that he'd not heard the story before.

"President McKay said he 'recommends this arrangement most highly for those who like to sleep in church,'"[65] Ginny beamed back, pleased to beat Father to the punch line.

Father chuckled. "Perhaps I'll use President McKay's bed-sitting idea in my Sunday School class. That way the members won't have to pretend to be awake."

"You know no one would dare sleep through your lessons, Poppa," Ginny said, not at all deceived by Father's protested modesty. "Besides," she added, impishly tossing a sly look at Father, "that's why the Bishop has left you in that calling so many years. He wants to make sure *you* stay awake and don't fall off *your* chair."

Father gave a good-humored grin, then added fondly, "Virginia Elizabeth. God gave mortals short memories to use. File and forget." Ginny just waved a small hand, assured that Father was more entertained than offended. If Neal thought Father's comment was a strange view for a historian to hold, he didn't offer an opinion of his own.

"President McKay is an educated, highly literate man," Neal said, bringing the conversation back to the president. "He was an English teacher prior to his becoming a member of the Twelve and the Prophet. Have you read any of President McKay's personal writings, Diana?"

"No," I said, surprised by the question.

"Good," Neal said. While his response seemed odd, I didn't have long to puzzle. As soon as the dessert was finished, Ginny hurried us into the family room. After Ginny and Neal had exchanged their gifts, Neal handed me a square, green package. Receiving unexpected presents was becoming a regular occurrence this Christmas. Thanking him, I removed the wrapper and looked inside. It was a copy of President McKay's *Ideals For Living.*

"Thank you, Neal," I said, sincerely pleased. "I'll enjoy reading the writings of our prophet."

"Turn to page 564 first, Diddi," Ginny urged. A smile in my heart, I nodded. The collaboration between Neal and Ginny was apparent. After giving Ginny and Neal a hug, I turned to leave. Halting me, Neal motioned under the tree to a flat package wrapped in plain brown paper with no visible name on the cover.

"I believe that's for you, Diana," he said. "It was in your mailbox when I arrived." Neal bent and retrieved the parcel and handed it to me. The writing on the package was instantly recognizable. A picture of strong slender hands flashed into my mind. Heart racing, I accepted the package and retreated to my room before Ginny could make a fuss and demand to know who sent it.

Alone in my room, I sat on the edge of the bed, heart still pounding wildly, wondering if my eyes had deceived me, or if it really was Dr. Brantwood's writing. After a long moment, I removed the wrapping. Inside was a recording of the musical score for Neil Diamond's *Jonathan Livingston Seagull*. Written on the record jacket were the words, "For Skybird. Season's Best, G.L. Brantwood." If it was one thing consistent about Dr. Brantwood, it was that his were not predictable responses. With this man, if you couldn't expect the unexpected, you were open to a great many surprises. Ruefully, I had to admit that had been my lot. Placing the LP on the turntable in Father's study, I settled back in the large study chair and closed my eyes, grateful to lose myself in the music.

Chapter Thirty

He who binds to himself a joy
Doth the winged life destroy
He who kisses the joy as it flies
Lives in eternity's sunrise.[66]

—William Blake: *Eternity*

Thursday, the university was open. Many students were already back on campus, preparing for the second term. During the holidays, since receiving Dr. Brantwood's gift, my feelings had vacillated between cautious relief and a tantalizing elation of well-being that wouldn't be moderated, no matter how persistently I strove to hold a more sensible attitude. Each day I'd listened to the recording of *Jonathan Livingston Seagull,* and each day my spirit had taken wings. I had tried to phone Dr. Brantwood to thank him, but couldn't reach him. I knew it was just a gift—perhaps even a courtly disclaimer—but in spite of my efforts to subdue its buoyancy, my heart remained stubbornly betrothed to an illogical euphoria.

Thursday morning was spent in my carrel at Edwards. At noon, Adrianne and Warren dropped by to see me. They'd just arrived home from Los Angeles that morning. It was unusual to see Warren with Adrianne in Edwards. In fact, it was the first time in our four-plus years of university that I'd seen them together in the library.

"Hi, my lovely Dianosaurus," Adrianne greeted. "Still manning your post, I see. So glad you're not extinct, yet. I've so much to tell you."

"Hello, Adrianne. Hello, Warren. Glad you're both back safely. Did you have an exciting trip?"

"Sensational," Adrianne enthused. "Surely you must have felt the vibrations here, Diana?"

"Come to think of it, I did notice the earth reeling on its axis one or two times." That my world had strayed from its regular orbit was not the Eatons' fault, but perhaps a half-truth was better than no truth at all.

"Thank you for the Little Prince pin, Warren," I said warmly, rising and extending my hand. "It's a very special gift to me. One I will always cherish."

"Glad you like it," Warren said. "Addy told me Exupéry was one of your favorite authors, so when I saw the pin in Seattle last summer, I knew it had your name on it." The realization that Warren had bought the pin for me in the summer gave me something of a start. I wouldn't have expected him to think of me when he was on vacation.

At five thirty I left the library, intending to walk home as usual, but instead of entering the dirt path by the river, I found myself unaccountably standing in Room 39 in Arts. Distractedly looking at the barren table and empty chairs, I wondered how I got there. Had I subconsciously intended to make the pilgrimage?

Disturbed to find my mental processes clearly unreliable, I took myself firmly in hand. A gift was a gift. It wasn't a declaration of intent. Most likely it was Dr. Brantwood's way of saying goodbye. The Neil Diamond recording was just his polite way of easing us both out of a difficult relationship. Having restored some reason to my unruly feelings, I began to feel more in control. I was, after all, a mature and reasonable human being, not a giddy schoolgirl expecting a gallant knight to ride up and rescue me.

The door to the vacated classroom shut with a firmly resolute sound. Dr. Brantwood walked to the table and dropped his briefcase on the wooden surface with a solid thump. Folding his graceful hands together on the top of his black case, he surveyed me, a veiled expression in his casually noncommittal eyes.

"Will you allow me to make love to you tonight, Miss Collings-gate?" he asked matter-of-factly, with no more emotion than if he'd been asking me to turn in a term paper.

My mind in total disarray, I faced him silently. The white image of the austere lady in the mirror rose menacingly before me. I shut my eyes in a frantic attempt to dispel the pale semblance.

"Please," I said. "I'm fully aware you have no such intention."

The serene eyes regarding me with such distressing ease remained calmly unaffected.

"What do I have then, my queen?" he asked, leaning casually back against the blackboard, arms folded.

The word 'queen' struck quick pride. "You must understand," I said. "I realize I behaved foolishly . . . immaturely. I've never done that before. Didn't know I would."

Dr. Brantwood raised his eyebrows. "You mean with a prof?"

"No! Fainted."

"You mean while—"

"While nothing," I interjected. "I'm trying to explain. I had no intention of giving offense—of slighting your reputation."

"I see. You think it's all right to sleep on a man's couch, so long as he doesn't."

"Please. I'm trying to apologize."

"Yes. So I've noticed. But you are aware most gentlewomen faint from tight corsets and not restrictive principles? It's a question of not enough air, not one of not enough morality."

A perplexing, openly mischievous smile caressed the corners of his lips as he spoke. My own mouth was clamped shut in defiance of my need to exonerate myself from the charges of dramatically illustrated, self-generated hysteria.

Regarding me thoughtfully for a moment, Dr. Brantwood asked with respectful but frank curiosity, "Is being alone with me so dis-quieting to your religious soul?"

"No, Dr. Brantwood," I said, forcing my mouth to speak. "Not to my religious soul."

"Then what? Many decent people indulge the proclivity of hold-ing one another in their arms." Dr. Brantwood's eyes scanned me with unrestrained interest. He showed no embarrassment, but while he spoke his mind with charming, even seductive ease, his words vibrated through me like the systematic striking of a drum.

What did he expect of me? What? As if in answer, as I stood in silence trying desperately to regain my self-composure, from deep in the wellspring of my admiration for this unfathomable man, a new empathy was born. With the eyes of the self-contained lady in the mirror coldly calculating my worth, I looked down at Dr. Brantwood's clean, unmarked hands. There was a salty taste in my mouth.

"I don't know what you wish to know," I said quietly. "I can only offer what I know." My voice sounded pitifully inadequate, like that of a small child asking to touch another planet. I felt so exposed—so vulnerable.

"And that is?" Gathering my courage, I faced him, the words slipping softly to my lips.

"I . . . love you . . . that's all . . . I love you." They were humble, wobbling words, but with their saying, Dr. Brantwood's detached indifference vanished.

"Diana," he said warmly. Stepping swiftly around the table, he drew me into his arms. No longer under the necessity of secluding my love, I returned his embrace. With the wonder of sharing, awe came, wreathing my body and spirit in a dawning, tremulous joy. Dr. Brantwood's eyes were shining into mine with a warm, love-filtered light. Touching his lips tenderly to mine, he wrought the miracle. For the moment, the tyrant time was dethroned, and I didn't question the capricious trick nature might be playing. Dr. Brantwood knew of my love for him, his arms and lips reconciling all I had ever yearned to know of his regard for me.

With his loving touch, the aridity of my life dispersed as mist in sunlight, and I felt as though I was passing with it, was being blended by the presence and influence of one wonderful man, into all the feeling and felt things of the universe. In the harmony of the moment, I was becoming one with his world, when I realized he wished me to return to an independent existence, to leave his universe. But for the time I stood next to him, my head on his shoulder, his arms securing me gently to him.

Chapter Thirty-One

If there when grace dances, I should dance.[67]

—W. H. Auden: *Whitsunday*

For those taking the full-term, January and February were the busiest months, as well as the coldest. Loaded down with books and heavy winter clothing, students and staff looked like roundly contoured robots struggling through equally round drifts of snow.

Despite a severe cold spell in the second week in February, classes continued as scheduled. Adrianne took it upon herself to instruct Warren to drive me to and from the university during the worst siege of the weather. Always amenable, Warren didn't appear upset at having his time managed for him. As for myself, Warren's undemanding company was welcome. Although not as verbal as his sister, he was like her in many ways, and I liked him better for the similarity. Even so, there were notable differences. Where Adrianne was always late, Warren was always on time. Promptly at seven every morning, his red BMW would pull into the driveway at Collingsgate.

Aunt Amy had taken to getting up to see me off, but it wasn't to facilitate my departure. Her interest was to check on my young 'swain', as she called Warren. While I explained that Warren was still just a friend, Aunt Amy was dubious enough about his status to want to check for herself every day. When Aunt Amy made up her mind on something, she was hard to convince otherwise. Father just shook his head, thoroughly perplexed by Amelia's formidable mental bastions. Once Aunt Amy took a stance, she held it. I could hear

Dad muttering, "Admirable woman, Aunt Amy. Mind set like a pair of vice grips, but an admirable woman."

The last morning in January, Warren arrived right on time. As we pulled out of the driveway he asked, "Have you picked your date for the Wanita Formal?"

The Wanita Formal was Western's Sadie Hawkin's dance. There was one every spring. Many girls booked their favorite dates months prior to the actual event.

"No," I said. "Hadn't planned on going."

"If you change your mind, Diana, no one's asked me." Warren spoke calmly, but I noticed he held both hands firmly on the steering wheel.

"Not even Janice?"

Warren gave a manly snort. "Especially not Janice. She's been rather busy of late." After a short silence, Warren added, "I'd like to go with you, Diana. Have I waited too long to ask you out?"

Not wishing to hurt Warren's feelings, I nodded with a flicker of regret. Why did others have to be left out? Why couldn't everyone be happy?

"So it's hello goodbye then?"

"No, Warren. We're friends. Friends don't say goodbye."

"Is there someone special, Diana?" One thing about the Eatons, if they wanted to know something, they came right out and asked.

"Yes," I said, "there is."

"Anyone I know?"

"You might," I evaded.

"Are you asking him to the dance?"

"No." Warren was pushing. Until now, he'd always been so comfortable to be around. I did like him. Actually, I thought the world of him.

"Would you do me a huge favor, then?" he asked, turning the car smoothly into the university drive. He had a right to ask. I did owe him for the rides to and from university.

"Sure, Warren," I said, glad to return his service. He was a wonderful young man.

"Would you let me take you to Wanita? I'd like to think you went somewhere special with me." It was a gallant request, so like Warren. As it was a matter of friendship, I decided to accept.

"Sure thing, Warren. Why shouldn't friends go to a dance together? I'll be glad to go with you." There, I thought triumphantly. Ginny would be proud of me. Adrianne might construe more in the arrangement than was intended, but Adrianne would put her own spin on the world no matter how the axis tilted.

"Great," was all Warren said.

Three days later, on the night of the formal, Warren's red sports car again drove into the drive. Aunt Amy had apparently been watching for him from the front window. "Diana! Your young swain is here," she called up the stairs to me.

"He's a friend. Not a swain," I called back down, knowing the words would fall on deaf ears.

Looking quickly into the mirror to see if everything was straight, I went down. Ginny insisted that I wear my green Chiffon dress and the lace mantilla. I felt a little foolish in the mantilla, but decided it did look attractive. Also, I had no wish to offend Ginny by not cherishing such an exquisite gift.

At the entrance, I gathered my coat and pulled on my boots. As it was Friday night, Father was marking as usual at the university. Ginny was out for the evening with Neal. It was a relief to know Warren wouldn't have to run the gamut of both Aunt Amy and Ginny. As it turned out, Warren was not at all perturbed by Aunt Amy's obvious interest. Indeed, by the time we left, he and Aunt Amy were getting on so well they were practically betrothed.

Outside, I gave Warren a grateful smile. "Thanks for handling that so well, Warren. Aunt Amy thinks—"

"Aunt Amy doesn't think anything I might not be tempted to think myself, given a little help, Diana."

Warren opened the car door for me, and I climbed in. It always surprised me how normal it felt to be with Warren. We hadn't seen a lot of one another, but gradually we'd become acquainted. For the first time, I realized I held a very real sisterly affection for him.

Even in awkward situations as this one, Warren was remarkably at ease.

To keep the evening from becoming too searchingly personal, I asked, "So what made you decide to take Physical Education? Was it your sports scholarship?"

"Yes and no," Warren said. "It was the scholarship and the fact that I'm an empiricist."

"How do you mean?"

"I believe physical experience is the source of knowledge. That makes me an empiricist. As an empiricist, I have no other option but to take physical education."

I laughed. That was just the kind of illogically-logical remark an Eaton would make.

"Adrianne coming with Nelson tonight?" I asked. Now that Adrianne and I didn't have any classes together, I was seeing her less on campus.

"Yes," Warren said, noticeably concerned. "I think she'd rather not, but she asked him before Christmas, so she had to keep her word. I think Addy wishes she had asked John Cairn."

I mentally raised my eyebrows, but didn't say anything.

Warren eased his car into the one remaining spot behind the Phys Ed gym where the dance was being held. He opened the red car door for me with friendly courtesy and led the way into the dance. So much had changed in the past month. If I'd been attending a dance with someone as nice as Warren a few months ago, I would have felt excited. Now, I felt as though all the dances in the world couldn't compare with the new and powerful feelings stirring within me for Dr. Brantwood.

The band was playing "Knock Three Times" when we entered. I looked around for Adrianne but couldn't see her. Then my heart caught with unexpected delight. Dr. Brantwood was standing by the entrance. I'd told him I'd be going to the dance with Warren but never expected to see him there. He must have been asked to be one of the faculty reps. Realizing Warren knew nothing of my feelings for Dr. Brantwood, I looked away.

Warren took my hand for the first dance. It was a jive, "Rockin Robin." Perhaps due to his athletic training, Warren was a smooth dancer. We didn't talk, but just enjoyed the rhythm and the music. As of yet, there was still no sign of Adrianne or Nelson.

The second dance was another rock rhythm. I had learned to do most of the modern dances plus the Latin dances at Young Women's. I found myself wondering why had I stuck so severely to my studies. It was fun dancing with Warren. He did a mean rock and roll; although, I couldn't lie to myself. I knew everything and everyone at the dance, including Warren, had become suddenly wonderful because Dr. Brantwood was there. It was the well-known principle of 'projected virtue' operating.

Just before the jive ended, Adrianne and Nelson showed up. They came over as soon as they spotted us. Grinning, Adrianne lifted the edge of my Mantilla with one small hand and dropped me a broad curtsy.

"Senorita Diana Deloros d'Estralita de La Vega," she addressed me with exaggerated formality. "I am honored." Not waiting for my reply, Adrianne leapt to her feet. Clicking her fingers like castanets, she twirled and stamped, her arms and posture expressive of a fiery flamenco dancer. Eyes glowing with passion, Adrianne danced joyously, half singing, half chanting, "'Aye Torrero, she is here! Aye, Matador.'"[68]

Warren, picking up his cue, extended his arm to Adrianne and added, "'And I will be Numero Uno, Torero fino. She'll dream tonight of me.'" Both sang the chorus in raucous abandon, stamping around one another, "'O lay, O lay, O lay, Vainga, Viva El Matador.'"[69] Warren, not to be outdone by Adrianne, stomped and postured like a proud Spanish Toreador. Adrianne, changing roles, ran menacingly at the imaginary cloak in Warren's hand.

It was then I noticed that Warren was dressed entirely in black, right to his smart black satin tie with the gold pin. Surprisingly, he looked natural in the color. Together he and Adrianne were causing quite a display, arousing no little interest on the part of other students. Adrianne always enjoyed the spotlight. Throwing in their support, the band, perhaps in playful continuation of the Eaton duo's charming dance exhibition, struck up the Latin rhythm "La Bamba."

Standing stiffly straight and extending his arm toward me like George Chakiris, the actor who played Bernardo, Maria's brother in *West Side Story*, Warren gave me his hand and led me onto the floor, his bearing befitting a true matador. This socially smooth, suave mystique was a side to Warren I'd never seen, never would have suspected. He was Adrianne's brother, but he'd always seemed so laid back and casual. The evening had supplied some major surprises in more ways than one.

After the set, I noticed Nelson Cruthers standing laconically to the side, a visibly bored expression on his face. Seeing my glance, he shrugged and led Adrianne over to chat with some other students. It was obvious he and Adrianne would sit the next set out. Adrianne would be disappointed to miss out on the dancing. It didn't bode well for their evening together.

After "La Bamba," the band played "Besame Mucho," followed by "Tea For Two," and then "Let's Twist Again, Like We Did Last Summer." As with the Latin dances, Warren had no difficulty making his tall, broad body conform to the dance; although, he himself laughed at his efforts. The set ended with Elvis's ever-popular "Hound Dog."

The third dance set was about to begin when Janice, looking glamorous and feline in body-hugging black silk, commandeered Warren. For the first two dances of the set, I was content to sit quietly, watching the other dancers. It was tempting to look in Dr. Brantwood's direction, but I managed to refrain. Just as the third dance of the set began, Karen Carpenter singing "Close To You," the ballroom became inexplicably still, and I listened with new understanding to the words "Just like me, they long to be, close to you."[70]

I felt more than saw Dr. Brantwood's approach. Drawing near, he offered me his hand. The movement was easy without affectation.

"We could dance in the modern style without touching, if you would prefer, senorita," he said, the corners of his mouth begging a grin.

Accepting his hand, I shook my head. "Any style will do, so long as you put your arms around me," I whispered, surprised at my overtly bold response.

A smile spread across his face. "I'll see what I can do," he said.

On the dance floor, his hold was relaxed but sure. As we moved together to the music, I couldn't help laughing. Puzzled, his smiling eyes grew wide in pretended concern.

"Do you always find your partners amusing?" he asked, bending his head toward me.

"No," I said. "It's just . . . I'm glad you don't dance as adversarily as you converse."

His laughter bonded us together and we finished the set in silence.

Though I waited the rest of the evening for Dr. Brantwood to reclaim me, he didn't come. Janice was intent on securing Warren for every dance she could, which was puzzling in the light of Warren's comment earlier in the evening. Janice was apparently very interested in him. Daphne Englesby was also at the dance, vying openly with Janice for first dibs on Warren. Between the two of them eager to intercept Warren at every opportunity, I spent a good number of dances sitting out.

It really didn't bother me, as I had no interest in dancing with strangers. A few of the young men did break the 'girl's-choice' rule and ask me. Dr. Banescroft's son, Allan, introduced himself during the second half of the evening. His friendly manner was an appreciated change from the scrutinizing glances of Daniel Creighton who attended anthropology with me. Danny's antiseptic manner put me in mind of an immaculate lab tech peering through his microscope at a specimen on a slide. I wondered why he bothered to ask me to dance.

Beyond this, my impressions of these strangers and theirs of me didn't matter. My heart was with a tall, slim man who did not come. As the Wanita Formal neared its close, what was at first only a vague apprehension, became an urgent need to know if Dr. Brantwood was somehow offended. Certainly he was free to choose his company. He had no binding commitment to me. Father often plucked a rose and discarded it; selection was part of progress. Still, I couldn't reconcile my heart to his absence.

At ten to eleven my composure failed. I could no longer remain at the dance without knowing. Catching Warren away from Janice, we danced a set together.

"It's been fun, Warren. Really. But I have to leave. There's something I have to do."

Warren looked at me closely, honest concern in his eyes. "Glad to help you do it, whatever it is. I'm about danced out myself," he offered gallantly.

"No. Thanks, Warren," I said, ashamed to leave him at the dance. "I have to do this alone. It's . . ."

For the second time that evening, Warren amazed me with his Adrianne-like perceptivity.

"Yes. I saw him leave. Are you sure you can handle this, Diana?"

"Yes, Warren. I can handle it." In point of fact, I wasn't certain, but needed to muster sufficient poise to attempt.

"Well, if you're sure," Warren said. "But I'll be glad to stick around and give you a lift home. You might need me to defend your honor."

I gave Warren a grateful hug. "Thank you, Warren. You're a sport. Dad's working late tonight. I'll catch a ride home with him, if I need it." Warren nodded gravely, and we parted.

Putting the lace mantilla over my head, I grabbed my coat at the garment check and hastily exited with as much grace as tensed nerves would allow. Determined, I began to walk toward The Manse, but long before the sound of the orchestra died in the distance I was running, my feet flying as they had on that day in November.

I opened the front door of The Manse and proceeded rapidly across the dimly lighted foyer. The heels of my shoes clicked hollowly on the marble flooring, the formless sound reprimanding me for trespassing. In the pensive dusk of the vestibule, Dr. Brantwood's lights were not visible. However, from the sound of the music floating down the hallway, there was little doubt that he'd returned to his room.

Reaching his door, I stood marveling. Dr. Brantwood was not playing the grand. Instead there was an orchestral arrangement of "Granada" on the turntable. The rhythmic music did much to calm me, but still I hesitated. I knew it was a risky thing I was doing. I had no right to presume upon Dr. Brantwood's company at this late hour, mutual affection notwithstanding. Even so, I needed to know his mind; needed him to know my love was loyal.

There was no honorable retreat. Nothing to do but knock and hope he would understand. I knocked, the sound echoing all too loudly along the corridor. Momentarily, the door opened and Dr. Brantwood stood silhouetted in the muted light. My mouth moved in explanation, but no words came.

"Diana," he said, his eyes smiling warmly into mine. Stepping toward me, he took me in his arms, and gracefully guided me to the vibrant strains of "Granada." The lift to my heart when I'd first seen him at the dance returned in full measure bringing with it a feeling of sweet belonging. When the music ended, I stepped back from him, breathless but content.

"You're not annoyed," I said, relieved. "You left and I thought—"

Dr. Brantwood gathered me again into his arms. Feeling the comforting warmth of him, I reached my own arms up to encircle his neck and laid my head on his shoulder. Heedless of time, we stood together in the doorway. When I could bring myself to part from him, I again stepped back.

"Goodnight, my love," I whispered softly.

"Goodnight?" he repeated, bending toward me with a remonstrating gesture. "Is my moon goddess slipping back into the night sky so soon?"

"I must. It's late. Too late to be . . ." I nodded goodnight, turned, and walked quickly down the hall.

Before I reached the top of the stairs at the end of the long corridor, the imprecating strains of *Egmont Overture* reached me, breaching the silence. The notes were familiar, but the music had no dynamics;

it was completely devoid of expression. In an instant, all the chaffing taunts ever directed to me seemed bundled into that purposely bland sound. Baffled, but determined, I retraced my steps to the still open doorway. In the room, Dr. Brantwood sat playing at the grand.

"I'm not a fake," I said quietly. Dr. Brantwood stopped playing and looked hard at me.

"I see you are not," he said seriously. "A fake would have stayed." He took his coat from the alcove and closed the door. "I think Lord Gordon better see you safely home," he directed gently.

"So that's what the initial G stands for?" I dared to ask, all wounded pride dispelled.

"Greensleeves is what the G should stand for," he tossed back, giving me one of his droll, but thoughtful looks.

"No," I prompted. "Is Gordon your Christian name?"

"G could stand for many things," he said. "It could be gadfly, or gladiator, or gambler."

"You are none of these," I responded, picking up the game. "But it could be gypsy, or gallant, or great." The flight of fancy melted away on the wings of a more serious thought. "Or it could stand for God."

"Or godless," he parried easily. "But what would you like *your* G to stand for, Diana?"

Looking into his eyes, there was only one response.

"Gordon."

The smile on Dr. Brantwood's face was replaced by an inquiring seriousness.

"Gordon Lawrence," he said kindly. "Didn't you know?"

I shook my head, blinking to keep back the tears that threatened to tumble to the surface in a sudden release of feeling. Breaking into laughter, Dr. Brantwood looked at me appraisingly.

"You loose woman," he said with gentle, but genuine surprise. "You mean to say you spend time with me, let me put my arms around you, kiss you—even, heaven forbid—converse with you, and you don't know my Christian name? What will your bishop think?"

"I don't think—" I stopped, realizing Gordon was baiting me, however playfully.

His laughter continued with a richness that draped my world in velvet. When it subsided, he said amenably, "Never mind, my paragon. It's just like you not to ask. Silent Selene. Moon Sylph. That's my Diana."

"I'm not loose, Gordon," I said firmly.

"Diana, my Queen. If any man knows you're not a loose woman, I would be that man. While your real condition isn't lethal, Lord Byron knows I've done what I can to prevent it."

"Gordon." I laughed. "You've been reading too many English novels."

"Diana, Diana." He turned to me, an appraising look in his eyes. "You're as lovely as your name. My Diana." He said my name appreciatively, as if tasting the sound, then added reflectively, "It is my mother's name."

"Oh? I'm delighted," I said sincerely. "And were you named for your father?"

"Of course," Gordon said, without missing a beat. "That's what the L stands for in Lawrence. Love for Diana." He looked at me fondly. Affirmed, but also a little unnerved by the intimate earnestness of Gordon's straightforward avowal, I countered in kind.

"I was named in spite of my father. I mean, I was called Diana Lynn Esther because Father wanted to call me Mehitabel Hepzibah, and Mother wouldn't let him. We had a stalwart ancestor called Mehitabel, and Hepzibah is biblical. Father wanted us to have upstanding names to remind us of who we are."

"And are you reminded?" Gordon asked, his voice low, his eyes searching mine in that curiously probing way of his.

"Yes. I am," I answered, daring to return Gordon's gaze with equal vigor. His lips smiled briefly. Perceptive eyes inviting, he bent his head, kissing me gently.

"Still reminded?" he asked softly.

"Still reminded," I heard myself respond from far away.

"Still now?" he prompted, taking me in his arms and kissing me with an intensity even the most uninitiated could not misunderstand.

I rested my forehead on his chest, heart racing, my arms still around his neck.

"Gordon . . . ."

"Okay," he laughed. "Passion stores well on chilly nights. But walk close beside me. I'll keep your reputation safe, and you can keep me warm."

His arm around my shoulder, we walked down the steps and across the parking lot to the road. The three miles home faded too quickly and soon the man himself was gone. At the gate, under the overhanging trellis, I stood alone in the moonlight, watching his tall figure recede in the distance, as he walked back to the university.

With Gordon's commanding presence no longer beside me, an overwhelming sense of our differences unexpectedly cascaded down upon me, like the swiftly falling petals of roses in a storm. *He has chosen his way,* I said firmly to myself. *Respect requires—*

The self-deceiving thought collapsed in a deflated heap on the rigid, rock bench. The stone was mercilessly cold to my touch.

In that moment I knew Adrianne's accusations were true. I was trying to people an artificial world with flesh and blood entities. My nice control was a defense. At the dance, and after, when Gordon had held me warm against him, I had felt the forces of our lives drawing us together, even while pushing us apart. Most importantly, in those brief wonderful moments, I had come to know the profoundness of love. Gordon had addressed my entire being, and I had awakened and answered him, no longer a naive, immature girl, but a woman: a woman astounded at the dimension and marvel of her own created desires, a woman bewildered at the powerful wealth of emotion Gordon's love engendered.

Chapter Thirty-Two

A thousand fantasies
Begin to throng into my memory.[71]

—John Milton: *Il Penseroso*

Monday following Wanita, I met Adrianne at SUB lounge. Not ready to talk about my developing relationship with Gordon, and hoping to forestall whatever Machiavellian conclusions Adrianne might be construing, I asked, "So how did the evening go with you and Nelson?"

"Just fine! Nelson neatly set Darwin's theory of evolution back two million years. Perhaps in another two million he'll crawl out of the swamp."

"Darwin?"

Adrianne eyed me warily. "You know who I mean."

"That bad?"

"Worse. I knew I shouldn't have gone to Wanita with Nelson. But that's okay. I gave him the frozen rat's heart from my Bugs lab. He got the message."

"You gave Nelson a dissected rat's heart? The real thing?"

"I did. I popped it in a box and presented it to him this morning."

"It does beat a Dear John letter," I acknowledged, looking with respect at the nonchalant young woman beside me. We walked together in silence across campus, my mind intrigued by what Adrianne might pull next. I didn't have long to wait to find out. Coming to Edwards, Adrianne caught my hand in hers and holding it to her heart, raucously began singing the chorus from the song "People Will Say We're in Love."

"By the bye, Sly Di, did you enjoy your tango with The Bramblybriar? Need me to pull any brambles out of your hide or pride?"

I laughed. "No. No life-threatening punctures."

"You're sure of this?" Adrianne asked. It would have been more honest to confide in Adrianne, but the time didn't feel right.

"You know, Diana," Adrianne said, "I've always urged you to loosen up, but—"

"Yes," I interrupted, laughing. "'Keep one foot in Zion. But do a little tap dance now and then in the world!' Did I get it right?"

"You got it right, Eliza. But when I say tap dance, I don't meant slum in public. You do know Professor Aslan Higgins, or whoever you think Bramblybriar is under that wolf-shepherd skin of his, is not a tame lion."

"One dance with Dr. Brantwood isn't slumming. And how can you mix up *Chronicles of Narnia*, *My Fair Lady*, and *Uncle Remus* all in the same breath?"

"Easy, I just open my mouth and see what comes out."

Adrianne was nothing if not honest, her translucent personality just one of her enviable charms. I stood perplexed at what to say to this vexingly insightful, if overly inventive, friend of mine. Seeing my dismay, Adrianne smiled contentedly. Dropping her chin in the prizefighter stance of readiness, she peered at me speculatively, while polishing the nails of her right hand on her red cardigan.

"See you at Tiffany's for breakfast, Diorama. And don't forget to bring along your pepper spray. Our campus seems to be having an outbreak of sheep-loving lions." Adrianne turned and struck off for her next class. Relieved that was over, I turned my steps to my next class, also.

As is the norm on any large campus, once a class is disbanded contacts between students are few, and as expected I didn't see many of the students from English 550 in second term. Adrianne would pop by my carrel in Edwards when the spirit moved her. Kumari and Mr. Stewart frequented the library, as did Lois Weiss.

Most importantly, I continued to see Dr. Brantwood. Most Saturday afternoons we would spend our time together walking by the river. My whole week's activities were becoming exquisitely attuned to those special times with Gordon. In those first warm weeks of love's awakening, if I'd evaluated my feelings honestly, I would have been cautioned by the rapturous anticipation that filled my mind and spirit waiting for those precious moments with Gordon. In my heart I could not condemn our continued association. My love would not be censored; it was so new, so fresh, and so wonderful.

What could be wrong? Ours was an honest, open-minded association: the mutual attraction of two mature individuals. No one would be hurt. Without my being aware of it, I was becoming more than slightly adept at rationalizing.

It was early morning, Father's special time of day. We walked side by side a few steps apart. I could always tell Father's footprint. It was heavier in the toe, due to the extra push just before lift-off, and it was always pointed straight ahead.

Looking at Father's footprints in the snow, I could hear him saying, "Why walk down the road of life blindfolded when you can keep your eyes open and save your shins a lot of bruises?"

That was Dad. With Father it was always *plan ahead*. Plan ahead had become the 'Collingsgate Catechism.' Thinking of Father's testy tirades against those who were determined to go through life "accruing interest on tomorrow's sorrow," I felt an inward surge of affection for the colorful, eminently sane man who was my father.

Perhaps he was right. Perhaps too many people *did* "clamber up fool's hill with buckets over their heads." Did I have one over mine? I hoped not. Father wouldn't condone anyone in even a semi-conscious state failing to consider the consequences of their acts. "Look before you leap, or leap at your peril," he would mutter sadly when observing the shambles of some of the lives around him. It was a sobering thought.

It wasn't my custom to walk to the university with Father. Our individual schedules didn't leave much time to spend together, so I valued the rare moments alone with him, even when he was silently engaged in his own thoughts. Rounding the corner of Admin behind Father, I saw Gordon coming down the bare, broad steps. He gave no sign of surprise on meeting Professor Collingsgate and myself together. Although we had never talked of it after the encounter in Admin, I assumed Gordon knew of our relationship by now. Father also sighted Dr. Brantwood and waited for him on the walk.

"I understand my daughter had the honor of being numbered among your flock last term, Dr. Brantwood," Father greeted him affably.

"I did try to get that idea across to Diana, Professor Collingsgate," Gordon said warmly, extending a chilly, ungloved hand first to Father and then to myself.

"I sympathize," Father concurred. "At home we have to rope and tie Diana up before she will condescend to learn a thing." Between these two men, both of whom I loved, it was a standoff. They knew it, also. Seeing Father and Dr. Brantwood grinning wickedly, I smiled with them.

"Do you suppose, Gordon, we could persuade Diana to leave us in peace long enough to go over the panel discussion on *Truth or Myth*?" Father asked.

"Perhaps," Gordon said, the warm light from his eyes encircling me securely. "If you have a piece of that rope you use, there's a good sturdy oak at the back of Arts."

"I'm going. I'm going," I said, laughing.

Alone in my carrel, preparing a paper for anthropology, I paused to rest my eyes and gazed out the west window toward the mountains. The snow-capped summits stood starkly outlined against the pale sky. "Anyone can dream," Father would often say. "Dare to do."

With a great resolve of will, I went back to work. In half an hour, I was again looking out the window, but this time not as far as the mountains. With the center green mantled in piling snow and the barren trees no longer sheltering students from the northern winds, the campus looked whitewashed. A high banking drift of snow had formed white peaks along the walk by Arts, making the theater entrance impassible. The Arts bench, on which I had first encountered Gordon's amazing drive to know my mind, was nearly buried under a blanket of white. *Snow towers of the mind*, I thought.

Looking left between Arts and Admin where Father and I had met Gordon earlier, I could see the oak tree stalwartly guarding the lonely outpost. As I considered the winter scene, the stretch of ruffled snow began to look more like an expanse of white-capped water. Similarly, the lower branch of the oak appeared to transmute into the gangplank of a ship. Father and Dr. Brantwood stood on the edge of the wooden arm jutting over the freezing water. Bowing formally to one another, the two men were exchanging artful pleasantries, each trying craftily to trip the other off the plank into the frigid water below.

I had to blink twice to dispel the illusion. Then I laughed. There was no need for concern. Drs. Collingsgate and Brantwood were well matched.

Three hours later, once again at my carrel after attending my first two classes, I felt a familiar gaze upon me and knew without looking that Gordon was near. He came to my carrel and looked down with interest at the large green book in my hand.

"I'm reading Margaret Mead's case study on violence in primitive cultures," I advised.

"And?"

"And I suspect violent societies are not all primitive."

"Undoubtedly there will always be societies that prefer war to peace," Dr. Brantwood granted. "You don't have to be primitive to delight in bloodshed."

"I mean," I said, "this particular society mistakes vice for virtue. They believe violence expresses affection."

"You suggest they're fond of violence, as a pig is fond of its wallow, or a nun is fond of her cloister?" Gordon parried.

Puzzled, I didn't answer.

"Would you rather the nun thought her fitting habitat the mire and the pig resided in the nunnery?"

I looked at Gordon leaning with such charming ease against the carrel and a question worried my mind. The bantering light left

Gordon's eyes. Glancing reflectively into my own, he bent over and kissed my forehead gently.

"You should never frown, Professor Collingsgate," he said warmly. "You're justifiably proud of your father, and he of you."

After he left, I felt the place his lips had marked with my fingers. It was as if I would always feel his kiss there—tender, approving. I felt a burgeoning impatience, a fervent desire to throw caution to the wind. It was an unworthy feeling, and I pushed it away. Even as I did, I knew I couldn't long delay the reckoning that must come. In my mind, in my body, in my spirit, I was beginning to know the yearning of mortality: the need of the flesh to become one with the beloved with no separation in cell or sinew.

I still knew little of Gordon's life—of the experiences that had helped to shape his mind and thought. His bantering words filtered into my mind, *Would you rather the nun thought her fitting habitat the mire, and the pig resided in the nunnery?* Why did this earnest man press so hard against the parameters of my reason? Was it only his mind soaring? Or was he asking me to consider carefully the path ahead of us?

The cumulative effect of generations is generally more significant than the experience of a single life. This I knew. Yet Dr. Gordon Brantwood's single life was having more impact upon my own than all I had ever read about or learned from the myriad lives of generations of noble men and women. I would need to love him wisely, indeed.

As the days passed and the steady gray somberness of February gave way to the turbulent youth of March, I found myself more and more in Gordon's company. The man, who a few short months before had been a stranger, was the single most important force in my life. And while I knew I was borrowing on the promises of hedonism, every vital instinct I possessed longed to be with Gordon, to fill every moment with his presence, and to live for him alone. He had become so much more than an inspiring intellectual, a detached symbol of academic prowess. He was a whole, unique, responsive human being. The challenge he offered now was not merely to my mind, but to my entire being. He made me love life as I had never loved it before, and I yearned to take up his banner and cause and make his dreams mine.

I could no longer rationalize my love for Gordon as only deep respect. I knew it was worlds more than that. It involved my whole being, my goals, my aspirations, my ideologies. Most particularly it involved my theology. Whether I willed it or not, I knew I would soon have to choose between love and belief. With Gordon there would be no halfway. He had been honest with me from the beginning—urging me, compelling me to come to terms with our differences in looking at life.

At no time had he deceived me or sought to do so. While I hadn't always understood his approach, he had from the onset addressed our association with absolute integrity. He wasn't asking for half my love. He was asking for all I had to give, but he wanted it given with no regrets. Even knowing this, I closed my ears to the wise small voice within, telling myself I was a mature individual and in no danger of falling under a personal Babylon.

The spirited, impetuous days of March did little to still the enraptured song of love in my heart. As boisterous as the spring days, inside my harvest was full and rich, a joyous open-hearted hymn—my whole being singing in harmony to the sublime strains when Gordon was near. With all the ethereal madness of the poets, I knew love.

Chapter Thirty-Three

In what ethereal dances,
By what eternal streams.[72]

—Edgar Allan Poe: *To One in Paradise*

The first two weeks in April, Gordon had to leave campus for a short lecture series in Toronto. In an effort to regain my footing and bring some order to my feelings, I found myself spending more of my free time at home.

The poems in my hands were a total surprise. The work of a mature mind, the written words graced the page with the poise of elegant swans. It wasn't a hoax; it was Virginia's handwriting. She had a highly personalized writing style. My focus kept returning to one simply stated but engaging poem that Ginny had written about Mother and Father, her written images riveting my attention.

A lady, radiant and young
Walked up the aisle in blue
And stood beside my father there
While whispering a silent prayer
Then softly said, "Oh, yes. I do."

Her lacy veil fell to her feet
And fluttered as they raced
Across the chasms of the past
Until they entered at long last
The dreams of "I love you." [73]

"Virginia Elizabeth, these are good. They have . . . vision. I never knew you wrote."

"I do," Ginny confessed happily. "Neal likes them, too. But he likes everything I do."

"When did you start writing?"

"After Momma died. It helped."

"Thanks for letting me read them. I didn't know you had a secret life."

Ginny laughed. "Neal said the same about you, Diddi."

"Oh."

"Neal said underneath that gray flannel reserve you always wear, there's real silk. He said you ought to wear your inside on your outside more. Let others know what a nice person you are." Ginny took her poems from my hands and regarded me with sisterly affection.

"You will, won't you, Diana? Father will need you when I'm gone." Impulsively, Ginny threw her arms around me and laid her head on my shoulder.

"I think you're a queen," she said earnestly. "A sky queen, just like your namesake." Letting go of me, Ginny took her favorite place in the kitchen rocker and wrapped her arms around her knees.

"Lately, you're even quieter than usual. I'll bet you're having a perfectly fascinating affair."

I looked with new respect at the petite lady opposite me.

"Come on, open up," she enticed. "Let's hear all the delicious details. The guys at school must be mad about you. They probably all carry stolen snapshots taped to their hearts."

A white visage appeared starkly in my mind's eye at Ginny's innocent words. As I stared at the unresponsive mental image of myself, I knew it was not conceit that drove people to exile themselves from others' love.

"I guess we build fences as much to keep ourselves in as to keep others out," I said chastened. Turning away, I walked across the kitchen to the stairwell. Pained at the deception I knew to be in myself, I paused on the landing.

"We'll talk later," I said. I knew we wouldn't. The owl clock on the stairwell knew it, too.

Ginny's candid appraisal of Neal's regard for her was not exaggerated. He proposed, and she accepted. Virginia Elizabeth Ellen Collingsgate and Neal Edward Allen were to be married in the Cardston temple on April sixteenth. A small reception for family and close friends would be held later that day at Collingsgate.

Neal was eight years older than Ginny, but that wasn't important. Father was ten years older than his Elizabeth Kathleen. What was of concern was that Ginny wouldn't be finished with her senior year at Hazelmere High. The wedding couldn't be postponed, as Neal had to leave immediately after finals for McGill to article for his admission to the bar. Consequently, Neal had arranged for Ginny to complete her term work in Toronto by correspondence and take her finals there. Father was firmly set against the idea of Ginny leaving before graduation, but Ginny had made up her mind not to be left behind. And so it was settled. She and Neal would be staying with Aunt Gladys until Neal found a home for them. With Neal's responsible head, that would be a couple of days at most.

With the important day so close, there were many preparations to be completed in the short time before the wedding. Predictably, there was little confusion, as The Jinn switched permanently into her White Tornado identity. Ginny knew what she wanted done, and she knew how she wanted it done. To her credit, her virtuosity with home management shone in the responsible way she prepared for her wedding. Amy Mom was, as usual, loyally at her side, but then Aunt Amy had always been Ginny's right-hand woman. Whatever Ginny had her heart set on, Aunt Amy was involved in up to peak capacity.

It was going to be a hard separation for them both. Ginny had given Aunt Amy's life focus and meaning. I wondered if after the honeymoon Aunt Amy wouldn't be invited to live with Ginny and Neal. In any event, Carlyle would be going. The canary would never survive without his mistress' adoring ministration. The thought occurred to me that if Aunt Amy left, so would Mephistopheles. I didn't mind that so much. The cat and I were on speaking terms most of the time, but just barely. And so the days prior to the wedding passed.

The season of graceful lilies, daffodils, and hyacinths came with the blessing of renewed life. On Good Friday, Gordon called to say he would be detained another two weeks. I knew he couldn't attend the Temple wedding, and in all likelihood wouldn't feel comfortable at the reception, but still the delay in his return wore on my nerves.

Easter Sunday was robed in radiant sunshine, as the recently showered fields unfolded their newly blooming flowers to receive the sun's warmth. The garden space in front of the church already sported a modest array of red tulips, yellow daffodils, and purple crocus. The whole earth was awakening, fresh and new. I could see and appreciate the beauty, and yet this spring it was extraneous—beheld only from the outside. It was as if the season of rebirth was a stranger to me. The thought was troubling.

Inside the chapel that Easter morning, the spirit of the congregation was in harmony with the season, but I could not feel part of the grateful communion. Rather, I felt separated.

The service passed in graceful simplicity. In her place in the alto section of the choir, Ginny, in glowing expectation of her coming marriage, looked as fresh and beautiful as the spring morning itself. It was then I noticed that Spencer Dykie was unusually intent upon his music. At nineteen years of age, Spencer was a mature musician of exceptional talent. He always performed well, but on this morning, his flawless technique lacked heart.

A silent compassion for Spencer welled up inside me. Directly following the closing hymn and benediction, Spencer got up from the organ bench and left the chapel. His organ solo had moved many in the congregation in spite of his perfunctory performance. Is it possible to appreciate a person's music and yet hold no compassion for the person himself? I wondered.

The story of Guarneri, the violin maker, came to mind. Although he was a master craftsman, the great Joseph Guarnerius del Gesu had a difficult time selling his violins. Competition from Stradivari was stiff, popular opinion favoring Strad violins. So while Stradivari grew wealthy and famous, Guarneri lived and died in poverty.

Perhaps it was true. "Murder a man's work and you murder the man." That this could be so wasn't hard to believe. Take from a man the work (or person) he most delights in and sets his heart upon; deny him the right to contribute what he was born to contribute, and you largely murder his reason for living. It was a sobering thought, the implications of which were all too clear.

I thought of Gordon and a lonely defiance welled in my mind. What need had I of religion to make me whole? With Gordon I was more than whole. There was no duplicity. Gordon needed my love, not God. Walking resolutely to the organ, I picked up Spencer's music and placed it in the organ bench. I wanted to believe my act was a genuine response to the sympathetic bond, which at Easter as at Christmas, unites in loving fellowship, all those who believe in the grace and the fathomless mercy of God, but I knew it was not.

Determined to get a grip on myself, I decided to walk home. The fields, softened from the recent rains, were difficult to cross on foot. Fortunately, there was an old road apart from the main artery, whose roughly graveled surface afforded a passable route without the intrusion of heavy traffic. Private and picturesque, the road was lined with poplar trees standing in sturdy dignity, their budding branches stretched in grateful awe toward the heavens. Above the trees, the spring sky was a generous expanse of purest blue with only the occasional ivory cloud.

In the simple honesty of nature, my spiritual agitation subsided—the trees, the sky, the open air, and the greening fields supplying a welcome reprieve. The words from the hymn we had just sung in service popped into my mind. "Earth with her ten thousand flowers . . . all around and all above, bear this record, God is love."[74]

The gentle words momentarily helped restore my perspective. There was no need to escape from my beliefs. What was needed was time. Time to reaffirm myself. Time to look down the road ahead. I thought of Ginny. She would find in marriage to Neal the fulfillment of her most cherished goals. Hers, like Father's, would be a passionately loyal marriage. Ginny didn't need to fear the exchange of private freedom for the more bountiful freedom found in the union of two individuals whose faith was already united. Ginny didn't need to defend or curtail her beliefs. When she pledged her troth, it would be not only to Neal, but to God. Could I do the same? The thought brought bitter comfort.

A yellow monarch fluttered across the road. Following the lightly etched wings, my mind lifted in butterfly fashion from the present into the past. Bridal silk for the moment laid by, Ginny smiled up at me in the pink angora of childhood. Virginia Elizabeth Ellen had been a dimpled, thoroughly affectionate toddler. Seeing her again in her infant charm, I wished I'd spent more time with her. My self-styled life was not intentional neglect. I had no desire to cause Ginny unhappiness, but if my separateness from her as a young woman could be justified, the regret I now felt would remain a testimony against the distance I'd kept from her in childhood.

I opened the worn wooden gate of Collingsgate and entered the long walk through the budding garden. Grateful to be home, I halted by the pond to take one more breath of fresh air and look again at the awakening earth. Spring always brought a certain mixture of feelings, but this spring every vibration of spirit and mind was intensified many times over. Ginny was born in the spring on the second of April. Mother had died in the same month ten years later. Now, once again it was April, and Ginny was leaving. And Gordon . . . Ginny hadn't met . . . might never know Gordon. I leaned against the rough wood of the trellis to steady myself. That one cruel, flagellating thought plummeted down upon me, dispelling all the lightness and beauty of the day.

Time sped swiftly along. Two weeks had passed since the Temple wedding. Ginny, Neal, and Carlyle were established in their own home in Toronto. Ginny, who saw life as a reflection of her own optimistic spirit, phoned Thursday to say she was well pleased with her beautiful new surroundings. For Father, the first few weeks of adjustment to Ginny's absence were a period of many demands on his time. His numerous duties in the garden, as well as a heavy schedule at university finishing the year's work, helped fill his time.

Aunt Amy had left for a visit with her brother Dennis in Colorado, so Father and I were left to fend for ourselves. In point of fact, our fending amounted to little more than getting our own meals when we were hungry, neither of us caring to be around the house now that Ginny and Aunt Amy were absent. Absorbed by personal adjustments, we spent the time largely in our own pursuits.

I hoped Dad found the solace he needed in his private studies. The coming of spring and my deepened love for Gordon had wrought a change in my usual responses. The sanctuary I had always found in books was missing. Indeed, as the spiritual debates with myself continued to intensify, my studies became a burden. The Edwards library, at one time so comforting, seemed a spiritless tomb, the rows of stale books full of lifeless white pages inert as corpses. The atmosphere weighed me down, as if the air itself were trying to suppress my desire to live life on equal terms. With neither refuge nor haven, I spent the days during Gordon's absence wandering directionless and disenchanted along the river.

Chapter Thirty-Four

I saw Eternity the other night,
Like a great ring of pure and endless light,
All calm, as it was bright; [75]

—Henry Vaughan: *Silex Sintillans*

Gordon came home the following Monday. I met him outside Arts at Queen's Bench. *Queen's Bench* was Gordon's name for the place where we'd had our first encounter. Gordon greeted me, hungrily gathering me into his arms, and I knew the time of reckoning could no longer be postponed. Yet still I stalled, confident the delight we felt in each other's company was sufficient reason for delay.

Gordon had the afternoon free and suggested we go for a hike. With study becoming more and more difficult, I was glad to have a reprieve from my books. We walked north along the river and then climbed till we reached the summit of a hill overlooking the river valley. For a while we stood side by side, gazing together in appreciative awe at the lovely view below.

Sensing my happiness, Gordon turned and drew me into his arms. For a timeless moment I felt Gordon's love encircling mine, and the joy that flooded my awareness made me want to kneel on the broad back of the hill and thank God that Gordon lived—that I had come to know him. Then, as Gordon's lips sought mine, the feeling of unity was shattered by doubt, and I drew back.

"Please," I pleaded. "Let everything stay—"

"Attainable?" Gordon supplied, quickly reading the line of my thought.

I looked at him gratefully. "Yes. Attainable. Let the cobwebs cluster over the mantle till the dream is caught so fast it can never escape."

"There's something to be desired in that," he said, with what seemed a tinge of regret in his voice. He looked searchingly across the valley, his arms folded loosely in front of him. "Our dreams— the reality of a personal world—can't be entirely shared. Mostly, we dream alone."

"But surely there are dreams enough to share?" I asked, desperately willing him to retract. It was as though Gordon's words had once again swept me helplessly out to sea on a tiny raft while he remained on the shore.

"There are as many dreams as there are brokers to peddle them," he said without emotion. "But another's dream won't do for your own. It must be your own."

Gordon turned away toward the river. I understood his words. He spoke his mind too clearly for there to be doubt. People may share their goals, but what they do with these goals is up to the individual.

Gordon turned and faced me. His face held a thoughtful frown.

"You put me in mind of a gelding I had that would sooner leap a fence than cross through an open gate," he reflected.

"If your horse had been ordinary, would you remember him now?" I asked.

Gordon ignored the question with characteristic composure. In place of an answer, he offered me his hand, looking at me with tranquil, smiling eyes. Gordon's expressive eyes always tantalized my mind. That moment, as he looked soberly at me, I felt secure, sheltered. Relaxing, I basked in their compassionate depths. Enveloped by his love, I felt renewed, just as I always did resting in the clearing by the river, or pausing under the protective mantle of a summer sky.

Yet there had been times, not entirely forgotten, when Gordon's eyes were a merciless, brittle hazel, reflecting a crucifying intelligence against which I could support myself by only the strongest effort of will. At such times, the gulf between us widened to an almost incontestable breach of natures. Just when I needed to understand him most, I understood him the least.

It was time. Time to know Gordon's mind regarding us.

As if reading my thoughts, Gordon took my hand and led me beside him along the rim of the hill. Walking was easy. Except for the occasional gopher burrow, there was no underbrush or outcroppings of rocks to obstruct the way. Directly in the path of the northern wind, the barren hill was still modestly attired in winter brown. While undeniably plain, it did give a breathtaking view of the valley below—a valley which as a microcosmic cradle of nature, was bursting into new life in an unveiled panorama of spring.

We stopped walking and simply looked. Standing motionless, side by side, gazing out over the valley, Gordon answered all my questions. "Are you afraid I wouldn't love you well enough?" he asked, a new warmth of tenderness in his voice.

With his words, the world of nature became wholly still. In the stillness I knew his love was not in question; he would love me well. As the light of morning releases the dark night, he would love me beyond fear—even beyond myself. How could the success of my personal dreams compare with what he offered? When I didn't speak, Gordon continued, a somewhat hurt tone in his voice.

"Diana," he said softly, "I'm proposing marriage . . . not living in sin."

Surprised, I looked into his eyes. Gordon had just asked me to marry him. It wasn't the proposal I'd envisioned, but it was like Dr. G. L. Brantwood to be matter-of-fact.

Taking my hand and raising my fingers to his lips, he continued with charming irony. "If my aim was to seduce a Christian, I'd choose one who didn't practice her beliefs." He looked at me with unmasked sincerity.

"I love you because you know who you are. You know where you stand on things."

When I still couldn't respond, Gordon tried a different approach, but he was tacking against the wind, with no help from the strongly divergent currents that were dividing me from the desires of my heart. When he spoke again, his voice held an unspoken, but urgent appeal.

"Think, Diana. Use your mind. You have one. I've seen it in your papers. Coupling your life with mine won't destroy some eternal design. Non-believers do marry. In holy union, they beget children just like everyone else. Surely you don't require God's permission to marry me?"

Think? Why would Gordon bring up my need to think in connection with a proposal of marriage? Instead of the heavenly elation, the complete rapture I'd imagined I'd feel from a proposal from this man I loved so deeply and respected so entirely, I felt disoriented—emotionally disabled by the interchange.

Distressed by my inability to respond, my mind flashed back to a picture of myself as a small child taking the bus to Wildemere Elementary. It was six weeks into my first year. The bus driver, Norman Bennett, was a kindly person. Smiling at me over his shoulder one Monday morning, he had asked sociably, "So, Miss Diana. Are you going to learn to think today? Not everyone can do it." Not knowing what to reply, I'd remained silent—as silent as I was now. Realizing Gordon was rightfully expecting some sort of response, I faced him.

"Think means?" I asked, feeling as though my life's blood was somehow being drained away.

"This is the real world, Diana. If you need religious certitude, fine. But use your mind as well."

"You mean use *your* mind."

"No. I'm not asking you to think like me. Just loosen up. Show some flexibility, some tolerance for other opinions." His words, though calmly spoken, hurt.

"I've always respected your opinions," I said softly.

Gordon sighed in exasperation.

"Kant was able to reconcile, 'The starry heavens above . . . the moral law within.'[76] Why is it so difficult for you to contract some working compromise? Kant is at least mildly comprehensible. Kierkegaard is not. Faith that requires the submission of will without clear understanding is not rational or moral."

"You would pit man's reason against God's morality?"

"Of course not. Just don't ask me to deny reason."

"I don't think that's what Kierkegaard had in mind by his leap of faith, Gordon." Helplessly, I felt a numbing coldness engulfing my mind. Gordon jerked his hand through his hair.

"With Soren, it's always the paradox. Don't you see, Diana?" he appealed. "If to become a knight of faith, one must embrace the unknowable, the exercise is absurd."

"Perhaps what the writer meant was that the finite mind cannot comprehend the infinite."

"That's only too obvious. Why grasp at the incomprehensible?" Gordon looked at me, a discerning awareness in his eyes.

Desperately, I wondered who was I to instruct the instructor? Aware of the incongruity, I stumbled on. "As Kierkegaard suggests, Gordon, there may be more than one interpretation for what happened on Mt. Moriah between Abraham and God."

"So what was Kierkegaard's main premise do you think?" I could feel the intensity of Gordon's searching intellect focused in his question; his passion to know my mind clearly visible on his face.

"I'm not sure," I admitted. "Perhaps that there's more than one path to faith. Perhaps as a mortal mind approaches the absolute, that mortal mind also becomes more incomprehensible—more impossible to understand. Kierkegaard never claimed to understand Abraham. Only to admire him."

Gordon stood a few feet away and contemplated me quietly. Dismay and doubt mingled in his expressive eyes. "If not Abraham's path to faith, if Abraham is incomprehensible, then why follow his, or Moses', or any other person's path to Sinai? Why make the pilgrimage at all?"

"The witness of faith comes though the Holy Spirit," I testified softly. "To receive that witness, we have to make a personal investment. A sacrifice." The words sounded preachy, sermonizing. Inwardly, I was groaning under the relentlessness of Gordon's interrogation.

"Give all, get all." Gordon summarized succinctly. He jerked his hand through his hair again, shrugging his shoulders eloquently.

"But to sacrifice reason is not rational, Diana!" he said, his honest eyes searching mine. "Faith built on supposition can only lead to fanaticism. Faith, which leaps beyond reason, is untenable."

Gordon was pushing unusually hard against my mind, his keen intellect willing mine to shed constricting patterns of thinking. I felt my hands growing damp, a severing distance seeping into my perceptions. Even now with a full admission of mutual love between us, the tension that Gordon's focused questions always engendered had not lessened. If anything, as the bonding love between us grew stronger, his demands upon my intellect increased. There were demands upon my spirit and body as well. Each time he held me, the intensity of his embrace grew—his kisses beginning to feel like living fire. I was becoming well acquainted with the exacting demands of the flesh.

Feeling Gordon's desperation for a response, I tried rephrasing. "A contrite heart and a humble spirit is the sacrifice most normally expected. Most of us aren't called upon to sacrifice our kin or our sanity for faith."

Gordon smiled with disbelief. "But if your will is not God's will, what then? Abraham's son and Jarius's daughter were lucky. Captain Jephthah's daughter was not so fortunate. She wasn't reprieved from her fate. Faith is no guarantee."

Gordon's knowledge of the scriptures surprised me. He was a widely read scholar, but I hadn't supposed he'd studied the Bible.

"The Savior tread the winepress—"

Gordon waved my words away with a dismissive gesture of his hand. "Alone," he interrupted quietly. There was a tone of painful frustration never before heard in his voice. His next words, though barely a whisper, held an acid flavor. "Is that what you want, Diana? To go on alone?"

A paralyzing numbness spread through me. At last I knew Gordon's mind, and I knew my heart; yet still I couldn't answer his plea as we both desired. Trying desperately to say the words that would cut the bands of aloneness and join us together at least for mortality, I kept seeing the naked, bleeding hands rising above the rushing waters of the gorge in my dream.

"Would you like to go back?" Gordon asked abruptly, looking wearily across the valley to the pale crystal mountain beyond. His mouth was set in a grim line.

I nodded, my heart heavier than I could ever remember. The wind to our back, we began the long descent to the university. As we retreated, I didn't see the spring-crowned countryside. Instead, I saw the image of Icharus, son of Daedalus, once again plummeting fatally toward the sea, his wings of wax melted from flying too close to the sun.

Back in the ordinariness of everyday pursuits, I had increased cause to regret my lack of responsiveness on the hill. Dropping my pen, I raised my head from my books. With tired eyes and tired mind, I looked out the window beside my carrel in Edwards, seeking to ease the searing spiritual turmoil—the strain on spent nerves. After the full revelation of Gordon's heart, I was filled with an increasingly anxious, turbulent dismay.

Gordon had opened the way. I was free to accept his challenge. The world would not condemn our love. Marriage was entirely within the bounds of the moral law. What overly polite pretense within me was causing delay?

I rested my head on my hands. Why continue the futile debate? God would understand. I hadn't chosen to love Gordon. Or had I? At any rate the decision was made. Love had come gently and gradually, Gordon's mind and insights filling me with such marvelous wonder. And now? Why must love be strangled in infancy, entombed behind the cold, rocky dikes of some pitiful need to share religious conviction? Mature love was generous—tolerant of others' views and opinions. It was especially tolerant of others' beliefs. In the final analysis, love was the ultimate giving. Was joining my life together with Gordon's, in an acceptably lawful relationship, an abomination before God? If so, belief was hideous. If so, God was not love.

I stood up defiantly. It was no good. Study was just one more test of endurance. Holding my books against me, I strode out of the library and walked briskly across campus. If my only affinity was with nature, then that was where I would be. Biting back the bitterness that threatened to consume me, I looked at the weed covered path. Instead of taking the direct route home, I chose the dirt road that led past an old, deserted church.

Walking with seeming direction, in my mind nothing meshed, nothing fit. One thought, half born, broke against another. They both died. Could the mind bleed?

I tried reciting poetry, but my own words, *I do not call religion bondage*, burst in and shattered the illusion I was attempting to create. "Not bondage?" I asked a silent sky. The words from Neil Diamond's song "Lonely Looking Sky" rushed in to fill the void in my heart. Feeling lonely never made *what* not right? I looked at the unseeing clouds and pulled my scarf closer around my throat.

That was the problem. Earthly love couldn't live in the sky. That was an affectation of those who mistook dreams for reality. Cervantes was wrong. It was an "impossible dream"—an empty, impossible dream.

I stumbled against something in my path. It was the front step of the abandoned church. Shamefully, I turned abruptly away. Then, with an impulse born of a higher nature, I turned back, opened the unlocked door, and went inside.

The musty interior of the chapel was coldly silent, the shaded light of day only just filtering in upon the small altar at the front. I looked at the faded, deteriorating, once-white lace of the altar covering and found myself upon my knees, my head bowed. I dearly wanted to pray, to make supplication to God for both Gordon and myself, but could not. I felt lifeless. There was no prayer in me, nor were there any tears to cool the burning in my spirit. I looked out the window behind the altar to the subdued gray of the sky and stood to my feet.

Who would my marriage harm? To join my life with a nonbeliever wouldn't make the earth reel off its axis. The stars wouldn't drop from the heavens. Gordon viewed belief as unreasonable. He would be exempt from whatever penalty must be paid; condemnation would fall upon me alone. If I perished from the faith, what was that to anyone but me?

I raised my hand to my forehead; it was hot and flushed. Then my arm dropped limply to my side as I heard clearly in my mind,

. . . "that they may always have His Spirit to be with them."[77] The words filled me with shame. In the enforced honesty of the moment, I knew I wanted to believe a lie. I wanted to love Gordon more than God. "He that loveth father or mother more than me is not worthy of me."[78] As much as I had attempted to bury that knowledge in the empty rhetoric and despair of the world, there was a gulf between Gordon and I, a gulf that might, because of our present differing perspectives, be forever fixed.

Chapter Thirty-Five

The heart has its reasons which reason knows nothing of. [79]

—Blaise Pascal: *Pensees*

The ring of blue spruce around Collingsgate looked unnaturally excluding when I wearily made my way into the front yard. Grandfather Richard seemed to glower down on me, his branches hostile and unwelcoming. Father was nowhere to be seen, so I sat wearily down on the stone slab bench.

The bench was brutally cold. In C. S. Lewis's brilliantly allegorical book, *The Lion, The Witch, and the Wardrobe*, Aslan had been sacrificed on just such a cold stone bench as this. Pain had pierced my own heart when that foul deed was done. Quickly I got up and made my way to the side door. There was no self-deception. I knew I was fleeing not from Aslan's betrayal at the hands of his enemies, but from his betrayal at the hands of his friends.

After supper, I randomly selected a book from the library in Father's study. Open on Father's desk was the book Neal had given him at Christmas: *Markings* by Dag Hammarskjold. Father had illuminated a passage with a yellow highlighter.

> *"God does not die on the day when we cease to believe in a personal deity, but we die on the day when our lives cease to be illumined by the steady radiance, renewed daily, of a wonder, the source of which is beyond all reason."* [80]

I looked from Mr. Hammarskjold's book to the volume in my hands. It was *The Pursuit of Pleasure*. Perhaps the U.N. Secretary General's writings presented a case for the pursuit of understanding.

Exchanging my selected book for Hammarskjold's, I made my way to the family room. Curling up on the lounge, I tried to read, but my eyes saw few words. Frustrated by the struggle to concentrate, I looked over at Father. He had also, for some reason, decided to spend the evening out of his study. It was the first time we'd sat together since Ginny and Neal had been married.

Father rested in the big chair with Aunt Amy's afghan around his shoulders, his rose catalogue open before him. After twenty minutes of fighting with the meaningless, flesh-colored pages, I laid my own book down. Unnoticing, Father read steadily on. Tonight his sameness and predictability were agitating. With Father it was always history, books, and roses. I looked at his graying hair and wondered if he had ever felt, in his remarkable self-sufficiency, cut adrift from life's moorings.

"Do you really believe in God?" I asked presently. Father turned dispassionately to a new page in his rose catalogue.

"Why not?" he returned unperturbed. "God believes in me."

Why not? I thought hopefully to myself. If that was so, then God believed in Gordon, knew Gordon, wanted Gordon to believe in Him. Still unsettled, I tried a new approach.

"The Sinai prescription for morality is a little dramatic, don't you think?" Especially, I thought to myself, the providentially concealing cloud and Holy Mountain with its refining fire.

Father looked up from his catalogue. "You're wondering whether the commands of God constitute a valid guide for living?"

I nodded. The dissent I felt was transparently close to the surface.

"I imagine that depends on whether you want them to be," Father said calmly. "The commandments seem to have been important enough to God to make them." There was a note of finality in Father's voice. I sat and stared at the afghan. His answer wasn't good enough.

Feeling a desire to be alone, I picked up my book and got up from the couch. As I passed the landing to go to my room, the words on the wall plaque leapt toward me, "The heavens declare the glory of God and the firmament sheweth his handiwork."[81] At the bottom were the words, *"God is Love."* I had read those words at least twice a day for almost twenty years, but never had they been forced upon my mind with such hydraulic, pain-transmitting power. I moved up the stairs. On the landing, I paused and looked out the hall window toward the university.

Love? Then let me love! I noticed that the large intent eyes of the owl clock seemed to focus searchingly upon me. "You tell me," I told him silently, without emotion.

Once in my room, I dropped wearily on my bed, not bothering to take off my clothes. The night dragged dismally on. I couldn't sleep. The hands of the wall clock pointed to three fifty-five; the air in the room was heavy and oppressive. Shoving my blankets back, I got out of bed. The polished, wooden floor was cold and hard under my bare feet. In the bottom of the dresser, I found a pair of coveralls and slipped them on over my clothing, then pulled on my shoes and donned my coat and hat.

Outside, the pre-dawn world was a lusterless, gray darkness. The seeping night mist pressed damp, chill fingers against the earth, making the trees appear as only indistinct huddling clumps. In spite of the gray solitude around me, I felt a surge of grim independence lift my spirits. Half to the sleeping world and half to myself, I exclaimed, "We make our own heaven by living! By following our dreams!" The sound of my voice quavered briefly in the mist and was lost in the night. Bereft of my false courage, I stood irresolute on the unwelcoming riverbank. Blanketed in shadow, the colorless water was not beautiful. Mesmerized, I looked at the cold black surface of the river.

Why would any reasonable being become a prisoner by choice? The heart should not be incarcerated. Let me out of my self-imposed exile from the world! Let me grapple and cope! Let me live my life as I choose, not just stumble over some rocky path faith prescribes.

The dawn came, but it was empty and uninspiring. I sat on a rock by the river, hoping the sounds of the lapping water and the early morning warmth would dam the painful flood of raging indecision inundating my senses. Plunging my foot into the cold brine, I stirred the water in the shallows along the edge of the bank with my foot and watched the dislodged silt and mud discolor the water. It was all unreal. The naked, bitter turmoil in my mind was unreal. The silt, the rocks, the river, the earth, the sky—this was real. Surely in this real world, sensible people were above this gripping inner chaos, this fruitless warring of mind and spirit.

In rising frustration, I kicked the stones with my foot. Stones—blind, senseless stones. "'What fools 'we' [sic] mortals be!'"[82] The Bard was right! I jumped to my feet. I would not be a stone—rigidly self-righteous, beyond feeling. I would not live my life in lonely exile from the loving relationship I craved. "Gordon," I cried across the river. "Gordon!" But the echo reverberated back—God! Humbled, I bowed my head, fell sobbing to my knees beside the river and prayed. "Dear God. Thy will be done."

As the days dragged on, Gordon did not contact me. He had issued his challenge, his invitation to join my life with his. It was my serve, and still I could not reconcile my need for religious certitude with my feelings of unconditional love for Gordon.

In Father's garden, the tangerine-pink buds of the Mission Bell were just beginning to appear. Other early blooming roses, the White Knight and Santa Anita, were also starting to show. Soon the flower garden would be radiant with white, a true bride of spring. It was a time of intense botanical involvement for Father, who watched over the first delicate buds with the devotion of a parent for a child.

The afternoon Sacrament service was over for the day. It was a great relief to be outside in the garden. Father, for once not wearing his brown jacket, was spraying roses. He was using malathion; although, he used lindane or rotenone or anything else he thought might rid his precious roses of aphids. By mid-June, the budding for the early flowering roses would be over, and Father could relax his vigilance until the next batch of blooms. He put his spray can next to the Eden rose and came over to the stone bench where I was sitting.

"Time to fumigate the house again," he said, a tired tone in his voice. "Ginny should have waited a little longer to become a 'stranger in paradise.'"[83] Ginny's outspoken objections to the annual house fumigation were well known to Father. It mattered not. Each year the houseplants were dreadfully fumigated to keep the rose pests from finding a safe environment to multiply and infect the garden.

Father was looking decidedly older since Ginny left. The silent weariness that comes with age was beginning to show. He stood looking at the newly opened petals of the Eden rose. Compassion surged through me as I grasped for something to say to lighten his growing solitude.

I was about to speak when Father himself spoke. "Do you recall the Greek philosopher Heraclitus, Diana?"

"Was he the one who said you can't walk through the same stream twice?"

Father nodded. "Heraclitus had a disciple. The disciple, in blind reverence to his master, decided to advance Heraclitus' theory one step further. So he declared you can't walk through the same stream once. In stipulating such a law, he prohibited motion."

It was clear where Father was headed. The foolishness of Heraclitus' myopic protégé was, perhaps, not unlike my own.

Reaching over and placing his hand on my shoulder, Father looked at me searchingly, but there was tenderness in his eyes. "You see?" he said. "It is possible, however sincerely intended, to shoot beyond the mark, Moonlight. To go beyond what is eternally ordained. There are principles in existence that govern not only the movements of the planets, stars, and other spheres in their proper course, but also determine the regulation, the rules, the times, and the seasons of man's existence and mortality. Deny those laws and they still exist. You can't go beyond them. If you do, you deny more than motion, you deny God himself."

"Yes, nihilism," I said, comprehending Father's direction. "The doctrine that denies any basis for truth. Taken to the extreme, it denies existence."

Father nodded and put his hand on the back of the bench. We sat in silence together. After a time, he spoke again. "You will always be a Collingsgate, Diana. But make no mistake. He is a man to be valued."

Father's words flew straight to my heart. Father, my father. He knew. He knew of my deep internal conflict—of my desperate battle to maintain my faith—but did not condemn. Nor would he choose for me. I alone must decide.

The slanting rays of the evening sunlight fell softly upon the rose garden, illuminating the still-to-flower Black Prince by the gate. Near the Black Prince, the Camelot rose was ready to burst into its first bounty of blooms. Father, seeing my attention on the Camelot, began singing in his gravelly base, "'A law was made . . .'"[84]

Weakly, but gratefully, I joined him in the chorus. ". . .a distant moon ago, here . . .'"[85]

"Moonlight," Father said, interrupting our ballad and putting his arm lightly on my shoulder, "do you remember seeing your first Aurora Borealis?"

I nodded, smiling at the recollection.

"You look a little now like you did then," he said mildly. We both smiled. I let my head drop against Dad's shoulder.

"I can well imagine how I must have looked," I said, my mind going back to that night long ago when I was just four years old.

Father had slipped into my room to awaken me. Helping me into coat and slippers, he led me swiftly outside, where I was abruptly thrust onto the threshold of eternity. All around, the heavens were plunging in great rifts and sheets of metallic iridescence toward the earth. Long luminous streamers shot close to the ground, and then veered sharply back into the heavens, shooting so high it seemed they would bring the entire sky down with them. My child's mind was paralyzed with fear at the awful wonder of the sight. It was obviously the end of the world.

Unable to take my eyes off the glorious, frightening scene for even a second, I heard Father ask without apparent fear, "What do you think of it, Diana?"

Although soulfully afraid, I somehow found enough courage to answer, "I am glad it is beautiful."

"Yes," Father said enthusiastically. "It's one of nature's most beautiful works. Do you know the name of it, Diana?"

"Yes," I whispered, determined to stand on those very steps until it was all over. "Yes. I know. It's called the Final Judgment."

Father's loving laughter had shattered the terror of the night as he swung me up into his arms. "You are my own self, Diana," he said seriously, when his laughter subsided. "Little and misinformed as you are. We are the same. The Final Judgment, as you call it, is less imaginatively known as the Northern Lights or Aurora Borealis. And it is shown for the benefit of saved and sinner alike."

Chapter Thirty-Six

Where is the quiet hand to calm my anguish?
Who, who can understand? He, only One.[86]

—Emma Lou Thayne: *Where Can I Turn For Peace?*

The final exams were scheduled for the last week in April. Rallying my wavering interest, I forced myself to concentrate on the papers before me. Gordon and I had agreed to give each other some space for a while. As soon as term ended, he would be heading back to Ryerson to teach a spring and then a summer session, so we'd decided to let things ride until he returned. Even so, knowing he was still on campus, it was only by the sheerest force of will that I didn't seek him out. Each day was a contest of endurance; each hour I yearned for a glimpse of him. Soon he would be leaving, and I wouldn't see him again for twelve long weeks.

Rationally, I knew the time apart was seriously needed to sort out the confusion of thought and feeling bombarding my mind and emotions. My love for Gordon was not the difficulty. It was the question of differing ideologies—a house divided—nagging incessantly at the back of my mind. And it was something else; something I couldn't get my mind around, perhaps because my emotions were so inextricably involved.

"Thinking is best done with the mind, not the hormones," Father was wont to say of youth who intemperately let their hearts rule their heads. Yet it didn't quite fit. While it was one thing to be governed by desire, it was quite another to be spiritually ill at ease. Somehow, in silent torture, the two weeks prior to Gordon's leaving passed.

The day before he was to leave for Toronto, I could endure the separation no longer. Once again I found myself knocking on his studio door. The door opened and Gordon stood before me. He was wearing a rumpled wool sweater, and his unruly hair was in more than normal disarray. There were dark circles under his eyes that I'd never noticed before, and yet, to my eyes, he was the most beautiful person in the world.

Gordon didn't seem glad to see me, and a constricting fear gripped me that perhaps it was over between us. For a moment, as though separated by a dark glass, we stood silently regarding one another. Finally, motioning me inside with a movement of his sculptured hand, Dr. Brantwood perfunctorily offered me the chair beside the lounge. For the first time since I'd known him, Gordon was ill at ease, not seeming to know what to say or what to do.

"I had to see you," I said, reaching my hand tentatively to touch his arm. Inwardly, I prayed he would know how much I meant the words. "I couldn't face another twelve weeks without . . . I had to see you before you left for Toronto."

"Does that mean you're going with me?" Gordon's eyes focused hopefully on mine.

"You know I can't go with you, Gordon."

He gave me a wounded but unsurprised look. "It takes three days to get a marriage license, Diana. Unless you have to get your president's consent?"

"No. I don't need his consent. I just wanted to see you . . . tell you I love you."

"So you've said."

"Where will you be staying? I asked, gathering my emotional reserves. Is there a number where I can reach you?"

"I have your number, Diana. I'll call you when I find a place." Gordon seemed as though he was turned to stone.

"Gordon," I cried. "Gordon. I would marry you this moment, with or without a ring, wedding dress, or minister . . . if . . ."

He looked up warily, unveiled skepticism in his eyes.

"If only I knew it was the right thing to do. That no one would get hurt." The tears were running uncontrollably in my mind, but I was aware nothing showed on my face.

Gordon looked at me as though he believed none of it. "Come over here and tell me that," he challenged quietly, his eyes raking my feelings with the knife-like pain of emotional rejection.

Knowing absolute honesty was the only hope of restoring understanding between us, I forced myself to return his coldly penetrating gaze.

"Gordon," I said, "I love you. I want you. You. You alone. I desire your companionship, your association, your arms always around me. I desire your love more than I ever thought it possible to desire anything on Earth. You've come into my life and filled my mind—my spirit—with wonder. But in so doing, you've turned my world upside down. Things I thought would never be challenged have been challenged. Things I thought would never be doubted have been doubted. Your mental brilliance has made me—compelled me—to question. Now I doubt. Now I question—even the very existence of God. Please . . . please . . . give me more . . ." Unable to explain further, a sob escaped.

Coming quickly across the dark gulf that separated us, Gordon gathered me into his arms and held me warmly against him. In soulful relief, I returned his embrace, pressing my face into his shoulder. In his arms, relief cascaded through every bruised and bleeding ligament of my spirit. *Please don't let us lose one another again*, I prayed silently.

After a long moment, Gordon drew slightly apart from me, his arms falling around my waist, his chin resting lightly on my forehead.

"Come to me, Diana. Come to me," he invited gently, his voice filling me with life-renewing hope. "Must we remain strangers?" Tenderly he touched my hair. There were obvious tears in his eyes.

Eyes and heart soaking in his, I said fervently, "Our souls aren't strangers."

I didn't wait for him to kiss me, but began at his chin, gratefully, fervently kissing every corner and angle of his wonderful, intelligent face, until his laughter stopped me.

"Enough. I need this face in some sort of shape, if I'm to lecture with it." He looked at me shrewdly, but warmly. "If loving teaches me to 'rhyme and to be melancholy,'[87] I should at least look like a professor." It was a quote from Shakespeare's *Love's Labour's Lost.*

Friday after my last exam, I saw Gordon off at the airport. It was a somber parting, but not without hope. I was sincerely glad that I'd followed the inspiration to see him Thursday. It would be a difficult twelve weeks, but at least Gordon had come to a clear understanding of why I needed time to think.

His last words were, "I'll meet you at Queen's Bench when I get back, Esther. Keep it warm for me."

Chapter Thirty-Seven

Hopes, what are they?—Beads of morning
Strung on slender blades of grass;
Or a spider's web adorning
In a straight and treacherous pass.[‡‡‡]

—William Wordsworth: *Inscription on a Hermit's Cave*

Saturday, May second, the day after Gordon left for Toronto, members of the University Symphony and Chorus gathered in SUB foyer. Those involved in the annual concert tour, which would take in Alberta, Saskatchewan, and British Columbia, were committed for eight days and sixteen performances. The object of the tour was to reach as many small communities as possible. In so doing, the Greyhound charter would follow a circuit of over 1,800 miles. If all went according to schedule, the students would be back on campus in time to prepare for graduation ceremonies.

With spring exams over for another year, students exhibited a notable resurgence of energy and were in high spirits for the tour. For myself, the trip was simply a duty I had to perform. Right up to the moment of boarding, I debated if going was a wise choice. Leaving campus this year seemed ungrateful, as if I was deserting. Was I betraying a loyalty?

Adrianne came sprinting up just as the bus was getting ready to pull away. She was in proper slap-dash form. Clanging onto the bus, her bags and purse banging against her legs, her gray woolen skirt swishing in protest at being bustled along in such a hurry, she fell into the seat beside me with a relieved sigh.

"Thank heaven for janitors," she exclaimed. "Alarm didn't go off. But praise be to Victor Frank, here I am."

"I'm glad The Hole janitor looks out for you," I said sincerely. "I was getting worried."

Adrianne's cross strata friendships, her social networking, was paying off. Perhaps this was because her idea of what constituted real class wasn't confined to the bigotry of who's who on campus— or anywhere else. She believed, like Father, that our university Duck Pond was just another duck pond, so why put on airs? No point ostracizing the ducks without degrees who wanted to splash around in it, too. I was genuinely pleased Addy felt this way.

Apart from the momentary lift Adrianne's arrival provided, it was a disheartening departure. In my mind, I could see Gordon waving briefly from the boarding lane at the airport, a look of quiet resignation on his face. Remembering our parting, I felt a chilling premonition that we were just postponing the inevitable. Forcing my thoughts to remain positive, I attempted to focus on the events at hand.

Figures of students and parents stood shivering in the brisk spring wind, waiting for the bus to pull away. Their bodies banked against the lacerating air, their faces and hands drawn up under hoods and sleeves, they had the semblance of immaterial beings. I wondered if they were the ghosts, or if we were. Father had driven me to SUB, then departed for Collingsgate, as his days off were precious time to him. There was no need to fuss. I was a big girl and could see myself off. We were all big boys and girls and we were only going for two weeks. Did those so frantically waving goodbye think we would disappear into the broad expanse of the prairie and never return?

Near the city outskirts, the bus picked up speed and soon we were out in the country, watching the undulating prairie under the morning clouds. Finding little to interest me in the unvaried landscape, my thoughts slipped back to Gordon. Suddenly an annoyed tug on my elbow disrupted my reveries.

"Dynamism," Adrianne prodded, "are you going to sit staring out that window the whole trip like a shish kebab skewered on a stick? If you don't want anyone to play in your garden, okay. But this trip is supposed to be fun, eh?"

I turned from the window, repentant that I was blighting Adrianne's pleasure in the trip. The miles and the time had flown by as I wrestled with my dilemma. "I'm sincerely sorry, Adrianne," I apologized. "I was thinking. Have some things to sort out."

"No doubt you do," she said, "but you've been sorting them for hours. Don't you think it's time to shake off your solitary delights and join the group? I'm sure Bramblybriar can manage on his own without you mooning over him every minute."

"Adrianne," I said wearily, "his name is Gordon." Then betrayed by my own suppressed feelings, I confessed, "I don't even know how old he is." I hated sounding plaintive, but there it was.

Adrianne frowned, but her alert eyes took on a softer light. She reached over and took my hands in hers. The touch was comforting, defense-reducing.

"Gordon is thirty-three, Di Brains. Ever heard of asking?"

I shook my head, feeling both relieved and foolish.

"That how you found out, Adrianne? By asking?"

"Certainly. His Bucksworth is on the board. There has to be some perks in being related to one of the campus digs." By *digs*, Adrianne meant dignitaries. Professors were not included in that stellar appellation.

The Greyhound slowed and pulled into a garage by the highway. We were a few miles from Medicine Hat. For the moment, the rest stop terminated Adrianne's carefree chatter. Students piled off the bus for washroom and refreshments. Set on the rolling prairie, the service station was thoroughly modern, replete with simulated rock siding and a plastic canopy extending over sleek pumps. I decided to stretch my legs.

The cold wind had ceased, and the air was clear and fresh. It was good to walk and ease my cramped body, free from the noisy commotion of the bus. I entered the restaurant and walked to the blacktop counter to buy a pack of red licorice for Adrianne and some peppermints for myself.

Taking my purchases outside, I was glad to be able to breathe in the fresh air away from the stuffiness of the bus. The pungent scent of Mentha avensis, wild mint, was in the air, testifying to the presence of a creek or marsh nearby. I wondered where? I should have been able to see it. The flat countryside offered freedom for the eyes to wander in any direction giving a sense of unbounded visibility. *Unbounded visibility.* Wouldn't that be an asset? Lifted by the thought, I looked to the east where the dark purple bowl of the earth met the lighter violet of the sky in a firm, straight line. There was equality between earth and sky on the prairie—room for people to be themselves.

"Frogs are putting on their own community concert tonight," Mike said, grinning. He walked past me a short distance to a small hummock. "It would be a grand place to set up the symphony," he mused, looking out across the expanse of shadowed flatland.

"Yes," I agreed. "You come from around here?" Something in Mike's tone indicated pride of ownership.

"Just over that rise. That's where the house is. The land beyond the fence line, extending to the stream at the base of the hill, belongs to my parents."

"That's a large area. But I thought the land was flat?"

"It gives that impression," Mike agreed. "But you should try to find stray cattle on the prairie, and you would learn differently." In his apparent attachment to the land, Mike's face expressed a depth of selfless concern that was charming.

"Parents coming to the concert tonight, Mike?"

"Wouldn't miss it," he said proudly. "They've been a great support to me in my schooling. They think education is the key to getting up in society." We both laughed in recognition of the doubt many students harbored on that account.

"Then I'll try not to miss the second entrance to the *Requiem*. Last two times, I seem to have lost my place."

"So I noticed. But you always get back to the score before Eagle Eyes can spot your lapse. You're a good player."

"Not as good as you, Mike. Did you start playing when you were very young?"

"First thing I remember doing. My dad gave me a violin before I had teeth and said, 'Here, Mikey boy! Fiddle for your supper.'"

Laughter rippled, cutting through the early evening dusk. It was Adrianne.

"Wondered if you two had turned to salt pillars," she teased. "I was beginning to think you and Mike were going to spend the rest of the tour standing sentry on this clump of sod."

There was a cunning twinkle in Adrianne's eye. "Discussing unanimism?" she asked innocently. A puzzled look on his face, Mike nodded politely to Adrianne and left to board the bus.

"What's this about unanimism? I asked. Since when did you take up with Romains?"

"Since you've been in my care and keeping, my darling antisocial dove. You should give Romain's idea of 'merging with the collective consciousness' a try.[89] Give yourself a treat. Now get on board and don't give me any more lip."

I did as I was told. Once on board, Adrianne settled back in her chair.

"Should be in the 'City of Passion' in less than an hour," she enthused. "Then on with the show."

"City of Passion? I thought we were going to Medicine Hat?"

"We are. Haven't you heard Johnny Wayne and Frank Shuster's description? 'City of fashion, city of passion, Medicine Hat.'[90] You should watch more television, Dia Mia."

Pleased to have an audience, Adrianne began a spontaneous imitation of Maestro Schmidt, the chorus conductor.

"If you vill be zo kind peepulz. Puleeze to lizen up! Ve must deport ourzelvez like ladeez and gentlemenz! Ve must zing mit our zouls! Ve must tink ze muzic, here!" Adrianne smote her chest over her heart with an agonized expression, but her preposterous impersonation gave her away.

"You like the maestro, don't you, Adrianne?"

"Yes," she admitted, realizing her game was up. "He eez a reeel muzeesshun!"

I looked over fondly, enjoying the moment with my sporting friend.

"So," she asked, "how are Ginny and Neal doing? What do you hear from them?"

"Not a whole lot," I conceded. "I believe they're in what's termed the 'honeymoon phase', so they probably won't surface for a while."

"Prof Riki miss The Jinn?"

I nodded. "He couldn't very well help missing her. Ginny was his second mother." Ashamed of the ungracious words, I looked away. Thankfully, Adrianne changed the topic.

"Like a paper?" she asked.

"No, thank you."

"You sound defiant."

"No."

"But you should read the paper. Or is it too loud for your delicate webbing?"

I looked helplessly out the window. When Adrianne was in her investigational mode, there was no avoiding her.

"I seldom read a paper," I said quietly, looking into the night, "because I can't see the advantage in peddling anxiety."

"So who peddles? Facts are facts."

"Don't you think society would improve if things were told like they could be, instead of how they are?"

"Dreamer," Adrianne chided, once more the protectress. "That's idealization, not news. When are you coming out of your eggshell? There's a whole world outside of your secluded, porcelain existence."

"You mean calcium existence," I corrected mildly. "Eggshells are made of calcium." Adrianne ignored my petty remark, picked at a thread in her gray pleated skirt, and banged one dainty foot against the footrest.

"Even if the news were whitewashed, who's going to candy-coat the world? Next thing, you'll be demanding packers fillet sardines."

I smiled. A point Adrianne instantly seized upon as admission of guilt.

"Oh, no, Dio! You don't?"

"Well, yes. I do."

Adrianne laughed and chanted, "Armadillo Di. Likes to paint the sky. But with her head under her bed. She'll neither do nor die."

"Adrianne!"

She looked at me, pleased she'd elicited a stunned response. I couldn't blame her. Widely divergent on many topics, we would never hold exactly the same view of things. Laughter and humor were Adrianne's way of breaking even. Her emotional volatility was a stopgap tactic she used to bridge our differing worlds.

Switching topics, Adrianne said slyly, "I hear Suffocating Suffolk's having an affair with Dr. Banescroft's son, Allan. You know the one that teaches physics? Now what would make a person lose their balance over a prof?" Adrianne's eyes sparkled.

I looked at her closely, trying to determine if she was driving the stake in on purpose. She *was* enjoying the moment, but it was also apparent she was trying to give me an opening to express my feelings. Not yet able to share, I turned toward the window.

"Affairs are outdated, wouldn't you say, Di?" Adrianne pressed, not to be deterred. "Today people usually settle for less."

I knew what she meant. The one night tumble was not a novelty on campus. Ignoring the inner warning that there would be greater wisdom in silence, something too long repressed made me speak.

"That would depend on your definition of an affair, Adrianne."

"Oh, great, Di. That's rich. Let's just say there are 'affaires d'amour' and 'affaires d'honneur' and one is not the other."

"Never?"

"Never. You know Bramblybriar will never be happy outside of his briar patch."

"Meaning?"

"Meaning he's not the type to set out the garbage every morning and retrieve the paper every evening. And he certainly won't be disposed to face Mecca and pray three times a day."

"Adrianne!"

"I'm sorry, Di. It's just . . . why walk a mile when you could easily trip over what's already at your feet?"

"Meaning?"

"You know Warren cares for you."

"As a friend, yes," I said, still faintly hoping that was true.

"As a person."

"Warren's a nice boy," I hedged, wishing the conversation wasn't happening.

"Boy?" Adrianne scoffed. "Warren's past puberty, or haven't you noticed?"

Adrianne was beginning to chaff sincerely. It was indisputably time for some gold-star diplomacy.

"What's Warren doing this summer?" I asked, hoping to ease our exchange of its dangerous burden of feeling.

"Back to B. C. More reforestation." Adrianne gave me an undeceived glance and shrugged her shoulders. Offering me a piece of red licorice, she said wryly, "Here, bite on this. It'll help you stand the pain. Now that we've mastered adolescence, later when you're feeling up to it, we'll discuss adulthood." I gave her a grateful smile and meekly accepted the licorice peace offering.

As I collected my things to disembark from the bus and begin the concert, a smile rose in my heart. At such times, when our dialogue reached a deadlock, Adrianne could be so affectedly callous, she was almost too tender. I did wish with all my soul that I might confide in her, might open my heart to her and tell her of the beauty and depth of my devotion to Gordon. But how could she understand when I myself could not? Until the inevitable choice was made, I was forced to remain silent. The silence was mandatory. Instead of being able to shout the beauty of my love from the housetops, I must allow it to be suffocated under those precipitous, glass cliffs of towering silence. I was a lone traveler in a silent dream. Everything was unreal, and life was not as I imagined.

The first night concert went well. Somehow I managed not to lose my place in the "Requiem" and the evening finished successfully. There was a social after, but I didn't stay, remaining only long enough to meet Mike's parents. Mr. and Mrs. Morrison were kindly people, and I was glad Mike had invited me to meet them.

"Your son is a fine violinist," I said sincerely. "I don't know how he puts up with me for a partner." Mike's mother smiled gently, nodding her head with humble pride in her son.

Mike's father said, "Mike says the same thing about you, Miss Collingsgate. I understand your father's a professor at Western?"

"Yes, he is. Not a music professor though—history. And you have a farm here near Medicine Hat?"

"Yes. How did you know?"

"Mike showed me the land as we came into town. Managing such a large area must take sound horticultural skills."

"Dad took horticulture at the University of Regina," Mike intervened proudly. "He runs a very scientific, advanced operation. I hope to do the same someday."

"I can see you all love the land," I said, genuinely impressed with their passion. "My father grows a few roses in his spare time, so on a smaller scale, he'd appreciate your feelings."

Mikes' parents nodded smiling. Knowing Mike had other friends waiting to talk to him, I excused myself and left for my billet. I was asleep by the time Adrianne got in from the social.

We boarded the bus at five the next morning. Adrianne promptly fell back to sleep, her tousled head falling companionably against my shoulder. Feeling her warmth, I was filled with gratitude for Adrianne's loyal, if tempestuous, friendship. She was a great blessing in my life, especially the last few weeks since Ginny had married and moved to Toronto.

A question disrupted my brief peace of mind. While Adrianne had given me so much, had I been the same support to her? Why was it that I had not been able to share my faith with her? When Adrianne and I first met, I'd invited her to church with me, but Adrianne had shied away from organized religion, feeling it was phony. At least that explained why she could torment me mercilessly about my unusually "high level of religious saturation."

"Almost makes you believe," Adrianne observed quietly, lifting her head and peering over my shoulder through the bus window at the vibrant morning sky. I looked in the direction of her gaze. The sunrise was indeed breathtaking, reflecting shimmering silvers, crimsons, and violet hues with startling radiance. I hadn't known Adrianne was awake. Feeling renewed remorse for my recent personal doubts about God, I didn't respond.

"I think I see why you worship," she said thoughtfully. There was a new reverence in her voice as she spoke. So the silence last night was right. It was necessary. No good would have come of sharing doubt. *Let the first seeds of Adrianne's believing find fertile soil,* I prayed fervently.

Aloud I said, "I should have woken you."

"No, you shouldn't have. You need time to be alone with your God." I felt a ring of shame at her words.

"And you?" I asked.

"Give me time, Di," Adrianne returned smiling, her newfound reverence still reflected in her voice. "I only just met Him."

For the first time since knowing Adrianne, I realized that the solemnly piquant face looking steadily out the window from the chair adjoining mine was not as sure of life as she pretended. Astoundingly, Addy was, at the moment, almost transparently vulnerable.

As if sensing my thoughts, Adrianne bent and took her transistor radio from under her chair, and attempted to tune in a station with the small silver selector knob. Unfortunately, even with the volume turned up full, there seemed to be only one station clear enough to understand. From this cite, the poorly defined voice of a minister sputtered into the bus.

"Some cheerful Charlie's spreading religious doom and gloom," Adrianne sighed. "Why don't these zealous do-gooders let people worship God where he belongs—in the heart?"

My friend's moment of reverence for the creations of God obviously didn't extend to His ministers. She did not, however, turn off the radio, and the voice of the cloth continued on in an uneven, wavering tone.

"In its nearsighted lust for pleasure, society has lost the quality which ensures its continuance: the quality of belief in a power beyond man's own. Greedy for superficial excitement, bereft of value outside the self, the individual is stretched taut between the poles of gluttony and graft. We live in a society whose rigid, inelastic heart allows only one response—ennui. Wishing to feel everything, we feel nothing. Modern man has lost his ability to respond positively. Running indolently from experience to experience, with loud and empty laughter, men seek gratification of every whim until the carnal appetite, satiated with temporal pleasure like a water-logged tree stump, becomes the whole man."

Adrianne shook her head and snapped off the transistor, replacing it firmly under her chair. "The world is full of myths, Charlie boy," she said, "and they range from simple-minded sentimentality to calculated deceit. But don't worry, you're as creative as anyone."

"You don't think pleasure has become the world's guiding dictum?" I asked. "You don't think the world is bored?"

"Generalizations are boring," Adrianne returned spiritedly. "Look, Di. I know that some are bored, and some are pleasure seekers, but there are many more young people taking part in international competitions, serving in UNESCO and CUSO, carving useful contributing careers. There are middle-aged and older people engaged in scientific research for advancing cures for illness and improving health and longevity. Others give their time and talents to help build developing nations. Still others explore new fields in sea and space. These people are involved and participating in life. They're not self-serving or bored." Adrianne paused in her energetic affirmations and pointed thumbs down to the radio under her chair.

"You want to know who's bored? I'll tell you who's bored. Charlie's bored." I reached over and squeezed her hand, quietly proud of my strong-willed friend. Adrianne would always be Adrianne, but her indomitable wit arose from a genuinely caring heart. For all her vivacious charm, she was authentic.

By four o'clock on the fifth day of the concert tour, the sky was already lightening in the east. By five, the prairie was left behind, and the mountains towered around the bus. Tolerating our passing with silent reserve, the mountains enclosed a world far different from that outside their protecting walls. In the vastness of the snow-clad reaches, awe was still known. Respect and wonder still held a place in the heart of mountain canyons and cascading waterfalls.

As we rounded a bend in the road, heaven and earth seemed momentarily to coalesce, the distinction that separates them utterly disbanded by a generous embrace of land and sky. Pearl clouds clung in milk-white opalescence low to the earth. Like wanderers seeking a place of rest, the clouds sought succor against the mountain's majestic breast.

For some miles, the clouds continued pressing against the earth, every now and again parting in places to reveal a gray mountain peak lifting above a ridge streaked with red iron oxide; then closing again, shrouding the mountains with softly floating, diaphanous bodies. Though the clouds veiled much of the mountains, it was still possible to see many signs of habitation, even at this early hour.

Smoke arose from a cone-shaped incinerator on the boundary of a lumber camp behind the pine trees to the right of the road and mingled with the clouds in a filmy haze. A logging truck, piled high with rough-hewn logs, slowed in front of the bus and turned off to the mill, swiftly disappearing into the mist. Two hitchhikers, a man and a woman wearing brightly embroidered ponchos, appeared out of the mist and waved to the bus. Catching only a glimpse of their tired, white faces as the bus drove by, I felt a uniting compassion with them. I wondered how many of those wan faces, that appeared out of the fog and then vanished, were fighting unseen battles silently within their own souls? How many lonely people passed by other lonely people in the fog? Did they, like me, require strength beyond their own?

I shut my eyes but couldn't dispel the image of those two valiant faces. At least, God, my spirit cried, rescue these dear plodding souls from the torment of fearing they fight a losing battle alone. Grant them the faith they need to endure.

By six o'clock the clouds had begun to lift, but they still covered a great portion of the mountainsides, weaving the tops of the trees with a puffy webbing of purest white. The morning sunlight was beginning to break across the mountains in brief patches through the clouds. Then unexpectedly, with perfect celestial timing, at the summit of Rogers Pass the clouds broke apart, rent asunder as if by some divine command. And there, framing a large oval of bright, clear sky were two well-defined, intensely white clouds shaped like great white hands—the sculpted fingers of one hand touching the fingers of the other at the apex of the arch.

The cloud hands holding up the heavens were breathtaking, so clearly delineated were they against the deep blue of the surrounding sky. I pressed my face against the window glass, straining for a better view. Quietly the hymn words "that hand which bears all nature up shall guard his children well,"[91] rejoiced into my mind. With the life-restoring thought, a shudder of renewed faith kindled, trembled, and spread like burning flame through my entire being. Tears washed in uncontested abundance down my face as truth filled my soul. *There is a God! Now and forever. There is a God!*

Chapter Thirty-Eight

This narrow isthmus 'twixt two boundless seas,
The past, the future,—two eternities! [92]

—Thomas Moore: *Lallah Rookh, The Veiled Prophet of Khorassan*

Sunday morning, the day after arriving home from the concert tour, Adrianne dropped by Collingsgate to ask if I cared to drive up to the mountains with her and John Cairn. It wasn't surprising to see Adrianne and John together. She'd been leaning in his direction since the election in the fall.

"So you won't go?" Adrianne pouted sweetly. "Instead of spending this heavenly day with us, you're going to scour your soul in another spiritual steam bath? I had hopes that Bramblybriar— Gordon—would cure you of your sublime devotion to duty. Never mind," she sighed. "When John and I get to the mountains, we'll say hello to God for you."

I smiled, surrendering to Adrianne's perplexing intuitiveness. With a blend of tenacious psychology and genuine concern for others, she possessed an unerring empathy that couldn't be masked by even her sagacious wit.

"I'll phone when we get back, Di Love," Adrianne promised over her shoulder as she swung down the walk beside John. Pausing in the rose-covered archway by the gate, she called back cheerily, "And don't forget, Dia Mia. You'll always be my favorite armadillo!"

Adrianne's copper hair glittered brightly in the sunlight as she turned aside from the walk and took the path to the car with John.

She wasn't as tall as John's shoulder, yet she looked as natural by his side as if they'd always been together.

Adrianne didn't keep her promise. She did not phone. In her place, Warren telephoned with an urgent request to meet him at Xavier Hospital. Adrianne had been injured when the car she was riding in collided with a truck in the foothills west of the university. She was unconscious and in critical condition with a severe concussion. John Cairn, the driver of the car, was dead. He had swerved to avoid hitting two hitchhikers, who'd been straddling across his lane just around a mountain bend, and inadvertently driven into the truck.

I received Warren's call on the phone that hung on the second floor landing. The sun's rays came through the hall window, striking the hands of the owl clock at six forty-seven, and seeming to hold them rigid at that time for an eternity.

The trip to the hospital has become one with the past, but the vigil waiting for word in the lounge at Xavier remains distinct. Adrianne's parents, Howard and Dianne Eaton, held hands silently as they waited anxiously in chairs close to the reception desk. Warren sat next to me, but neither his presence nor that of his parents seemed as real as the picture of the Madonna and Child that hung on the lounge wall. The newborn Christ had an expression of compassion on His face that made Him appear, in spite of His cherubic features, much older than His Mother Mary.

As the minutes and hours passed, the lovely portrayal of the Virgin Mother and the Holy Son of God held my eyes and spiritual focus. There was no deception. The cloud vision had rightly proclaimed. There is a God. There is a compassionate, powerful deity who rules and presides over the universe. I would not doubt again.

The accident occurred at six thirty p.m. A few minutes after dawn, Adrianne Eaton's vibrant, incredibly beautiful soul passed from mortality forever beyond the veil. The sky hands had claimed her for their own.

Warren drove me home from the hospital. He was controlled, but he seemed much too big for the small red car. In fact, nothing about him fit. His running shoes overrode the gas pedal like a giant's foot in a kiddy car. His jacket was too short in the sleeves, allowing his wrists to extend far beyond the cuffs like those of a growing schoolboy. His hands, like his feet, were much too big for either his arms or the steering wheel. His shoulders were too broad, his head too small, and even the cap, which attempted to cling to his disordered thatch of red hair, was the wrong size for his head.

At Collingsgate, Warren helped me out of the car and walked with me to the steps. Lifting my chin with a big awkward hand, he looked numbly into my eyes, attempting to smile. "I'm here for you, Diana," he said haltingly, his voice husky with unshed tears. "I'm here."

Seeing the misery in his eyes, I put my arms around him. In my arms, Warren was not missized, but only a small, wounded boy. In some infinitesimal way, I was able to give him the courage he so generously tried to give me.

Chapter Thirty-Nine

Why meet we on the bridge of Time
to 'change one greeting and to part? [93]

—Sir Richard Burton: *A Translation, The Kasidah of Hagi Abdu El-Yezdi*

Spring passed. Just as Adrianne had come without warning into my life, so she departed from it. And her departing left a void that could not be filled.

Adrianne's funeral was held in the Whyte Avenue Chapel. Mr. and Mrs. Eaton, who didn't have a close affiliation with their church, had requested that the service be held in our building. Bishop Mark McBride presided. The service was well attended. Sitting beside Warren and Aunt Amy, my thoughts wandered numbly where they would.

Howard and Dianne had asked Father to give the eulogy and requested me to give a violin solo. Not emotionally up to it, I asked Mike to stand in for me. The Eatons graciously accepted the substitute, requesting that Mike play Massenet's *Meditation from Thais*, one of Adrianne's favorite pieces. Mike accepted the honor gladly.

He played well. It was a relief to listen to the sweet melodic strains as they eased, for a moment, the sadness in all our hearts. Lifted on the gentle music, a mosaic of memories, ebbing and flowing, gathering and dispersing, engrossed me with the sights, the sounds, the mortal impressions of Adrianne.

"You tell me who you think you are, and I'll tell you who I'm not," she had enticed enigmatically on that first meeting, her bright eyes sparkling with the energy, the mystery of life. And now, a scant five years later,

those same bright eyes, once so filled with the fire of living, were closed for the final time on Earth in the mystery of death. I put my hand involuntarily to my heart. Looking at Warren and seeing the same feelings of bereft longing in his eyes, I took his hand and pressed it warmly in my own. Soon, it was Father's turn to speak:

Whence this pleasing hope, this fond desire,
This longing after immortality? . . .
'Tis the divinity that stirs within us;
'Tis Heaven itself, that points out an hereafter,
And intimates eternity to man.[91]

Father continued, directing his remarks specifically to Adrianne's parents and family.

"Though there is always intense grief, when our loved ones are taken from us in the prime of life, death itself should not be feared. Death comes to all sooner or later and is as Nancy Byrd Turner suggests, only *'an old door set in a garden wall.'*[95] The flowers on this side of the gate will dim in comparison to the incomparable beauty that awaits us in the garden across the veil."

"For those who serve and care for others in this life, there will be great joy in the next stage of existence. Those who love their fellow men and women, love God. Adrianne showed her love of God, by loving others."

"Some people remain folded all their lives. They never flower. Adrianne not only flowered, she blossomed abundantly. She gave herself to life with a generosity that has blessed us all. In reaching out to others, Adrianne lived a valiant life—a life that inspired others to reach higher. We who know her best, love her best. We know her indescribable worth, her infinite value as a beloved daughter of God, heiress of the kingdom, soldier of the crown."

"Let us not mourn for Adrianne more than our souls can bear; but rather let us, as she would want, remember her youth, her vitality, her joy in living. Let each of us live worthy lives, so that we will be, when it is our time to 'cross over the bar' to the sunlit joys beyond, worthy to meet her."

"Our Lord and Savior, the creator of the universe, has atoned not only for our sins but also for our suffering. In all our sorrows, we can be assured that He who intimately knows and understands our pain will ever be with us."

"*For none of us liveth to himself, and no man dieth to himself. For whether we live, we live unto the Lord; and whether we die, we die unto the Lord: whether we live therefore, or die, we are the Lord's.*'[96]

Following the service, those assembled gathered in the cultural hall to offer words of consolation to the bereaved family. Many from university were in attendance. Kumari, Bernie, Lois, Neila, Jack, and Harris, all offered what comfort they could to Warren. It was then that I noticed Daphne Englesby. As she came up to speak with Warren, I observed with surprise that her eyes were red with weeping. Laying her hand softly on Warren's arm, Daphne looked up at him with genuine compassion.

"Adrianne was . . . she was . . . incomparable."

Warren smiled his appreciation, and Daphne continued. "I regret that I personally didn't have the courage . . . to read the original translation while she was with us. I would have liked to have known Adrianne better." The gentle gracefulness of Daphne's words and manner moved Warren's heart. Chivalrously, he bent and gave Miss Englesby a grateful embrace.

Daphne was nice. She was thoughtful, just as my perceptive friend had surmised. I smiled and gave Daphne a warm hug, also. "That's from Adrianne, Daphne," I said, swallowing my tears. "I think she'd want you to have it." Daphne smiled as we three walked to the door and stood together in silent farewell to our beautiful friend.

Chapter Forty

. . . reason's glimmering ray
Was lent, not to assure our doubtful way,
But guide us upward to a better day.[97]

—John Dryden: *Religio Laici*

Adrianne's funeral had been on Tuesday. The day after, Father said unexpectedly, "Care to go for a walk by the river?"

I readily agreed, glad to have an opportunity to get out of the suffocating closeness of the house. We walked south, away from the university, without speaking, each engrossed in our own thoughts. Every once in a while, Father would spear a tattered wrapper or other piece of litter with a sharp stick and stuff them into his side pack. In spite of the raw, boundless aching in my heart, I smiled. How often had I heard Father comment, "Nature is not a litter box. Nature is a gift of God. For those to whom this hasn't been revealed, I have two hands."

After a while, Father began humming, "'Good night Irene, Good night Irene, I'll see you in my dreams.'"[98]

"It seems much like the day your mother went adventuring across the veil. Do you remember the man we met after the funeral, when we were walking together?"

"Yes," I said, my mind going back eight years to that painful day frozen in time. "I remember. The man kept raving, 'There ain't no living in the city. Ain't no livin' in the town. So I'll take my livin' to the backwoods and drink my whiskey down.' I also recall he smelled like mildewed turnips."

Father gave a wry smile. "Yes. That's the one. Do you know who he was?"

"No. I thought he was just a vagrant."

"No one is 'just' anything, Moonlight. Everyone is someone. He was Roger Chronkhite, a colleague of mine. Used to teach in the history department. Lost his wife and infant daughter in a car accident the year before Elizabeth Kathleen went looking for them."

"Then I hope Mother found them for Mr. Chronkhite," I said contritely. Repentant of my uncharitable attitude, I was sincerely sorry for the life that had departed from Mr. Chronkhite's spirit before his body ceased to breathe.

Father and I continued to walk in silence. The sky was overcast and a slight wind was blowing. Motioning to me, Dad took a seat on a log sprawled across the path. I stopped some feet away and looked across the river. After a moment, Father joined me where I stood by the bank.

"Funny thing about humans," he mused. "Their shelf life never exceeds their inner life. Once you give up inside, it's all downhill. Spiritual stamina determines our quality of life more than we know."

"Where is Mr. Chronkhite now?" I asked, sincerely hoping he'd been able to rekindle his interest in living.

"He's in a home across the river," Dad said slowly. "I go to see him every couple of weeks."

"Is that where you go Thursday nights?"

"Yes. There or home teaching."

I nodded. Father never missed his home teaching.

"Would you like to come and see Roger with me tomorrow, Diana?"

The invitation took me by surprise. "I . . . I guess so."

In view of Adrianne's unexpected passing, and the difficult choice with Gordon yet to be made, it wasn't hard to be sympathetic with a man whose loss of family had caused him such devastating pain that he'd completely lost his interest in life. Father nodded, and we walked back to Collingsgate in silence.

It was late Thursday afternoon. I was in the kitchen making supper and thinking of Adrianne with great longing and sadness. She had always adjusted so quickly to every new experience. Would she adjust as easily to being across the veil? A spasm of self-pity shook my reverie. Were all my dearest friends and loved ones to vanish from my life? Would there be no one left?

As I looked from my chores to the picture of Grandmother Carolynne's hands, I became intensely aware. It was as if Adrianne, although gone beyond mortal sight, was trying to get my attention. I felt her uncontainable spirit addressing mine—her keen intelligence finding a way into my consciousness. This would be so like my friend. It had never been Adrianne's way to remain silent. Wherever she was, she would make a statement. Having passed beyond mortality, she was still irrepressibly Adrianne.

When supper was ready, I went eagerly to get Father. I felt an urgent desire to know his opinion. With so many soul-wrenching issues to sort out, I was determined to know if Dad believed mortals could receive impressions from those in the next life.

Father was working on the white Innocence rose in the center of the pond when I approached. Seeing me, he leaned meditatively on his spade and waited for me to speak.

"I had a talk." I paused, wondering if I should proceed. When Father merely listened in silence, I decided to go ahead. "With Adrianne today. I mean she . . . had a talk with me. Actually, she was scolding me—like usual—on a peccadillo of mine."

Dad nodded his head. "Go on," was all he said.

"She asked me why I was moping about, acting as if I'd lost my best friend forever. If I couldn't stand a little distance between us, how loyal was that?"

"You listening to *Jonathan Livingston Seagull* in spiritual mode, Moonlight?" Father asked mildly, giving me a searching look. Since Ginny's leaving, Dad had reverted more often to calling me Moonlight.

"Yes," I admitted. "It's my favorite part."

Father listened as I quoted the passage from Richard Bach's tender moving story. When I'd finished, he leaned reflectively forward, for the moment in a sober frame of mind. The irreverent thought occurred to me that perhaps Dad and Roger Chronkhite had much more in common than was apparent. Neither one was very often seriously sober. But today, Father surprised me.

"My guess is that's how it works," he said thoughtfully. "What we read or hear, which uplifts or inspires our mind with truth, the Holy Ghost brings to remembrance in time of need."

"Yes, Dad, but it was Jonathan like I've never read him. It was Jonathan written on the very tablets of my heart. Like Adrianne was there beside me, talking to me in that revitalizing offhand way of hers—half in jest, half-serious, half . . . half Adrianne."

"She was in her instructional mode?" Father suggested, smiling.

"Yes. I guess, but more." I hesitated, but something in the events of the last few weeks had made it easier to talk to Father, so I waded ahead.

"Is that how it was with you and Mother? Is that how you kept going? Did you sense her near?"

"Elizabeth Kathleen seems very near at times," Father said quietly.

"Then it's more than simply carrying Mother in your memory?"

"Yes. Our loved ones do live in our hearts, but they also have their own independent immortality. If it's one thing your mother's taught me since she went gallivanting off on her own, it's the 'permanence of personality' after death. I guess it's that knowledge that keeps me plugging along."

"You've never seemed to plug along to me, Dad," I ventured, getting bolder.

"No? Well, I do. Mostly in the rose garden. That's my plugging-along place."

"You mean your laughing place, Brer Rabbit?"

Father smiled. "Yes. But it's more. It isn't just feeling Elizabeth Kathleen's presence from time to time that keeps me going, or the roses, or even my work at the university. I've got to keep pace. With that insatiable curiosity of your mother's, she'll be up there learning so much—expanding her awareness of the created universe so quickly—I'll be left behind if I don't keep struggling to keep up down here."

"You want to keep pace with Mother's growth?"

"Have to. At least as much as possible. Elizabeth Kathleen can get as smart and sassy as she likes. She's not getting away from me."

The words may have sounded like a reprimand, but as they came from Father, the veiled tenderness was apparent. After a moment, perhaps thinking he'd revealed too much of his own personal feelings, Dad reverted to a more normal mood.

"Elizabeth Kathleen would go on her purging rampages. I'm afraid if I don't keep pace, when I walk into paradise, your mother will stomp all over my lovely theories and incite all her pet elephants to help."

"You think there are elephants in the spirit world?" Delight caressed my mind at the thought.

"Elizabeth Kathleen is there. Rest assured—there will be elephants."

"Dad," I objected, "Mother was only five-feet tall. Smaller even than Ginny."

"Only on the outside. On the inside she was gigantic. Do you realize if her new body matches her soul, I'll have to build her a home the size of a football stadium?"

I smiled and walked into the house. When Father was threatened, he always diverted to the absurd. It was his way of equalizing the odds. I'd been equalized many times before and knew when to concede defeat.

After supper, as promised, I accompanied Father to see Roger Chronkhite. I wanted to find an excuse not to go. While Gordon would not be home for some weeks yet, I felt the time was needed to prepare myself for the challenge ahead. Fortunately, as the weeks had passed, I had become more spiritually calm. I sensed a new strength within myself that could only come from one source. My prayers and supplications had been answered. My decision was made: I would cleave to my legacy of faith.

It would now be up to Gordon to choose between man's reason and the majesty that existed beyond the minds of men. Gordon would be the one who would choose whether to sever the newly formed, untested threads of love that held us tentatively together, or to go forward as husband and wife.

At quarter to eight, Father asked me to come into the living room for a prayer prior to our leaving to see Mr. Chronkhite. I always appreciated Father's prayers. When Father prayed there was no layering, no artifice. Father knew better than to take on God. He never presumed to instruct or to tantalize his Maker.

As my first real appreciation for my father emerged that day by the river with the Monkshood, so today I realized that one of Father's greatest strengths was his knowing where his sphere-of-influence ended. He was humble. However much Professor Collingsgate's mental jousting at windmills may drive his family, friends, and colleagues to distraction, Father never contested with God.

Dad pulled the green Chevy out of the garage, and I got in beside him. The drive would take a half hour. I needed the time, feeling uneasy that I'd let myself be talked into visiting a man I'd met only once years ago as a child.

"What do I say to Mr. Chronkhite?"

Dad wrinkled his face at me. "What you'd say to any sentient being. Hello."

"But then what? What if he'd prefer to see you alone?"

"Roger is always alone. Your being there, or mine, won't make any difference to him."

"Then why do you go? I mean, if your being there doesn't matter?"

"Because the person that gave his life for Roger, for all of us, commands that I do."

I felt a ring of shame at Father's quiet reprimand. "Is the Savior always with Roger, Father?"

"Now that's a question He leaves open."

"How do you mean?"

"We are going to see Roger. That takes care of part of the time. What the Christ does with the rest of the time on His and Roger's hands is up to the Lord."

Not wishing to puzzle that circumvention out, my mind turned to Gordon. I had talked about so many things today with Father, I thought one more subject wouldn't 'upset the apple cart', as Aunt Amy was fond of saying.

"Dr. Brantwood has asked me to marry him," I blurted out, with no more poise than a five-year-old. My hands felt moist to the touch, my tongue sticking to the roof of my mouth.

"I believe that's been established," Father said, raising his still dark eyebrows.

"You knew then?" My breath exhaled in surprised relief.

"Dotter, there is such a thing as honor among thieves, even at the Pre-Cambrian level of university professors," Dad said dryly.

"You mean Gordon—that is Dr. Brantwood—spoke to you?"

"That's a reasonable supposition to make." Dad's combat mode of avoidance was kicking in, as it always did when someone asked a foolish question.

Unable to restrain my curiosity, I asked, "What did he say?" I knew it was rude to ask about a private conversation, but the intense emotional pressure of the past weeks had loosened my tongue and my manners.

"If you must know, Dr. Brantwood—that is Gordon," Father said slyly, "asked if I had any objections to your switching faculties. I told him since you'd already chosen English over History, I didn't see how it could be avoided."

"Dad!" I said, perturbed. "It isn't a foregone conclusion. He didn't think—"

"Gordon doesn't assume anything with regard to you or to your answer, Diana. He's too smart to jump to conclusions, and far too vulnerable." Father was speaking in a no-nonsense tone I'd seldom heard him use.

"Vulnerable? How do you mean?"

Silently, Dad pulled the car over to the curb in front of what must have been the institution where Mr. Chronkhite was a resident. Turning off the car, Father faced me with a look as serious as any I'd ever seen on his benign countenance.

"Yes, Diana. Vulnerable. Do you think that while Dr. Brantwood has had such an undeniable impact upon your mental perceptions, that you've had no effect upon his? He fears absorption by your ideology, the same as you've feared becoming convinced by his. That is what happens when people respect one another's intelligence. They reassess their conclusions about life." Father looked steadily at me a moment, his blue-gray eyes sincere, and then added, "Most Christians convert by choice not coercion."

Father had expressed this viewpoint before, but I had not, until this moment, seen its application to myself. While previously there had been a marked respect in Father's voice when he'd said, '"He is a man to be valued," now I was hearing something more. Something stronger. I understood. Father was cautioning me to allow Gordon the space and time he needed, not just demand it for myself.

"I've never pressured Gordon to believe," I said quietly. "He's free to follow the dictates of his conscience."

"I'm not telling you what to do, Diana. Just don't prostitute your mind. Don't prostitute Gordon's. Prostituting your body would be destructive enough, but when you prostitute your mind, you go whoring against reason. If you, or any person, are made to accept what you believe is spurious ideology, whether it's true or false is irrelevant; you have debased your mind."

"What you are saying is that faith unclocks our understanding, it does not contravene it?"

"Exactly so. Spiritual knowledge confirms, expands reason. It never refutes true logic."

"Thanks, Dad," I said meekly. "I mean, thanks for staying sober. I needed to hear that."

"Why God saw fit to bless me with four fastidious females," Father said in feigned remorse, "is an eternal mystery." Bowing gallantly, he held the door of the car for me.

"Shall we cross the Alps? Hannibal is waiting." Our conversation concluded, we went in to visit with Mr. Chronkhite.

Friday morning six weeks later I rose early. Spring and summer had passed. In seven days Gordon would be home. Putting on my wool sweater to ward off the morning chill, I left the house and began the walk to the university. In my heart I carried a prayer for strength. Although the autumn was now in its maiden glory, I was oblivious to the beauties of nature. No matter; now wasn't the time to reflect on earth's loveliness. Now was the time to steady my mind and emotions for what lay ahead. As surely as I lived, I knew the hour of reckoning had arrived. If everyone must face their own Abrahamic trial, this was mine.

Kierkegaard was right about our toughest spiritual decisions being filled with agonizing paradoxes. Since that moment on the hill when Gordon had declared his desire to marry me, I'd experienced turbulent, even paralyzing conflict within myself, but thankfully, the challenge now was not one of faith. That trial had passed. The test I would soon be facing would be one of obedience. If necessary, would I have the strength to sacrifice love for belief? Could I remain as steadfast as Abraham? What if Gordon would not, or could not, walk toward the light? What if during the long, lonely intervening weeks, he still could not see any reasonable, logical rationale for belief?

I stopped by the log in the clearing and looked out over the river. The sunlight caught by the spray from the ripples of the water was diffracted into a myriad of tiny, shining rainbows. The light from the rainbows seemed to leap into my mind, pouring strength into my soul. My self-doubt lifted.

At that moment I knew that the desire for spiritual union was put into the hearts of men and women for a reason. As we are to be one in precept with God, so we are to become one with our eternal partners. For me, physical union with Gordon would not suffice. To be only bone of his bone and flesh of his flesh would never be enough. I wanted to be thought of his thought and spirit of his spirit.

I stepped over a tree that had fallen across the path. Kierkegaard's premise was not without contradiction, but I couldn't deny its truth. Gordon must make the leap of faith himself. Only he could do this; only then would he have intellectual confirmation. Looking up at the blue sky overhead, a statement by President David O. McKay slipped gently into my consciousness, bringing a resurgence of hope.

"God is the center of the human mind, as surely as the sun is the center of the universe."[99]

The prophetic power of President McKay's healing words sank deep. Whether or not Gordon was aware of it, God was the center of Gordon's mind, also.

Gordon was all in a man I'd ever loved, ever wanted to love. But I knew now I couldn't circumscribe Dr. Brantwood's reason within my own desires, any more than I could my own. Whether our future would be together or apart would be, as I had known for some time, irrevocably Gordon's choice. He, alone, could make his own reasoned leap of faith.

Chapter Forty-One

Th' unwearied sun from day to day
Does his Creator's pow'r display,
And publishes to every land
The work of an Almighty Hand.[100]

—Joseph Addison: *Ode*

The twelve long weeks of waiting for Gordon to return from Toronto were finally over. Convocation had come and gone. Without Adrianne, Ginny, and the man I loved, it was a stiffly formal affair, but that was of little consequence. What was important was that Gordon was home.

As arranged, I met Gordon at Queen's Bench. A cool September wind was blowing, and for the first time since the season began, I noticed with a surge of awed surprise the never-diminishing wonder—the indescribable beauty that is the fall.

Coming directly to meet me, instead of first going to his office suite at The Manse, Gordon looked more rumpled than usual. His greeting was cautiously reserved, but it was far from cold. With a surge of renewed hope, I gladly returned his welcome. In his hands he held our future.

My own hand securely in his, we walked across the lovely autumn campus and angled down the long hill to the river's edge. Without intending to head in any particular direction, we found ourselves in the protected clearing, where almost a year before a new professor on campus had gallantly followed me to return my purse.

"It seems the same," Gordon said, a reminiscent smile on his lips. "Except this time I didn't have to chase you here."

"It was kind of you," I responded warmly. For a moment I argued with myself whether to reveal the whole truth. The remembered reflection of beautiful hands on the water decided for me. "You see," I said, "I loved you then."

Gordon rewarded my admission with one of his rare personal smiles. Placing his hands firmly but reassuringly on my shoulders, he said seriously, "Why didn't you write or call me when Adrianne died? I would have come."

"I'm truly sorry," he continued. "Truly sorry. Adrianne was a brilliantly gifted student. Our loss is great." Stepping back, Gordon moved closer to the river and stood in silent reflection looking over the water.

After a time, his back still toward me, he spoke. "Do you read Ruskin, Diana?"

"Some," I replied truthfully.

"Anything strike you as odd?"

"You mean about his religion of humanity? Ruskin's idea that salvation is found in working?"

"About the man himself," Gordon clarified.

"Not odd, but certainly coincidental."

Gordon didn't reply, apparently lost in thought as he continued to gaze over the river.

"Ruskin's last home was called Brantwood," I ventured. "Is that what you mean?"

Gordon smiled at me sideways and shook his head. I searched my memory, frantically seeking for an odd thing about Ruskin, apart from his inconsistent philosophies.

"I have noticed that you and Ruskin take a strikingly different view of the relevance of fairy tales to real life," I said tentatively. The memory of the disconcerting 'Jack and the Beanstalk' discussion was still etched clearly in my mind.

"Ah yes. The 'imagination fantastic,' he mused. "You refer to the *King of the Golden River*, which Ruskin wrote?" Gordon had surmised correctly, but still he continued to stand with his back toward me, his gaze riveted firmly on the softly rippling water.

"Yes," I said hopefully. "Ruskin's parable about the transforming power of love: the triumph of good, through kindness, over evil."

My astute friend spun around to face me, unmasked eagerness in his glance. Folding his arms, he leaned back against the trunk of a tree in a typical Brantwood stance. The engaging smile that I had come to partially anticipate and wholly delight in, even as I distrusted it, played around his mouth.

"What makes you think Ruskin and I differ? Are my opinions so ungenerous?"

"Your criticism of me for not reading mature works."

"As you pointed out with Exupéry's *The Little Prince*, Diana, literary fairy tales like Ruskin's *King of the Golden River*, or Oscar Wilde's *The Selfish Giant* serve a far greater purpose than to beguile children. I never intended to disparage sound literary masterpieces, only to secure your reasons for your references." Gordon paused, focusing his glance on me to ensure I would recognize his sincerity, then shrugged boyishly, shoving both hands into his pockets.

"I'm astounded that the art of polemics would be so greatly despised by a Collingsgate, Diana. When I've questioned you closely, did it never occur to you that I might simply wish to spar with you? Elicit your views?"

"A few times, yes," I admitted.

"Only a few? My examinations must have made you consummately uncomfortable." The comment was a statement, not a question. Gordon's voice was low, his manner enticing me to confess. I hesitated, searching for the insight to bridge our worlds. Was Gordon still asking me to view conversation from his perspective? Was his concept of conversation as a 'war of words,' a serious exercise for high stakes, the clue that was needed?

"I think I see what you mean," I said, taking heart. "Ruskin, besides being a celebrated art critic, was well known for his polemical ability: his skill with controversy and argument to defeat opposing points of view."

"Go on," Gordon said encouragingly.

"You suspect Ruskin may have defeated himself. He may have, at the end of his life, precipitated his own disbelief?"

I waited tensely for Gordon's response. The supposition that men through men's reason can confound themselves may mean Dr. Brantwood was admitting that reliance on human logic alone wasn't enough. It was a necessary risk, a gamble I had to take. On this question, our future depended.

Except for the beating of my heart, the clearing was unusually silent and still, almost as if nature herself was listening. Neither the lapping of the river water, nor the birds, nor the wind, made any sound. When Gordon didn't speak, I tried rephrasing.

"What you are saying is that reason, to be without flaw, requires a source outside the human mind?" Gordon stepped eagerly toward me, his visual focus holding mine.

"That's what I've always admired about you, Diana," he said gently. "You may have to be driven to the wall to state your opinions, but you do understand the inferences. You pick up the nuances in a conversation like a piranha scavenging for food."

Gordon regarded me quietly through fondly appraising, violet-shaded eyes. As he did, it was as though I was seeing him clearly for the first time. I had been so overwhelmed, so overawed by his wonderful intellect, that I'd missed seeing his heart, just as I had missed seeing Adrianne's hidden vulnerability until the very last.

What little I had perceived of Dr. Brantwood's personal depth, had been only his outward appearance. Now, for the first time, I was seeing his true substance: the inner man sincerely struggling with all the power of his God-given intelligence to understand this magnificent universe and all its workings. He was indeed a man to be valued.

Relief flooded through my being like the breaking of water in a dam. Gordon did not lie. And he had just said, in his own enigmatic way, that he could now accept the necessary existence of a guiding intelligence beyond the power of mortal minds. It was a quantum leap forward. He had acknowledged the key issue; he would walk toward the light. In so committing, he had opened the door to our future together.

Dr. Gordon Lawrence Brantwood took a last determined step to where I stood. When he spoke, his voice held no shadow of doubt or turning back; his decision was made.

"So, Diana Rhodora Nemorensis, my Lady of the Wood. What now? Advance? Retreat? What's your royal will, Esther? Come to me, or consign me to my miserable fate? Love me, or leave me?" There was only one reply.

"Good morning, Dr. Brantwood," I said firmly. Had the life-renewing tears not been flowing so copiously down my face, gratefully obliterating the cold aloof image of the fading white lady in the mirror, I might have managed a more eloquent response. From the look on Gordon's face and the grip of his arms around me, there was no concern that he had misunderstood.

Why thou wert there, O rival of the rose!
I never thought to ask; I never knew;
But in my simple ignorance suppose
The self-same Power that brought me there, brought you.[101]

—R. W. Emerson, *The Rhodora*

Derivation and Origin of
Names of Main Characters

Diana
The Goddess Diana: Diana Nemorensis

Diana Nemorensis (Diana of Nemi), also known as "Diana of the Wood," was an Italic form of the Goddess Diana. Nemi was a lake in Italy, reputed to be Diana's mirror.

The name Diana has many historic roots. In Italic mythology, Diana is known as the Roman goddess of the moon, the hunt, and of childbirth. She was the child of Jupiter and Latona and Apollo's twin sister. Diana was a virgin sworn never to marry and had the ability to talk to animals and to nature. As goddess of the hunt, Diana is often depicted carrying a bow and arrows. She was reputed to be both beautiful and, as far as mythological divinities go, good.

In Grecian mythology, Diana was known as Artemis. One of the seven ancient wonders of the world, Artemis' temple was built at Ephesus, the capital of Asia Minor. In Acts 29: 23-41 we read of the riot at Ephesus, where the citizens yelled "Great is Artemis of the Ephesians," for two hours in an attempt to keep the Apostle Paul from bearing testimony of the Christ. The people feared that if Paul's Christian faith spread, it would destroy the immense trading benefits that came from the worship of the Goddess Diana. Silver craftsmen profited by making small replicas of Diana's temple and selling them to believers.

Biblically Diana would mean luminous or perfect.

Brantwood

"Brant" is derived from Norse and means "steep." Brantwood was the name of the home of the renown art critic and thinker, John Ruskin from 1872 until the artist's death in 1900. Brantwood, built at Coniston Water in the famous Lake District of England, is now a famous resort museum.

John Ruskin's battle to define and maintain faith is possibly well known. That he had an extremely analytical mind and was a master of polemics is perhaps not as well observed. A polemic is an argument devoted to a particular thesis. Unlike debate, where good is often verified in opposing points of view, in polemics, one point of view is confirmed as true. Also unlike apologetics, which is usually employed as a strictly intellectual defense or destruction of faith, polemical arguments have a strong emotional component.

Symbolism in Story

The use of symbols as a means of investing meaning and expanding concepts has long been an integral part of communication through the written word. The employment of a physical object or fact to represent an idea, virtue, or human characteristic helps make immaterial qualities such as these more concrete and thereby more readily understandable.

In "Good Morning, Dr. Brantwood," symbols are specifically used to bridge what can be unchartered territory between the fictional contrivance of the story and plot and the very real and salient issues that this particular work of fiction is designed to explore. One widely used symbol in literature is that of hands. Depending on the intent, hands may represent many different desirable traits such as charity, compassion, or they may represent the other extreme of punishment, retribution, or cruelty. Hands may also represent skill, capability, and profession or work.

In the event that hands may be seen to symbolize positive qualities, they also acquire characteristics of beauty and usefulness as vehicles of service to other human beings. The focus of the hand symbols depicted in this story is on the positive aspects they represent. In the case of Grandmother Carolynne Collingsgate, hands represent loving toil and labor on behalf of her family. Dr. Brantwood's hands symbolize skill, intellectual power, and tenderness. The hands representing the Savior's atoning sacrifice and loving majesty are concrete links to faith.

Other symbols used in the story include roses, particularly the Black Prince and the white Innocence rose, the changing seasons, nature and animals—notably the armadillo, which for purposes of this story represents social isolation and benign, goal-focused introversion.

Doctrine and Theology

As far as the doctrine and theology of the Church of Jesus Christ of Latter-day Saints goes, no attempt has been made by the author of this story to expound upon principles, or to establish any precedent or practice whatsoever for this faith or any other.

While it is the author's considered opinion that personal revelation is required in the difficult decisions in life, as far as the advisability or inadvisability of marriage to a non-member is concerned, the righteous and wise counsel of L.D.S prophets to marry for eternity as well as time, is not disputed in any way. Rather, it is endorsed. There is no intent to suggest or to predict that marrying out of the gospel setting will bring happiness. There is no attempt to validate or to invalidate marriage to a non-member, or to pretend to prophetic insights the author does not possess. The beliefs of all faiths, (Christian or otherwise) as well as that of those who have no faith, are respected absolutely.

Credits and Comments

[1] William Wordsworth (1770-1850) "The Solitary Reaper," Lines 25-26, Vol.11, 1815.

[2] Maltbie D. Babcock(1858-1901) "This Is My Father's World," 1901, Westminster, John Knox Press.

[3] Rembrandt, Harmenszoon van Rijn (1606-1669) Attributed Quote.

[4] Samuel Taylor Coleridge (1771-1834) "Kubla Khan," lines 1-5, "The Complete Poetical Works of Coleridge,"1912. Kubla Khan was the grandson of Ghenghis Khan. Xanadu was the Mongol palace.

[5] William Wordsworth, "Lines Written Above Tintern Abbey." Full Title: "Lines Written a Few Miles Above Tinturn Abbey on Revisiting the Banks of the Wye During a Tour," July 13, 1798.

[6] William Wordsworth, "Preface to Lyrical Ballads," 1798, explains Wordsworth's idea that poetry should use simple language. Lyrical Ballads was a pivotal work, heralding the Romantic Period of Poetry which focused on topics such as beauty and truth, using nature as a basis to explore and expand human emotion.

[7] William Shakespeare (1564-1616) *Julius Ceasar*, Act 1, Scene 11. "Yon Cassius has a lean and hungry look; He thinks too much: Such men are dangerous." Yes, he was dangerous. He instigated Ceasar's death.

[8] Joe Darion (1911-2001) Used by permission, copyright 1965, words by Joe Darion for song, "I Am I Don Quixote," in screen musical *Man of La Mancha* (1964) based on Miguel de Cervantes *Don Quixote*, (Alonzo Quihana) 1605. Joe Darion also penned the inspirational song, "The Impossible Dream."

[9] William Wordsworth, "London," 1802, Line 9. Sonnet written in praise of Wordsworth's hero, John Milton.

[10] William Shakespeare, *Macbeth*, Act 2, Scene 2. Dr. Brantwood infers by this quote that he, unlike Macbeth, has neither murdered sleep nor music, both of which give him respite from worldly care.

[11] James Hilton, *Time and Time Again*. Reproduced with permission of Curtis Brown Group Ltd. London on behalf of the Estate of James Hilton, Copyright James Hilton 1953.

[12] Socrates (469 - 399 B.C.) Apology 38a, "The unexamined life is not worth living." Words attributed to Socrates at his trial for corruption of youth. Interpreted to mean he would choose death over living, if living meant foregoing the right to seek understanding through a reasoned examination of life.

[13] Walter de la Mare (1873-1956) *The Three Mulla Mulgars*, 1910. Characters: Three Royal Monkey Brothers: Thumb, Thimble, and Nod. Theme: A Heroic Quest requires perseverance. A magic Wonderstone helps.

[14] Ralph Waldo Emerson, "Nature" (1803-1882) *Addresses and Lectures*, Ch.5, "Discipline." Theme: A study of nature helps man understand his universe. First pub. 1836 in Boston by James Munroe and Company.

[15] William Shakespeare (1564-1616) *A Midsummer Night's Dream*, Sc. 5, Lines 7-17. This may well be one of Shakespeare's funniest lines, as he being both a poet and a lover, could then easily empathize with the lunatic.

[16] Robert Frost (1874-1963) "Choose Something Like A Star," Lines 24-25, pub. 1947.

[17] Robert Frost "Choose Something Like A Star," lines 24-25, pub. 1947.

[18] C. S. Lewis (1898-1963) *The Allegory of Love*: A Study in Medieval Tradition. London, 1936.

[19] Summary of information on Courtly Love from Wikipedia.

[20] Diaz Gomez, "The Chivalric Ideal." *This work, so far as I know, is not in print, but something was needed to corroborate Mrs. Weiss' honorable view of the Code of Chivalry in practice.*

[21] Baldassare Castiglione (1478-1599) *The Courtier*, Book IV, pub.1528, focuses on the qualities & behavior of the ultimate accomplished gentleman. Women's conduct is also delineated.

[22] Stephen Leacock (1869-1944) *Guido the Gimlet of Ghent*, pub. 1911. Public Domain. The Canadian humorist, Stephen Leacock, begins, "It was in the flood-tide of chivalry. Knighthood was in the pod." While Castiglione describes the Knight-errant in a serious way, Leacock makes him the object of humorous satire. The adjective "errant" means wandering, presumably in search of chivalrous adventure.

[23] William Butler Yeats (1865-1939) *The Wild Swans at Coole*, #28, "The Baloon of the Mind," pub.1919. Used by Permission.

[24] Thomas Carlyle (1795-1881) A Scotsman, historian, essayist, satirical writer, teacher, and philosopher. Believed in rule by strength rather than by democracy. Was not an advocate of letting the common people rule.

[25] Al Capp (1909-1979) L'il Abner, 1st pub. 1940. "What is good for General Bullmoose, is good for everybody," in comic strip became "What is good for General Bullmoose is good for the USA." in film.

[26] Alfred North Whitehead (1861-1947) "The art of progress is to preserve order amid change."

[27] Henry David Thoreau (1817-1862). Along with Emerson, Thoreau belonged to the school of transcendentalism. Difficult to define, it encompassed religion, philosophy, and literature.

[28] Michel de Ghelderode (1898-1962) Belgian playwrite who wrote in French. Was born Adhemar Martens, adopted the name Ghelderode in 1931. Took inspiration from history of the Middle Ages and the Renaissance.

[29] A. L. Tennyson (1809-1892), "In Memoriam A.H.H.," CVI, Lines 1-4. *In Memoriam* (1849) was written as a tribute to Tennyson's friend, Arthur Hallam. It is an examination of Tennyson's personal grief caused by Hallam's death. Tennyson ponders on life, death, the afterlife, and whether God and Nature are really at war.

[30] Alfred, Lord Tennyson, "Locksley Hall," Lines 181-182, pub. 1842. While Locksley is a fictitious place, the poem deals with the very real aspirations, strengths, and deficiencies of youth.

[31] Aristotle (384 B.C.E. – 322 B.C.E.) Brilliant scholar and philosopher. Founded zoology, formal logic, laid groundwork for Christian scholasticism. Attributed Quote.

32 Charles Dickens (1812-1870) *Hard Times For These Times*, 1854. First published as a serial in magazine called "Household Words." *Hard Times* deals with the effects of mechanization and economic deprivation (poverty) on personalities. Also, in Thomas Gradgrind, who both dislikes and distrusts capitalism, we see content and teaching style distorted by a worship of facts.

33 Jean-Jacques Rousseau (1712-1788), "Preface to Narcissus," (The Lover of Himself) 1752. This preface, pub. 1856, largely deals with Rousseau's defence of his work which he wrote at the young age of eighteen.

34 Antoine de Saint-Exupery (1900-1944), *The Little Prince*, pub. 1944. *The Little Prince* (Le Petit Prince) was written in 1942 in French. However, it was first pub. in 1943 in English. This fable-allegory tells of a pilot's (the pilot had crashed in the Sahara desert) encounter with a little prince from a distant star.

35 William Blake (1757-1827) "The Little Black Boy" in *Songs of Innocence*, "The Complete Poems," Penguin Books, pub. 1977.

36 Al Hoffman, Dick Manning, "Hot Diggity, Dog Ziggity," popularized by Perry Como in 1956.

37 George D. Spindler (1920-). Editor, anthropologist, considered to be the father of Educational Anthropology, Stanford University. A paraphrased summary of his views on "emergent" and "traditional" value interaction in society.

38 George Spindler, Ibid

39 Henry Winthrop, "The Sheltered Generation," printed 1969. Term refers to those born too late to participate in either WWI or WWII and who missed the worst effects of the Great Depression; those who are not vocal protestors, but who maintain the status quo.

40 Henry Winthrop, "The Sheltered Generation."

41 Original Source Unknown

42 Oscar Wilde (1854-1900), "A Test of Friendship."

43 Hannah Arendt (1906-1975) *Life of the Mind*. A political theorist, Arendt's views were first delivered as a presentation to the Gifford Lectures in 1973. The book, *Life of the Mind*, was published later. It is a wonderful exploration of thinking, willing, and judging.

[14] George Orwell, *The Animal Farm*, Copyright George Orwell 1945, by permission of Bill Hamilton as the Literary Executor of the Estate of the late Sonia Brownell Orwell and Secker & Warburg Ltd.

[15] Robert Wright & George Forrest, song "Rhymes Have I," *Kismet*. Broadway musical 1953, film 1955. Musical Score adapted from Alexander Borodin. Story based on book by Charles Lederer and Luther Davis, which was in turn built on the 1911 play "Kismet" by Edward Knoblock. Quite the evolution.

[16] Samuel Johnson (1709-1784), "Vanity of Human Wishes," Line 157, pub. 1749 Thesis: Humanity wishes to become great, but to do so requires incorporating Christian values.

[17] Hugh W. Nibley, *The World and the Prophets*, Deseret Book Company, p 178, pub. 1974 Permission to quote granted from Deseret Books.

[18] Joseph Smith (1805-1844) Articles of Faith #6, "The Pearl of Great Price." The Articles of Faith, first published as a letter to editor John Wentworth in 1942, outline the basic beliefs and theology of the LDS faith.

[19] Rudyard Kipling (1865-1936) "The Recessional," Stanza #2. Composed for Queen Victoria's Diamond Jubilee in 1897.

[50] Laurence Binyon (1869-1943), "For the Fallen," Ode of Remembrance, 4th stanza. First pub. "The Times," September 1914 . Written to honor and show respect to the great number of soldiers lost at the beginning of WWI.

[51] Alfred Adler (1870-1937) Attributed Quote.

[52] T.H. (Terence Hanbury) White (1906-1964). *The Sword in the Stone*, 1938. Permission to use by Harold Ober Associates.

[53] William Wordsworth's imaginative power as a poet was deeply affected by nature, the contemplation of which he felt would elevate man's finer sensibilities.

[54] Robert Wright & George Forrest, *Kismet*.

[55] Robert Wright & George Forest, *Kismet*.

[56] Ralph Waldo Emerson, "Rhodora," Lines 9-12 Sub title: "On Being Asked Whence is the Flower?" Emerson, was a poet of the Romantic School, and thus interested in exploring both the beauty and power of nature.

[57] Robert Wright and George Forrest, *Kismet*, "Sands of Time." While the imam prays in the mosque, Hadji, the poet/beggar decides to go to Mecca. Marsinah dreams of her gardener/caliph.

[58] Robert Wright & George Forrest, *Kismet*. Hadji's soliloquy.

[59] Rabindranath Tagore, *The Sheaves*, "The Invitation." Tagore was a Bengali poet and musician, known as "The Bard of Bengal." He received the Nobel Prize for Literature in 1913 for his best known collection, *Gitanjali*. Tagore's works have a noted spiritual dimension. Quote: "Faith is the bird that feels the light when the dawn is still dark."

[60] John Ruskin (1819-1900), "Modern Painters," Vol.3, Part 4, Ch. 16, Sect 28.

[61] Henry David Thoreau, *Walden*, pub. 1854, Essay One: "Economy." "The mass of men lead lives of quiet desperation. What is called resignation is confirmed desperation . . . But it is a characteristic of wisdom not to do desperate things."

[62] Thomas Wolfe (1900-1938) *Look Homeward, Angel*. Wolfe's first novel.

[63] John Dryden (1631-1700), "All For Love," (The World Well Lost) Prologue, 1677. The play itself is a heroic tragedy about the last hours of Antony and Cleopatra and is Dryden's most performed play.

[64] Dave Dreyer & Herman Ruby, "Cecelia." Popular song written in 1926. Full title: "Does Your Mother Know You're Out, Cecelia?" Chet Atkins,1956, and Frankie Vaughan, 1962, were among the famous recording artists.

[65] David O. McKay (1873-1970), "Gospel Ideals," Ch. 40, p564, IE, 24: 769-777 Used by permission Cor-Intellectual Property.

[66] William Blake (1757-1827) "Eternity." Blake drew inspiration from his inner vision rather than nature, and did, in fact, experience a number of actual visions concerning the life of the spirit.

[67] W. H. Auden (1907-1973). Last line from poem "Whitsunday in Kirchstetten," (1962) found in "About the House," as quoted in Cox, "Feast of Fools." Whit Sunday (White Sunday) is Pentecost, the seventh Sunday after Easter.

[68] Jane Bowers & Irving Burgess, Song: "El Matador." Made popular by the Kingston Trio in 1960. Lord Burgess, as he styled himself, also

wrote Harry Belafonte's "Jamaica Farewell," "Day-O," and "Island in the Sun."

[69] Jane Bowers & Irving Burgess, "El Matador."

[70] Burt Bacharach & Hal David, (They Long to Be) "Close to You."

[71] John Milton (1608-1674) "Il Penseroso," (The Serious Man) Line 205, (1645-1646.) "The Poems of Mr. John Milton," both English and Latin, published by Humphrey Moseley. Basically Milton contended you have to be sad in order to write well. Hmm.

[72] Edgar Allen Poe (1809-1849) "To One in Paradise," Stanza 4 wherein a lover mourns the absence of his love, presumably passed to a better realm.

[73] Author unknown.

[74] Thomas R. Taylor (1807-1835) Thomas C. Griggs (1845-1903) "God is Love."

[75] Henry Vaughan (1621-1695) "Silex Sintillans" (The Flashing Flint) 1950, The World. Vaughan was an Anglican Christian who is credited with modeling Silex Scintillans on Hezekiah's Song in Isaiah.

[76] Emmanuel Kant (1724-1804) *Critique of Practical Reason*, pub. 1788. While Kant's *Critique of Pure Reason* dismissed the possibility of knowing God through reason, his "Critique of Practical Reason" seems to suggest it may be possible. Kant is difficult to understand at best, (you can't can Kant in the sense of reducing his thought to a neatly packaged evaluation) so draw your own conclusions

[77] Joseph Smith, *The Doctrine and Covenants*, Section 20, Verses 77 & 79, April 1830.

[78] Holy Bible, King James Version, Mathew 10:37: "He that loveth father or mother more than me is not worthy of me: and he that loveth son or daughter more than me is not worthy of me."

[79] Blaise Pascal (1623-1662) "Pensees," Section IV, No. 277. "Pensees" means "thoughts", or in this case, "arguments for Christianity."

[80] Dag Hammarskjold (1905-1961) (Secretary-General U.N. 1953-1961) *Markings*, "Night is Drawing Nigh," p 64. Book is Hammarskjold's thoughts about his spiritual responsibility/work.

[81] Holy Bible, King James Version, Psalm 19.

[82] William Shakespeare, "A Midsummer Night's Dream," Act 3, Scene 2.

[83] Robert Wright & George Forrest, *Kismet*, "Stranger in Paradise."

[84] Alan Jay Lerner & Frederick Loewe, *Camelot*. Opened on Broadway 1960. Based on T.H. White's, "The Once and Future King," a heroic epic satire comprising four books, written 1958.

[85] Alan Jay Lerner & Frederick Loewe, *Camelot*.

[86] Emma Lou Thayne, "Where Can I Turn For Peace?" Used by Permission. Copyright 1973, LDS.

[87] William Shakespeare, *Love's Labour's Lost*, Act IV, Scene 2, Line 70: "By heaven, I do love, and it hath taught me to rhyme, and to be melancholy."

[88] William Wordsworth, "Inscription on a Hermit's Cave," 1818, pub. 1888.

[89] Jules Romains (1885-1972). Began the Unanimism Movement in French literature in the 1900's. Primary work on unanimism, "Men of Goodwill." Philosophy extolled: "Group consciousness transcends individual awareness; the whole collective consciousness provides greater insight than the part."

[90] Johnny Wayne & Frank Shuster, Description of Medicine Hat, Alberta in T.V. comedy routine.

[91] Phillip Doddridge (1702-1751) Hans G. Nageli (1773-1836) "How Gentle God's Commands," 2nd Verse: "Beneath his watchful eye, His saints securely dwell; That hand which bears all nature up shall guard His children well."

[92] Thomas Moore (1879-1852) *Lallah Rookh*, "The Veiled Prophet of Khorassan." Oriental Romance. Heroine Lallah Rookh (Tulip Cheeks) is engaged to the prince, but falls in love with the poet, only to find, he is the Prince! Similar romantic plot in Kismet, where Marsinah thinks the Caliph is the gardener.

[93] Sir Richard Burton (1821-1890) A translation: "The Kasidah of Hagi Abdu El-Yazdi," I.

[94] Joseph Addison (1672-1719) *Cato* (A Tragedy) Act 5, Scene 1, 1712. First Performed 1713. Roman Senator, Marcus Cato, was a Republican who defied Caesar and lost. General George Washington had the play performed for his troops in 1778 at Valley Forge in defiance of a ban on theatrical productions.

[95] Nancy Byrd Turner (1880-1971) "The Best Loved Poems of the American People," Doubleday & Company, 1936.

[96] The Holy Bible, King James Version: Romans 14: 7-8.

[97] John Dryden, (1631-1700) "Religio Laici" (A Layman's Faith) 1682, "The Poems of John Dryden," 1913. Dryden believes, "Reason has its limits, with regard to faith," but still, Dryden does seem to infer men can be "reasoned into truth." In the Preface Dryden writes, "We have not lifted ourselves to God by the weak pinnions of our reason, but he has been pleased to descend to us . . . They who would prove Religion by reason, do but weaken the cause they endeavor to support: tis to take away the Pillars of our Faith and to prop it only with a twig . . . "And then there is his view expressed in the funeral quote that "reason guides us upward to a better day."

[98] Gussie L. Davis, "Good Night Irene," (1888-1892) popularized by Lead Belly in 1940's, has its main origins in folk music. The line, "I'll see you in my dreams," gives some optimisim to an otherwise sad song.

[99] President David O. McKay, *Gospel Ideals*, p 23, CR October 1925, p 106-107. Used by Permission Cor-Intellectual Property.

[100] Joseph Addison, "Ode." Main premise: The sun, moon, stars, planets, and nature all bear record of a divine creator. The last stanza reads:

In Reason's ear they all rejoice,
And utter forth a glorious voice,
For ever singing, as they shine,
The Hand that made us, is Divine!

[101] Ralph Waldo Emerson, "Rhodora," Lines 13-16, (1834-1839.) In Emerson's book, "Nature," the writer suggests reason is the connecting link between the world of matter and the world of the Spirit, by which is meant the world of the Creator.

About the Author

Taryn Peters is the pen name of
Opal M. Court.

Born and raised in S. Alberta, Opal, a retired
English teacher, gives credit to her parents for
introducing her to the wonderful world of books.
In addition to her interests in reading, writing,
music, and gardening, Opal's life is filled and
blessed with four children, ten grand-children,
and a "cutie patootie" great grandchild.
Her greatest loves and pleasures in life are her
family, friends, and flowers.

Sister Court is sustained in good times, and
in adversity, by her belief in and love for the
Great Creator. Her personal philosophy of life
can best be summed up in the words of Paul
as recorded in 2nd Corinthians 4:8

"... we look not at the things which are seen
But at the things which are not seen; for the
things which are seen are temporal;
But the things which are not seen are eternal."

Made in the USA
Columbia, SC
13 September 2017